Praise for Mari Hannah

'Terrific police procedural by the inimitable Mari Hannah.'
Ian Rankin

'Mari Hannah writes with a sharp eye and a dark heart.'
Peter James

'Thrilling, exciting and kept me on the edge of my seat.'
Angela Marsons

'I was transported to the dark waters of Kielder from the very first page. A true police procedural with heart. I loved it.'
Sophie Flynn

'Terrific writing. Gripping and intricately plotted, compassionate, funny and wise.'
Kate London

'Of course there's a pacy plot, as we'd expect from Hannah, and of course a real authenticity in the police background, but more importantly we explore a cast of characters who have complexity, humour and depth. These are people with whom I'd love to spend an evening in the pub!'
Ann Cleeves

'Not many crime writers can master authenticity, plot and character but Mari Hannah always delivers on all three.'
Trevor Wood

Mari Hannah is a multi-award-winning author, whose authentic voice is no happy accident. A former probation officer, she lives in rural Northumberland with her partner, an ex-murder detective. Mari turned to script-writing when her career was cut short following an assault on duty. Her debut, *The Murder Wall*, (adapted from a script she developed with the BBC) won her the Polari First Book Prize. Its follow-up, *Settled Blood*, picked up a Northern Writers' Award. Mari's body of work won her the CWA Dagger in the Library 2017, an incredible honour to receive so early in her career. In 2019, she was voted DIVA Wordsmith of the Year. In 2020, she won Capital Crime International Crime Writing Festival's Crime Book of the Year for *Without a Trace*. Her Kate Daniels series is in development with Sprout Pictures and Atlantic Nomad.

Also by Mari Hannah

STONE & OLIVER SERIES
The Lost
The Insider
The Scandal
Black Fell

KATE DANIELS SERIES
The Murder Wall
Settled Blood
Deadly Deceit
Monument to Murder (aka Fatal Games)
Killing for Keeps
Gallows Drop
Without a Trace
Her Last Request

RYAN & O'NEIL SERIES
The Silent Room
The Death Messenger

THE LONGEST
GOODBYE

A Kate Daniels novel

MARI HANNAH

ORION

This edition published in Great Britain in 2024 by Orion Fiction,
an imprint of The Orion Publishing Group Ltd.
Carmelite House, 50 Victoria Embankment
London EC4Y 0DZ

An Hachette UK Company

3 5 7 9 10 8 6 4 2

A CIP catalogue record for this book is
available from the British Library.

ISBN (Paperback) 978 1 3987 1595 0
ISBN (eBook) 978 1 3987 1596 7

Typeset by Input Data Services Ltd, Bridgwater, Somerset

Printed in Great Britain by Clays Ltd, Elcograf, S.p.A.

MIX
Paper from
responsible sources
FSC® C104740

www.orionbooks.co.uk

To my family, at home and away.

Prologue

Before the phone rang, Kate Daniels' shitty day was like any other in the murder incident room, until Pete Brooks came on the line. Normally cool in a crisis, the control room operator seemed rattled. There was a lot of background noise too. She knew instantly that a major operation was in full swing; a manhunt he called it: PolSA, a firearms team, dog section, the works.

Finally, he managed to get the news out.

'Officer down, guv. Shot in the back.'

Kate felt sick.

An injury to any colleague, on or off duty, was a tragedy. This one was as serious as they came. Potentially life-changing. Kate's stomach took a dive, convinced that he was about to tell her that the officer concerned was one of hers . . . before he told her that it wasn't. The duty Senior Investigating Officer had been called out.

So why was Pete calling if she wasn't required?

'It's Georgina, boss . . . I'm so sorry.'

He was sorry?

What the hell did that mean?

Sorry was something you said if you bumped into a stranger, accidentally knocking them sideways; sorry was a word people used when they had been unkind to a loved one and wanted to make nice; sorry was an overused coverall for bad behaviour, a throwaway comment that followed a minor mistake, a meaningless sentiment. Why was he sorry? He hadn't pulled the trigger.

Paralysed by his words, Kate's mind raced through all the possible outcomes, none of them good. Georgina had to live. She had to. That improbable hope died in her heart as the controller spoke again.

1

'She didn't make it, boss.'

Death is something we all face. It was a constant in Kate's life, but Pete's words took her breath away. Ceasing to exist was final. The end of the line. No going back. That's it. End of. There was nothing else.

Racing to the scene with coordinates for Rothbury riverside, she called for an update. There was none. Forty-five minutes later, in an area flooded with police activity, she pulled up sharp, got out of her vehicle and climbed into full forensic kit. Terrified of what came next, she sucked in a breath, wiped her face with her hands, then slammed the tailgate of her Audi shut.

All eyes turned towards her.

A uniformed officer pointed her in the right direction. With a sense of urgency, she moved towards the River Coquet. Woods fringed the water's edge, a pretty path she'd walked a million times with Georgina, though never for exercise.

They got enough of that at work.

Now she was running along the dirt track. It was then she saw it, if not the crime scene, a deposition sight, a white crime scene tent erected to keep prying eyes at bay, hers included. Lifting the tape surrounding the inner cordon, she was immediately confronted with a problem.

The SIO, DCI Gordon Curtis, tried to block her way. 'What are you doing here?'

'Minding my own business.'

'Get the hell out of my crime scene.'

Ignoring his request, Kate stepped aside.

He grabbed her arm.

She glanced at his hand, then at him, a hostile expression. 'Get the fuck off or you'll regret it.' She shrugged herself free.

He didn't try to stop her.

She approached the tent, her heart kicking a hole in her ribcage by the time she reached it. She stood there, adrenaline pumping, a cold sweat forming on her brow. She was in danger here. Professionally, not physically. Protocol dictated that she turn around and return to base.

She couldn't do it . . .

She wouldn't . . .

Some things were more important than regulations. Pure desperation was driving her to see for herself that those who'd found the body were not guilty of mistaken identity. Wanting it to be true didn't make it so. An officer had been murdered. If not Georgina, then another colleague whose family would suffer.

The last few steps felt like a mile.

And still Kate clung to the hope that an error had been made.

Opening the flap of the tent, she stepped inside, in no doubt that she was breaking every rule. She was past caring. Even though she knew what to expect, it was a shock to view the body of a much-loved colleague lying face down on the ground, arms splayed out, a dark patch of blood across her back. Kate knew instantly that it was Georgina. She'd entered the wood, alone and unprotected, with no police-issue radio on which to call for help.

A sitting duck for anyone who'd do her harm.

The pathologist, Sue Morrisey, was on her knees, in the middle of her examination, recording her initial impressions that the SIO should've been there to witness. Pausing the audio device, she glanced over her shoulder, her blue eyes managing to convey sorrow and compassion non-verbally through the narrow slit between cap and mask. She looked at the body, then at Kate, an expression the detective chief inspector interpreted as confusion over who would oversee the investigation.

'Are you taking over, Kate?'

'No . . . I had to come.'

Morrisey's nod was almost imperceptible. 'I hate to ask, but would you mind helping me turn her over? Curtis stepped out. I don't know why—'

'Well, it wouldn't be for police work, would it?' Taking a pair of gloves from her pocket, Kate pulled them on.

'Ready?' Sue said.

Kate was not ready. How could she be? This was Georgina, daughter to Molly, wife to Nico, mother to Charlotte and Oscar, all of whom she knew personally, a family whose lives were about to implode.

For them and for Kate, life would never be the same.

On autopilot, her eyes scanned the scene to see what it would tell her, drifting to a point two yards from Georgina's body – to something that did not belong to her. Kate imagined a female inspector, shocked and out of breath, crouching down, checking for signs of life, instinctively removing her hat before doing so, forgetting to collect it when the doc arrived. The hat lay upturned on the ground, the cap badge upside down, symbolising a fallen colleague.

It was the small things that got to you.

A tear fell from Kate's eye.

She wiped it away.

'Kate?'

'Sorry . . .' She cleared her throat. 'Where do you want me?'

Sue noticed Kate's chest rising and falling heavily, evidence that she was under immense stress, mentally unprepared to carry out her request. 'Nowhere. I don't know what I was thinking. Step out. I'd be grateful if you could find Curtis for me.'

'No . . . please,' Kate begged. 'I'd rather it was me.'

'Oh, Kate. Georgina would want that.'

It took all Kate's resolve not to bawl. She wanted to gather Georgina up in her arms and take her home to her family, for no other reason than to avoid what was coming: a post-mortem, identification, trauma for all involved. Sue would be as gentle in her handling of Georgina's lifeless body as any doctor would a live patient. Still, Kate the friend, not the detective, wanted to spare her that indignity.

Resuming her running commentary, and with Kate's help, they rolled Georgina over, Morrisey noting that there were no other injuries on the body as far as she could tell . . . 'There's mud on her uniform trousers, a lot of it, ingrained, more than I'd expect to see if the victim had fallen, clear evidence that she'd been kneeling when shot.'

Kate was broken.

This wasn't murder, it was an execution.

1

Three years later

Jackson's emotions were all over the place as the vehicle he was travelling in approached the city centre. The journey south had been a blast: a short stop for a Big Mac, a crateful of Ouseburn Porter to wash it down with, a welcome home gift his mother called 'Mobile Happy Hour'. Only in Newcastle would you find four grown-ups wearing Santa hats without a hint of embarrassment.

The miles had flown by.

As the car drove down the hill toward the Tyne, there was a lull in conversation. In the distance, the arch of the Millennium Bridge changed to the colour purple. Jackson's gaze shifted to the slow-moving, inky black water beneath, the cityscape beyond reflected on the surface, a mirror image underlined by a thin slither of light from the underside of the pedestrian walkway. He'd never been able to put into words his attachment to his birthplace, except to say that a vice closed around his chest every time he left, a feeling that was even more profound when he returned. After a three-year absence, all he'd dreamt of for weeks was this moment.

He felt deeply touched being there.

Raising his mobile, he zoomed in, capturing the image of the iconic bridge, marking his return to home soil. The Quayside was rammed tonight, everyone having a lush time as they sang and danced drunkenly in both directions, from one of the many nightspots on either side of the river.

In a few minutes he'd be joining them.

'Good to be home, son?'

The question had come from Jacob, the best chauffeur in

the business, his mother's driver for as long as Jackson could remember, ferrying him to and from school until he was old enough to go by himself. Unable to speak, he nodded at the sympathetic eyes looking at him through the rear-view mirror.

Picking up on what had become a friendly staring contest, his brother Lee gave Jackson's arm a solid squeeze, slurring his words as he spoke. 'Comin' unstuck again, young 'un?'

Jackson looked away, embarrassed. 'Does my head in every time.'

'Hey! We've all been there, haven't we, guys?' Neither man in the front answered, or if they did, Lee didn't seem to hear them. He was too busy yanking the ring-pulls off two more beers, shoving one in Jackson's hand, clinking cans. 'Get your crying over with. We're local heroes going home, right?' He put an arm around Jackson's neck, pulling him into a tight hug that felt like an arm lock, adding his voice to Chris Rea's 'Driving Home for Christmas' as it bled into the car from the radio.

Jackson pulled away.

Lee mumbled into the ear of the front seat passenger: 'Get what I asked for?'

Tony hadn't said a lot since their journey began. He'd allowed Jacob to entertain the brothers in the rear on what was and had been going on in the party city locals called The Toon. Jacob was comedy gold, Tony the exact opposite. He couldn't crack a smile if his life depended on it.

His mother's money man was hard to read, mild-mannered one minute, ruthless the next. Reaching into his breast pocket, he retrieved a folded envelope, passing it into the rear without a backward glance.

Lee handed it to Jackson.

'What's this?' he asked.

'An early pressy, from me to you. And while we're on the subject, I have another surprise for you. We're not going back to Spain. When the New Year arrives, we're staying put—'

'But, I thought Mam said—'

Lee pointed at the envelope. 'Get it open, man.'

Intrigued, with Lee breathing down his neck, Jackson slid a finger under the flap to get at the contents: two match-day tickets in the posh seats – Newcastle United home game at Christmas – every Geordie's dream. When he looked up, the tears were back. As gifts go, this was right up there.

He fist-bumped his brother.

'Game on!' he said.

2

They practically fell out of the car when they reached Livello, a late-night cocktail bar that stayed open till three. The queue to get in snaked its way halfway down the street and round the corner. Lee stood a moment eyeing up the girls, most dressed in sparkly tops and short skirts, with bare legs and killer heels, some with tinsel in their hair. Unlike him, they seemed not to notice the plummeting temperature.

Doormen were allowing one out, one in, regardless of party size. It might cause a riot, but Lee was hoping they might make an exception. One of them was a good mate. Realising that his ride hadn't moved off, he turned, knocking on the driver's window. It wound down slowly, Jacob's brown eyes staring up at him, awaiting instructions.

'You guys can knock off,' Lee said.

'Not going to happen. Your old lady—'

'Isn't here. Go on, get lost, or I'll tell her you called her that.'

'Taxis will be non-existent later.'

'Fair enough, but we're not ten, so stop acting like we are. We've come all the way from Spain without a babysitter. Don't know about Jay, but I have a reputation with the ladies to protect. I'm also hypothermic, so go find yourself a beer so we can get inside. We'll text you when we're ready to leave.'

The place had been humming all night. It felt good to hear the familiar twang of those who celebrated Christmas and those who didn't. Jackson didn't care either way, so long as everyone was having a good time. They were doing that with bells on.

Some would never see a turkey tomorrow.

Checking the time on his mobile, he sent Jacob a text to collect them. As he looked up, Lee was about to approach the bar for the umpteenth time, flashing his cash, one for the road, the third since midnight, the curfew their mother had set for them. Amazed that he was still on his pins, Jackson tugged at his sweat-soaked shirt, pulling him out of the queue, tapping his wrist.

'It's late. If we don't get a move on, Mam and Dad will think we're not coming.'

'Yeah right . . .' Lee's voice, hoarse from singing and shouting, was lost as the deafening blast of Taio Cruz' 'Dynamite' boomed out through speakers to the delight of everyone in the room. One girl who'd jumped on a table to dance was yanked off by a staff member. She threw her arms around his neck, planting a kiss on his cheek, so he wouldn't eject her.

Jackson couldn't hear himself think.

He raised his voice above the din. 'What did you say?'

'I SAID, they'll be necking champagne. You think Mam would go to bed knowing her boys are in town?'

'Stay then, I'm out of here.'

'Nah, c'mon!'

Jackson headed for the exit to avoid a row. Surprisingly, Lee followed, without making a big deal of it. Lighting up once they got outside, he turned to face his brother, offering him a smoke. Jackson shook his head. Across the road, Jacob was waiting. Jackson gave him the nod to start the car. When he turned around, Lee was high-fiving a couple Jackson hadn't seen before, wishing them all the best for New Year. The girl stepped back, raising her mobile to capture the moment. Lee draped an arm around his mate, a big smile for the camera.

Quick as a flash, Jackson stepped forward, placing a hand over the lens.

'What the fuck?' The girl gave him a hacky look.

'No photos.'

'What?'

'You heard me.'

She glanced at Lee. 'Who is this tosser?'

Lee didn't answer. As the couple moved off, he turned to face his brother.

Jackson glared at him. 'Still think we can hang around?'

3

The journey was short and quiet. Tony had taken Lee's advice and knocked off early. Jacob followed their mother's instructions to the letter. His was a good job, one he couldn't afford to lose with a wife and kids to feed. Two miles east of the city centre, in the suburb of Heaton, he pulled to the kerb, turning to face the brothers, his left arm hooked over his seat, waiting until they gave their full attention.

'This is where you get out and walk,' he said.

'Walk?' Lee said. 'You're 'aving a laugh. I can hardly stand.'

'Two blocks down, turn right.'

Jacob gave them the name of a street and a house number. As soon as they got out and slammed the door, he took off at speed. Minutes later, following his directions, they arrived outside a typical two-up-two-down red-brick property at the end of a Victorian terrace, surrounded by a thick hedge and garden railings.

'This is it,' Jackson said.

'Fantastic.' Lee was being facetious.

It was not the fancy home they had left behind. Not even close. Their parents were slumming it, a temporary measure, they'd been told. Nowt to do with a cashflow problem. They were lucky bastards when it came to money. It never had been an issue growing up. They'd had the best it could buy – and then some.

They glanced up and down the road, before heading through the garden gate. The curtains of the property were drawn, coloured tree-lights visible through the thin material, a welcoming sight. Lee's eyes sparkled in the darkness, his breath like a cloud in the cold night air. He'd never admit it – and couldn't hide it – but he was as emotional about this homecoming as Jackson had been when they arrived on the Quayside.

'Right,' he said. 'Let's play Santa.'

'Got their presents?'

'Oh shit!' Lee tapped his pockets frantically, laughing as panic flashed across his brother's face. 'Chill out, divvy. I'm winding you up. Know any good carols?'

'Carol Thompson from my class . . . pure evil, bro.'

Lee grinned.

Jackson didn't. 'You're not seriously expecting me to sing?'

'C'mon!' Lee nodded toward the door. 'It'll make her day.'

'You choose then.'

A male voice came from behind. 'Try "Silent Night". It's one of her favourites.'

The brothers turned, a split second of recognition.

Jackson didn't hear the shot that killed him, didn't feel the bullet that passed through his head from front to back, spraying his mother's front door with brain matter. He was gone before he hit the deck.

Lee pulled a gun, returning fire.

Taking one in the chest, he joined his brother on the ground, unable to shift his body weight or reach for the weapon that had dropped on the ground. In his peripheral vision, Jay's dead eyes stared at him, his neck at an odd angle, jammed against the front step. As warm blood seeped across Lee's chest, pooling beneath him, he heard the door open, his mother's piercing scream. Someone grabbed his feet. He was on the move, being dragged across frozen ground before blacking out.

4

Christine Bradshaw knew Jackson was dead before they got him inside. Throwing herself on the living room floor, she let out a sob, begging him to wake up, even though she knew he was beyond help. Beside him, her firstborn was unconscious, barely hanging on, his face grey. Over her shoulder, she screamed at his father.

'Do something!'

Don Bradshaw rushed across the room. With tears streaming down his face, he got down on his knees. Pulling open Lee's jacket, he yanked his bloody shirt up, exposing his injured chest. Despite a weak pulse, his son's heart was pumping blood from a gunshot wound. His father watched it fade to a trickle, then stop. He froze, before a futile attempt to revive him.

Defeated, he sank back on his heels. 'He's . . . gone, Chris.'

'You useless piece of shit!' Her eyes were hateful.

He couldn't look at her. 'I'll call an ambulance,' he said quietly.

'They are NOT taking my boys away,' she yelled. 'Not like this. There'll be a post-mortem. You want that, do you? It'll be months before we get them back. The pigs would love that. If they want them, they're going to have to come through me and that fucking door and get them.'

Don didn't move, didn't argue either.

Christine had seen him shellshocked before, but never like this. Dropping his head in his hands, he began to wail. Sensing her indifference, he looked up, sadness replaced by anger.

She could read him like a book.

He'd been slow to work out what she'd known from the moment the first shot was fired, what she was now ranting about. 'It's the middle of the night. It's been three years since the kids set foot in the UK and they're shot the moment they arrive home. One of our crew has talked – the question is, which one?'

'Who would dare?'

'I dunno, but they won't live to spend the blood money.' Christine glanced at the lifeless bodies on the floor. 'Search their pockets.'

'What for?'

'Do it!'

He carried out her instructions, finding two tickets for the upcoming NUFC match in the pocket of Jackson's jeans. In Lee's jacket, he found a long box wrapped and with a blood-soaked label attached. In gold metallic ink, he could just make out the writing: Happy Christmas, Mam x

Christine wept as he handed it to her. Not for long. Realising that she'd not heard sirens, she nodded toward the window.

'Check the street.'

Again, Don did as he was told, inching open the curtains. 'Squad car. Two uniforms approaching next door. Time we left.'

'I'm going nowhere without the kids.'

'You're not serious!'

'I said no!' There was a bottle of whisky and shot glasses on the sideboard. Ignoring her bloodstained hands, she poured herself a stiff drink. Without offering him one, she downed it, then turned to face him.

'Did you pick up Lee's gun?'

Nodding, he pulled the weapon from the back of his pants. Turning it round, he held it out, the grip facing her. She didn't take it. He knew why.

She wasn't that dim.

'Is it loaded?'

With her breathing down his neck, Don checked the weapon. The magazine was in. Keeping his finger off the trigger, he slid the lock back, checking the chamber. She saw brass. He made the gun safe.

'Take it off.'

He stared at her. 'What?'

'The safety . . . take it off.'

'Chris, you're not going to do anything stupid—'

'No, but you might.'

5

Kate Daniels' temporary office was a far cry from the one she usually occupied at one end of the Major Incident Room. When Hank entered, she was on her feet, standing with her back to him, staring blankly out of the open window. Their guv'nor was five thousand miles away; an overdue, extended vacation, after spending a week rubbing shoulders with the LAPD, leaving his responsibilities as Northumbria's head of CID in her capable hands. The knock-on effect was Hank acting as DI, taking her role in charge of the Murder Investigation Team.

In the distance, church bells struck the half hour.

Kate seemed not to notice them or the fact that she wasn't alone. She was deep in thought, a spiral of smoke drifting from the cigarette she was holding in her left hand.

'Kate? What the hell are you doing? You don't smoke.'

'I do now.' She turned to face him. 'It's not been the best of days so far.'

'If the fags don't kill you, Bright will.'

'He won't know. I'll bribe the cleaners.'

He pointed at the only thing on her desk. 'What's that?'

'An acorn shell—'

'Yeah, I got that. Why is it there?'

'Jo gave it to me ages ago. It fell out of my coat pocket . . .' Kate walked over to the desk, picked up the empty shell by its stalk and spun it in her fingers. 'It's symbolic. The only mighty oak growing round here is a pile of bloody paperwork that'll take me three hundred years to process.' She sat down, putting her feet up on their guv'nor's desk.

Hank smiled. 'Mission control suits you.'

'Don't take the piss. I never wanted the job.'

'You won't say that when your pay cheque arrives.'

'Don't need the money either. What's happening?'

'In the MIR? Not much, though you look ready to commit murder so that could change.'

'Why are you here?'

'I miss having my ear bent.' What he meant was, he missed her. As her bagman, they were inseparable. 'The truth is the team are restless, as bored as you are. In case you hadn't noticed, it's Christmas Eve. Can I send them home?'

She looked past him. 'I think you spoke too soon.'

Hank turned to find DS Lisa Carmichael racing towards the door. Without knocking, she entered, so out of breath she might just have completed the Great North Run. His good humour vanished, along with any chance of knocking off early. He knew it was serious before she opened her mouth.

'What's up?' he said.

'Have you been smoking tabs?' Carmichael screwed up her face. 'It stinks in here.'

'Since when did you care about health and safety?'

'I don't—'

'So, what do you want?'

Lisa switched her focus to Kate. 'Guv, I take it you saw the firearms incident on the log this morning?'

'I did. What of it?'

'An anonymous 999 caller reported three shots fired in quick succession. A shoot out is how she described it. Control traced the call to an East End address and sent a patrol out to see her. Officers got no reply at the door. Fearing for her safety, they gained entry through a rear window. They found her hiding in an upstairs bedroom, scared to death. Her name is Ella Stafford. She claims she heard shots and saw nowt. She's terrified of the couple next door and wants no further involvement.'

Under Kate's scrutiny, the newly qualified detective sergeant shifted her weight from one foot to the other, a look of panic on her face. It was unlike Carmichael to react this way. Under normal circumstances, nothing fazed her. Surprised by her rigid body language, Kate's initial intrigue was now bordering on concern.

Whatever she was about to reveal was serious.

'I take it the neighbours from hell are known to us?' Kate took in Carmichael's nod. 'Do they have names?'

'They do now,' Carmichael said. 'Don and Christine Bradshaw.'

6

Breathe. Breathe!

Blindsided by Carmichael's revelation, Kate had gone to a very dark place. It hadn't passed her by that today was the third anniversary of her friend and former colleague Georgina Ioannou's murder, an ongoing investigation in which the Bradshaws' offspring – Lee and Jackson – had quickly become the most likely suspects. Kate tried to pay attention, but the walls of her temporary office began to close in. Sucking in air, trying to remain calm, she got up and walked to the window where life went on as normal, today as it had then. Her despair over Georgina's murder had never gone away. It never would. She was irreplaceable. Since the day Kate joined the job, she'd always been there as the voice of reason. Now she was gone, Kate was powerless to suppress the memory of that fateful day.

Get a grip.

Georgina had left an indelible mark on Kate. Even so, she'd buried her grief before the funeral, sealing it deep within her psyche, the only way she could cope with the horror of that day. In truth she was scared to let it out, afraid that if she did it would destroy her, weakening her resolve to carry on doing the job she and Georgina both loved. Had the roles been reversed, that's what she'd have done too.

'Kate?'

Hank's voice brought her back into the room. She didn't know how long she'd been standing at the open window, keeping him and Carmichael waiting. She turned to face them, on autopilot once more. 'If someone took a potshot at the Bradshaws, payback for what their sons are alleged to have done, this shooting incident could blow up in our faces.'

'Guv, this not what you think it is,' Carmichael said.

'Come on then, we need to be across it.'

'After reassuring the witness, Ella Stafford, first responders found blood spatter on the Bradshaws' door. There had been an unsuccessful attempt to wipe it away. There were also drag marks from the garden path into the house. Firearms were alerted. Ash Norham, the OIC, established that shots had been fired into and away from the house. A guy who lives across the road saw the whole thing.'

'Are Don and Christine OK?'

'They weren't the victims.'

Carmichael's panic now made sense to Kate. 'Jackson or Lee?'

'Both.'

'And the shooter?'

'No sign.'

'Why am I only hearing about this now?'

Carmichael hesitated. 'Neither the initial caller nor the eye-witness had a clue who lived there, so it didn't immediately flag a link to fugitives on the run, not until Ash's crew completed the usual checks. The tenant signed her name as Hazel Sharp, a smackhead who's in the system as no fixed abode and heavily in debt to the Bradshaws. According to the landlord, she only moved in last month and paid her rent upfront, in cash, to the end of January.'

'I happen to know she doesn't have two pennies to rub together.'

'It's a cover address, guv. The Bradshaws were expecting company—'

'A bit of forward planning, right on time for their kids to crawl from under their stone and sneak home before Santa came down the chimney,' Hank said. 'Shite like time off as much as we do.' He glanced at Kate, a rhetorical question on his lips. 'We're not getting any now, am I right?'

She ignored him. 'I still don't understand why I wasn't alerted sooner.'

'A witness saw Don Bradshaw retrieve Lee's weapon from the front garden,' Carmichael said. 'Aware that it was in his possession, and that he might well use it, Ash decided to hold off and call in a negotiator. There was a stand-off for almost five hours.'

'Still, he knows the drill. The Bradshaw boys are suspects in a fatal shooting. There's a warrant in place—'

'Guv, there was no marker on the address—'

'I don't give a shit.' Kate fired up her computer, waiting for the incident log to load, eyes on Carmichael, fingers tapping impatiently on the desk. 'Images of the Bradshaw boys are pinned to noticeboards in every area command. Who do you think will be in the firing line when the press gets hold of this? If there are newspapers tomorrow, *POLICE TAKE REVENGE* will be the headline, *Five-hour delay while the shooter disappears.*'

Kate noticed Carmichael's unrest.

'What are you not telling us, Lisa?'

'When Ash got in there, he found Lee and Jackson dead on the living room floor.'

'Where they belong,' Hank said.

Kate rounded on him. 'Not funny—'

'It's what we're all thinking.'

'And some of us have the sense not to say it out loud. I'll have to deal with this shitshow. I don't need adverse publicity, so keep it buttoned.' Kate switched her attention to Carmichael. 'Lisa, I know Ash is a mate, but I want him in here to explain what happened. I hope he's covered.'

'Guv, I don't know the ins and outs of it, but Don pulled a gun. Ash shot him, one to the torso. And that's not all. Before anyone could restrain her, Christine clobbered Ash with the baseball bat. She's in the cells and he's in the RVI if you still want to speak to him.'

Kate frowned. The Royal Victoria Infirmary was not Northumbria's specialist emergency care hospital. Ash deserved the best medical attention. She asked, 'Why there and not Cramlington?'

Carmichael shrugged. 'It was closer, I guess. All I know is, he's had a few stitches in a head wound. They're keeping him in for observation.'

'And Don?'

'Died in the ambulance.'

7

'Jesus!' Kate rubbed at her temples, a headache developing. 'I don't even want to think of the ramifications down the line. Ash will have some explaining to do for using lethal force on a man whose sons are the prime suspects in the murder of an off-duty police officer.'

'Doesn't sound fair, does it?' Carmichael said.

'Body cam will cover him,' Kate reassured her. 'He did what he's trained to do, what any firearms officer would do in the circumstances.'

Carmichael bit the inside of her cheek, unconvinced.

Kate missed her reaction. 'Hank, I'll concentrate on Georgina's case. You take the lead on the shootings. You've waited a long time for this.'

'Yeah, because you're Wonder Woman and never go sick.'

'I'll be hands on but won't step on your toes.'

'You mean, until we link the incidents . . . which we will. You're twice the detective Curtis was.' The man leading the hunt for Georgina's killer had since retired, leaving the case unsolved – something Kate would never do unless she was being carried out in a box.

'As are you,' she said.

'Appreciate the compliment,' Hank said. 'I don't get many.'

Kate gave a wry smile. 'I'm not here to give out gold stars. Get your priorities in order. First stop, the scene. While you're there, interview your eyewitness, then get over to the morgue. Christine Bradshaw can wait. If she keeps her fists to herself while she's in custody, the best scenario would be to bail the mouthy cow, otherwise it'll look like persecution of a crime family we have a personal beef with.'

'Understood.'

Carmichael was halfway to the door.

'Lisa, hold on,' Kate said. 'If you're up for it, you're Hank's 2ic.'

'Thanks, boss. I won't let you down.'

'Make me proud, both of you.' Kate gave an encouraging smile. 'I'll let you know if there's any update on Ash. Before you leave, tell Maxwell I want everything we've got on Georgina's murder on my desk by the time I get back. We all know Curtis made a balls-up. Now the prime suspects are deceased, proving a case against them won't be easy. One of you, find out if Charlotte and Oscar Ioannou were on duty last night – discreetly, please.'

Hank frowned. 'You don't think—'

'I don't know what to think, except they'll top a list of suspects. Let's hope they have a cast-iron alibi.' Kate stood, pulled on her coat, wrapping a checked scarf around her neck. 'Oh, and while you're at it, get Andy to contact DS Zac Matthews and give him the heads-up that I need an urgent word with him—'

'Didn't he put his ticket in?' Carmichael said.

'Yes and no. He took his bit on the Friday and re-joined ROCU on Operation Strike on the Monday as a civilian.' The Regional Organised Crime Unit was a collaboration of three forces: Northumbria, Cleveland and Durham, dealing with organised crime, cybercrime, assessment recovery and regional intelligence.

Carmichael frowned. 'What's the point in that?'

'A salary and a pension,' Hank said.

'Yeah, and no time to enjoy it.'

'I'm sure Zac had his reasons,' Kate said. 'Anyway, he stuck his neck out to complain about the way Curtis was running the initial investigation. I need his input urgently. And get someone to trace Georgina's ex too please, Lisa.'

Hank looked at her oddly. 'She had an ex?'

'We all have them, even you.'

'You have a name?'

'Crawford, Alan. They weren't together long. That's all I know about him – other than the fact that she broke his heart when she met Nico. Georgina tried to let him down gently. It didn't end well. He stalked her for a while. I never met him – it was before my time. He was obsessed, apparently.'

'You're suggesting he still is? She was married to Nico for three decades and has been dead three years—'

'The man was in love. Believe it or not, there are circumstances in which love never dies.' Kate gave him a pointed look. 'I'm *suggesting* you cover all the bases, old boyfriends included, especially the weird ones. You need a TIE action on him.' She meant trace, interview and eliminate Crawford.

'I'll add it to my list then, shall I?' Hank said.

Kate made a face. 'You're the SIO.'

'Where are you going?'

She scooped up her keys. 'To call on Nico before someone else does.'

8

Kate burst through a set of security doors and out into the car park, pointing her key fob at her vehicle as she raced towards it. As she pulled out of the Northern Area Command HQ, nicknamed Middle Earth due to its situation on Middle Engine Lane – traffic slowed, last-minute travellers hoping to spend time with friends and family clogging up the road. As her vehicle came to a halt, Kate was back in the past, in a long line of cars making their way into the West Road Crematorium and Cemetery, trying to put on a brave face, every painful second of that day etched on the inside of her brain.

Kate looked on as the coffin draped in the Northumbria Police flag slid out of the hearse, the force logo emblazoned upon it. On top was a single white wreath; next to it, Georgina's uniform hat. That image broke her, a reminder of the inspector's hat she'd seen lying upturned in the crime scene tent. Despite the pain she was feeling, others were feeling worse. Out of respect, she kept watching as Georgina's casket was lifted onto the shoulders of her grown-up kids, Oscar and Charlotte, her shift inspector, and another female colleague – all cops who wore dress uniform, white gloves, and grim expressions. They were dry-eyed, though visibly shaken.

Every step they took seemed to happen in slow motion.

Over two hundred lined the path into the west chapel. Heads were bowed, each mourner profoundly upset, hugging those around them. Kate hung back, holding on to her emotions, Jo Soulsby by her side.

'You OK?' she said.

The nod Kate gave in return could so easily have passed for a shake of the head.

In the car, staring out the windscreen, Kate wished Jo was with her now. They'd had a row before Kate left for work, nothing serious, just sounding off. What was happening today, what had happened in the past, was a stark reminder that life was fragile, too short to waste on meaningless gripes.

'Call Jo,' Kate said as traffic moved off.

'Calling Jo,' her in-car system informed her.

Taking the slip road onto the A1 north, the Audi moved into the outside lane, picking up speed. The call rang out unanswered, which meant that Jo didn't yet know what was going down in the Major Incident Room. Despite her role as Northumbria's criminal profiler, Hank would have locked down the investigation to ensure that nothing leaked out before Kate made it to Rothbury.

If he'd taken Jo into his confidence, she'd have picked up for sure.

Disconnecting, Kate made a mental note to try again after she'd spoken with Nico. On this day of all days, he'd be struggling. She anticipated that the conversation might take time. She could hardly blurt out the narrative Carmichael had given and leave. Nico deserved her full attention. Kate would make certain he got it. The rest of her journey was a blur.

'Kate, how d'you want to play this?' Hank said as they waited for Georgina's funeral to get underway. Like her, he'd held off, allowing other mourners to enter the chapel before them.

She swung round to face him. 'Follow my lead. A swift dispatch was not the Bradshaw boys' MO. They were known for taunting their targets, torturing them, letting them know what was coming, delighting in watching their enemies sweat. They would have done the same to Georgina. She stood no chance. I may not be the SIO, but I'll make damned sure they don't get away with it.'

'Careful,' Hank said. 'That sounds like a threat.'

'Wrong. It's a promise.'

A delegation of their team stood by awaiting instructions.

Kate pulled Carmichael to one side. 'All set?'

Lisa nodded. The covert camera concealed in the button of her coat was up and running.

'Good. I won't point, so listen carefully. I want you to recce the place. Check out the waiting room first, then wander around the car parks like you're taking a moment of meditation. Take the footpath to the east chapel, along the cloister, through the archway beneath the clock tower and into the garden of remembrance. Then come this way and in through the west chapel entrance. Clear?'

'Yes, guv.'

'Go.'

Lisa took off.

Kate turned to face her crew, addressing them collectively, keeping her voice low to avoid being overheard by friends and family of the deceased. 'This is a dreadful day for all of us. I'm asking you to mourn Georgina in your own time. This is not our investigation and you're not here to pay tribute. You're here as spotters. So, when we're at the house afterwards, no taking advantage of a free bar. Move around, talk to people. Keep your eyes open. If anything looks or sounds odd, I want to hear about it.'

Their silence was broken by an uncharacteristic grumble from DS Andy Brown. 'The case is open and shut, guv. We all know who did it. No disrespect, but Curtis needs to get a wriggle on. It's been three months already.'

'He has to find them first,' Kate reminded him.

'He couldn't find his way home. Did you ask the Chief if we could work the case?'

'I didn't ask, I begged. She's having none of it.'

'Where the hell is Curtis anyhow?'

Kate cut him off. 'Watch your mouth, Andy. Chief incoming.'

9

The pretty village of Rothbury was cloaked in thick fog when Kate arrived, though she could see festive trees lit up through the windows of the houses she passed. She entered Hillside, pulling up outside an impressive home with a sweeping driveway and mature borders. Unlike the house next door, there were no decorations visible through the windows, no lights of any kind on inside.

Christmas was a muted affair in the Ioannou household.

Kate sat for a moment, shutting her eyes, composing herself. Something was troubling her about the day Georgina was laid to rest, a comment made by the man she was about to call on. It remained out of her grasp. To access the memory, she walked her way through that day, as if she had been conducting a cognitive interview with an eyewitness.

At the funeral reception, Georgina's relations stood around talking in hushed whispers, trying for brave faces, failing miserably. Kate could see that many close friends were still raw, unable to believe what had happened.

She could relate.

Attending these events felt like an intrusion on family grief, though each copper present had an uplifting story to tell about Georgina, in or out of the job. That had always been the way they handled goodbyes, whether a colleague was dead or alive, retired or serving, killed in the line of duty or not.

The living room resembled a florist's shop. Kate read a few of the condolence cards, so many beautifully written messages of sympathy from coppers Georgina had worked with, some containing police humour making Kate laugh, many more making her cry. Jo caught her eye. Kate looked away, resisting the temptation to make her excuses and leave.

Charlotte arrived at her shoulder. 'Thanks for coming, Kate.'

Embracing her, Kate found her voice. 'Where else would I be?'

Charlotte pulled away. 'Can I get you anything? Tea, coffee, something stronger?'

Kate held up her glass. 'I have water. Is there anything I can do for you?'

Charlotte pointed across the room. 'Can you stop my twin from downing shots like there's no tomorrow? He's not been sober for days.'

Kate followed her gaze.

A changed man since his mother's death, Oscar was already half-cut, scowling at anyone and everyone, making his mouth go if they so much as looked like they might approach him to offer condolences. Andy Brown was doing his best to calm him down. Oscar was having none of it.

Kate turned to face Charlotte. 'He's going to regret it in the morning—'

'Yeah, well as bad as he feels, he shouldn't behave like that in front of his family. Look at his wife and kids. They're grieving too. What an idiot! Excuse me, Kate.'

Charlotte walked away.

Kate took the opportunity to check on her team. As instructed, they mingled with mourners, every detective looking for anyone who stood out as particularly nervous, as a guilty person might, even though Andy Brown had already made the point that the Bradshaw brothers were the only suspects. While Curtis had good reasons for that belief, Kate intended to tell him what she thought, and pass on the video of the funeral, whether he welcomed it or not.

Hank had read her mind. He was the other side of the living room, viewing the many photographs of Georgina, scrutinising the faces of those featured with her, looking for potential culprits should it turn out that someone other than the prime suspects had a motive to kill.

Stranger things had happened.

Nico waved, making a beeline for her.

An emotional man, he'd coped far better than Kate had expected today. It wouldn't last. When the house was empty, when everyone had gone, he'd be in pieces, as she would in the privacy of her own home later.

She managed a weak smile as he reached her side.

He leaned in, dropping his voice to a conspiratorial whisper. 'Kate, have you got a moment?'

'Of course.' She put down her glass. 'What is it?'

'Outside please.' He turned, heading out through open patio doors into the garden, Kate following. They sat down in the sun away from everyone. Nico didn't say anything for a while, though there was clearly something bothering him. Eventually, he found his voice. 'I wanted to thank you.'

'For what?'

'Being honest when I asked you what the process was with undetected murders. I had other questions, but Curtis failed to return so many of my calls, I stopped trying to contact him.' He paused. 'I found stuff on the internet that said laying a loved one to rest might bring complications if the killer remained at large.'

'Nico, you shouldn't be thinking about that now.'

'Is it true?'

'Why don't we do this in a few days—'

'Please, it's preying on my mind.'

'I already told you. A post-mortem independent of police has been carried out – the one thing Curtis did right.' Kate felt the blush of shame creep up her neck, burning her cheeks. 'And, for the record, his absence today is appalling—'

'No reflection on you though.'

'I disagree. It casts a shadow over the whole department. No matter how the investigation is going, he should be here to offer support—'

'He wasn't invited . . .' Nico's expression hardened. 'Oscar

33

told him to stay away. As you saw inside, there would've been hell on if he'd turned up. Kate, I'll be honest, we want him off the case.'

'You have every right to ask for that . . .' Kate paused. 'I must warn you that the request might not be granted.'

'Why?'

'He has friends on the top floor.' Seeing Nico's anger rise, she changed the subject. 'We seem to have drifted off the point. What is it you want to know?'

'Curtis warned me of the possibility of exhumation when the offenders are caught should a defence barrister request one. I asked him what the odds were of that happening. He wouldn't answer my question, so I'm asking you.'

'Slim,' Kate said. 'But not impossible.'

Nico looked right through her – an icy expression.

10

Now Kate remembered – only she wished she hadn't. She climbed out of her car, walked up the garden path and knocked gently on the door. She waited. No one answered and Nico's vehicle was not on the driveway. She was about to turn away when his face appeared through the stained-glass panel in the centre of the door, his expression lifting when he saw her standing there.

He didn't know . . .

Or perhaps he did.

He opened the door, ushering her inside. 'I was expecting you.'

His comment threw her initially, then she relaxed. There was no anger or distress in his eyes. There would have been had someone got there before her. The reason he'd said it was clear. She'd called on him last Christmas Eve and the one before that and the one before that to comfort him the day Georgina died.

Kate entered the house, glad not to have to fight her way in. The press would arrive as soon as the story broke. There was no hug in the hallway. In some circles, even good friends and family had stopped doing that. Kate gave him a compassionate smile instead, letting him know that she was aware of how he must be feeling.

He'd be feeling a lot worse soon.

In the living room, he picked up a bottle of red, already uncorked. 'Will you take one . . .' He spotted her reticence. Rarely did she drink on duty. 'For Georgina?'

She gave a half-smile. 'Always.'

As he poured it out, Kate cast her eyes around the room.

There was no tree, but more cards than she'd ever seen

in one house. Nico handed her a glass, toasting his beloved wife, inviting Kate to sit on a high-backed leather chair, one of two placed either side of the mantelpiece where a log, a foot long, burned gently in the grate. He'd offered her the view, the seat facing the window with a panoramic outlook across the Coquet and the Simonside hills beyond.

This was a special place, Georgina's haven away from the grim truths she unearthed, though her garden was a mess, many trees missing, a massive pile of logs where they once stood. At the end of November, hurricane-force winds had brought down hundreds and thousands of trees and heavy snow had paralysed the region. Storm Arwen had thrown everything at the northeast and Scotland, devastating the countryside, knocking out power, changing the landscape forever, including Georgina's lovely garden and those on either side.

'Jesus,' Kate said. 'I had no idea you were hit this hard.'

He looked over his shoulder. 'I was luckier than my neighbour. No damage to the house, though the power was out for six days. I moved in with Oscar for a while.'

'How is he?'

Nico's shrug spoke volumes.

Kate dropped the subject, keen to prepare him for what was to come – probably a media circus with TV and radio crews parked outside, his phone ringing off the hook with journalists wanting his reaction to the deaths of Lee and Jackson Bradshaw. She couldn't afford to hang around.

'Nico, I have something to tell you I'm afraid you're not going to like.' Kate repeated what Carmichael had told her earlier, that the two suspects in his wife's murder had been shot and killed. Nico remained silent as she spoke. His dark eyes had grown moist by the time she stopped talking.

He said nothing in return.

'I'm taking over Georgina's case file,' she said.

In a flash, his mood became sour. 'A bit late, isn't it? I begged you to do that three years ago.'

'I did try—'

'Not hard enough.' His tone was scathing. 'Instead, your lot threw us under a bus.'

Kate held her tongue. That wasn't quite how it had gone down.

There had been plenty of times that Kate had stared down senior officers over the years, going head-to-head over issues they disagreed on, sometimes passionately. They hadn't always resolved a problem to her satisfaction, but her own guv'nor had listened and given her opinion a lot of thought before pulling rank. She respected that in anyone. Today was different. Today, she was facing the new Chief, a woman who, for reasons unbeknown to Kate, didn't rate her, despite an exemplary track record.

'Ma'am, with respect, the victim is one of our own. DCI Curtis doesn't have the investigative experience.' She wanted to say is incompetent, but that would get her nowhere. She had to tread carefully.

'In your opinion.'

'It's the only one I have, ma'am.'

'Why are you really here, Detective Chief Inspector?'

'Sorry? I don't understand. I told you why.'

'And I told you no.'

'This isn't a case of professional jealousy, if that's what you're suggesting—'

'Isn't it? You're not the only DCI who has sound judgement and intelligence. What Curtis lacks in that regard, he makes up for in other areas, such as the ability to follow orders and adhere to protocol.' The Chief crossed her legs, relaxing into her chair, her expression impenetrable. 'You think I didn't hear about your unauthorised visit to the crime scene? Think again.'

'So, he's a snitch as well as being useless.' It was out of Kate's mouth before she could stop it.

'Did I say it came from him?'

Kate stood firm. 'I know it came from him.'

'I gather threats were made. You're bloody lucky he didn't make it official.'

'Sounds like he did, ma'am.'

'I've made my decision. On the grounds of continuity, I'll stick with Curtis. Was there anything else?'

'You're making a mistake, ma'am.'

'Which is mine to make. You're dismissed.'

'I'm sorry,' Nico said. 'But with three officers in the family, we deserved better.'

It was hard for Kate not to take the dig personally. Besides, he was right. The family had been treated badly. Curtis should never have come within a million miles of such a high-profile investigation. Kate was convinced that he'd been given it because it was 'a straight' where police were not looking for anyone else. Lee and Jackson Bradshaw were a shoo-in. They had made threats against Georgina at court.

All Curtis had to do was find them.

The Chief's decision to keep faith with him had backfired spectacularly. He'd neither found the offenders, gathered evidence to secure a conviction, nor considered alternative scenarios. Kate met Nico's steely glare. Haunted by the past, he'd aged ten years in three. The only thing that remained the same was his dark curly hair.

'You must know that your name was mentioned,' he said. 'What the investigation needed was someone with a clue.'

'As I said, I did try.' *Tell him.* She took a moment. 'It was my fault and I'll carry that guilt until the day I die.'

'What do you mean?'

Kate blew out a breath. 'When I heard about Georgina, I let my heart rule my head. I went to the crime scene. The Chief found out and refused my request to work the case. Had I not done that, chances are the investigation might have been over long ago and the person or persons responsible would now be serving life.' She looked away, then back at him, on the brink of tears.

11

Hank saw what he was expecting when he arrived in Heaton: a typical crime scene, screened off from the garden railings to the front door. More screens fanned out at a forty-five-degree angle across the street to the house where the eyewitness Martin Alexander lived. Apart from Ella Stafford, he was the only person who'd come forward to help police. There would be others who'd seen the incident unfold who, for whatever reason, preferred to stay off police radar. And some who wouldn't recognise community spirit or social conscience if their lives depended on it.

There were no security cameras visible outside any of the houses, including the Bradshaws' property, though it was yet to be determined if there was internal security that might prove useful. Uniformed officers were guarding the outer cordon, keeping the public at bay. A forensic team were busy, on hands and knees, undertaking a fingertip search. CSIs were taking measurements, checking the exterior walls of properties across the road, looking for damage from the shot the witness Alexander claimed had been fired in his direction.

Hank pulled up behind forensic vans and other police vehicles.

Craig Bell, a thirty-something, recently promoted crime scene manager, acknowledged him with a nod. Kate hadn't taken to the civilian. As good as he was at managing and supervising a crime scene, and feeding back to the MIT, she had no time for egotists.

As the window went down, Bell approached the pool car with his trademark swagger, ducking his head to see who else was in the vehicle.

'Hank, Lisa.'

'Craig.'

Hank was checking out the driveway. Even with the CSI tent in situ there was room for a small car. It was empty. Shame. Satnav might have shown him where the Bradshaws had been recently. He was out of luck. His eyes shifted, first to cars parked on the street, then to a uniformed officer making notes on a clipboard. He was around six three, fit looking, older than Bell.

'Who's that?' Hank asked.

'House-to-house manager.'

'Name?'

'Rob . . . Banks. I'm not joking.'

'Easy to remember. Can you ask him if any of these vehicles are registered to the crime scene address or to a Hazel Sharp?'

Bell wandered away to chat with Banks.

Hank craned his neck, glancing into the empty lane that ran down the side of the building with access to the rear. There was a camera on the gable end, he pointed out to Lisa. 'Raise an action to see who that belongs to.'

Bell re-joined the detectives at the car.

'Any joy?' Hank asked.

'He says not.'

'I assume you want us to enter at the rear?'

'Please,' Bell said. 'I warn you, it's a mess in there. My crew will be here a while. They're not complaining, and neither am I. We're on overtime and already three-nil up—'

'Don't be a prick,' Hank said. 'In case you forgot, it's three-one.'

'Get out of bed the wrong side?' Bell's chuckle was short-lived.

'Nah,' Hank said. 'I learned the difference between funny and inappropriate.'

The CS Manager made a short transmission on his radio. 'Watch your backs. Gormley and Carmichael heading in. Meet them at the rear, someone.'

A female member of his crew answered. 'Will do, boss.'

Bell turned to face Hank. 'You're good to go . . . sir.'

Hank reached for the car door. 'Step away.'

Raising both hands in surrender, Bell walked off, muttering under his breath, the demeanour of a man who knew he'd overstepped the mark. Hank was an amiable man unless you rubbed him up the wrong way.

Watching Bell slope off toward the front door of the house, Carmichael swivelled in her seat, a big smile on her face. 'You know you're my hero, right?'

Hank moved off. 'He's a waste of space.'

'I think he got the message. When we get back to base, I'll pull up the details of all vehicles registered to this postcode. Don and Christine weren't the type to take public transport . . . or walk. If they were at home, their car won't be far away. If it's around here, we'll find it.'

'You'd be wasting your time.'

'They could be using Sharp's vehicle.'

Hank roared with laughter. 'Ever seen her behind the wheel?'

'No.'

'If you ever do, watch out. No, Lisa. Bradshaw wouldn't be seen dead in anything Sharp owns, whether it moves or not. You won't find her DNA in that house either. She'll have got the key and given it straight to Christine who, incidentally, prefers high-end vehicles to ferry her around. If she owns any, they'll be registered to members of her crew, not some drugged-up mug-punter they're using to hide behind. Christine's people are spread out, citywide. There'll be no paper trail leading to her.'

'Isn't it worth checking?'

'Knock yourself out.'

12

Kate waited for Nico to calm down following her revelation. She worried that he might push her away as he had when she called to pass on her condolences after Georgina's murder, offering to visit, to do something practical to help him and the family she'd grown to love. Respecting his right to privacy, she'd backed off. Now she'd ask the questions she hoped Curtis had already put to him during the early stages of the investigation, to uncover something he'd missed.

If Nico would let her.

Right now, he had other things on his mind. 'Georgina never told me the Bradshaw boys were out. If I live to a very old age, I'll never understand why.'

'She may not have known herself.'

'Not true. Her supervision received a call from the prison. He gave her the nod on the day she died.'

'Would it have made a difference if she'd told you?'

'Of course. I'd have talked her out of going to the riverside . . . or gone with her.'

'Let it go, Nico. You're not responsible—'

'Then why does it feel like I am?'

'You're not. If Georgina were here, she'd tell you the same—'

'Then why risk going there when she'd been warned of their release?'

'What was she to do, hide for the rest of her life? C'mon, that's not fair.'

'Isn't it?' He turned his head away.

Kate leaned forward, elbows on knees, hands clasped together. 'Nico, don't do this to yourself.'

Slowly, he turned to look at her, his jaw set like a blade. 'Solitude was her thing, not mine. She spent so much time at the river, I began to think that it was a rendezvous, that she was cheating on me—'

'Are you serious? She adored you.'

'Not enough to confide in me.' The light left his eyes.

'She wouldn't want you worrying. Neither would she allow the Bradshaw brothers to dictate the rest of her life.'

Nico spat out a response. 'Yeah, all twenty minutes of it.'

Kate took a moment. Her eyes scanned the pretty garden, remembering a birthday party one summer to which she and Hank had been invited. She pictured it now, Georgina crossing the lawn in a stunning navy and white figure-hugging floral dress, laughing, a crowd around her, as always, Nico barbequing fish and souvlaki behind a curtain of smoke. The memory was so clear, she could almost smell the marinade.

Nico's voice pulled her back into the room. 'You have questions. Ask them.'

Turning to face him, she chose her words carefully. 'How was Georgina before she went on shift that night? Any sign of nervousness?'

'None. You know Georg . . .' He choked on her name, then cleared his throat, regaining his composure. 'Over dinner, I'd been banging on about our retirement. I'd planned a road trip in a campervan, seeing more of the Med before settling down in our bolthole.' The couple owned a house in Greece. Nico was born in Halkidiki, a Macedonian seaside resort. He met Georgina when she was on holiday there. They fell in love and were married soon after, Nico following her to the UK, opening a restaurant in Newcastle many years ago. 'I wanted to go home, spend time with my family. I thought she'd love the idea.'

'She didn't go for it?'

He shook his head. 'She said she'd rather die.'

In a moment of pitiable sorrow, their conversation evaporated.

Kate got up.

Placing a hand on his shoulder, she gave it a gentle squeeze, then turned to face the window, unable to meet his gaze. Her emotions were so close to the surface, she could almost reach out and touch them. She'd do anything, anything, to protect him from more pain. It wasn't looking good.

It was Nico who broke the silence.

'Georgina apologised afterwards. She said she was willing to compromise, even though it would be a wrench to leave the kids, especially the little ones. As it happens, they were all for it, with plans to join us often. None of that will happen now.'

Kate sat down. 'You should make it happen. I'm sure that's what she'd want, Charlotte and Oscar too – and the grandkids.'

He didn't respond.

'I didn't mean to upset you,' Kate said gently.

'You didn't. Georgina and I had words before her last shift. Not a row exactly, more a difference of opinion. Handing in her warrant card meant more time with the grandkids, not less. My plan came as a shock I suppose.'

'Occupational hazard,' Kate said. 'We cops have a lot of catching up to do.'

'Exactly what *she* said. She was mortified that I'd been scheming to drag her away from all that. She said that a community of ex-pat saddos whose evenings consist of bingo and karaoke was her idea of hell.'

Kate smiled. 'I can hear her saying that.'

He rolled his eyes, emotions now in check. 'I told her it wouldn't be like that. I, we had family there. They're a bit crazy. Good people though . . . like you.'

'Crazy or good?'

For the first time since she'd entered the house, Nico managed a smile. 'You two were so alike. She said the day she met you was like looking in the mirror.'

'For me too.' Kate swallowed hard. 'She was a one-off. Few women gave me the time of day when I joined up. Georgina did, asking nothing in return. I didn't get that from other female officers, some of whom acted like mean girls at school.'

The flashback arrived from nowhere. Kate should have been buzzing when she reached the station. All she felt was exhaustion. Fresh out of training school, she'd been deployed to stand guard outside a crime scene, told to let no one in unless they were a bone fide detective with a warrant card to prove it. That boring duty in sub-zero temperatures had turned out to be so much more than she'd ever thought possible.

Strung out and sapped of strength, she pushed open the door to the parade room and was met with a round of applause. She hadn't yet got her feet under the table and didn't know how to respond.

An officer she didn't know smiled at her with kind eyes. 'Blimey, that was a baptism of fire. Congrats. You're Kate, right?'

'How did you—'

'See anyone else covered in blood?'

'I was told to find Georgina. She's going to bag my stuff.'

'That's me. Have you been swabbed for DNA?'

'Yeah, soon as I got here. CSIs found skin under my nails and hair on my uniform that doesn't belong to me.' Kate glanced at the tunic she'd proudly pulled on twelve hours ago. It was covered in mud, blood. A button was missing. One minute she was surrounded by dense fog, spooked by an eerily quiet street, a feeling that she was not alone; the next, she was on the ground, scrapping with a violent man who'd come out of the crime scene where he'd hidden undiscovered by those first entering the premises.

'Kate, are you OK?' Georgina said.

'What? Yes, I'm fine.'

Georgina told her to breathe. 'It's the shock beginning to register. We heard the chase on the radio . . .' She held open a large evidence bag. Kate dropped her jacket into it, the older officer sealing and signing it, adding the time and date. 'You put in quite a shift. A murderer as a first collar is nothing short of extraordinary.'

'How lucky can you get?' The spiteful comment had come from another female officer.

'Back off,' Georgina said, then to Kate: 'You'll get used to the cynics. Amy has a degree in jealousy. Can't compete workwise. Most days, she doesn't even try. The truth is, none of us can live up to what you achieved tonight. Be proud.'

'Thanks. Do you know what's happening upstairs?'

'The suspect is being questioned by MIT detectives. Word is, he's keeping schtum. Wise move, if you ask me. Because of you, he'll be wearing a lifer's vest for the rest of his days. Anyway, let's finish bagging your kit and get you showered. You need that head wound seen to at A&E.'

'Florence Nightingale will take you,' Amy said.

Georgina gave her hard eyes. 'Rather me than you.'

Kate was beginning to like her new best friend.

13

'Georgina taught me that not all twats are men,' Kate said. 'I was ambitious. Some of my colleagues saw it as a threat. Every time I put my hand up for an assignment, they took it personally, passing snide remarks that I was being given special attention, accusing me of sleeping with the enemy – all of whom were male, in case you were in doubt, high enough up the chain of command to do me good in exchange for a quick shag.'

'How wrong could they be?' Nico was teasing her.

'Either they were too thick to realise I was on the other bus, or arrogant enough to think that they could save me from the devil.' Kate laughed. 'If Georgina had her suspicions in the early days, she never voiced them. She was different from the others, smart and funny, prepared to give me a leg-up. All she wanted was my friendship. Even when I got the next rank, there was no animosity between us, never any resentment from her. I couldn't have loved her more.'

'Me either.'

'I know.'

A wave of grief washed over Kate then.

She missed Georgina more than she could say.

As months turned to years, their relationship flourished, and just as Kate was harbouring a deep secret, it emerged that Georgina was doing the same. Behind the laughter Kate saw a tortured soul. It was like looking at her own reflection. She couldn't reach Georgina then. Now she never would.

Nico said, 'Georgina believed that everyone deserves a second chance, Kate. I disagree.'

Was he trying to tell her something? She couldn't bring herself to ask a question she didn't want the answer to. 'I need to go. You should probably call the kids before the press do. What I need to ask can wait.'

'No, please. Don't leave.' He was almost begging. 'It helps to talk – especially to someone who's listening. Georgina was a statistic to Curtis, a crime number. He couldn't even pronounce her name and didn't try. How hard is I-O-NOU? I couldn't look him in the eye, let alone engage with him, on any level. He should've been sacked.' Nico looked blankly at her. 'Oscar was ready to swing for him. Have you any idea what losing his mum did to him? Charlotte too, though she's come out the other side . . . I hope.'

'An enquiry would—'

'We don't want an apology, Kate. It's too late for that. What we wanted was respect and justice for Georgina.'

And now you have it, Kate thought but didn't say. 'You do understand that the investigation into Georgina's murder must go on.'

'What? Why?'

'I must satisfy myself that it was the Bradshaw brothers who killed her. Their guilt must be clear and unequivocal before the case can be closed.'

'Kate, they haven't been seen or heard of since her murder.'

'That's true, but—'

'Have you forgotten that her evidence sent them to prison, that they threatened her in open court? One of them drew a hand across his neck from the dock, remember?'

'Yes, I know. We discussed it.'

'She used to have nightmares about the threats they made. She'd wake in a cold sweat, lashing out, like they were in the room with us. I cannot understand why the authorities let them out.'

'They were serving a determinate sentence. Legally, there was nothing anyone could do to keep them inside when that term of imprisonment ended.'

'They had no contact whatsoever with the authorities when

they got out. I accept that there are failings in the criminal justice system, but we were never notified when they failed to show at the hostel, a condition of release which could have seen them returned to prison. Shouldn't we have been the first to know? Didn't we deserve that?' He didn't wait for answers. 'Curtis said it was all circumstantial—'

'It was.'

'Then answer me this: why else did they go to ground?'

'On its own it wasn't enough to nick them.'

'Kate, they left the country within hours of the shooting. How much of a pointer do you need?'

'I'm sorry, but suspecting they were responsible and proving it are two very different things. Now they're dead, that'll be doubly difficult. I must prove guilt, or the file remains open.'

Nico stood up, poured himself another drink, held up the bottle.

Kate shook her head. She wanted to get off the subject of the Bradshaws' innocence or guilt. It wasn't helping him come to terms with last night's events. 'I promise you I'll do everything in my power to close the case. In the meantime, Hank is leading the investigation into last night's shootings. It looks like a professional job, an execution. I'm sorry, but he'll want to know where you were in the early hours of this morning.'

Nico didn't blink. 'I was at work till one a.m.'

'Good to know.' Kate paused. 'I didn't think you were that hands on these days. Didn't you tell me you'd employed a manager?'

'It's our busy time. We'd had many bookings cancelled, but there are always walk-ins at this time of year, even this year. I was needed front of house.'

'Till closing time?'

'Yes.'

With all her heart Kate wanted to believe him. He was a gentle soul, friendly and generous. The sudden death of his wife had changed him immeasurably. 'Where did you go afterwards?'

'Are you asking as a friend or a detective?'

That stung. Kate looked away, then at him.

Seeing how hurt she was, he apologised.

'No, you're right,' she said. 'You and I are too close to be having this conversation.' She didn't mention that Don Bradshaw was also dead. 'It's not for me to question you. Forget it. I came to warn you of what was happening. You need time to process this shocking development. Better if Hank takes your statement.'

'I hope he does a better job for the Bradshaws than Curtis did for Georgina.'

'He will.' Kate stood. 'That I can promise you.'

'Curtis walked away without having the decency to introduce us to his replacement, Kate. No proper handover. The coward sent an email.' Nico used his fingers as inverted commas "Open-unsolved, no designated SIO unless further evidence comes to light." It was like a punch to the gut. Whoever killed the Bradshaws, it wasn't me. Sod the expense to the taxpayers. I wanted those two to suffer, to spend the rest of their depraved lives locked away.'

14

Hank and Carmichael jumped out of the car, Lisa opening the rear door, hauling a kitbag from the passenger seat. Hank walked round the vehicle and took it from her. Even standing outside the house, he knew he wasn't looking at the main residence of a criminal family. There was little security. No bars across the flimsy back door. No razor wire fishtailing over the wall that ran around the property to the rear lane to prevent an assault by police or a rival gang.

Something was off.

Had it been a permanent address, it would've been locked down tighter than a Bank of England vault. The only authentic thing about it was the rubbish piled up in the rear yard. The detectives pulled on forensic kit. Signing in, they timed their entry before moving through the kitchen. It was hard not to notice shop-bought food set out on the table with bottles of expensive fizz, one in a plastic ice bucket, and four glasses waiting to be filled. Hank looked up at two balloons suspended by yellow ribbons from the overhead lights.

'Christ, I've seen it all now. Anyone seen an old oak tree?'

'Homecoming party?'

'I'd say so.' Hank eyed a half-eaten plate of finger-food at the head of the table, next to an empty bottle of beer and another, half full. 'Looks like Don started without them. If we had a mind to, we could probably add aiding and abetting a fugitive to Christine Bradshaw's charge sheet, though I doubt Kate would go for it.'

In the living room, the detectives moved past the crime scene photographer, trying not to disturb him. There was a distinct lack of technology on display, no computer on which to carry out illegitimate business, another giveaway that the Bradshaws weren't living there, though Hank spotted a couple of burners which might prove useful in tracking their movements.

Where had they stashed their paraphernalia and their drugs? That question would generate a myriad of enquiries for his team. Whether she knew it or not, Hazel Sharp – the woman who'd taken on the tenancy – was in grave danger. The Bradshaw crew would cover their tracks, leaving no loose ends. They had been in and out of the house, putting up a Christmas tree, getting ready for their sons' arrival.

The Bradshaw boys lay face up in the middle of a carpeted floor, a coffee table pushed against the settee to create space. Lee was closer to the detectives, eyes shut; Jackson further away, near the wall, eyes open.

'God, they're so young,' Lisa said. She'd only seen photos of these two, never met them in the flesh. 'Lee was alive when they pulled him into the house.' She was stating a fact, not asking a question. She excelled at reading a scene.

Hank stepped sideways, inviting her to take his place. 'Tell me what you see.'

'What is this, a test?'

'It's important that we're on the same page.'

Lisa crouched down beside Lee's body, took a moment, then looked up. 'An attempt at CPR by one of his parents?' To demonstrate, she used the heel of her gloved right hand to press down on the left, holding it over the body to simulate chest compressions. 'The ends of my fingers don't match the pattern of blood on Lee's skin. Yours would, so I'm guessing it was Don who tried to revive him.' Lisa pointed to a small amount of blood on Lee's face. 'He used mouth-to-mouth too, I reckon?'

Hank nodded, in complete agreement.

'A father's worst nightmare.' Carmichael had no kids. Hank had a son. 'There are no similar marks on Jackson. His death must have been instantaneous. There's a fair amount of blood on the lower part of both brothers' jeans.'

'Yeah, looks like Don took the full impact of the shot that killed him, fell backwards landing across their legs.' A camera flash lit up Carmichael's pale face.

'You OK, Lisa?'

'Yeah, wondering how Ash is.'

15

Nico had asked Kate to leave, then begged her to stay. Their friendship meant too much to fall out over something beyond their control. Kate kept her coat on, asking if they could sit in the garden. It wasn't only that she was claustrophobic in the house. She had an ulterior motive for choosing to go outside. He made coffee and brought it out onto the decking where a frameless glass balustrade ran around the terrace sheltering them from the prevailing wind. The sun had come out, but it was icy.

'You want a blanket?' he said.

'No, I'm fine, thanks.'

'Tell me that in ten minutes.'

Handing her a steaming mug of froth, he'd only just sat down when they both heard a vehicle pulling onto the driveway. Excusing himself, he got up again. Sliding open the patio doors, he went through the house to see who was arriving. Kate suspected that a raft of visitors would call on him today.

She was keen to avoid them.

Glancing over her shoulder, she could see through the living room into the hallway. Oscar was at the door, laden with festive parcels, a last-minute shopper. He showed no signs of anxiety or upset. His father said something, causing him to peer out through the window.

Kate waved.

Oscar made a beeline for her.

She was on her feet by the time he reached her, wishing her a Happy Christmas, a greeting she returned. He was barely recognisable: pale, much thinner than he'd been when she'd last seen him. He smelled strongly of alcohol. He wouldn't pass a breathalyser. As if he'd read her mind, he pointed at her coffee mug, then grimaced at his father.

'Papa, it's Christmas. Surely we have something stronger.'

'We had wine already,' Kate said.

'Baklava?'

'I'm fine, thanks.'

Oscar's impeccable manners and good humour melted away as he realised that the mood between his father and Kate was awkward. 'Am I interrupting?' He jumped to the wrong conclusion. 'Oh, please . . . let's not do this again.' He meant get upset about his mother. 'Fuck's sake! I'm seeing the kids in half an hour. I've been ordered to arrive with a smile on my face.'

'This isn't a welfare visit.' Nico glanced at Kate. 'You'd better tell him.'

'Tell me what?' Oscar eyed her with suspicion.

As she explained the reason for her being there, she studied him closely. He became tense, his agitation clearly visible. Then confrontational, rudely interrupting her in full flow. Before she could finish what she started, he turned, going back inside, helping himself to a stiff drink that he gulped down before returning to the garden.

'Papa, I'm off—'

'Don't go on my account,' Kate said. 'I'll be leaving myself shortly.'

'Yeah, well, I'm not listening to any more of your shite!' For a long, uncomfortable moment Oscar stared at her with hard eyes. 'Oh, now I get it. You think one of us is responsible.' He lost it then. 'Well, fuck you, Kate.'

'Hey!' Nico said. 'Mind your mouth. Kate's here because—'

'Save it for someone who gives a shit, Papa.' Oscar pulled out his car keys.

'I'll call you a taxi,' Kate said.

'No, you won't.'

'Then let me give you a lift.'

'So you can take me in? That's why you're here, right?'

'Oscar, why are you so angry?'

'Why do you think?'

Unsettling questions were jostling in Kate's head. Had he been patient, biding his time, waiting to deliver justice for his mother? Or, fearing that the case would be shelved due to lack of evidence, the file left to gather dust in the corner of the incident room, had he realised that Lee and Jackson would eventually surface, providing him with the opportunity to take the law into his own hands? Was that why he'd been acting weird since his mother's death, allowing his temper to get the better of him, unable to handle the idea of shooting the Bradshaw boys in cold blood?

Before Kate had time to say more, he stormed out.

Nico apologised for his behaviour. 'Give him time, Kate. He'll come round.'

She hid her scepticism, turning her eyes to the horizon, the light fading over the hilltops in the distance. Time and again the family had been assured that Georgina's case would be reallocated. It hadn't been. Every day, the news spoke of mounting stress on the police service and the judiciary. Understaffed and under enormous pressure, the criminal justice system was on its knees.

The idea that Oscar might have taken advantage of the Bradshaw brothers' return in the dead of night was pushing the boundaries of credibility. That didn't make it impossible. That's what had been niggling Kate all morning and why she'd asked Nico to sit outside, hoping it might jog his memory when she raised the matter.

Nico sat down and so did she.

Ask him.

She hesitated, unsure how to broach the subject. In the end, she decided to go the direct route. Slowly, she turned to face him. 'Do you remember the conversation we had out here on the day of Georgina's funeral, about exhumation?'

'How could I forget? The prospect of that happening terrified me.'

'Did you ever repeat that to anyone?'

'Only to Oscar.'

That didn't surprise Kate. Charlotte would have thrown herself in the grave rather than let anyone dig up her mum after she'd been laid to rest. No family wanted that. If the Bradshaws were guilty, and it could be proven beyond a reasonable doubt, that wouldn't now happen. Kate's stomach took a dive. In helping Nico understand the process, had she inadvertently given one or all of them a motive?

16

Hank and Lisa spoke briefly with Ella Stafford, the woman who'd called the control room to report that shots had been fired. No further forward, they kept it short, crossing the road to meet with the eyewitness, Martin Alexander. His house was identical to the Bradshaws', only better kept with a well-tended garden and recently painted front door. Hank thought the man who opened it looked familiar. He was late forties, fit body, rugged features, dark hair, dark eyes, designer stubble.

Carmichael held up ID. 'Mr Alexander, I'm DS Lisa Carmichael and this' – she thumbed in Hank's direction – 'is DS Hank Gormley, the SIO investigating the incident you witnessed during the night. Can we go inside?'

'Sure.' He stepped back to let them in.

The house was warm and cosy inside. The smell of a fry-up wafting along the hallway made Hank's stomach rumble. He'd overslept, leaving no time for breakfast. When all hell let loose, he'd missed lunch too. He was hoping that whoever was cooking might arrive and offer to fill the hole in his stomach.

He was out of luck.

'Will this take long?' Alexander said. 'I'm due in Cramlington in a couple of hours.'

'Shift-worker?' Hank asked.

'Paramedic.'

'We won't keep you long. We need to go over what you saw and heard. It would be helpful to know exactly where you were when the shooting happened.'

'Front bedroom.' He pointed up the stairs. 'Help yourselves.'

'Sir, we need you with us,' Carmichael explained.

'You go up, I'll only be a second.' Alexander excused himself to turn off the cooker.

At the bottom of the stairs, Hank glanced into a room leading off the hallway. A huge festive tree dominated the living room, decorated with great care, a small pile of gifts beneath the bottom branches. He was unlikely to see his own decorations this holiday. Julie had invited friends over for Christmas dinner. He still hadn't called to tell her he wouldn't be able to join them.

It wouldn't go down well.

He led the way, Lisa following him up.

'Friendly, isn't he?' she said.

'Unless he's the shooter.'

'Point taken.'

At the bedroom window, they looked down on the street below. CSIs were hard at work, dusting for prints, looking for shell casings and other items that may or may not turn out to be of evidentiary value. Inside the railings, the front door was visible, though a dense laurel hedge obscured the small garden from the road. The perfect place for a shooter to lay in wait for two cocky kids who'd eluded police for too long.

Behind them, Alexander mounted the stairs.

Hank turned as he appeared in the doorway, a bacon butty the size of a doorstep in his right hand, a bite-size shape missing from it. Clocking his interest, Alexander swallowed what was in his mouth and ran his tongue over his teeth before speaking. 'Mind if I scoff while we talk?' He held up the sandwich. 'If I don't eat now, I may not get the chance.'

'No, get it down you.' Carmichael eyed Hank.

He was sulking.

'Don't mind us,' he said. 'We run on fresh air.'

The witness shrugged. 'It's what we all signed up for, right?'

'Absolutely.'

He *was* right. All three expected to be busy handling those who would overindulge on drugs or alcohol, who got into a fight and came off worse or, the saddest of all, tried to end their own lives. Emergency services were always at full stretch during the festive season. When most of the world were happy celebrating, others were desperately sad: suicides and murders more likely in the next few days than at any other time of the year.

'There's no bacon left,' Alexander said. 'You want toast?'

'No time,' Carmichael said. 'We're good, thanks.'

Hank was tempted to tell her to speak for herself. He could murder a slice. 'My 2ic is right. We'd love some scran, but we're on the clock.'

'You do know I gave a statement to the house-to-house team?'

'We do.' So, Alexander was aware of police procedure. Grateful that he wouldn't have to explain every step of a journey that would one day end in a courtroom, Hank entertained the notion that his witness was ex-job, as many paramedics and ambulance crew were. If he was, he chose not to mention it. 'Can you show us exactly where you were standing last night?'

Alexander walked to the right of an open sash window. 'Here.'

'Why there?'

'My kid, Bethany, was out. I told her to be in by midnight at the latest. Me and the missus came to bed early. She fell asleep, I didn't. I can never rest till I know our daughter is safe. I took a shower, rang her a few times. She didn't pick up, let alone appear. I was looking out for her.'

Hank pointed up the street to the left. 'A taxi would bring her in that way?'

'Yeah, the road is closed off at the bottom. And that's when it all kicked off.'

'Describe what you saw.'

'Two kids approached the house, both pissed. I remember thinking they might need an ambulance if they were heading for a party. A shot rang out. One went down. The other got a shot off in return. A third shot took him out too. I was worried that Bethany would get caught in the crossfire.'

'Back up.' Hank already knew the answer to the question he was about to ask. 'I want you to think very carefully about the sequence of events. The victims. Were they facing the door when they were shot?'

'No, they walked up the path. When they reached the door, they turned, as if someone had called out to them. I ran downstairs to see if I could help the casualties.'

'And did you?' Carmichael said.

'No. As far as I knew, the shooter was still around. I didn't see him come or go. I wasn't about to find out, was I? The door opened across the way. The woman who lives there came out. Screamed. Her old man ran out of the house, dragged her and the injured kids inside, along with a firearm he picked up on his way in. It was all over in seconds.'

'So, you knew he was armed?'

'Yeah, that's what I told the firearms team.'

'There were no further shots fired when the tenants came outside?' Hank asked.

'None.'

'How did you know they were kids?' Carmichael asked. 'I mean, it was dark. The house is between lampposts. The curtains were closed and there's no security light on the front door. Hard to see, right?'

Alexander hesitated. 'I didn't know, I assumed. They were wearing hoodies.'

'I wear hoodies and I'm not a kid,' Carmichael said.

'So do I . . .' Alexander shrugged. 'What can I say? They looked like kids. They walked like kids. The one who returned fire didn't look that old.'

'What angle was his arm?' Hank said.

'What?'

'Was he pointing the gun directly towards your house, to the left or right of the front door? I'm trying to place the shooter.'

'To the right.'

'Don't suppose you got your phone out?'

'No, it was downstairs charging. The shooting was all over in seconds. I'm bloody glad I wasn't walking across the street when the door opened. The guy who lives there might've taken me for the gunman. This is a quiet street, or was till they moved in.'

'Did you ever speak to them?'

'No, she looked like a million dollars, but she had a foul mouth on her. Anyway, they were never there. I mean, I saw them receive a food delivery, a Christmas tree and stuff, otherwise there's been no comings and goings I'm aware of.'

'How did they transport the tree?'

'What?' Alexander frowned.

'What vehicle did they use?'

'I don't know. Someone dropped it off, I think. I couldn't swear to it.'

'Have you ever seen them drive up?'

'No, come to think of it. I saw them get out of a taxi once or twice. I don't remember which firm. It was a private cab. Hard to tell who's legit and who's faking it these days, trying to make a buck in the run-up to Christmas.'

Hank would put money on the Bradshaws having dodged up a vehicle to appear as if it was a cab and that the driver of said cab would be a heavy on their payroll. 'You had no idea who they were?'

'Still don't.' Alexander didn't ask and Hank didn't tell.

'You didn't think to call us?' Carmichael asked.

'No, I assumed the guy who lived there would. I mean, he was hardly going to drag two strangers inside, was he?' Alexander paused. 'Look, there are times you keep your nose out of other people's business. This was one of them. I got caught up in my own drama. Bethany called me as I went upstairs, smashed off her face. One of her mates had fallen at a party in town. The restaurant owner called an ambulance. They took her to the RVI. Bethany went with her. She said she couldn't get a signal to call home until she left the hospital. By the time

I got the story out of her, the firearms team were crawling all over the place. I identified myself as a paramedic and offered to help. The OIC told me to sling my hook. He wouldn't let me anywhere near the scene.'

Carmichael said, 'Can we speak to Bethany?'

'Not here you can't. She stayed out to look after her mate. Well, that's what she said. I suspect it was to avoid me.' He shook his head. 'Bloody kids. I've never met one who could do as they're told. They're probably sleeping it off as we speak.' Alexander took another bite of his sandwich, then put it down on the bedside table to write on a notepad.

Hank stared at it, salivating.

Alexander handed the note to Lisa. 'Bethany's number. I warn you, the state she was in, it'll be like trying to raise the dead.'

17

Hank and Carmichael left the morgue with exactly what they had hoped for: confirmation that Jackson Bradshaw died from a single shot to the head – Lee hit in the chest: Amen. A small calibre handgun, ten a penny on the street if you knew where to look; an estimated time of death – approximately 3 a.m. – confirmed by Ella Stafford who called the incident in, eye-witness Martin Alexander, first responders and the firearms callout from the control room. Formal ID of the deceased had been made at the scene by their mother, confirmed by finger-prints stored on the PNC database.

'Lee and Jackson didn't get that tan in Heaton or from a bottle,' Carmichael said as she walked with Hank towards their pool car. 'In my book, that's conclusive proof that they've been living abroad. What I don't understand is how. They had no social security or dole money and they're lazy, not the type to do an honest day's work. Who do you know who could afford to live for three years without income? I couldn't.'

'Drug money, Lisa. They'll have had plenty of readies stashed away, picked it up the day they got out, murdered Georgina, then fled. Or their mum was wiring it via a relay of banks so we couldn't trace it.'

They climbed into the car.

Hank started the engine, waiting while she strapped herself in. 'When we get to base, raise an all-ports action. No, cancel that. Get Maxwell to do it. If we can establish where the Jackson boys re-entered the UK, we might get a handle on where they've been hiding out. Costa del Crime is about the extent of their imagination. You never know, we might get an early break.'

Carmichael made the call, then hung up.

Placing her phone on the dash, she thought about Hank's comment. 'You think there's an alternative explanation for their deaths than the one we've all been avoiding?'

He stopped at traffic lights, glancing into the passenger seat. 'Such as?'

'Well, wherever they went, they'd be up to no good. That's a given. Isn't it possible that they upset a lowlife abroad, bit off more than they could chew, were followed home and taken out—'

'Keep dreaming, Lisa. You don't believe that any more than I do. We're looking for someone closer to home, someone who's been planning their demise for a very long time.'

'If that's the case, how would they know when and where to strike?'

'Not the first time we've lifted a fugitive who'd come out of hiding to visit family at Christmas, would it? Any cop with half a brain knows that.'

It was dark by the time Kate left Rothbury, the A1 still busy north and southbound. She called Hank, arranging to rendezvous with him away from their area command where they were likely to be overheard. The pub they had chosen was heaving when she arrived, a happy, well-dressed crowd of partygoers beginning a night out at their local. Kate took a seat near the door to wait. She was about to text Jo to see if she was still in the office when one pinged in. Jo had beaten her to it:

I'm making dinner. Tom and James are joining us. Four is nice. Two is better. Lucky for us, they're heading out to meet mates. ☺

Kate smiled. She'd give anything to have Jo to herself, a chance to make up for their harsh words that morning. She keyed a reply.

> In the middle of something. ☹
> Can't you get away?
> Unlikely . . .

Guilt was eating Kate up. She could go home. Should do so, but Georgina's file was calling out to her, the only thing on her mind. What was so urgent that it couldn't wait? Nothing, was the answer, except her team were working flat out. How could she slope off to spend Christmas with her family while they could not? The argument going on in her head was unresolved when another text arrived . . .

> I'll make it worth your while.

Kate was about to add an apology when three images appeared on a muted TV above the bar, all with the surname Bradshaw: Donald, Lee, and Jackson. Moving text along the bottom of the screen angered her. The revolving caption was designed to shame and told only half the story: *Breaking: Police marksman shoots to kill.*

She sent another text.

> Turn on your TV.

There was a short pause before Kate received a reply:

> Oh, Kate. Any arrests?

Negative. Gotta go. Hank's here. Tell you later.
Be careful. x

Hank ordered at the bar and brought the drinks over, raising a glass to welcome in the so-called season of goodwill before they turned their attention to work. Kate gave him a lot to consider and pointers on what he should do next. 'I want the team to put their heads together and come up with a list of everyone they remember seeing or speaking to at Georgina's funeral, in or out of the job.'

'Wasn't Carmichael wearing a covert-cam?'

'That doesn't mean she captured everyone there. She turned the evidence over to Curtis, right after the service. He told me later that he'd interviewed everyone he could identify. I want to view it myself. If necessary, I'll raise actions to have them all seen again.'

'That's a hell of a job.'

'I'm in charge of the budget now. If I need a task force to hunt them down, so be it. I must be certain he didn't miss anyone. Did you find out if Charlotte and Oscar were on duty last night?'

'Charlotte was off duty.'

'And Oscar?'

'D rota East End.'

'Shit!'

'Yeah, I know. Less than a mile from the crime scene.'

'Did he take any time off?'

'Not that I'm aware of. He was single crewed all night, though I wouldn't read too much into it—'

'I'm not so sure, Hank. I saw him earlier. He's an angry man.'

'So why didn't you ask him?'

'He flew off the handle when I told him the Bradshaw boys were dead, and walked out before I got the chance. Besides it's your case until I say otherwise. He worries me, Hank. Friendships count for nothing in situations like these. He's not going to like it when you pull him in for questioning.'

'Thanks for the heads-up.'

'Least I can do. Any problems your end?'

Hank shared his run-in with the CSI manager. 'He got the message to keep his big mouth shut. Officers are canvassing house-to-house. ANPR are checking vehicles within a mile radius of the crime scene.'

'Good. How did it go with Alexander?'

'Fine. I'm sure Lee and Jackson were the targets.'

'Based on what?'

'His account. No shots were fired at Christine or Don when they came outside. If a rival gang had been responsible, they would have finished the job. Alexander should make a good witness.'

'You seem conflicted.'

Hank pulled his glass away from his mouth. 'There's something off about him. He's a paramedic I thought I'd seen before. Thing is, he wasn't driving an ambulance at the time. Mind you, he's the double of Clive Owen, so maybe that's why he looked familiar. I've been racking my brains and still can't place him.'

'Go with your gut, Hank.'

'I am. Lisa's running his name through the system. The guy didn't flinch when I walked in. If we've met before, he hid it well.' Hank continued to fill her in on his first impressions of the crime scene and what he'd learned from it that he could put to Christine Bradshaw in interview.

Kate bit her bottom lip, considering.

'What did I miss?' He pointed at her mouth. 'You always do that bitey thing when something does or doesn't add up.'

She gave a wry smile. 'Did Alexander mention the Bradshaws carrying luggage?'

'No, why?'

'Not even a backpack?'

Hank shook his head.

Kate took a moment. Thinking time. 'You said the table was set for a party as if they were expected home. No luggage would suggest they hadn't come straight from the airport. Or they travelled light in case they were spotted and had to make a run for it. They wouldn't necessarily bring owt with them.

Christine would have a pile of knocked-off kit waiting for them. Did you find any at the house?'

'No,' Hank said. 'But CSIs were still in the throes when I left.'

'My point is, if Oscar was cruising the East End alone, he may have seen them and flipped.'

'He'd hardly be driving around with a firearm in the glove box of his squad car, would he?'

'I supposed not.' Kate sifted alternatives, none she wanted to believe. 'Maybe he saw them earlier, kept obs on them and did something about it. Maybe he'd seen Don and Christine moving into their temporary home. Much as we'd like to, we can't ignore the possibility that he was in the right place at the right time.'

18

Zac Matthews had been waiting patiently outside Bright's office for Kate's return. He stood as he saw her approach from the corridor. He was fifty-seven years old, hair silver at the temples, not much up top, and a face that had seen enough trauma in his career to last a lifetime, every line representing another victim, another family in distress.

'Zac, apologies for keeping you hanging. It's good to see you.'

He smiled. 'It's been a while.'

'You know why you're here?'

He nodded.

'Come in . . .' He reached Bright's office door before she did, allowing her to enter first. In better light, he looked as tired as she felt. 'Make yourself comfortable. You want coffee? I need one . . .' She pointed at a fancy machine in the corner. 'Cappuccino, latte, espresso, you name it, I have it.'

'As it comes.' He took a seat on the other side of Bright's desk.

'I've been giving Nico the lowdown on what happened over-night before the press break his door down. It took longer than expected. He had a lot to say about Curtis—'

'He has every right. The man was . . . is a moron.'

'How the hell did you end up as his 2ic?'

Zac showed surprise. 'You don't know?'

'Know what?'

'Bright put me there to keep an eye on him. After your spat with the Chief, he needed evidence that she couldn't ignore. That's why Curtis left and why she shelved the case for lack of evidence to prevent you taking over.' He shook his head. 'She's a piece of work.'

'Never repeat that outside of this office.'

He grinned. 'Which bit?'

'Any of it.' He hadn't so far, or she'd have known about it.

'Is the guv'nor still away?'

'Not for much longer.'

'How is Nico?'

'Angry . . . as is Oscar. I've yet to see Charlotte.' Kate sat down, handing him a small posh cup. He peered into it, as if searching for contents, making her laugh.

He eyed the murder file on her desk. 'What do you want from me?'

'I won't keep you long tonight, but I'm short on manpower. Are you up for a temporary transfer?'

'I'm up to my eyes, Kate. I'm here now. What do you need?'

She placed a hand on the file. 'Before I read this, I'd like a handle on what went on before Georgina died.'

He drained his cup in one go, a pause before diving in. 'Geoff Mather was Georgina's shift inspector. He gave her the heads-up that the Bradshaws were out before roll call at 22:00 hours the night before she died, a warning he advised her not to ignore. She refused his offer to take the night off, so he made sure she was double-crewed. She had a difficult shift: some minor assaults, I forget how many; a stranger rape, a nasty stabbing. She left that victim at A&E at around six a.m., returning to base to write it up and hand over to the CID. His injuries were potentially fatal. She left work at eight fifteen, two hours later than expected.'

'Did anyone confirm that?'

Zac nodded. 'Given the circumstances, Geoff hung around that morning and walked her to her vehicle. Georgina was ultra-cautious, checking the car park for anyone hanging around. He waved her off and was first to hear of her death. Curtis was on call, then I gather the control room notified you.'

The controller's last words echoed in Kate's head:

She didn't make it, boss.

19

Carmichael was at the vending machine in the corner of the incident room. Seeing Hank approach, she dropped more coins into the slot and pressed for black coffee. She waited for it to dispense, then handed him a steaming paper cup.

He waved it away.

'Drink it. And when you have, you might like one of these.' She pulled half a packet of extra strong mints from her pocket. 'Christine Bradshaw's brief arrived. You don't want to go in there smelling of beer.'

'Thanks.' He took them from her. 'Who did she get?'

'William Montagu. He's in conference with her now. He sent a message via the custody sergeant that he has another engagement and can't hang around. He's ready to proceed if you are.'

Montagu was thin, of pale complexion, with silver hair and a full beard. A solicitor of standing, he was impeccably dressed in a tuxedo, a crisp white shirt and black bow tie, on his way out for the evening by the looks of it. He was escorted into the interview room, along with his client. Christine Bradshaw dwarfed him by eight inches. She'd arrived at the station in an expensive cashmere coat, leather gloves and knee-length boots. Now she was wearing a forensic suit – her bloody clothing having been retained as evidence.

Christine knew how to dress . . .

What she had difficulty with was stopping what came out of her mouth.

Hitching up his suit trousers, Montagu sat down. Christine took the seat next to him, her bodybuilding pecs visible through the flimsy material of her suit. Her arms could hold a copper in a headlock until his or her eyes popped. She'd always been a gym freak, a woman only a stranger would cross. Since Hank last saw her, she'd had work done.

She'd wasted her money.

Her venomous eyes flitted between the detectives waiting to question her. She and Hank went back a long way. She'd never had any dealings with Carmichael and gave her the once-over.

Taking a legal pad and fountain pen from his briefcase, Montagu set them down on the table, waiting for Hank to state the time and date, identifying himself and Carmichael, before giving his own name and profession. The suspect ID'd herself as Christine Elizabeth Bradshaw. Hank delivered the caution, asking her if she understood why she'd been arrested.

She said nothing.

'For the benefit of the recording, Ms Bradshaw declined to answer.'

'It's hardly surprising . . .' Montagu's piercing eyes fixed on Hank. 'The fact that we are sitting here with someone who lost three members of her family in the early hours of this morning is nothing short of an outrage.' He shut down Hank's response by lifting a hand. 'Allowances should have been made for the fact that two young men, my client's sons, were lying dead in her home when a firearms team entered her premises, one of whom then shot and killed her husband.'

Here we go.

Hank extended his condolences to Christine.

'Shove it up your arse,' she said. 'I've been here all day!'

'Because you were pissed and fighting,' Hank said. 'We thought we'd give you time to calm down.'

'You fuckers are all the same.'

Montagu snapped his head round, a non-verbal warning to his client to keep it civil.

'Don't shush me. Look at them. They're enjoying this.'

'Really?' Hank raised an eyebrow. 'There are places we'd rather be—'

She cut him dead. 'Did you orchestrate this shitshow, Hank?'

He turned to face Montagu. 'Sir, I accept everything you say. However, Ms Bradshaw and her late husband must bear full responsibility for the position they are now in.'

'You mean on a cold slab?' Christine interrupted.

Hank didn't bite. 'They ignored the police negotiator—'

'So what?'

'And failed to open up when asked to do so,' Hank continued as if she hadn't interrupted. 'The officer in charge waited several hours for them to cooperate before giving the order to enter. Before the scene was properly secure, Don Bradshaw pointed a loaded gun at the officer, threatening to blow his head off. Perceiving an immediate threat to life, he made a split-second judgement no officer wants to make.' Montagu was about to speak. 'Let me finish please. Police witnesses will testify that the OIC's actions were fully justified—'

'That's a lie,' Christine exploded. 'And not for you to say. You weren't there.'

'Ms Bradshaw has a point,' Montagu said. 'The matter will be referred to the Independent Office for Police Conduct and Northumbria's Directorate of Professional Standards in due course.'

'I don't need a lesson on what comes next from you, sir,' Hank said.

'I'll be their star witness,' Christine crowed.

'And the IOPC will discover that Don was in unlawful possession of a loaded firearm that had recently been discharged.' Hank paused to let that sink in. 'Forensic swabs taken from him will confirm gunshot residue on his hands.'

'That proves nothing. It was used outside the house. He took it in for the safety of the public.'

'You crack me up, Christine. Always did. Not to be unkind, but your old man and consideration for others don't go hand in hand, so shut up and listen for once in your life and stop trying to deflect the blame.' Hank leaned in. 'There was a paramedic standing by to help your sons. If you'd let the officers in, Lee or Jackson might still be alive, Don too. Our lot did everything they could to save anyone else from getting hurt.'

Though he tried to hide it, Montagu thought so too.

To avoid looking at either of them, he checked his watch, then raised his head, impatiently tapping his pen on the table. 'Can we stop wasting time and get on with the business at hand?'

'With respect, I didn't bring the matter up,' Hank said. 'I'm pretty sure you did.'

'Yes, and I'd be failing in my duty as Ms Bradshaw's legal counsel if I didn't provide context. That's what I'm here for, to set the record straight and explain the extenuating circumstances to the charge my client is facing. Surely, even you can see that she acted out of grief and desperation.'

Carmichael bristled; an acid tone to her voice, as she spoke: 'There's no mitigation for striking a police officer with a baseball bat from behind, splitting his head wide open. That firearms officer is no longer on duty. He's in hospital receiving surgical treatment for a nasty head wound and concussion.'

'I hope he dies!' Christine blurted out.

'You want to hope he doesn't.' Carmichael was dead calm. 'Clearly you have no regrets. I'll make it my business to repeat that when your case comes to court. Lack of remorse isn't going to play well, is it?'

Christine was playing blink first with Carmichael. A casual observer would describe the look she gave the detective as pure hatred. She was trying to intimidate. It wasn't working. Lisa was stronger than that. She held her bottle. There wasn't a hope in hell that she'd let this woman get the better of her.

Montagu said, 'I'm sure my client didn't mean that—'

Christine rounded on him. 'I fucking did.'

20

Despite her promise not to keep him long, Kate and Zac remained deep in conversation, unpicking the enquiry into Georgina's death, sometimes referring to the original murder file, sometimes not. It was as time-consuming as it was exhausting and distressing for both detectives. Several times during the conversation, tortuous thoughts arrived in Kate's head: images of inside and outside the crime scene tent; Curtis's fury; Georgina's lifeless body; her bloody uniform and the softly spoken voice of pathologist Sue Morrisey interpreting the victim's plight through her own forensic lens.

She'd been kneeling when shot.

Looking away, Kate closed her eyes: *focus.*

Zac's voice bled into her thoughts. 'Even shite know that most people are creatures of habit: drinking in the same pubs, jumping on the last Metro home – in Georgina's case taking the same path through the woods. Nico told us she walked there a lot, before and after work – a ritual, he called it.'

On occasion, I went with her, Kate thought.

'My theory is, they were counting on her going there and that's exactly what happened. She played into their hands, Kate. It looked like they had got away with it, until someone took them out this morning.'

'Nico can't understand why she went to the riverside that morning, given what she knew.'

Zac said, 'Would you?'

'I don't know. Maybe she underestimated the threat, though I doubt that. She knew what they were capable of. She felt safe there. Maybe she needed time to get her head straight before telling Nico.' She met Zac's eyes across the desk, hoping to persuade him to join the MIT, if only for a short while. 'If only she'd called me, I'd have taken her home and gone with her.'

'You guys were close?'

'Very.'

'Kate, I'm sorry, I had no idea.'

She moved on. 'Tell me these theories were raised with Curtis.'

'They were, but when Lee and Jackson skipped the country, he saw it as an admission of guilt and never looked past it. He was unwilling to listen to anyone who disagreed with him – and there were plenty of us who did. Believe me, we spoke up.'

'There's no mention of it in his notes.'

'Nothing went in there that he didn't want others to see.'

Kate studied him. 'The Bradshaw brothers used fists, knives, baseball bats. This time they used a gun. Did no one think that odd?'

'Less messy. Less risk of getting caught.'

'Yeah, I get that—'

'You're not suggesting that they weren't responsible?'

'I have to prove that they were.'

'Kate, Georgina's evidence sealed their fate at court. It cost them the best part of four years. They were hell-bent on revenge. A snout told us Lee had extra reasons to want her gone. His lass scarpered the minute he went down, taking their baby to a place of safety, far enough away so she wouldn't be found.'

'Hardly Georgina's fault.'

'Not the way Lee saw it. He was a bully with a quick temper, Jackson the weak one. I'm betting he pulled the trigger. Lee used him for serious grunt work. They had to be sure Georgina didn't live or they'd spend the rest of their lives banged up. Smart move. One clean shot. No witnesses. A military operation In. Out. Job done. We found no physical evidence linking them to her. That's not to say there was none. I'd love to help you find it.'

21

Hank studied Christine. There were no visible signs that she'd even shed a tear since the shooting. She was the matriarch of the Bradshaw family, as hard as any offender he'd come across, male or female. All she cared about was how much money she could make from organised crime.

'Let's not trade blows,' he said to Montagu. 'Ms Bradshaw has already demonstrated that she's on a short fuse with no off switch. Her lifestyle choices are well-documented. She's a recidivist offender with a long history of importing and distributing drugs, not to mention violent behaviour, including separate incidents of GBH and one of attempted murder.'

'Which I was found not guilty of.'

'On this occasion the cameras were rolling. You don't have a leg to stand on.'

'We'll see.' She was smiling as she said it.

'You're not helping yourself, Christine.' Crossing his arms, Hank leaned back in his chair, let out a heavy sigh. 'How long have we known each other?'

'Too long.'

'Have I ever been unreasonable?'

'Are you serious?' she scoffed.

'I'm offering you more time to consider your position before we proceed. DS Carmichael and I are in no hurry—'

'I am,' Montagu said. 'So, stop scoring points and get on with it.'

'I assure you this is not a game,' Hank said. 'Perhaps Christine would like to offer an explanation for her actions?'

'Like hell.'

'Thought not. You're aware that there was an existing warrant out for your boys, weren't you?' Hank waited. No response was forthcoming. 'Too hard a question? Then let me help you with that. Following the murder of Police Constable Georgina Ioannou, you were informed of the warrant and questioned by murder detectives over the whereabouts of your sons.'

'Interrogated, you mean? Yeah, I remember.'

'You declined to help—'

'You don't say.'

Hank didn't miss a beat. 'This afternoon we found evidence in your house that suggests you were expecting them. Their names were on Christmas presents under the tree, Christine.' She glared at him. He continued. 'I don't need to remind you that harbouring fugitives from justice is a criminal offence. You've done it before, more times than I care to remember. What I don't understand is why you didn't call an ambulance when your boys needed urgent medical intervention.'

'No comment.'

'It would be every mother's instinct, surely?'

'No comment.'

'Were you hoping they'd survive, that you might spirit them away before we reached the scene? Our response times are down, not out. We'd have made a special effort for you.'

'Don't get too cocky, Hank. Lee lived long enough to tell his dad that he was ambushed by a cop.'

'He did?' Hank was being ironic. 'Care to enlighten us?'

'Are you disputing my client's account?' Montagu said.

'Absolutely.'

'Sounds like hearsay to me.' Carmichael couldn't help herself.

'Was it shite,' Christine said. 'I heard it with my own ears.'

'Did he give a name?' Carmichael pushed.

'My lad has . . . had, a sixth sense.'

'We deal with facts, not feelings,' Hank said.

'Lee knows a pig when he sees one. Is that clear enough for you? Don said it was a dying declaration.'

'So, you didn't hear it,' Hank said. 'You've been watching too much telly, Christine. This is the real world.'

'Perhaps you'd like to return to it then,' Montagu said.

'Certainly. I'll leave you to explain what constitutes a dying declaration to your client in case she wishes to use it as a defence in the future. Let's move on, shall we?' Hank eyeballed Christine. 'Did you strike the firearms officer with a baseball bat?'

'No comment.'

'I can see we're wasting our time here.' Hank scooped his papers off the table and glanced at Carmichael. 'We're done . . . for now.'

'For now?' Montagu was desperate to leave. 'Given the tragic circumstances that took place prior to this interview, I assume you'll bail my client.'

'That's yet to be determined,' Hank said. 'There's no need for you to wait around. You have somewhere you need to be, as do we. We'll take good care of Ms Bradshaw. As you can tell, we're very well acquainted. She'll be held in the cells to give her time to reconsider her position while we follow protocol.'

'And do what?' Christine said.

'It's called a risk assessment. It'll help me decide what to do with you.'

'Risk to who?'

Hank glanced at Carmichael. 'Would you like to explain?'

Lisa opened the file in front of her in which she had made extensive handwritten notes while Hank was liaising with Kate. She turned the first page, then another, taking her time, making their prisoner wait, then slid the relevant section across to Hank. He gave a nod, her cue to carry on.

She looked at the accused. 'Last time we let you out on bail, you went straight to the pub, drank yourself stupid and laid into the first person who looked at you the wrong way, with a beer glass. Her injuries required major surgery.'

'Do I look like I give a fuck?'

'Not content with that, it says here that you poured petrol over your solicitor's car and set fire to it.' Carmichael didn't need to look at Montagu. His anxiety was palpable. 'A repeat of such volatile behaviour would reflect badly on our department—'

Christine smirked. 'If you keep me in, your life won't be worth living.'

Carmichael met her gaze. 'Are you threatening me?'

'I'm warning you.'

'Good, because retribution didn't go well for your boys now, did it?'

Carmichael flinched as Christine leapt from her seat without warning, almost upending the table, sending plastic cups of water and the detectives' notes flying. Lisa's face paled as she scrambled to pick them up. Seeing her reaction, Hank took charge, managing not to yell.

'Sit down or I'll have you removed,' he said.

'Go to hell.' Christine stood her ground.

'As you wish . . .' Hank made a show of checking his watch. 'This interview is over. Mr Montagu, given your failure to control your client, we'll resume first thing in the morning or whenever it's convenient for you to get here.'

Christine wasn't having that.

She sat down, leaning in, intimidating Carmichael as she retook her seat. 'When I appear before a magistrate, within shouting distance of the press bench, your pissy evidence will collapse under the weight of the horror I've experienced at the hands of police, a public relations own goal for you, the OIC who shot my old man and the cop who murdered my sons. How does that sound? And just so you know, my voice is so loud you'll hear it in your dreams.'

22

It was good to have Zac's insight. When he left Northern Area Command, Kate logged onto HOLMES; the national management information system created to aid major investigations. Fed by specially trained indexers, the electronic tool collected and collated paper-generated data. Anyone who came up during the enquiry into Georgina's murder – witness, suspect or police officer – was listed there.

Kate had been flipping between screens for an hour and three quarters, referring to Curtis's notes at the same time. His policy document included over-elaborate diagrams. Pretty, Kate thought, but meaningless to his crew. Murder detectives familiar with the system were programmed to recognise the difference between white noise and intelligence of real value. If they were any good, they homed in on what was important, short-circuiting the crap.

Switching from the digital file to his policy book, the first thing she noticed was how flimsy Curtis's stuff was, most of it unnecessary, designed to make him look good to those upstairs. His scrappy handwriting was beginning to blur in front of her. She turned the page, happening upon something that caused a sharp intake of breath, a report she had to read several times, just to make sure she hadn't read it wrong.

She hadn't.

This was a new low, even by his standards.

Kate took off her glasses and sat back, shutting her eyes for a moment, then pushed on. It was obvious that Curtis thought he knew the who and the why of her live-unsolved case. The names Lee and Jackson Bradshaw were the only suspects in the frame from the outset, revenge for putting them away being the obvious motive. From what Kate had read so far it was clear that she'd have to start from scratch and consider other theories.

Had Curtis given in to pressure from within their organisation? He wasn't the only one who'd been quick to jump to conclusions. The brothers had threatened Georgina, skipping town since her death, but in their line of work, they may have had other reasons for going to ground. Both had made enemies. Either way, it required balls to take them out on the doorstep of one of the region's most prolific, not to mention dangerous, criminal families. Available evidence suggested that this was no drive-by shooting. Whoever had killed them had hidden outside the house with no fear. Kate was asking herself why.

'Brave,' Kate whispered. 'Or stupid.'

Instinctively, she knew it was personal, someone with a grudge, someone who wanted those boys to see the whites of their eyes before drawing their last breath. She got up to stretch her legs, then opened Bright's drinks fridge, helping herself to a bottle of spring water from his private supply.

Sitting down, she unscrewed the top, took a long drink, then resumed her work.

On the face of it, there seemed nothing wrong with the file chronology. Georgina had been found by a jogger, ITV presenter Mark Trewitt, whose shocking discovery was all over the news by nightfall. Her body was in full view, no attempt made to cover it up.

Reading that detail triggered another gut reaction in Kate.

She pulled Curtis's policy document towards her, turned a few pages to a note he'd made, suggesting that because Georgina was in uniform, she hadn't gone home before her walk along the riverside. Picking up her pen, Kate scribbled a note that he'd not pursued that line of enquiry.

This bothered her.

She wrote in the margin: Unproven?

It was clear that she was going to need help. No detective

could work alone to review a historical murder case from start to finish.

A knock at the door startled her.

Carmichael was standing there.

Kate beckoned her in. 'Ah, the very person I want to see. I won't ask how it went with Christine Bradshaw? You look wrung out.'

Carmichael nodded. 'She has that effect on people.'

Kate looked past her to the door. 'Where's Hank?'

'Giving her time to cool off. She's pretty wound up.'

'As am I.' Kate tapped the file in front of her. 'I should keep reading but my eyes are shot. I'm knocking off now and will be in early doors tomorrow. As soon as you bail Bradshaw, I suggest you and Hank do the same.'

'That's undecided. We may keep her in.'

Kate raised an eyebrow. 'It'll invite a lot of flak if you do.'

'From the press?' Carmichael was undaunted. 'I'm up for that and so is Hank.'

'There's more at stake here than the two of you, Lisa.'

Carmichael bristled. 'Yeah, Ash is still in hospital.'

'Oh, God.' Kate held up her hands in apology. 'With all that's going on, I forgot to update you. He's doing fine and will probably be discharged tomorrow.'

Relief flooded Lisa's face.

Kate felt guilty for not putting her mind at rest sooner. 'What I meant was, the department might suffer. With three of Christine's family in the morgue, if we keep her in custody, the press will have a field day. That doesn't bother me too much, but I won't be the one in the middle of a shitstorm, Hank will. It would be a shrewd move to bail her. We'll learn more if she's out and about with an obs team watching her every move.'

It was a calculated risk that might well backfire.

23

Scaffolding shrouded Kate's house, despite a promise that it would be down by Christmas. It had been there for months following an arson attack by an offender determined to stop her looking into his affairs. The upside was that he too was now living in a cage – only his was much larger and more permanent.

In his case, life would mean life.

With no access to the front door, Kate used the rear entrance, locking it behind her, taking off her coat, dumping it on a chair in the newly fitted kitchen, before walking into the hallway. Many of the original features had been destroyed by fire, the internal staircase rebuilt, the ornate newel post and spindles copied. Without the wear and tear of a century of use, they would never bear the history of a home built in the 1800s. The stairs were uncarpeted, the walls newly plastered. The place was a bomb site, and something precious was missing . . . Kate's beloved motorcycle, wrecked in the explosion.

After the fire, Kate would have moved into Jo's house had it not been sold within days of the estate agent putting it online. They had been in temporary digs, a tenancy they gave up when the builders said they'd be finished by Christmas, then broke that deadline, landing Kate and Jo with a dilemma: live in a building site or find alternative accommodation. They chose the former.

Kate found Jo in the living room, curled up on the sofa, a glass of wine in her hand, the TV on. She patted the seat beside her. Kate walked towards it, apologising for her lateness. An outside broadcast was on the late evening news, a voice-over providing details of the shooting Hank had been dealing with all day, flashbacks of a critical incident in full flow, a stand-off, dangerous for all involved.

The images showed a police negotiator, deployed at short notice in the dead of night, utilising a loudspeaker to talk to those barricaded inside, trying to defuse a serious incident that could, and did, escalate – a futile attempt to save lives.

Kate bent over and kissed Jo gently on the lips. 'Sorry I missed Tom and James. Did you have a lovely dinner?'

'We did. They were buzzing. Said to wish you a Merry Christmas.'

'I don't deserve you or them.'

Physically and mentally drained, Kate sat down, her eyes drawn to the TV. On screen, a jump cut to Ash Norham using hand signals for his team to move in, a critical decision he'd taken a hundred times without a hitch. This time, he was un-lucky. Still, it could have been a lot worse if Don Bradshaw had managed to get a shot off. The screen switched to a day-time image of CSIs, a gathering crowd of nosy neighbours and media types, then body bags being loaded into a coroner's van.

Sensitive to Kate's mood, Jo slid a hand into hers, squeezing it gently. 'So, what's the story? Or would you rather not talk about it?'

Kate reacted angrily to the TV presenter. 'Did you hear that? He described it as an assassination. He's wrong. The term involves victims of importance, not some gutless vermin like the Bradshaw boys. It was an execution, just as it was for Georgina.' Kate looked at Jo. 'Sorry for ranting. What did you say just now?'

'I asked if you wanted to talk. You obviously do.' Using the remote, Jo killed the set.

'We don't know much,' Kate said. 'We have a witness who claims the shooter wanted his targets to know exactly what was coming. Apparently, when they reached Christine's front door, her sons turned, as if someone was standing behind them.'

'You think the shooter spoke, then fired?'

'Sounds like it. Makes you wonder what was going through his or her mind at the time. What I need is a good profiler.'

'C'mon, there's nothing I can tell you about the mindset of a killer. I would have thought you'd seen it all by now.'

'Well, give it your best shot or you'll be out of a job.'

Jo smiled. 'A lot has been written, most of it unproven. I'm not saying no one is predisposed genetically or psychologically to murder. Profiling is never that simple though. Looking at this case, a layman might think the shooter lacked self-control. My professional opinion is the exact opposite. We all possess the violence gene. Everyone can snap. Self-control is the difference between us. What's your theory? Another OCG, infighting within Christine's crew?'

'Off the record?'

'Need you ask?'

'This one has all the hallmarks of a revenge attack. I'm wondering if someone close to Georgina has been wrestling with a dilemma, to kill or not to kill, finally snapping on the third anniversary of her death. Top of that list would be Nico, Oscar, and Charlotte. Unless you count three and a half thousand Northumbria officers with a grievance against the Bradshaws. There's a queue of people who believe the death sentence is appropriate. Most of them are in my team, some who'd look the other way if the Ioannou family had played the vigilante card. I'm not one of them.'

'I know . . .' Jo was used to Kate offloading and tried to distract her. 'You eat, then we'll talk. I kept you some dinner.' She made a move to fetch it.

Kate caught her wrist, stopping her. 'I'm sorry, I'm not hungry. Sit with me . . . I've been dying to see you all day.'

Jo sat down, smiling as only she could, putting an arm around Kate.

Kate snuggled into her, then her phone rang, killing the moment.

In a flash, the magic had gone.

Jo had every right to feel pissed off. She wasn't the only one. Irritated, Kate pulled her mobile from her pocket. Recognising the number, she winced. 'I'm sorry, it's the custody sergeant. I'll have to take it.'

Jo's expression spoke for itself: *Don't you always.*

'Daniels.'

'It's Finn Adams, guv.'

'I can see that. What can I do for you?'

'I can't get hold of Hank. I tried his home. His missus said he's not there. He's not in the building either . . . or, if he is, he's not answering his mobile.'

'He'll be tied up with Bradshaw.'

'He's not, guv. That's why I'm calling. She's going apeshit, whipping up a riot. It's like Cell Block H this end. I told her to shut it, but she's not having any. Can I tell her she'll make bail later?'

Kate rolled her eyes at Jo and spoke into the phone. 'Seriously? You called me at home because a prisoner is giving you earache?'

He didn't answer, though she could hear the bedlam going on in the background.

Jo passed a glass of red to Kate, whispering: 'Calm down.'

Kate softened her tone, while remaining firm. 'You're the custody officer. Deal with it.' The notification of another caller trying to connect wound her up further. Adams was falling over himself to apologise. Her phone bleeped again. 'Finn, it's been a tough day and I have a call waiting.'

Hank was in the parade room, using the landline. He was about to disconnect when Kate came on the line, full of hell by the sounds of it. There was no friendly greeting, nor enquiry of how things were going. He'd hoped that having spent time with Jo, she'd be in a good mood, not ready to rip his head off.

'Speak!' she said angrily.

'Sorry to disturb you at home, boss—'

'Yeah? Why did you?'

'I'm unhappy about bailing Christine.' Hank whispered to Carmichael 'She's not happy,' then went back to Kate. 'With Ash still in hospital, I'm not convinced it's the right move. Do you really want to take that chance?'

'Jesus! Am I the only one who can make a decision tonight?'

'What d'you mean?'

'Doesn't matter . . .'

'Does to me.'

'I've just had Finn on the line complaining because Christine is throwing a tantrum in the cells. Hank, I'm not ordering you to release her, but prepare to face a media storm in the morning if you don't. The press won't give a toss that she's the godmother of an organised crime family. They'll see a grieving widow, a recently bereaved mother suffering police oppression on the eve of Christmas.'

'That doesn't bother me.'

'Well, it should.'

'You sound more like Bright every day.'

'Excuse me?'

Carmichael was shaking her head, urging Hank to apologise. Realising he'd crossed the line between professional restraint and familiarity, he should make amends. Kate had let him get close, more than any detective she'd worked with. She wouldn't allow him to take the piss.

He didn't get his apology in quick enough.

'You're the SIO,' she said. 'Start acting like one. Make your call and stick with it. I really don't care.'

'Yes, you do. Look, I'm sorry, you didn't deserve that any more than Bradshaw deserves bail.'

'And you don't deserve to be painted as a vindictive, inhumane arsehole, with too much on your plate to make the right decision. You think I want her out there? I'd like her rotting in a cell for the rest of her days but, as I told Lisa, there's a bigger picture.'

'Yeah, she said. We even set up an obs team. They're await-ing instructions—'

'So, what's your problem?'

'If they lose her, she's in the wind.'

Hank looked at the phone, then at Carmichael. 'She hung up on me.'

24

Montagu instructed Jacob to bring Christine's passport to the nick. Surrendering it was a bail condition. Her driver was told to hang around and pick her up at the main entrance. She looked exhausted and furious as she walked out into the darkness and jumped in the front passenger side, slamming the door, telling him to move off. He did so at speed, putting his foot through the floor, throwing her around in her seat, incurring her wrath.

'Oi! No drawing attention. I'm in enough trouble.'

He eased off the accelerator. 'Where are we going?'

'Short stop on Chilly Road, then the safe house.'

If safe houses were good enough for police, they were good enough for Christine. Hers was a newbuild, complete with pool, gym, sauna, triple garage. She'd bought a plot for next to nowt. It had stood empty and unloved for years. A local architect had designed the perfect home for her sons to live in.

They had no use for it now.

Jacob had read her mind and turned to face her. 'Boss, I'm so sorry about Lee and J—'

'Don't you dare!' she yelled. 'When I find out who betrayed my boys, they're fucking dead.'

Hank lifted his radio: 'We're on,' he said. 'Target vehicle is a Black BMW. Registration: November. Lima. Seven. Zero. Tango. Tango. Papa. Two up. Driver ID'd as Jacob Burrows. Bradshaw is in the front. The rear windows are blacked out. Unclear if there's anyone riding with her.'

'Mike 3459. This is Unit 1. I have the eyeball. Travelling south on Middle Engine Lane. Maintaining speed limit. Taking a left left . . .' There was a short pause in the transition. 'It's a stop at the roundabout . . . Moving off . . . Target vehicle taking the third exit, joining the Coast Road. Passing Battle Hill playing fields. Two car cover.'

Hank said, 'Do not lose her.'

The loss of her family was beginning to hit Christine hard. All she could think of was what was happening at the morgue. She slammed her fist on the dash, letting out an ear-splitting scream as the BMW picked up speed . . . thirty-five, forty, fifty miles an hour. 'Get Tony to meet us there. Tell him to bring the dogs. We might need them. I want to find those murdering bastards before the police do.'

Jacob made the call, then hung up.

'ETA?' she asked.

'Twenty minutes.'

'Good. He'll be there before we are.' She pointed off to her left. 'Pull off at Chilly Road.'

Jacob moved quickly into the inside lane.

'Unit 1: Target vehicle has veered onto the slip road. I repeat, target vehicle has taken the slip road. Unit 2, take the eyeball please?'

'Unit 2: Negative. Too close for us. We're going to have to follow you. Unit 3, can you cover?'

'Unit 3: Affirmative. I have the eyeball. It's a left left onto Chillingham Road. Hold on. The target vehicle is now stationary. I'll drive by and take a look.' He made the manoeuvre, dropping an officer off the second he rounded the corner onto Ravenswood Road. 'All units, 2644 now on foot.'

'2644: I have the eyeball. Target vehicle's rear door is open. One young male exiting. Mid-twenties. Approximately six four. Dark bomber jacket. Tracky bottoms. White trainers. Built. Like an advert for a gym. Too far away to make an ID.'

'Unit 1: Any chance of an image?'

'2644: Sending now. He's approaching an off-licence. Target vehicle's engine is still running. Appears to be waiting. Hold on.' There was radio silence for a few tense moments '2644: The male is now out of the shop. Jogging back to the car. He's in. Target vehicle is on the move. I repeat, target vehicle on the move. Driver has done a quick U-turn. Taking a left left on to the Coast Road. Heading your way Unit 1.'

Blowing out a breath, Hank turned away from the window. He'd lined up a Level One team, the best he could hope for at short notice. Across the room, Carmichael looked like she wanted to kill someone. She vehemently disapproved of the decision to bail Christine. The radio chatter had made her even more nervous.

She approached with a slapped-arse face. 'Have we got enough?'

'Two high-powered motorcycles, several cars and vans.'

They would be super quick, not super shiny, all with front and rear dash cams, a mix of local and national registrations to make them blend into their surroundings, with personnel chosen to appear like casual motorists, be it two males or females together, a male-female combo, with or without someone in the rear.

'What about foot soldiers?' Carmichael asked.

'Thirty plus.'

'I saw Collins move out dressed as an old lady in a head-scarf, Chalky White as a teenager with AirPods in his ears and a peaky cap. They were having a great laugh. You'd think they were off to a fancy dress party. I hope they're taking the op seriously.'

'Relax, Lisa. The surveillance team know who their target is and why they're following. The only thing they're not aware of is her destination. Go and get your head down. I'll update you in the morning.'

'I'm not tired, I'm worried. The boss must realise that

Christine will have a false passport in a dodgy name should she choose to make a run for it. Her kids proved it's possible to slip through the net.'

'I have it covered, Lisa.'

'Do you?' She glared at him: 'You have more faith in airport security than I do.'

25

Kate hadn't slept well. Once up and dressed, she tiptoed downstairs trying not to wake Jo. Yesterday's *Guardian* was on the kitchen bench: *Keep your celebrations small, doctors urge Britons*. In her case, small meant non-existent. The headline was as sad as it was depressing. Everyone had hoped that this year's festive season would be better than the last.

She considered calling Hank to find out if he'd released Christine, but he'd let her know soon enough. Her management technique didn't include treading on toes or anything else that might knock his confidence. She needed him on his game. Shrugging on her coat, she withdrew a pen from her pocket. She was about to leave a note for Jo when she wandered into the room in her festive PJs.

'Morning . . .' Jo yawned, barely awake as she gave Kate a cuddle. 'I'm sorry, I didn't hear you get up. Why didn't you wake me?'

'You were out for the count.'

'Hung-over you mean.' She made a grim face. 'Still am.'

'Overindulge before I got in, did you?'

'Might have.'

Kate smiled. 'Your offspring are a bad influence.'

Jo pointed at the Aga. 'Any coffee in that pot?'

Kate reached for it.

With her back turned, Jo slumped down on a chair, fishing a small, boxed gift from her pocket. It was lovingly wrapped in sparkly paper and tied with a silver bow. She placed it on the kitchen table, sliding it closer to Kate.

Draining the pot, Kate turned from the cooker and held out her drink. 'Here, get this down you, then do yourself a favour and go back to bed . . .' The gift box caught her eye. 'What's that?'

Jo gave her an odd look. 'You know what day it is, right?'

Kate made the face of Edvard Munch's *The Scream* – hands pressed to either side of her face.

'You forgot, didn't you? I'm wearing Santa pants and you still forgot?'

'As if . . .' Kate chuckled. 'I may be a rubbish partner but I'm not totally useless. I haven't had time to wrap yours yet.' She pointed at the gift on the table. 'I hope you're not expecting me to open that and run.' She put on her best begging face. 'Would you mind keeping it for later?'

'As in later today, this week, before or after New Year?'

'Today. This afternoon, I promise. I must go in this morning, you know that.'

'You're the big cheese. You can do what you like. Bright wouldn't have gone in, would he?'

'He would, given the circumstances. It's not the work. It's Hank. If he has bailed Christine on my advice, the MIT won't be happy . . . with him or me. I'm not leaving him to face that alone. He has enough to do.'

'I thought today of all days, I might top your priority list.'

'That's not fair, Jo. Anyway, it's not that. It's what kept me awake half the night. If Ash isn't discharged today and Christine is out on bail, I need to organise security. He shot and killed her old man. She's crazy enough to do something stupid. I can't have that on my conscience, you must see that—'

'OK, OK, you made your point. Don't yell, it's too early. Ibuprofen o'clock by my watch.'

'The sooner I get there . . .' Kate left the remainder unsaid.

'Crack on.'

'You sure?'

'You missed the shops if you're sneaking out to buy me something.'

Kate laughed.

Jo added, 'And whatever you do, don't forget to ring your dad.'

Picking up her car keys, Kate leaned in for a kiss that lasted longer than she intended. 'Merry Christmas, gorgeous. Bed-head is a good look on you. Think you could hold onto it till I return?'

'Might do. Go on, get out of here.'

26

Kate's intuition was spot on. The MIT were up in arms. Hank had left a note on her desk warning her that one or two detectives began making their mouths go as soon as they realised that Bradshaw had been bailed. Hank didn't name names. That was not his style. The tip-off was an olive branch so that she could prepare herself. She made off down the corridor at a fast pace, ready to do battle in the incident room, primed to support his decision. The minute she walked in, she noticed a group huddled around the vending machine, which usually meant dissenting voices. The team hadn't yet realised she was observing them, so the whispering continued:

He's off his head.

What the hell was he thinking?

Crazy, if you ask me.

Yeah, but his decision to make.

'You're right, it was,' Kate said loudly. 'The suggestion was mine.'

Detectives scattered to their desks, Andy Brown among them.

She was far from done. 'Don't hold back, guys. Have your say, then you can all get on earning double time. If you want to complain, do it when you're off duty. If you want to make it official' – she thumbed over her shoulder – 'there's the door.'

No one spoke.

Resentment filled the space.

Hank walked towards her, trying his best to hide the I-told-you-so expression on his face. Waiting for the MIT to settle, Kate made sure he received a reply: *it was the right thing to do.* She gave detectives the rationale behind her game plan and waited for the blowback. It arrived instantly, as vociferous as before, from several detectives.

After a few minutes, Hank put a stop to it. 'Guys, we have no time to indulge your arguments, now move the fuck on or leave. I want to update everyone on the ongoing surveillance operation.' He caught Kate's eye as he took centre stage, letting her know that he still had her back.

She was never in any doubt.

'Now then,' he said. 'Christine Bradshaw left here as a passenger in a BMW driven by Jacob Burrows, who she affectionately refers to as The Tank on account of the time he'd spent in the army, not his size. The exact details of the car and the route it took is in your briefing sheet. It made one stop only, on Chillingham Road where a young male the obs team couldn't immediately identify exited the vehicle for a short time, maybe to do some business, maybe to buy fags. They ended their journey on Runnymede Road, Darras Hall. It's a gated property you can't see into, but we're one up. We've learned something.'

'They haven't moved since?' Andy asked.

Hank shook his head.

'How do we know that if you can't see in? Christine wouldn't go anywhere unless it was both defendable and escapable, would she?' Despite her own misgivings, Carmichael had refrained from joining the others in publicly denouncing Hank's decision to bail the woman who attacked Ash Norham.

She was making a valid point, not scoring one.

Hank reassured her. 'The property backs onto the River Pont and farmland beyond. There's one way in, one out by car. Christine is in there with Burrows and the young unident I mentioned. The obs team leader sent his image to ROCU, which is why Zak Matthews has joined us this morning.'

Inviting him forward, Hank thanked him for nipping in for the morning briefing.

As he was about to speak, Kate's phone rang.

Zac hesitated. 'You want to take that, guv?'

Kate looked up from the screen. 'No, it's my dad. If I answer, he'll expect me to go round. We'll row. He'll sulk. I won't hear from him until he needs someone to kick . . . metaphorically speaking.'

Zac frowned. 'I met him once. He seemed placid.'

'So does a polar bear till you poke it.' Everyone laughed. 'The floor is yours.'

Zac turned to face the squad. 'The young guy the obs team couldn't ID is Harvey Armstrong. His mates call him The Arm. Make of that what you will. He takes care of Christine's street ops, trap houses, the buying and selling of illegal firearms. Her runners are shit-scared of him. It's alleged that he took over Lee's role before Christine sent him packing.'

'Really? We thought it was Bullock.'

'No, it was Harvey,' said Zac. 'He's a class-A thug who made himself very popular in Lee's absence—'

Carmichael cut him off. 'Then Ash is going to need close protection.'

'Taken care of,' Kate said. 'Two firearms officers on the door round the clock . . .' She'd accessed the overnight log at home, noting that Christine was out with a surveillance team on her tail. 'And before you asked, I called at the hospital on the way here. They're under no illusions that the patient is one of ours.'

Carmichael relaxed. 'How was he?'

'Asleep. Best thing for him.'

Andy's hand was up. 'Harvey has a strong motive for the shooting then?'

'Correct,' Zak said. 'And he's not the type to step down without a fight.'

27

The MIT took a short break then reconvened. Though she hadn't planned to attend Hank's briefing, Kate decided to hang around. Carmichael had something important to say. For the benefit of everyone else, she stood to do it. 'Hank raised an action to find the owner of the camera on the gable end of the terrace where the shooting took place. I found out that it doesn't belong to the property to which it's attached, but a house further down the street.'

'That's odd . . .' Kate's eyes narrowed. 'Can't imagine my neighbours allowing that.'

'Yeah, worth investigating. The man we need to speak to is Paul Johnson. He lives at number 24.'

'Make that a priority. Anything else?'

'Yes, I also spoke to Bethany Alexander. She confirmed everything her old man told us about where she was, and until what time. She sent me screenshots, including the ambulance men attending to her mate, hospital admission and time of discharge. All the screenshots and documentary exhibits are linked with the action.'

'Great work,' Hank said.

The smile Carmichael threw him was weak.

Kate was concerned about her. While she was doing a great job, she'd been distant of late. Christmas wasn't, and never had been, a good time for her. Her parents were killed in an avalanche in France when she was a kid. She'd been brought up by an aunt who'd since died. While Kate's mother had also passed away, she counted herself fortunate to have Jo and her sons in her life.

The acorn shell on Bright's desk caught Kate's eye as she walked into his office, acting as a reminder to be grateful for her newfound family. Picking it up, she wished she was home with Jo, making up for leaving her on Christmas morning. Like Lisa, Kate was not in a good place. She felt disassociated, unconnected to her surroundings, out of kilter with everyone she cared about, a stranger in her workplace. She'd spent less than a week subbing for Bright.

Already, it felt like a lifetime.

She scanned his office walls; an impressive display of international police badges he'd collected and framed over the years. On the opposite wall, a blown-up image of him standing in a line of cops, each wearing ear defenders and pointing a gun. Detective target practice was unheard of in the UK, except for specialist officers. Like Kate, Bright didn't fit into that scene. In fact, it surprised her that he wanted others to see what she considered to be a sexed-up version of himself.

He didn't need it.

His impressive reputation spoke for itself.

She wished he was here now so she could take advantage of his wisdom.

Once upon a time, she'd harboured an ambition to step into his formidable shoes, to lead the department from the front. Now she wouldn't have it gift-wrapped. Despite a pleasant view and a few fancy extras, his office and his work depressed her. The rank would never give her the adrenaline rush she craved. She needed her team, the buzz of the MIR, the laughs, the camaraderie, her own office. The MIT might have been grumpy this morning, but she'd swap that for this.

She'd had enough.

Grabbing her personal belongings, she left the room, heading to the MIR and the office Hank was currently occupying. He'd been disrespectful last night, and full of simmering resentment earlier, but he could never stay angry for long. Walking down the corridor, she felt like a kid dragging her teddy into her parents' room, about to climb into their warm, comfy bed. She couldn't wait to get there.

28

Kate studied the murder wall on her way in. It made grim reading. Bloody crime scene images of Jackson and Lee Bradshaw were prominent. A straight line linked them to a photograph of their mother, one that had been taken from her criminal record. Christine wouldn't approve. Next to it was a note that she'd been released from custody. Another line led to her husband, now deceased. Don Bradshaw was not included as a victim in Hank's murder investigation.

There was no dispute over who shot him.

Also on the home screen were the names and numbers of key personnel – first responders, CSIs, firearms officers – witnesses too. No suspects, she noticed. If Kate knew Hank, he'd keep the Ioannou family out of the frame until there was a damned good reason to put them there. She approved wholeheartedly.

He wouldn't go slinging mud at a copper or his family without hard evidence. On the other hand, he'd follow the trail of a killer wherever it took him. If a police officer had taken revenge against the person or persons he or she thought were responsible for murdering Georgina, then so be it.

That was out of his control . . .

It's what Hank would call the buggeration factor.

Remembering her promise that she wouldn't interfere until the cases were officially linked, Kate walked across the MIR towards her office, stopping on the way to take the temperature of the more vociferous members of her team who'd made their mouths go earlier.

They seemed over it.

Overloaded with files, she pressed on, bumming her way into her office. Dumping her coat and paperwork on one side of her desk, she perched on the edge, one foot on the floor, the other dangling free, hands resting lightly on her right knee. Hank didn't mention their altercation on the phone last night.

Their relationship was strong enough to survive that blip.

'I've been thinking,' she said.

He eyed her kit suspiciously. 'Are you moving in?'

'Haven't you heard? Lesbians bring everything on a first date.' He laughed at the tired joke. 'After much deliberation, I decided it would make perfect sense for you and me to work from the same office, given that our cases are interlinked, that's if you have no objection.'

He raised an eyebrow. 'I have a choice?'

'I'm not telling, I'm asking nicely. If you want the truth, I'm begging. I cannot spend another minute in that mausoleum Bright calls an office. What do you say?'

'His gaff is bigger . . . you can smoke in there, apparently.'

He ducked as she threw her acorn shell at him.

'Do I get to keep your chair?' He was pushing his luck. 'I rather like it.'

'You can sit on my knee if it makes you happy.'

29

They commandeered a second computer, another desk, pushing them together so they could sit facing one another. Half an hour later, the room was cramped but Kate felt at home as she rearranged her stuff as she wanted it, logging on to ensure she could access HOLMES. She'd missed Hank's input into her daily routine as much as he'd missed hers. Their difference of opinion was over. He was grinning like a loon. Satisfied with their efforts, they grabbed a brew and sat down.

In a better mood, Kate texted Jo:

> How's the head?
> Better.
> This isn't how I planned to spend our first Christmas together.
> So, don't.

Kate felt guilty as she typed a reply:

> On way soon.
> That's the right answer. ☺
> If you can't wait, Santa might have left something for you, if you can find it.

'You've got your social media face on,' Hank said.

Kate smiled, placing her mobile on her desk. 'It's my texting face, if you must know, letting Jo know that I won't be long. I felt guilty leaving her.'

'You should. This year you have no excuse. It's unheard of for the head of CID—'

'Don't start. Jo made that point this morning, though I have to say she didn't whinge about it. I will never understand how she puts up with me.'

'Me either.' He pulled a silly face, making her laugh. 'Get yourself away, Kate. I can handle things here.'

'Before I do, I'd like to run something by you. Georgina's file is thin, Hank. Curtis could write a good job, but he made lots of assumptions.'

'That's his signature.'

'Yeah, well it's not mine. I don't want to overload you, but there's stuff I found that you should know.'

He leaned back in his chair, hands clasped behind his head. 'Like what?'

'A couple of weeks after Georgina's death, Curtis had a run-in with the family. It almost came to blows. Oscar threatened him, told him if he didn't up his game, he'd hunt down the suspects and it wouldn't end well.'

'You think he made good on his promise?'

'I don't know.' She pulled a file towards her, from which she slid a flimsy A4 sheet of paper. It was an official complaint concerning Oscar. 'I found this inside Curtis's policy book. You need to see it.'

Hank read the document, then looked up with an expression of disgust. 'The useless nowt made a formal complaint against a murdered officer's kid. How low can he sink?'

'A lot further, believe me.'

'Meaning?'

'I have access to Bright's emails. He ordered Curtis to bury it.'

'Let me guess, he kept the report as insurance.'

'As you do,' Kate said.

'Thanks for the heads-up, Kate. This is news to me. It looks bad for Oscar. For all of them. I can see now why we need to move in together, in a manner of speaking.' Hank got up and walked towards the printer. Taking a copy for future use, he handed her the original and sat down.

Kate held up the complaint form. 'I'll keep my eye out for any more of these. To be honest, it didn't take me long to see stuff I'd have raised actions for, stuff Curtis took for granted. That impacts on you, which is why I thought we should be across each other's investigations, informally. I'm going to have to double-check everything.'

'You can't do that alone.'

'You're right, which is another reason why I'm here.' Kate paused. He wasn't going to like what she had to say next. She chose her words carefully. 'After Christmas, I'd like Lisa to work with me.'

'Why?'

'Haven't you noticed she's struggling?'

'She's working well enough.'

'She's a pro. I don't know if it's the time of year or the fact that she had to endure lockdown on her own when the rest of us had company, but she's not herself. I haven't mentioned anything to her. I wanted to talk to you first.'

'My need is greater, wouldn't you say? As personal as your case is, it's three years old. I have a fresh double-hander to investigate.'

'No one is indispensable.'

'So, take someone else.'

'I want Carmichael. Look, I accept that you have a complex job on your hands, but I'm reinvestigating a case where the evidence is considered ancient by anyone other than a cold case unit. It's a different animal altogether. I owe it to the family to get it right. Don't fight me on this, Hank. You have the whole team to focus on the shootings.'

'And you have Jo.'

'She's a profiler, not a copper.'

'Kate, I still need a 2ic.'

'That I can provide.'

'C'mon, no one can touch Carmichael.'

'Ordinarily, I'd agree with you—'

'Ordinarily?'

'Trust me, she's in pain and I need to get to the bottom of it. With so much on your plate you can't babysit her, no matter how much you might like to. I can. I'm protecting you as much as her. Of all the cases we've handled, none has been more high-profile. I want your mind on the job, not on Lisa.'

'And how will you sell it to her?'

'The way I sold it to you.' Kate smiled. 'If you're worried about telling her, don't be. I'll do it. As far as she's concerned, she's the best we have. I'm pulling rank, another reason for the team to be angry with me. I'm relying on you to back me on it.'

Hank gave her a filthy look. 'And who do I get? I'm not having—'

'Wind your neck in, will you? Given what I said about Curtis, I'm hardly going to hand you a dud. If she's available, you can have Ailsa.'

'Richards?' He frowned.

'I'll clear it with her supervision. I need to talk to him anyway.'

Now Hank was doubly confused. They had come across the Humberside officer while investigating the deaths of two missing children whose bones had been discovered buried on Bamburgh beach. With close links to the family of one of the girls, Kate had put Richards to work, first on her own patch in Beverley where the child was from, eventually seconding her to Northumbria's MIT. Without her, the case would never have been solved.

Kate nudged him over the edge. 'You rated her, didn't you?'

'Surely you don't need to drag in someone from an outside force.'

'I won't have to. She never went home.'

'Really?'

'It surprised me too, though I don't know why. Ailsa's single, no kids, no mortgage.' Kate smiled. 'Remember when I asked her if she had any commitments? She said she wouldn't even have to cancel the milk. I bumped into her the other day. She's a DC now, in the organised crime unit.'

Hank was impressed. 'Then she could be useful.' He still hadn't agreed to release Carmichael.

Kate would rather not argue over it . . .

She would if she had to.

'Level with me,' Hank said. 'What else is bothering you?'

She came clean. 'What if the Bradshaw boys weren't responsible for Georgina's death?'

He snorted. 'Are you and Carmichael a double act?'

'What d'you mean?'

'She said as much yesterday. I told her to keep dreaming. Lee and Jackson threatened to kill Georgina. She ended up dead and so did they.'

'You made my point. Even with a sterile scene, no witnesses or DNA, it's easy to jump to that conclusion based on circumstantial evidence alone. According to Zac, there's not a shred of hard evidence linking them to her death. Every copper living and breathing had them pegged as her killer, as did the media. Isn't it possible that a rival gang took advantage of a perfect storm to get rid of the competition when Lee and Jackson eventually showed themselves? Half the force is whispering about a vigilante killing when it may not be the case.'

'A rival would have finished the job.'

'Maybe they were interrupted—'

Hank cut in: 'According to Alexander, there was no one about. Christine's the mastermind behind the family's illegal operations, the one worth taking out. You think losing her boys will stop her? Not a chance. Chop her head off and she'll grow another. If it wasn't for this new kid Harvey Armstrong, I wouldn't put it past her to be drawing up a list of candidates to fill the vacancies created overnight.' He shook his head, continued to push his point of view: 'Christine knows fine well that Lee and Jackson killed Georgina. I'm one hundred per cent convinced of that. It's written all over her smug face. Why else would she be accusing us of a revenge attack?'

Kate's mobile rang, temporarily ending the conversation. She checked the screen and looked up. 'It's Carmichael, probably wondering where I am.'

'So why isn't she here?' Hank narrowed his eyes. 'I thought you didn't tell her you'd be working together.'

'I refuse to perjure myself on grounds that it may incriminate me. You OK with Ailsa as your 2ic or not? I need an answer and I need it now.' Hank was about to say more. She cut him off. 'I don't need this desk. I'll move to Bright's office.'

'I thought you hated it.'

'That's before I had Lisa.'

'Go on, rub it in,' he grumbled.

Kate took the call, her smile dissolving instantly.

Carmichael was distressed. 'Guv, I got a call from a neurosurgeon at the RVI. In the last couple of hours, Ash complained of a headache and blurred vision. His BP dropped off the scale, a rapid and sudden deterioration. A CT scan confirmed a massive brain haemorrhage. He's been moved to the ICU.'

30

Christine's night had been restless. Several times she'd dozed off through sheer exhaustion, only to wake soaked in sweat with a rolling image of her sons' bodies lying bloody and still on a patterned carpet in an unfamiliar living room. She was wide awake now, planning to get even. Through a crack in the curtains, the sun crept into the room. She rolled over to face the other way. It took a split second before she realised that Don wasn't there. It wasn't him she missed. It was the presence of a male, one who knew how to comfort her.

A super king was too big for one.

Don had been a good father. As husband and lover, he was useless. She'd hoped he'd improve over time. He hadn't. His weakness, in every sense of the word, had frustrated her for years. If he hadn't known so much about her business, she'd have seen him off years ago. She'd even considered a hit man to remove him from her life.

Ironically, the police had done it for free.

Christine got up, a smile developing. Don's death presented a welcome opportunity to start again. His replacement was already in her life, someone with a sexual appetite that matched her own. If that didn't work out in the long term, she'd continue to pay a professional until the right person came along.

Her head ached.

Taking a swim didn't help. She left the pool, showered, dressed, then went to meet with her house guests. They were already in the living room, waiting to discuss tactics.

Walking in, she studied each sombre face in turn.

'Fuck's sake! Did someone die?'

They didn't laugh.

During the night, Christine had gone through a long list

of her crew, trying to figure out who'd betrayed her. Only a close-knit circle knew of her sons' return to the UK. The top three on that list were staring at her. Jacob, she'd trust with her life. Tony had volunteered to drive to Spain to collect her boys. She'd declined the offer in case the UK Border Force picked them up. Had he been counting on that? Then there was Harvey, her lieutenant. He'd do anything for her. There was nothing in his body language that gave her cause for concern. He was connected, and ruthless, which was why she'd brought him on board. She intended to keep her enemies close – if that's what they were.

Of the three, Harvey stood to lose more than he'd gain from the lads' homecoming. He got on with Jackson but thought Lee was an arsehole for the way he treated his younger brother. That wasn't a bad description. Her eldest had always been spiteful. Nevertheless, someone with a big mouth had got him killed. She vowed that they wouldn't get away with it.

The question was, who?

She'd find out soon enough.

With that thought persisting, she poured herself a drink, then turned to face her crew with her focus on the future.

'So, what's the plan?'

'We need a description of the shooter,' Tony said.

'State the obvious why don't you?' She scowled at him. 'It's not often I suggest we start watching the detectives, but we might learn something if we do. The difference is, they follow regs while we play dirty. Set it up.' Her cold eyes found the youngest among them. 'Harvey, anything to add?'

'If you want eyes on witnesses, cops and journalists are your best bet. For that, we need cash and lots of it. Everyone likes a bit extra to play with at Christmas, right?'

Christine switched focus to Tony. 'Give him what he wants. My boys didn't deserve to die on the doorstep on their first night home. Whoever the shooter is will suffer a long and painful end. I want eyes and ears on the street. There's a paramedic who lives directly opposite. He was in that night. I saw him at the window, but he never came across the road to help. Make him aware he'll not be a paramedic long without fingers.'

31

Lisa was escorted to Ward 18. She had a word with the fire-arms officers at the door to a single patient cubicle. Ash was hooked up to all manner of sophisticated electronic equipment: IV lines, wires and cables monitoring his heart, BP and SATS, an alarming number of tubes administering drugs. She'd been asked to wait until medical staff cleared the room before entering.

Through an internal window she watched them work, grateful for the health professionals trying to save his life. It was clear that he was gravely ill and required constant monitoring. Lisa drew comfort from the fact that they knew he was a cop. If his life couldn't be saved, it wouldn't be for the want of trying.

She was overwhelmed by the care being taken.

She'd been warned that he was completely out of it.

It felt like she'd been standing there for hours while medics checked every vital statistic before finally deciding they could allow her to enter the room for a short while. After a discussion she couldn't hear, the medical team left his bedside and made toward the door. One nurse hung around, the last to leave.

In the busy corridor, he approached Lisa. He had kind eyes, cornflower blue, which was all she could see of him beneath his medical mask.

For once in her life, she was glad of hers.

'Mrs Norham, you can go in now.'

'I'm police.' She held up ID. 'I've been sent to check on him.'

'If you're not family—'

'I'll be in and out, I promise. My boss, Detective Chief Inspector Daniels, was here earlier briefing the firearms team. There's a significant threat to our colleague.'

'A few minutes. No more.'

As he moved away, Lisa gelled her hands at the door and stepped inside. Visually, through the window, everything looked bad: the sheer number of personnel around the bed; the serious expressions on the faces of the medical team; the frequent checking of equipment, her imagination in overdrive. Audibly, with the constant bleep of monitors, it was much, much, worse.

If panic was a sound, that was it.

Lisa closed the door and approached the bed.

Her eyes flew to the digital screen, the flashing LEDs that changed constantly with every breath Ash took. She was used to emergency rooms, but was so affected by what she was seeing, she was unable to make sense of the numbers. She hung on to the one thing she was sure of. Ash wasn't flatlining . . . yet.

32

Every detective, uniformed personnel and civilian on the force was shocked to learn that Ash had deteriorated. News spread like wildfire, telegraphed to those off duty. They would do their best to play happy families, but it would be a mountain to climb, impossible to keep up appearances, even for the sake of their hyped-up kids.

Kate exhaled as she wandered down the corridor. The MIT were even more pissed off about letting Christine go. As she entered Bright's office, she checked her mobile. No update from the obs team leader. Taking a seat, she called him. 'Steve, it's Kate Daniels. What's the state of play now?'

'Christine and Burrows are still in the house, guv. In the past hour, two vehicles have left the property, Harvey Armstrong in the BMW he arrived in. Tony Bullock in a grey Audi Q7. He must've been there already. We have eyes on everyone.'

'That's reassuring. Whatever they're up to, Christine will be orchestrating it. Keep me posted and let Hank know, please. It's his case, not mine.'

'Will do, guv.'

Kate checked her watch, then tried Carmichael's mobile. The call cut to voicemail. Kate was halfway through a message when her battery died. Placing it on a charger, she used her landline to call the RVI switchboard, asking for adult critical care – the unit specialising in neurosurgery for patients requiring intensive treatment.

The admin clerk went off to find a charge nurse.

A woman came on the line. Her interrogation technique was impressive. She wanted chapter and verse on Kate's relationship with Ash Norham, making it clear that she wouldn't discuss patient progress without it.

'I'm the SIO investigating the case in which he was critically injured.' That wasn't strictly true. Kate didn't care.

'Email a copy of your ID and I'll see what I can do.'

'Don't bother.'

Kate slammed the phone down as Carmichael walked through the door, averting her gaze, while shrugging off her coat. As she sat down, Kate's internal phone fell off its cradle. It began to emit an annoying reminder to put it back gently next time.

'Who was that?' Carmichael asked.

'A jobsworth at the hospital. Did they let you in?'

'Not for long.'

'How is he, or shouldn't I ask?'

'Not great, but in good hands. They're watching him round the clock—'

'He's strong, Lisa. He'll pull through.'

Carmichael dropped her head on one side, an expression that could only be described as an obstinate stare. 'You didn't ask me to work with you because Ash and I are mates, did you? Because if that's the case, I'm not going to fall apart like I did when Robbo died.' DC Robson's body had been dumped in the street directly opposite Northern Area Command as a warning for police to back off a previous investigation.

They wouldn't do it then.

They wouldn't do it now.

'Absolutely not,' Kate said. 'I told you. I need your expertise. I've also asked Zac Matthews to join us on a part-time basis until we get the enquiry to a point where we don't need him. He's snowed under but I'm hoping to persuade ROCU to release him until we wrap up our end of the investigation. You know each other, right?'

'Not well.'

'He's solid, in the CID most of his career: Crime Squad, Drug Squad – you name it, he's done it. It makes sense to use him, given his involvement in the initial enquiry. Between you and me, Bright put him in there to watch Curtis.'

'Then I can see why he left.'

33

Harvey coasted through the gates of Christine's new pad, stopping briefly to ensure that they closed behind him before driving off through dappled shade into bright sunshine. No white Christmas this year. It was a beautiful day – dry, bright, warm – perfect for a run he didn't have time for.

Thank fuck for global warming.

Dropping the visor, he put on his shades.

On the dual carriageway, he checked his rear-view for cops – all clear – and floored the accelerator. A Honda Fireblade flew past doing a ton. The lucky bastard was gone in seconds. Harvey loved to ride.

He was out of luck today.

On Christine's orders, everyone in the crew was grafting. Before Tony left, she'd flown into a rage, hurling a large vase across the room at him for daring to question Jacob's ideas, winding her up in the process. The chauffeur had been in her employ the longest and couldn't do wrong in her eyes. Harvey was wary of anyone who didn't get his or her hands dirty. While Jacob drove their boss around, he did the grunt work.

He was under no illusion as to what would happen if he didn't carry out Christine's instructions to the letter. Beyond unconditional loyalty, his unpredictable, volatile, uncompromising boss demanded action. If he didn't come up with answers . . . Harvey didn't want to go there. The last person to cross her, she'd stabbed fifteen times – fucking psycho.

It wasn't pretty.

No one knew where the bodies were buried.

Don would take her secrets to his grave.

It didn't take a lot to set Christine off.

The only time she cracked a smile was in the sack. She was

a great lay, but Harvey was beginning to wish he hadn't gone there either. Now her old man had croaked, she'd demand his services more often. Some words were taboo in her book: rejection was one of them. Kids his age had disappeared for less.

Mind on the job, he called one of his crew.

The burner rang out for ages. The fucker was probably high. If he didn't answer, he'd wish he had when Harvey kicked his door down. He shot over the roundabout, upsetting those with right of way. Tough. He was in a hurry. If he didn't have something to cheer Christine up – outside of the obvious – the vengeful cow would make him pay, even though with Lee and Jay gone, she needed him.

That was a sizeable bargaining chip.

The call connected, then cut off.

The mobile had been dropped.

Fucking prick.

Harvey redialled.

'Yeah?' The mouth breather rarely used two words where one would do.

'Picking you up in five. Be there.'

'K.'

34

Andy was bleary-eyed, hard at work acting on a tip-off from a criminal informant he'd bumped into at a city-centre pub at lunchtime. It wasn't often that intelligence fell into his lap, but three things conspired to lead him somewhere. First, the informant was shit-faced. He'd spent what money he had and was desperate for more. Second, he had knowledge that Andy was willing to pay for. Third, the informant had heard that the Bradshaw crew were out of action, that it was safe to blab without them cutting out his tongue.

Andy had no doubt that he was mistaken.

Acting on information received, he'd taken the initiative to track down Lee Bradshaw's ex-wife and child. They hadn't moved as far away as first thought, so he shot over there and paid her a visit, returning to the MIR with the swagger of a man who'd achieved his objective. He was rubbing his hands together when Hank arrived in the incident room, a tad gloomy. Unlike him.

'Something I need to know?' he asked.

Andy shared his intel. 'Suzanne Bradshaw reverted to her maiden name of Charlton,' he said. 'She's now living in Middleton-in-Teesdale.'

'Nice.' It was one of Hank's favourite places to visit.

'Yeah, it was a lovely run, an even better conversation.' Andy shoved his Maui Jims up to his hairline, dumping his car keys on his desk, along with his mobile. 'Suzanne has turned her life around. She's settled with a bloke who wouldn't know the inside of a police cell if he tripped over one. He's sound, Hank. A forestry worker.'

'They didn't give you any trouble?'

'No. Suzanne was shitting herself when I showed up, until I

broke the news that Lee wasn't going to hurt her any more and that she no longer needed a divorce.'

'She hadn't heard?'

Andy shook his head. 'Ever watch *The Good Life*?' He answered his own question. 'That's them. They don't even own a telly.'

'What's their place like? Remote enough to hide her ex and his brother?'

'Possibly, but hardly their style, is it? Lee and Jackson were street kids. I don't believe that's where they went to ground. For starters, there's not a nightclub in sight. And . . .' He pointed at the murder wall, specifically at the crime scene images of the two. 'They've been exposed to UV rays never seen in Teesdale.' Andy dropped his MJs onto the bridge of his nose. 'I didn't wear these to keep the sun from my eyes. I wore them to prevent frostbite. I wouldn't bet against a warmer destination. Anyway, the action is now with Harry. It's NFA as far as I'm concerned.' He meant that no further action was required. 'If there's any doubt, the office manager will flag it with you.'

'Cool.' Hank trusted Andy's judgement.

Leaving him to his work, he swung round to face the other way, expecting to see Carmichael. He was met with an empty chair; a sleeping computer monitor on her desk. Without her on the shooting, he'd struggle.

He crossed the room to Maxwell's desk.

'Any update from house-to-house?'

'One query.' Maxwell pulled it from his in-tray.

'What's it doing there?' Hank snapped.

'It doesn't amount to much. A woman who lives on the terrace that runs parallel to the Bradshaws' property got up in the middle of the night to let her cat in. Taxi pulls up. Two people get out. She can't tell if male or female. They're in shadow. They wait till the cab pulls away, then cut through the side street into the next terrace. Question is why?'

Hank was intrigued. 'Time was this?'

'She has no idea. Worth a follow-up?'

'Absolutely. You can't sit on it, Neil. It could be the Bradshaws arriving home or the shooter with a lookout. Find that taxi. It might produce a witness. If you get anything else like this, I don't want to have to come looking for it. What have we got on the all-ports action?'

'No one using the Bradshaws' passports entered via Newcastle International in the past week. I'm checking CCTV to see if I can spot them. If I get nothing there, I'll try Manchester, Edinburgh, Glasgow.'

'You're setting the parameters now?'

Maxwell blushed. 'I didn't mean—'

'I'm winding you up, man. Do it. Let me know if you get a sighting.'

Hank moved off towards Kate's office.

The word initiative was not one he'd normally associate with Maxwell. He was inconsistent and therefore not his go-to person when it came to following up on actions. However, Hank was beginning to realise that keeping *all* the troops onside was an important part of his new role. He couldn't work in a vacuum or solve the case alone.

His eyes lit up as Carmichael's replacement emerged from the corridor, a haversack on her back, a big smile on her face as their eyes met. Ailsa Richards was short, with fair cropped hair and an unusual green fleck in her left eye which was predominantly blue. Her nose was slightly crooked due to a run-in with an offender who'd beaten her to a pulp a few years ago.

'Hey,' he said. 'Welcome back.'

'It's good to be here . . . sir.'

Hank made a face. 'Leave it out.'

'Credit where it's due, Hank. Making SIO is a big deal where I come from.'

'It's a pain in the neck I hope won't last. To be honest, I don't know how Kate does it. Anyway, it's good to see you. We're down personnel-wise with more balls in the air than we can cope with.'

'I heard about Ash.'

Hank's nod was almost imperceptible. 'Let's grab a brew and I'll bring you up to speed. I hope you realise you're here to save the day.'

His phone rang.

He took the call. 'What is it, Steve?'

The obs team leader said, 'Thought you should know that Harvey picked up a kid on a street corner – eleven, twelve years old. Looks like one of his runners. They drove to Heaton. The kid gets out of the car. Knocks on Alexander's door, gets no reply and walks away. Harvey pays the kid, indefinite currency, then drives to Cramlington. He's sitting in the car park of the Northumbria Specialist Emergency Care Hospital.'

'He's still there?'

'He was five minutes ago.'

'Shit! We'd better warn Alexander.'

35

The digital clock above the murder wall clicked forward: 23:00 hours. Kate was surrounded by dead computer screens; personnel having finally knocked off after the mother of all shifts. Lights were dimmed in the incident room. No reason to stick around, though Kate couldn't bring herself to leave. All she could think of was Ash Norham lying in a hospital bed, clinging to life by a thin thread.

Kate sat down, alone and exhausted, using her mobile to call the hospital. This time she got through. Hanging up, she made another call. The woman she was so desperately in love with knew nothing of what was going on at the RVI. It was high time Kate put her in the picture.

Jo picked up immediately.

She'd have been expecting a key in the door. A phone call meant that something was up, a development in the case or some matter that required her urgent attention. Feeling guilty for letting her down, yet again, Kate momentarily lost the power of speech.

'Kate? Talk to me. What's happening?'

'Ash has taken a turn for the worst. The charge nurse said he's comfortable. No shit. He's in a fucking coma! Of course, he's *comfortable*. He's halfway to Neverland. Even if he makes a full recovery, I doubt he'll ever lead a firearms team in the future. He'll have a hard time coping with that.'

'Oh, Kate. I'm so sorry.'

'Look, I know I promised that I'd be home hours ago, but the RVI is a short detour on the way.' She didn't say that Ash came first, that the job and, on this occasion, even Jo couldn't keep her from looking in on him. 'I'm the one who should be sorry.'

'Don't be, I'll meet you there.'

*

Kate made the Royal Victoria Infirmary in eight minutes flat. Signs of other people's festive plans shone out from homes she passed on the way, twinkly lights everywhere she looked. A vision of a small box on the kitchen table popped into her head. It was waiting to be opened when she and Jo could enjoy a moment together.

There was a slim chance of that happening.

Kate pulled into a bay marked emergency vehicles only outside the Victoria Wing. Jo's Discovery had beaten her there. She was nowhere in sight. Once inside the building, Kate pressed the doorbell and waited impatiently for someone to come and let her in. Jo was sitting in the corridor, scrolling through her phone. She stood as Kate approached, a concerned expression.

'Where is he?'

'Kate, there's something you should know first—'

'Jesus! Am I too late?'

'No—'

'What then?'

'Lisa's here. I didn't want to disturb her.'

Jo pointed through a window separating the corridor from Ash's room. With trepidation, Kate approached the glass partition and was deeply moved by what she saw. Masked up – still a thing on IC units – Lisa was asleep in a chair, head resting on Ash's bed, their fingers laced together. Instantly, Kate made the jump. This was why her DS was so desperately unhappy. It was an image Kate would never forget. Not so long ago, she'd been where Lisa was now, clinging to the hope that a loved one would survive.

It almost broke her.

'Christ! I need this like a hole in the head.'

'Kate, calm down.'

'Wake her gently, please.'

'Why don't you take a moment?'

127

Kate moved towards the door.

Jo blocked her way. 'It's fine, I'll do it.'

Kate looked on as Jo stepped inside.

Carmichael jumped when a hand was laid on her shoulder.

She looked at Jo, then swung round, meeting Kate's gaze through the internal window. Hauling herself off her chair, she glanced at the figure in the bed before following Jo out into the corridor.

She was wiped out, her face lined with worry.

Instinctively, Kate stepped forward, pulling her into a tight hug. They held each other for a long moment, Lisa limp in Kate's arms. Pulling back, she kept hold of Lisa's hands. 'It's obvious what kind of evening you've put in. Go home and get some rest. You and I will speak in the morning.'

'Boss, I need to be here.'

'You need to do as you're told. You're no good to me otherwise.'

'I'm sorry. I should have told you.'

'Yes, you should. Now is not the time. You're excused from work until further notice.'

'Kate, please . . .' Carmichael begged. 'I need to work.'

'You need to be here, or you need to work? You can't do both, so which is it to be?'

Carmichael had no answer.

'Lisa, I appreciate your commitment, really I do, but you're in shock and that's perfectly understandable. Take the night to think it over. If you choose to work, I need your mind on your job, not wandering along a virtual hospital corridor, inventing worst-case scenarios.'

Carmichael was about to argue. Kate cut her off, delivering a stark warning. 'I expect your full attention. If I don't get it, you're out.'

36

Carmichael saw sense. Collecting her coat and bag from the floor of Ash's room where she'd dumped them, she bent over Ash, a quiet word in his ear no one else could hear . . . probably not even him. Leaving his bedside, she moved out into the corridor where Kate was waiting.

Carmichael said, 'Where's Jo?'

Kate lied. 'She needed some air.'

Catching the eye of the designated nurse heading in, Carmichael said. 'I'm nipping home for a while. Will you let me know if there's any change in his condition, however slight?'

'Of course.' The woman's smile was warm and sympathetic. 'You'll be the first to know. Try not to worry, Mrs Norham.'

Carmichael wept.

Outside, in the car park, Jo hugged Carmichael, telling her to take care and Kate that she'd see her at home, then peeled off in the direction of her vehicle. Carmichael seemed reluctant to leave the curtilage of the hospital site. Concerned that she might not be fit to drive, Kate offered her a lift.

She declined.

Kate took her arm, guiding her to her car.

Before they reached her parking bay, Carmichael stopped walking.

She swung round, under immense stress. 'Boss, I should have told you about Ash, but I'm not taking any flak for keeping it to myself. We'd decided to wait, until we were ready, until we were comfortable about telling anyone. Is that so wrong?'

'Forget it. Go home. We don't need to do this now—'

'Now? Fuck's sake! We don't need to do it at all! That's my point. Some things are more important than regulations. I thought you of all people . . .' She let the sentence trail off.

'I understand you're upset—'

'Do you?' Carmichael's eyes flashed in anger. 'You don't know the half of it. You never will. How could you?'

'I'm listening . . . Lisa, if you have something more to say, spit it out.'

'Boss, I respect you, you know that, but my personal life is not your concern. I seem to remember that you and Jo were once of the same opinion. Explain to me why Ash and I are any different. Or do you only lead by example when it suits you?'

Carmichael's parting shot had stung. She'd been skating on thin ice. If anyone wanted to piss Kate off today, they wouldn't have to try very hard, but she made allowances and let it pass, making sure Lisa drove away before moving off in the direction of her own vehicle. As she suspected, Jo hadn't left the hospital grounds. She was leaning against the bonnet of her car, arms crossed, watching Kate with the intensity of a cat as she walked towards her. Kate couldn't remember the last time she'd seen her so riled.

She braced herself for round two.

The minute she got close enough, Jo lost her shit, accusing her of being overly harsh on Lisa. Rarely did Jo turn on Kate . . . and never publicly. They were face to face in the busy car park, ambulances flying by in both directions on the road beyond the perimeter fence, worried visitors coming and going, one guy giving Jo a dirty look as he passed.

If she'd really been bullying Kate, the tosser didn't intervene.

'Keep your voice down,' she said. 'We have an audience.'

'I don't care.'

'Well, I do.' Kate unlocked her vehicle. 'Are we done?'

'Far from it. You have no clue how close she is to Ash or if he'll survive—'

Kate held on to the car door. 'You think I don't know that?'

A driver blasted his horn for her to move.

She stood her ground, yelling over the din he was making, Jo her only focus.

'My job is a balancing act. It doesn't include allowing your mates to sleepwalk into a situation they're not mentally equipped to deal with.' Climbing into her Audi, Kate slammed the door and wound down the window. 'I need eyes on the investigation and team security – so don't you dare lecture me on staff management. Christine threatened Carmichael. I'm trying to keep her safe.'

Jo didn't argue.

Kate was already driving away.

37

Traditionally Boxing Day was a relaxing, sit-on-the-sofa-and-eat-leftovers day, but there was no shortage of volunteers prepared to cancel their leave and lend a hand. A cynic might say they would be well paid for it, but overtime had never been mentioned. Goodwill still existed within the murder squad. Kate's team would stay late or come in early, for no pay if she asked nicely. They were devastated by the news that Ash's life was hanging by a thread, but his medical status would also drive them on.

Jo arrived with Kate's breakfast, a peace offering.

'Why didn't you come home?'

'I thought it might be best if I didn't.'

'Did you sleep?'

'For a couple of hours in the medical room. Well, I laid down. Can't say I slept much.'

'It was all my fault,' Jo said. 'I shouldn't have interfered.'

'Can we not play the blame game. Carmichael is on the way up.'

'I thought you said—'

'That was before she told me that if she didn't resume policing immediately, she might never do it. She begged for the opportunity to work. On the one hand, she's twisting my arm, ignoring advice. On the other, moping at home waiting for the phone to ring won't help her. Reluctantly, I agreed to let her stay where I can keep a close eye on her. For the record, I repeated what I said last night, she pulls her weight or ships out.'

There was a knock at the door.

Carmichael entered and sat down sheepishly at her desk.

'I'm staying too,' Jo said to both. 'One in, all in.'

Kate looked at her. 'You sure?'

'You don't need my expertise?' Jo looked wounded. 'I have cake if you guys want some, though I'll deny it if anyone else asks.'

'Nice shirt,' Kate said as Zac took his coat and jacket off. It looked new and was creased, like it had just been removed from its cellophane wrapper.

'Santa heard I was working with you.' He grinned. 'I lied. My iron broke.'

'Welcome aboard,' Carmichael said.

Already, Kate was worried. Her brilliant DS was bluffing, acting as if nothing untoward was going on in her life. Technically, with Zac there, Kate could manage without her. The incident room was a highly charged environment at the best of times. She'd soon know if Carmichael was fit for duty.

They sat down to a mini-team meeting, Kate explaining how she wished to proceed reviewing Georgina's murder file. 'Zac, I'd like you to precis the earlier investigation for Lisa? She knows some, not all, of what went down.'

'Fine, I was there from the off, same as you.'

'I didn't see you.'

'You weren't seeing anything but red that day as I recall. I was hoping you'd deck Curtis, to be honest.'

Kate used her forefinger and thumb as a small measure. 'Believe me, I was that close.'

'And after I've spoken to Lisa? What then?'

'I'd like you to go through Curtis's policy book and note down what you'd have done differently had you been in charge. Lisa, you're my clean pair of eyes. I'd like you to look at the evidence and let me know if anything jumps out at you.' Kate turned again to Zac. 'I'll speak to your guv'nor, see if he can spare you full-time.'

'With Ailsa gone, we're at full stretch, guv.'

'Our need is greater—'

'Not if Hank wants eyes on Christine's crew it isn't.'

Kate didn't like it, but Hank's side of the investigation was equally important. 'OK, crack on then. I'll review the situation in a few days.'

They all got to work, though time and again, Kate found herself checking on Carmichael. Aware that she had to pass the fit-for-duty test or be sent home on compassionate grounds, she hid her sadness well and no doubt felt under pressure to perform. Kate spent the next hour catching up on admin, stuff she needed out of the way so she could concentrate on her open-unsolved enquiry, rarely lifting her head. Carmichael seemed fully engrossed in her work, asking all the right questions of Zac.

Lifting her hands off her keyboard, she swivelled her chair to face Kate. 'Guv, there's crossover between Georgina's murder and the Bradshaw shootings. How do you propose we handle that?'

'Our priority is Georgina. We must prove the case against the Bradshaws before we link the incidents. If you find anything relevant to Hank's case, pass it on, otherwise we're separate entities.'

Carmichael gave a nod.

Kate tried to lift her spirits. 'For the record, he objected when I removed you as his 2ic. It's no longer an issue. I've put Ailsa Richards to work.'

'She's a good 'un,' Zac joined in. 'We've worked a lot together.'

'She looks well,' Carmichael said. 'I saw her on the way in.'

'It doesn't bother you that she's here?' Kate asked.

'Hell, no.'

Kate's eyebrow twitched. 'It did last time.'

The blood crept up Carmichael's neck.

Zac hadn't a clue what they were on about.

Kate struggled to keep a straight face. The dynamic between Carmichael and Richards had been interesting when the latter was on secondment to Northumbria. Lisa bristled every time the then Humberside officer – a wannabe detective – was commended for her efforts. Hank was Lisa's supervision at the time. To keep her on her toes, he made it his business to applaud Ailsa's efforts – not that she didn't deserve it. She absolutely did, proving herself an asset to the investigation. She was well-liked by all, including Andy Brown, who also happened to be Lisa's crime buddy, the two having come through training school together, another point of friction between them.

'I'd like to think I've matured,' Lisa said coyly.

'Does that mean you no longer sulk?'

'I outrank her now.' Carmichael smiled.

The pride she showed in her promotion was a reminder of how far the ambitious detective had come since she joined the MIT. Proof, if it was needed, that she'd be sticking around. To the casual observer, Lisa had aced her test with an A-star. Kate wasn't fooled. She was in pain, trying way too hard. The jury was still out.

38

Kate usually ignored calls from unrecognised numbers. On this occasion, she made an exception. As soon as she realised who was on the other end, her pulse quickened. She immediately excused herself, leaving Carmichael and Matthews to their work. Moving into the corridor, she opened the first door she came to and darted inside. Seconds later, she was hurtling towards her own office for an urgent word with Hank. The minute she entered the incident room, she was ambushed.

DS Harry Graham held a pivotal role within the MIT. He was the receiver, the office anchor. All intelligence that came into the incident room passed across his desk. Consequently, he knew more about the investigation than anyone.

He didn't look happy.

'Guv, can I have a word?'

'You can have two if you're quick.'

'Why are we not arresting Bradshaw for attempted murder?'

A scan of the room confirmed Kate's suspicion that he was the newly appointed spokesperson for the team. Detectives were keeping their heads down, avoiding eye contact. She refocused on their mouthpiece. She'd worked with Harry for years. He'd stepped out of line before, and would again, but she didn't have time for a punch-up.

'Harry, I gave you the rationale. It hasn't changed.'

'It hasn't? Ash is comatose.'

Kate checked the corridor in case Carmichael had followed her in. 'Wind you're neck in. I explained it nicely first time. I don't intend to repeat myself to you or anyone hiding under their desks, too bottleless to speak up. Do I really have to say in words of one syllable why it was important to let her go?'

He didn't answer.

'Harry, it's my job to consider all the angles and to offer Hank guidance. You need intelligence on Christine's organisation to solve the double-hander. In case you haven't noticed, we have a finite team. She has an army and the cash to open mouths, which gives her a huge advantage. With her out of custody, we're in play.'

'And so is she,' Harry said.

'Exactly where we want her.'

'It's too risky.'

'Think of her as an involuntary asset. If we are nowhere, she might be somewhere. Her crew are intimidating witnesses. If we hadn't followed her home, we wouldn't know that Harvey is watching Alexander's workplace.'

Harry continued to trade blows. 'Our attempts to warn him that he's exposed failed.'

'Then try harder.'

The room fell silent, the whole team looking at Kate now. She'd always led from the front, always managing to take them with her. Never had she faced such vehement opposition and challenge to her authority. Harry wasn't yet onside . . .

He had ten seconds to get there.

'There's a shooter roaming the streets, Harry. Assuming it's a male we're dealing with, if we don't get to him before Christine does, she'll take him out. Potentially, we can save another family from experiencing the trauma of losing a loved one, a situation the Ioannou family are still going through three years after Georgina's murder.'

'Alexander has a family too,' he said. 'His daughter, Bethany, isn't returning our calls.'

'I've had it with the criticism, Harry. It ends here . . . and that applies to all of you. Do your jobs or apply for a transfer. I'll gladly sign you off.'

Shamefaced, Harry backed down.

Kate walked into her office. Slamming the door behind her, she blew out a breath.

Hank eyed her over the top of his specs. 'I think they heard you in the Met.'

'Yeah, well, thanks for supporting me.'

'Didn't sound like you needed it.'

'I do, Hank. Always. But if I'm forced to justify my actions to the team once more, I'll swing for them, I swear.' Placing her hands flat on her desk, she leaned against it, a moment to calm herself. When someone knocked on the door, she exploded: 'Not now!'

Hank studied her, confused. 'Are you going to tell me what's eating you?'

She pulled up a chair and sat down. 'Hank, what I'm about to say is highly confidential. I'm only telling you because you've been Carmichael's mentor for so long—'

'What's she done?'

'It's what she hasn't done that concerns me. Late last night, Jo and I went to the RVI. We found Lisa asleep, practically lying across Ash's bed, holding his hand. She should've told me they were in a relationship. If she'd chosen to keep it under wraps for personal reasons, fair enough, but I suspect she kept quiet because she wanted in on the action. I'd have taken her off the case if I'd known.'

'Christ! She was in on the interview with Christine.' Hank was way ahead of Kate. 'And you're worried she might do something daft if we rearrest her?'

'Yes and no.'

'Kate, if Lisa takes a pop at her, in or out of custody, she'll get off at court.'

'That's the yes – a dead cert.'

'And the no?'

'Goes no further than this office, are we clear?' Taking in his nod, she dropped her voice to a whisper. 'The team may not appreciate Bradshaw's temporary freedom, but when we lock her up – and we will – it'll be on a murder charge. Ash's parents are his next of kin. They've been told to get to the RVI as quickly as they can. Medics will try and keep him alive until they get there. Then his life support will be removed.'

39

Hank was deeply disturbed on two counts: firstly, by what Kate had told him – and the fact neither of them knew if Ash's parents were even aware of Carmichael's existence; secondly, by the alarm Kate expressed over Alexander's safety. She wanted Hank to head out and look for him, to ensure that the witness was OK and clued up to the danger he might face if Christine's crew came looking.

Gathering Ailsa, he left Middle Earth to take care of it.

A stationary observation post had been set up in an unlet property opposite his house, an officer reporting on any suspicious movements. There were a few kids riding up and down the street, doing wheelies on new bikes, but no thugs arriving tooled up, ready to cause mayhem.

Hank could have shown Ailsa the CSI photographer's images of the crime scene, but none would replicate the experience of physically being there: taking in the street, the sights and sounds, the proximity of neighbouring properties, the area surrounding it and, importantly, entry and exit routes. What he was trying to do was circumvent her having to ask a load of questions by seeing it for herself.

Ailsa eyed the keys on the dash, attached to which was a label: SCENE KEYS that included a bunch of numbers pertaining to the investigation as well as the initials of the officer who recovered them – in this case, Craig Bell, the CSI manager Hank had clashed with on his first visit – and the exhibit number: CB35.

'Has the scene been cleared already?' Ailsa asked.

'Secured and alarmed. It's all ours.'

'That didn't take long . . .'

'Not as long as it's taking for this idiot to pull over.' A Golf driver was hogging the outside lane. Hank flashed his lights and still he didn't shift.

'I meant bearing in mind it was a triple incident,' Ailsa said.

'We're talking Christine Bradshaw, remember? She left us sod all from what I could see, apart from dead bodies. The scene is an RV point. She and Don were using it to hook up with their kids and let off a few fireworks, no pun intended. They weren't planning to hang around or put an offer in for the place.'

'Still, they're a notorious family. If crime scene investigators missed something—'

'Relax. They had a good team on it.' Hank was tailgating the Golf. The driver woke up and moved into the inside lane, allowing the detective to put his foot down. 'These ops are bog-standard. When they shut the door for the very last time, they know they have left nothing incriminating behind. Put it this way, if they found anything, I guarantee Christine put it there for us to find—'

'Why would she do that?'

'Misdirection. She's a game-player.'

'Well, she lost . . . Her family are all dead.'

'Yeah. And she doesn't like losing.'

Five minutes later, they arrived at the scene. Hank coasted to the kerb, stopping the car opposite the front door, pulling on the brake, allowing Ailsa a moment to check out the property while he knocked on Alexander's door. When he got no reply, he wrote a note on the back of a calling card, asking him to make contact urgently, before re-joining his stand-in 2ic.

With the CSI tent removed, the front of the house was visible. There was no small patch of grass. No pretty plant pots. Just a block-paved driveway, bordered by an evergreen hedge. The gate was closed, as were the curtains. The last thing Hank needed was images of the crime scene appearing in the local press or on social media.

'How long have you been working organised crime?' he asked.

'I joined the unit last year when I made DC.'

'You're proving to be invaluable,' Zac said.

'You been checking up on me?'

'I'm a detective. That's what I do.'

'Me too.' She made a crazy face. 'Hank, pinch me. I can't believe I'm even saying that. It was working with you, Kate and the gang that did it. I got the bug and it never left me. I don't think it ever will. Zac's been showing me the ropes since I joined ROCU, even though he has a lot on his mind—'

'Don't we all? I need you on your toes, Ailsa. Anything you're unhappy about, gimme a nudge. You don't know, you ask. Understood?'

She glanced at the property through the side window. 'I see what you mean about the house being unprotected. Not a steel door in sight. I have something to show you.' Accessing her mobile, she scrolled through her images and turned the device to face him. 'This is where the Bradshaws really live. Is that proactive enough for you?'

Hank was impressed. 'You been saving that up?'

'Consider it my Christmas gift to the investigation. My lot have a file this thick on their crew . . .' She held her hands a foot apart. 'We haven't the resources to keep every criminal family under obs twenty-four-seven. We do our best.'

'Even ROCU will have problems getting in there,' Hank said.

'I never said it would be easy. Christine has someone looking after the place, probably tooled up waiting for a raid, a snarling dog or six guarding the perimeter, automatic bolts on the door. Difference is, we'll have armed support if and when we go in. My guv'nor would love to empty the place and share his findings with the MIT. It's purely their business he's interested in. With Christine under pressure, there's never been a better time to close them down. His concern is nothing to do with murder – Georgina's, or anyone else's.' Ailsa stopped talking. 'Sorry, that came out wrong. I didn't mean it literally.'

'Don't worry, Ailsa. Kate is looking out for Georgina.'

For Carmichael too, he hoped.

40

For half an hour, Jo had been comforting Kate in her office. She was sitting very still, trying to compose herself, thinking through what she would say to Carmichael, trying to calm down. With the weight of Bright's job to contend with, the double-hander and the old case review rekindling her grief over Georgina's murder, Kate was in the worst place possible to deliver such devastating news. She pushed herself so hard, Jo had often thought she might snap.

'I've got a splitter,' Kate said.

'I can imagine.' Jo handed her a painkiller and water to wash it down with. 'Why don't you close your eyes for five. If Ash's parents aren't due to arrive for another four hours, you have plenty of time.'

'No . . .' Kate raked a hand through her hair. 'What I have in mind can't wait. I want Lisa to see Ash while he's still breathing. Once the parents arrive, they may not let her in.' Leaning forward, she dropped her head in her hands, then stood up and paced the floor. 'I keep thinking of her asleep on his bed. Poor sod looked utterly spent.'

'How close do you think they were? I've never known her date anyone for longer than a few weeks, have you?'

'You're not helping.'

Jo swore.

Kate looked at her. 'What?'

'Didn't you say one of the nurses mistook Lisa for Ash's wife? You don't think they got married under the radar, do you?'

'No . . . I bloody hope not.'

Jo stared at the woman who made her feel whole. When they first got together, everyone else faded from view. Kate felt the same. It was like no one else in the world existed. If

Carmichael was occupying that space, she'd be experiencing unimaginable pain.

Unable to speak, Jo got up and gave Kate a hug.

Pulling away, she turned and left the room.

Walking slowly down the corridor, she took a deep breath as she neared her temporary office. Whatever she was expecting when she opened the door, it wasn't this. Zac was alone, head down in his work.

'Where's Lisa?'

He shrugged.

'Let me guess.' Kate's tone was edgy, urgency in it. 'She asked you to cover for her, right?'

'No, I thought—'

'When did she leave?'

'Twenty, twenty-five minutes ago? She took a call, grabbed her coat, and legged it. You look like you're about to do the same, guv? Anything I can do?'

Kate's mobile rang. Ignoring the question, she checked the screen: Carmichael.

'It's her.' She walked out of the office into the dim corridor beyond, lifting her mobile to her ear, full of mixed emotions, anger and sorrow competing for space in her head.

Carmichael was weeping.

'Kate, he's gone.'

41

Kate burst through the double doors into the incident room, asking the Murder Investigation Team to pay attention. She waited for them to down tools and settle, sharing the dreadful news of Ash's death, and gave them a moment to process it.

It knocked them sideways.

Crushed by losing another colleague, so soon after Robbo and Georgina, some bowed their heads, grief-stricken, a moment of silent reflection; others glared at her, no attempt to hide their hostility.

Kate knew why.

Hank may have given the custody sergeant the authority to sign the bail form, but she alone was responsible for allowing Christine Bradshaw's release. She'd give her right arm to reverse that if it meant that Ash was still breathing. It was her job to lift her team now. It wouldn't be easy . . .

She could hardly lift herself.

Detectives were looking past her to a point over her shoulder. She swung round. Hank was standing there, a ghostly complexion, a rigid jaw. He wiped his face with his hand, trying not to look angry.

Kate knew him well enough to know different.

You could hear a pin drop.

'The obs team have confirmed that Christine remains at her mansion,' Kate said. 'She's going nowhere.'

Christine threw her mobile across the room. It bounced off the newly painted wall, leaving a dint in the plaster, and fell to the floor. She glared at Tony. 'The fucker died! Find Jacob and get me out of here.'

She'd planted a couple of her crew in the hospital canteen,

telling them to act like all the other saddos worrying about relatives, and to let her know if the armed officers stationed outside her victim's room showed their faces.

Fifteen minutes ago, one of her spotters was on the blower. She'd wandered up to the ward, drawn curtains preventing her from seeing into Norham's room, but the armed officer detail had been stood down. She was about to turn away, when DS Carmichael rushed out the door and into the ladies' loo, sobbing.

Christine needed no further proof. Wishing him dead was about to bite her on the arse.

She turned as Jacob arrived in the room.

'Move!' she yelled.

'I've organised a warrant and a firearms team,' Kate said. 'They're ready to head out as soon as we are. Can you deal, Hank?'

'I need to find Lisa.' Hank checked himself.

Kate covered for his mistake.

'She's tied up.' Detectives were unaware of Carmichael's relationship with Ash. That's the way it would stay until she said otherwise. Kate wanted to reassure Hank that she'd spoken to her, that as soon as he left Middle Earth, she would too. No priority eclipsed the need to look out for Carmichael. Had she been able to, Kate would have added that the best way he could help her now was to bring in Christine. Instead, she elaborated on her lie. 'I sent her to the RVI. Ash's parents' train gets in shortly. We don't need a delegation to overwhelm them.' She thumbed toward the exit. 'Go on, get out of here. Take your lead from the firearms OIC. I don't care how long it takes. Do as I ask, and don't return empty-handed. Be careful, all of you.'

Volunteers were picking up mobiles, shrugging on coats, Ailsa among them. It was as if they had already decided who would go and who would stay to cover the office. Kate reminded them that not a hair on Christine's head was to be harmed.

'She'll get what's coming in due course.'

Hank was already on the move.

She called out to him.

Turning away from the others, he retraced his steps.

She said quietly, 'You and I will regroup in the morning.'

They looked at one another. Unable to bear the silence, Hank tried to speak and choked on his words, dropping his voice to a whisper.

'Tell Lisa . . . to call me if she needs to talk.'

Tears pricked Kate's eyes. 'I'll tell her.'

42

Kate walked to her office to collect her belongings. Through the window she saw Hank climb into the front passenger seat of a personnel carrier, the rest of her squad jumping in the rear. As it followed the firearms van out of the secure car park, she ran down the stairs, bursting through the back door, unlocking her Q5 as she approached the vehicle. Firing it up, she sped off, heading for the RVI.

It was the least she could do for Carmichael.

Kate reached the hospital before Ash's relatives arrived, time enough to commiserate with Lisa and offer her condolences. Outwardly, she looked better than Kate had expected. Her professional persona had kicked in. She was one step removed – on autopilot – not fooling her boss. Deep down, Carmichael was dying.

They stayed put while Mr and Mrs Norham identified their son at the morgue, Kate ensuring that they had everything they needed afterwards, including a designated contact over the holiday period. Lisa was to have spent Christmas with Ash at his Gateshead flat overlooking the Tyne. Without disclosing how it came to be in her possession, she handed his parents her own key.

In their current state, they didn't question it.

Neither did they react when Lisa introduced herself. Kate took that to mean that she hadn't met them before, that her relationship with Ash was recent or, for whatever reason, the couple had chosen not to make it public at work or at home. A casual observer might argue that it would make things easier for Lisa going forward. Kate knew it would make matters ten times worse.

Grieving for a secret lover was brutal.

Kate had been there when Jo booked to fly to New York, a plane that ditched in the Atlantic Ocean a hundred miles short of its destination, killing everyone on board. It was days before Kate discovered that Jo hadn't boarded, that she was alive and unharmed. For Carmichael, there would be no such happy ending.

An overwhelming urge engulfed Kate. She felt compelled to tell Ash's parents that Lisa was so much more than an MIT detective there to convey bad news; that she was in love with their son. Only it wasn't Kate's place to interfere or break a confidence. If Lisa wanted them to know the nature of her relationship with Ash, she'd have told them herself. Instead, Kate supported the bereaved parents in practical ways, arranging a car to take them to Gateshead, taking the heat off Lisa in the process.

As soon as the cab disappeared, Kate led her to her vehicle and headed home.

There were no tears on the short drive to Jesmond, no conversation either, despite Kate's best efforts. When she pulled up outside the house, Lisa made no move to get out. She stared blankly through the front windscreen, as if the car was still moving and she hadn't realised it had come to a stop. Worrying that she'd bury her grief, rather than let it run its natural course, Kate placed a hand gently on hers.

Recoiling from her touch, Lisa turned to look at her: raw, exposed, at rock bottom. 'Boss, I don't quite know how to say this, but I have never felt so alone. I'm grateful for every day I've worked with you and Hank, but I can't do this any more – the job, I mean. It's taken too much out of me.'

It came as no surprise that she felt that way, though Kate hadn't expected it so soon and wasn't ready for it. She responded in the only way she knew how. 'Oh, Lisa, if I had a quid for every time I've said that over the years, I'd be a rich woman. After we lost Robbo, I wanted to curl up and die. I know you felt the same. You went on then and you will now. Besides, what would I do without you?'

Carmichael's eyes filled up.

Kate said, 'It's what we were born to do. We both know it.'

'I used to think so.'

'Give it time. You're in shock. You need to process what's happened.'

'I can't hack it any longer . . . I just can't.' A single tear rolled down Carmichael's cheek to the corner of her mouth. She wiped it away with a shaky hand. 'It wouldn't be fair on the team, Kate. It's time for a change of direction.'

'Lisa, you're a brilliant detective, one of the best I've worked with. It was tough losing Robbo, but Ash is more than a colleague. He wouldn't want you to give up now, I guarantee it. The MIT is better with you in it. The team need you. Hank and I need you. A few hours ago, we fought over you.'

Lisa laughed, then sobbed.

'Look, Hank would kick your arse from here to Sunderland if he knew what you'd just said. So, here's the deal: I won't tell him if you promise not to make any sudden decisions on your future. Your resignation will hit the bin if it lands on my desk anytime soon. You can honour Ash's memory by helping me to prove Georgina's case. He'd want that, you know he would, and I can't do it without you. What do you say?'

'I'll think about it.' Her reply was barely audible.

'C'mon, let's get you inside.'

43

ROCU did their best to investigate and infiltrate organised crime gangs who made money from extortion, blackmail, fraud, and drug running – harming every community they touched. Detectives on Operation Strike had tried and failed to take Christine Bradshaw down. They may never dismantle her organisation, but it would be a major coup to disrupt it while she was in prison. Vowing not to return to base until she was in cuffs, Hank pushed all thoughts of Kate, Lisa and Ash from his mind.

His adrenaline kicked in the nearer the personnel carrier got to its destination, the firearms vehicle turning slowly and deliberately into Runnymede Road. A moment or two later, it killed its lights and stopped. Easing off the accelerator, Hank's driver did the same, pulling up thirty yards behind. Behind that, the vet's car followed suit. She was there to dope Christine's dogs, should the need arise.

The radio in Hank's sweaty hand crackled.

'Unit One: Stand by.'

'Copy that.'

Hank watched armed support officers pour from the vehicle, fanning out as they hit the tarmac on either side of the front gate, others making their way stealthily down the side of the property and around the back. Using night vision binoculars to follow the action, he observed them take up their positions, swearing under his breath as the electric gate of the adjacent house moved slowly across the entrance, dipped headlights lighting up the street. So much for silent and deadly, under cover of darkness.

'Fuck's sake!'

All he was missing was a brass band to announce their arrival.

Unless . . .

Hank tensed.

Was this Christine making a run for it?

He half-expected her driver to come flying out of the neighbouring property in a Hummer, lights on full beam, blinding everyone, colliding with anyone who tried to stop him. Maybe that was why they called him The Tank.

Hank didn't need to warn the firearms team what was happening next door. Hardwired for danger, Unit One quietly instructed Unit Two to approach with caution. As he crept along the street, the car nosed forward.

In the glow of streetlights, Hank got a glimpse of the driver and passenger. Relaxing, he lifted his radio: 'Unit Two, I see one female driver and small child in the vehicle. I repeat. One female and a small child.'

The woman froze, in full-on panic mode, eyes wide with fear as Unit Two appeared on the edge of her driveway. He held up a hand – STOP – then pushed it repeatedly towards her, indicating that she should reverse. As she did so, the gate closed, plunging the street into darkness once more.

Unit Two parted the hedge, making sure her car lights were switched off and she'd gone inside. 'Unit Two: Neighbour secure in the house. Please hold.' He returned to where he'd been stationed. 'Unit Two: Now in position.'

'Unit One: any dogs on the prowl?'

A negative reply was echoed by other units, each confirming their positions and that they were good to go. North, south, east, and west sides of the residential plot were clear. The property was surrounded, each officer having a visual of colleagues on either side, like a daisy chain of weaponry.

Within minutes the fun would start.

In the kitchen, Carmichael slipped off her jacket and held on to it. She looked lost, like a child on its first day at nursery, wondering which peg she should hang her coat on, what to do or say next, waiting for an adult to tell her where to go. She'd been in the house many times, but seemed disoriented, unfamiliar with the place. She was there in body only, her mind unable to function.

'Here, let me take that . . .' Kate took her coat, draped it over a chair, then turned to face her. 'Can I get you anything? Cup of tea, something stronger?'

'No, thanks.'

She jumped as the door opened.

Jo had come to greet her.

'Lisa, I'm so very sorry.'

Pushing a rogue hair from her face, Carmichael tucked it behind her ear. Her bottom lip quivered, stemming a tsunami of emotion she'd been holding back. Stepping forward, Jo pulled her into an embrace, a sad smile for Kate over the young detective's shoulder. Lisa was rigid in Jo's arms, too numb to cry, too exhausted to speak. In time, she'd need to.

Kate and Jo would be there to listen.

Carmichael turned her head slowly, something shiny catching her eye, the gift box Jo had inadvertently left on the kitchen table.

'I should go, I don't want to intrude on your evening.'

'Hey,' Jo said. 'Don't you dare run off.'

'No, really.' Carmichael grabbed her coat. 'I'm fine.'

'Even if that were true, you just arrived.' The detectives had come to an accommodation in the car, but the shock was still to come. Kate recognised the signs. 'Listen to me, Lisa. This is no time to be on your own. You know I've been there recently. Without Hank to help me through it, I'd have gone under. You saw the state I was in.'

Carmichael hesitated.

'Please,' Kate begged. 'Let Jo and I do this small thing for you. Stay the night at least.'

Carmichael nodded.

'I need to crash.'

44

Hank's work mobile began to march across the dash. Armed officers had vanished, and the radio was ominously quiet. Keeping his eyes peeled on the street, he lifted the device to his ear.

'Gormley.'

'You wanted to speak to me?' It was Alexander.

'You pick your moments, man.'

'I've been busy. You tied up?'

Hank peered out through the window. 'You could say that.'

'Shall I call back?'

'No, I'll make it quick. Whatever you do, don't ignore what I'm about to tell you. You've had a visitor who may or may not have been related to the family across the road, know what I'm saying?'

Alexander swore down the line.

'Yeah, not what you deserve for helping us. Watch your six. You need anything, let me know.'

'Thanks for the heads-up. I have leave to take. I'll make myself scarce.'

The radio burst into life: 'Unit Three: I'm in the garden.'

Alexander said, 'What was that?'

'Nothing for you to worry about. I've gotta go.' Hank hung up, scooping the radio off the seat. 'Mike 3459. Repeat, please.'

'Unit two.' His voice was soft and low. 'I'm in the garden. House lights are on. No movement inside. Stand by.' There was a short pause. 'Two vehicles on the driveway: dark coloured BMW, Registration: November. Lima. Seven. Zero. Tango. Tango. Papa. Dark Audi Q7: Registration: Delta. Charlie. One. Six. Alpha. Papa. Kilo. Both engines cold.'

Hank pictured other units moving in, crouched down,

weapons at the ready, eyes scanning the dark corners of the garden, every movement and sound a potential threat to safety. Hank hoped there would be no shooting – there had been enough of that in recent days – but if Christine didn't come quietly, his armed colleagues were ready for her.

What concerned Hank was another bloodbath, another death. If that were to happen, Kate would never live it down, let alone forgive herself.

Her voice pushed its way into his head . . .

You and I will regroup in the morning.

He'd caught the 'stay alive' subtext but failed to acknowledge it. He was angry with her, something he now deeply regretted. At the time, his only concern was Carmichael. Thinking about her made him feel emotional. He'd taken her under his wing since the day she joined the Murder Investigation Team. He had no idea how she'd recover from this.

'Unit One. Go, go, go!'

Hank forced himself to focus.

Armed officers were on the move, lightning fast.

There was a loud crash as the front door was breached, officers yelling as they ran in: 'Armed police!' Then again as they cleared each room. 'Clear! Clear!' until Unit One confirmed that the house was secure.

Hank left the van and ran towards the property, followed by his team, pulling up sharp as he entered the driveway. 'What the hell?'

Ailsa arrived at his shoulder. 'Where are we?'

This was not the same house she'd shown him an image of at the crime scene, a classic design with a pillared front entrance and Georgian-style windows. What they were looking at was as modern a property as they had ever seen, an unappealing glass box.

Hank met Ailsa's gaze.

Christine had played them.

45

Tony poured Christine a stiff gin and tonic and took it upstairs as requested. She was in the bath, smoking an expensive cigarillo, her left arm dripping bubbles as she lifted it from the water to accept her drink. Her shapely legs were smooth and silky, crossed at the ankles, one foot resting on the corner of the bath. She didn't give a stuff that she was wanted for the murder of a cop.

'Is Harvey back yet?' she said.

Tony bristled. 'No.'

'What's with the twisty bracket?'

He straightened his face. 'Anything I can do for you?'

'You can take the night off. I don't need you any more.'

The double entendre was like a punch to the gut. He felt like turning her bubbles pink, but she'd be out of his hair soon enough. Then she'd beg him to take over. Harvey had muscle, but not the clout or financial acumen to run her operation. Tony had graduated to a position of power. He'd sit tight and bide his time.

'Can I trust you, Tony?'

'What?'

'You fucking heard me.' She took a long drag on her cigarillo, blowing a cloud of smoke in his direction. 'You wouldn't betray my boys, would you? Their absence created a vacuum in my business. It was filled temporarily, but Lee was keen to retake what was his.'

'I know, we talked about it.'

She paused, making him sweat. 'Someone around here is a cold-blooded killer. Couldn't be Harvey. I know exactly where he was. Couldn't be you, unless you're going to tell me you were a hitman before you got an education.' She looked up at the ceiling, thinking time. 'Maybe I'm looking for a snitch, someone lacking bottle, who'd need someone else to do the grunt work. Is that you?' Her slate-grey eyes terrified him. 'Well? No one saw you on Christmas Eve after Jacob dropped my boys at Livello. Did you take a taxi to Heaton and lie in wait?'

'I went home, Christine.'

'Can anyone verify that?'

'You know they can't.' His wife was long gone because of her. For years she'd picked up men and dropped them at will. Who would dare argue? 'I can't believe you're asking. How long have we known each other?'

Her face said: too long. 'I hope I'm wrong. I wouldn't want to lose you.'

Tony's stomach rolled over. She didn't mean lose, as in misplace. 'Aren't you just a tad worried about what the cops are doing?'

She smiled. 'I know what the cops are doing. They're searching the lads' house as we speak. I watched them on my phone. Hank Gormley is standing on the driveway looking forlorn, poor love.'

She sat up, exposing her beautiful breasts.

Putting her cigarillo out in the ashtray on the side of the bath, she hauled herself into an upright position, towering over him, white bubbles cascading down her body. Despite wrecking his marriage and casting him aside, she still turned him on.

What's more she knew it.

He held out a bath towel.

Ignoring it, she stepped out of the water and moved towards him, too close for comfort, enjoying herself. 'You seem to have drifted off, Tony. You are listening to me, aren't you?' Her tone became more combative, like flicking a switch. 'You better be, because if I find out you're the rat in my crew, I will kill you myself.'

Tony stood his ground. 'What can I do to regain your trust?'

Christine didn't do backchat. 'I'll think of something.'

'Christ, in what world do you think that Gormley is going to stop looking for you? He won't be turned. Neither will his boss. They will pursue you till the end of their days. If you want my advice – which is what you pay me for – you need to leave the country ASAP—'

'Shut your mouth. If I need your guidance, I'll ask for it.' She pulled on a white robe, tying it at the waist. Turning her back on him was a show of strength. The woman was fearless. She swung round, a smile developing. 'Now you mention it, how about you start with Hank? He needs to know that if I go down, he'll be joining me. Difference is, he won't get up.'

46

Hank didn't call Kate to update her as he normally would. Carmichael's need eclipsed his, and Kate could do without more bad news. So, he was on his own. Time to rethink his options. When Runnymede Road was first mentioned by the obs team as Christine's bolthole, Ailsa was at her usual post in ROCU, unaware that a request was in for her to assist the MIT. Tonight, she'd walked in late and knew only that they were going to make an arrest at a mansion in Darras Hall. Assuming it was the same one she'd shown Hank at the crime scene, she'd piled into the personnel carrier, a black Ford Transit with no windows in the rear, a series of events conspiring to waste precious time and resources. He was philosophical in the face of such a crushing disappointment.

No one person was to blame.

They watched the carefully mounted operation wind down, the firearms team making their way to their vehicles, gloomy expressions all round. Ailsa too was downcast, which was out of character. Even when things were not going well, she managed to stay cheerful.

Hank wandered over to speak to her.

She got in first. 'I'm so sorry, Hank. I couldn't see out of the van, so I didn't think to question the route.'

'Why would you? Even on big ops things go wrong. This is not your fault.'

'Yeah, but the boss is expecting a positive result tonight. She's taken so much stick lately. When the rest of the team find out Christine is on the fly, it won't help, will it? Who do you think Harry and the others will blame?'

Hank peered at her through the darkness. He'd do anything to prevent that from happening. Kate was under extreme pressure, professionally and personally. He didn't want to add to her woes.

An idea arrived in a flash.

'Call ROCU and get the postcode for the house you showed me. Do it now please.'

Ailsa made the call, asking for the information, then hung up. 'We're down but by no means out, Hank.' Accessing maps on her iPhone, she typed in the postcode, then handed over her mobile, a big smile on her face.

Using two fingers, Hank enlarged the map on screen. 'Yes! Come with me.'

Hoping to turn a negative into a positive, he took off in the direction of the firearms vehicle with Ailsa hot on his heels. Unit One was talking to the vet. They turned as Hank and Ailsa approached.

'Stu, Madeleine . . .' Mentally, Hank crossed his fingers for the right response to the plan formulating in his head. 'If I can get a warrant quickly, are you good to go again?'

'Fine by me,' Madeleine said. 'I've got nothing else on tonight.'

Stu asked, 'What did you have in mind?'

'Bradshaw has another address, two streets away,' Hank said. 'She won't be expecting us to rock up at her other place tonight. She'll be rolling on the floor laughing, thinking she got one over on us. With your help, I'd like to wipe the smile off her face.'

Stu's face lit up. 'I'm in.'

In possession of the warrant, Hank gave Stu the address, telling him to lead on. When they got there, everyone followed the same routine, scoping the exterior of the place before proceeding. This time the vet was required. Madeleine had done her job, tranquillising no fewer than four snarling dogs that now lay sleeping in the garden, clearing the path for a silent assault on the house.

The firearms team found no one on the ground floor. Upstairs was a different story. Units Three and Four bursting through a bedroom door on the floor above.

'Armed police!'

Christine was in the act, on top of Harvey. She swapped one type of moaning for another. 'You gotta be kidding me!' She was dragged unceremoniously off the bed, leaving her current squeeze exposed and with his hands in the air. Christine lashed out at the officers. 'Get off me, you fucking morons!'

'Oh dear.' Hank sauntered through the door, holding two hands in front of his face, peeping through his fingers, unable to wipe away the smile as he dropped his arms to his side, telling Bradshaw to get dressed. 'I do hope you enjoyed that shag. It's the last one you'll be getting for a while.'

47

As soon as Kate read Hank's text, she left Jo babysitting and drove to Middle Earth at breakneck speed to congratulate the firearms team and the MIT for their efforts. Everyone was overjoyed to learn that Christine Bradshaw was back in custody. Kate would have liked to interview her, but this was Hank's first case as SIO.

She wanted him to take the credit.

Sitting down in the observation room, she waited for the interview to begin. Christine was already there, a uniformed escort standing to one side, ignoring her. The prisoner leaned back in her chair, arms crossed over her chest, her usual bored expression absent, which Kate found curious. Sensing that she was under surveillance, Bradshaw lifted her eyes to the corner of the room, staring into the camera lens, directly at Kate.

What was going on in her head?

There was no middle-finger salute tonight, nor trademark you-can't-touch-me sneer. Unaware of what was going on in the MIR, she seemed highly agitated. Section 18 Wounding was one thing; being arrested on suspicion of murder another thing altogether.

Kate's phone lit up. Jo's number.

'Hey, thought you'd like to know that Lisa's still asleep.'

'That's good.'

There was a long pause, neither of them knowing quite what to say to each other. Kate was grateful to be in a room where she wasn't the focus of attention and wouldn't be disturbed. Ash's death had shaken everyone who knew him, not just Carmichael.

On the screen in front of her, Montagu entered the interview room. Due to legal professional privilege, Kate couldn't eavesdrop on the conversation, though she was wishing she could lip-read. The uniform cop moved outside, remained at the door as he'd no doubt been instructed. Prisoners tended to lash out at a messenger telling them something they don't know or didn't want to know.

'How's Hank doing?' Jo was asking.

'He's not started yet. Christine's brief is here, so we'll be underway soon.'

'OK, you sound busy. See you later.'

Jo hung up.

Montagu sat down, conveying the news that Ash Norham had died, that the police had all they needed to put Christine away for a very long time. Others might shrink in stature on hearing that they were about to be charged with such a serious offence. Not her. Once more she looked smack dab into the camera, lifting her chin, undefeated – a show of bravado against all the odds in case the pigs were watching.

Let the games begin.

'Yeah, yeah. I get it, Monty. What's the plan?'

'My advice is, be contrite—'

'Apologise? You're 'aving a laugh.'

'Christine, you have the means to employ the best legal counsel, but you're in more trouble than ever before—'

'Then I'll pay them extra. Fucking thieves.' She gave him hard eyes. 'You need to persuade the CPS to reduce the murder charge to manslaughter. If they won't, I want the best money can buy to swing a jury in my favour. Got that?' Montagu was nodding. 'I've dodged a murder trial before.'

His expression said: *this time you'll go down.*

'What? Don't tell me my luck's run out because I've been riding it for a very long time.'

'You heard the SIO. Bodycam footage will disprove a claim of self-defence. The officer had his back turned when you hit him – and it will take a magician to convince any jury that Don reached for the gun to hand it over for safekeeping before he was shot.' Montagu flushed in anticipation of repeating a swear word. '"I'll blow your head off" speaks for itself.'

'Norham shot my husband. I lost control.'

'As part of your defence team I'd avoid pointing the finger at a dead police officer. Victim-blaming rarely draws sympathy in court. Our defence will play on the extenuating circumstances that prevailed at the time the offence was committed and the trauma you are now suffering.'

'Cool. By the time you're finished, I'll sound like Mother Fucking Teresa.'

'It's no laughing matter, Christine. The law is a lottery. You can never second-guess a jury panel.'

48

Kate paid attention as the door into the adjoining interview room swung open. Hank entered and sat down opposite his suspect. He turned on the tape, ensuring that the audio was switched on, so she could listen in. Christine glanced at the empty chair beside him: *no sidekick?* He didn't explain Carmichael's absence, nor hang around. He kept the interview short, his tone steady and deliberate the whole way through. The fact that he knew the victim personally made no difference to the way he handled Bradshaw.

She was rattled by the end of it.

The balance of her mind had always been disturbed, in Kate's opinion. That wouldn't stop a clued-up barrister twisting the facts, casting doubt, pleading provocation, characterising her attack on Ash as unacceptable but arguably understandable, given her state of mind. Nor describing the actions of the police as a vendetta, a misuse of power against a woman whose family had been wiped out within the space of a few hours.

The police were used to bad press. Sometimes it was deserved. There had been an explosion of high-profile offences committed by serving officers that had fuelled an exponential growth of public distrust.

This not only worried Kate. It shamed her.

Like Georgina, Hank, Carmichael, and the rest of her team, she'd spent her working life helping victims, not creating them. The vetting process was to blame. Recruits had entered the service who should never have been allowed to pull on a blue suit, possess a warrant card, or carry a gun. Their despicable actions had scarred the reputations of thousands. These were the very officers who could be bought and who, for their own gain, would tip off serious and organised criminals like

Christine Bradshaw. Hank would be hoping to swing the pendulum the other way by removing her and her cohorts from the streets of the city he loved, protecting his community.

He eyed his prisoner. 'Do you have anything to say?'

Considering the question, Christine remained silent.

In the observation room, Kate leaned forward, zooming in on her. Gone was the characteristic bravado, the smug expression and downright contempt for Hank and everything he stood for. For the first time ever, the DCI saw a crack appearing in the detainee, a hint of panic in her slate-grey eyes. Bradshaw had blown it this time.

Hank and Montagu arrived in the corridor at the same time as Kate. She waited for them to shake hands and for the solicitor to move away before speaking. 'Well done,' she said. 'That was pitch-perfect. Now take off. I don't want to see you in here until tomorrow.'

He wasn't expecting that. 'You know I can't—'

'You can and you will. I'll walk you out.'

Hank followed her towards the exit. 'Kate, I have work to do. Taking Christine out of circulation was a massive time suck. I want to catch up on the shooting. There's still a dangerous offender out there with a firearm.'

She stopped walking and turned to face him. 'Who neither of us believe is going to hurt anyone else. Agreed?'

'I can't argue with that.' He hesitated, a sombre expression. 'How's Lisa?'

'She's with Jo. Go home, Hank. You've done Ash proud.'

49

Kate snuck out of the house at the crack of dawn so as not to wake Carmichael, Jo volunteering to look after her. If anyone could help Lisa through her grief, she could. It didn't turn out that way. Within the hour, Jo had arrived at Middle Earth, casually dressed in skinny jeans, a pair of brown suede boots and a chunky knit sweater, a warm coat over her arm. Her hair was tied in a loose French braid that looked complicated to achieve but had taken her minutes that morning. Kate spied her sneaking into her office with their dog in tow.

No sign of Lisa.

'Jo?' Kate caught the door as it swung shut. No greeting given, just an accusatory stare and a sharp tongue. 'What the hell are you doing here?'

'Don't look at me like that. I got bored.'

'Where's Lisa?'

'She wouldn't take no for an answer.'

'She's here?'

'In your office,' Jo whispered. 'What was I to do? She's a grown woman with a mind of her own.'

'Not going to happen. It's too soon.'

'Says the cop who couldn't keep away if her life depended on it.' Jo made a face. 'Was it too soon when your mother died? Or when Hank was shot in Spain? Was it too soon when you left your old man clinging to life after his coronary because you thought I'd perished on a plane? It's your fault. You moulded Carmichael in your own image. She's a workaholic with no life outside of the job. She could almost be your daughter. She's trying to live up to your high standards and prove that she deserves the faith you have in her. She needs something to take her mind off Ash.'

Carmichael ploughed on, trying not to think about the post-mortem that was, or would be, taking place today. The reasons for that were laid down by law: Ash's death was sudden, violent, and unexpected; he died after arriving at A&E with an injury, following an unlawful assault. Any suspicious or unnatural death involved investigation and deliberation by a coroner.

Resigned to that brutal fact, Lisa took out her phone.

She didn't have to scroll far through her videos to find one featuring Ash. He was in a clubhouse, clowning around with a bunch of rugby mates having scored the winning try against another force in the first game Lisa had the pleasure of watching. He turned to camera, toasting her with a pint of Black Storm. Only she could see that special message in his eyes, the one that spoke volumes, the one that told her she was loved.

Right now, she couldn't control her fury.

Zac rounded the corner, opening the door as Carmichael snatched up the internal telephone and punched in a number, her back to him. Not wishing to interrupt, he hung back. If this was a professional rather than a personal call, it might be connected to the enquiry, something he needed to know.

What she said next blew his mind.

'Finn, it's Lisa . . . Carmichael, MIT. What time is Bradshaw being transferred to court? Hank wants me to have a word before she leaves.'

Zac frowned. The only Finn he knew at Middle Earth worked in the custody suite.

'You're a star,' Carmichael said into the phone. 'Yeah, I'll let him know. No, it shouldn't take long.' A long pause in the conversation. 'The spiteful bitch! Did you kick her back?' Another pause. 'I would have . . . OK, yeah, thanks . . . I'll be down shortly.'

She blew out a breath, hanging onto the desk, using it as

a prop, taking a moment to compose herself, a woman under immense pressure. Zac had already made the jump. He could have stepped out when she hung up, forgetting what he'd heard. He chose not to. He had some advice to impart.

'You don't want to do that, Lisa.'

Carmichael swung round. 'Do what? And why are you creeping up on people?'

'Whatever it is you have in mind, believe me, Bradshaw's not worth it. You antagonise her, you'll be pinning a target to your chest.'

'Did I ask your opinion?' She gave him what was known in their circle as the Scotswood stare and didn't wait for an answer. 'You're no longer a cop, Zac. So do me a favour and keep your nose out of my business.' Zac held up his hands in surrender, but Carmichael wasn't done. 'I need a moment with Bradshaw face to face. What do you care, anyhow?'

'I hope you know what you're doing.'

She made for the door.

He blocked her way.

'Lisa, I can't let you do it.'

She shoved him backwards. 'Get out of my way!'

He hung onto her, as a father would a hysterical child, one you didn't wish to hurt, just talk some sense into. 'Please, Lisa. Sit down and take a moment. You walk out that door, your career is over. You'll be looking over your shoulder your whole life . . . and for what? Would Ash want that? Would Kate?'

Swallowing her grief, she eased away and turned her back on him, her face superimposed in the window of Bright's trophy cabinet. The reflection staring back at her was unrecognisable: gaunt, angry, an ugly version of who she was. Ash loved her, would do anything to protect her. Their time together had been brief, but also wonderful. Deep down, all Carmichael wanted to do was honour his memory. Going head-to-head with Bradshaw was not the way to do it. She owed Zac Matthews for stopping her.

She turned to face him. 'How did you know?'

'I heard the call and put it together. Finn might not be aware that you're no longer on Hank's side of the investigation. I am.'

'Thank you.'

'For what?'

'Saving me from myself.'

50

Kate had advised Carmichael that there was only one place to start looking into Georgina's murder and that was at the beginning, on the day before she died. Her car was recorded as leaving the station at 08.20 with her at the wheel, no passenger. Seven minutes later it was spotted by ANPR on the A19, then heading north on the A1 ten minutes after that.

Lisa imagined her heading home, unaware of what was to come.

She noted the estimated time of death as 09.15, not long before her body was found. She couldn't have been at the riverside long before being confronted by her killers, ten minutes or so after she'd have reached Rothbury. If only she'd gone straight home. If only Ash hadn't swapped shifts with a mate whose parents lived in the south. Life or death was a game of chance. Wrong time, wrong place. Tragic.

Lisa had scheduled a Zoom call with the man who'd found Georgina's body. It ended as Kate walked through the door with coffee and Christmas cake, a gift from Jo to keep them going. She shared them out, then pointed at Carmichael's monitor.

'Who was that?'

'Mark Trewitt.'

Kate sat down. 'What did you think of him?'

'He was very helpful. And has a sharp memory. It's not every day you come across a body, is it? The control room logged his call at nine thirty-six. He had nothing to add to the statement he originally gave to Curtis.'

'Didn't I read that he called his office immediately afterward?'

'Yeah, I checked that against the file. His producer gave a

statement at the time, confirming how shocked he sounded. It couldn't have been him, Kate. The woman walking behind him produces documentaries and runs with a camera. I watched the footage she handed in at the time. Trewitt almost tripped over Georgina's body, then looked around, scared to death. He wasn't faking it.'

Vaguely aware of the chat going on behind him, Zac stared at the open policy book on his desk. On the page he was reading there was a note of samples collected at the crime scene: discarded cigarette butts, a chewing gum wrapper, a paper cup, and other detritus. It reminded him of a young officer who'd come forward and was never taken seriously by his former SIO.

He glanced at Kate.

'Guv? I found something.'

She turned to look at him.

'Curtis took the view that as Georgina had been shot, with no bodily contact as far as he could tell, the search parameters didn't need to extend far. They were shorter than they should've been, in my opinion—'

'Shame you didn't tell him that at the time.'

'I did. He took no notice, of me or anyone. I've just been through samples listed in his policy book. Those taken from outside his designated search area are not included. And yet I know for a fact that some were taken by a uniform cop at the scene. Smart. Really switched on. As it happens, she knew one or both Bradshaw brothers – or knew of them.'

'Go on.'

'She collected samples from outside of the designated search area and brought them to Curtis's attention. He almost bit her head off. It doesn't look like they were ever sent to the lab.'

'Tell us you're joking,' Carmichael said.

'I wish.' Zac's face flushed as he refocused on Kate. 'Guv, I would have mentioned it to Bright, but there was no point. Curtis reopened the riverside. Any evidence would've been lost. I'm sorry, I don't remember the rookie's name.'

'Shouldn't be hard to trace her.' Carmichael was already on it, typing into her laptop.

'Have you spoken to Curtis yet?' Zac asked.

Kate shook her head. 'He's not answering.'

'No offence, but he'll not relish the thought of coming face to face with you.'

'Yeah, well he can count on it. If he thinks his involvement with the case is over, he can think again. North Yorkshire Police will be knocking on his door right about now. That's where I'm heading next, if you're up for it.'

'You'll get more out of him if I'm not there,' Zac said.

'OK, I'll take Lisa. You trace the rookie. We'll confer later.'

51

Ailsa familiarised herself with the interior of the crime scene, which was now practically empty, many items having been seized by crime scene investigators for further examination. After she'd seen everything there was to see, Hank took her outside with a plan to establish exactly how the shooting went down. To do that he needed someone else's help, a risky strategy given that the person in question had the means to keep tabs on the Bradshaws, not to mention take them out. Many a key witness had turned out to be the guilty party.

Hank secured the scene, pocketing the key.

Ailsa was about to head off.

'Wait a second, I need to make a call.'

'Something wrong?' Ailsa asked.

'Whatever I do next, play along.' Pulling his mobile from his pocket, he called Alexander's number, looking up at his front bedroom window as the call rang out. The curtains were drawn.

'Hello.' Alexander's voice was thick in his throat.

'It's Hank . . . Gormley. Sorry to disturb you.'

'You sound it. Is this tit for tat?'

'No, and I won't keep you long. I'm outside. Can you come to the window and stand exactly where you were when you were waiting for Bethany on Christmas Eve?'

'We've been over this. I gave you all I got.'

'Hey, I need your help. You might need mine one day.' Hank paused, trying his luck while the guy was half asleep. 'As ex-job, I thought you'd understand.'

'Nah, we never met. I'm good with faces. You're confusing me with Andrew.'

'Andrew?'

'My brother.'

'Ah, thought you looked familiar.'

The curtains across the way were yanked open. Alexander was standing there, bare-chested, in the middle of an enormous yawn, his hair sticking out at odd angles. He looked dog-tired. 'What do you want?'

'I'm standing where the victims were shot, right?'

'Give or take.' Alexander raked a hand through his hair. 'Move back a touch . . .'

He looked on as Hank shifted his position and stopped.

'A bit to the right.'

Hank followed his instruction.

'Spot on.'

'I'm going to ask my colleague to take up a position in the corner of the front garden. Give me a second. I'm going to put you on hold while I get her set up.'

'Make it quick. My heating's on the blink. I'm freezing my balls off here.'

Ailsa smiled, doing as Hank asked, then turned to face him.

'Come forward a bit,' he said. 'Not so close.'

'Really?' she said. 'If I was about to shoot Christine Bradshaw's offspring, I'd climb into the bloody hedge—'

'And transfer your DNA in the process? You need to think like a killer who doesn't want to get caught. This was a professional hit, not a numpty firing at someone's cherished pet with an air gun, as gross as that is. A pro who would know that leaves rustle when disturbed and could give the game away to a couple of jumpy exiles taking risks.'

Although Ailsa was taking her task seriously, Hank could tell she was enjoying the role play.

Hank unmuted Alexander. 'Martin, can you see my colleague from there?'

'No. Can't see her. Didn't see the shooter, I told you.'

'Hold on.' Hank spoke to Ailsa. 'Pretend you're going to shoot me.'

She raised her right arm, forming her hand into the shape of a gun, pointed it at him.

Hank prompted Alexander. 'Now can you see her?'

'No, not a thing.'

'Imagine the first kid has gone down.' Hank raised his right arm, pointing an imaginary weapon at Ailsa. 'How am I doing?'

'Move your body to the right . . . stop. Turn sideways. Now point the gun?' Hank did so. 'Aim further to your right . . . a bit more. There. Perfect.'

'You sure?'

'Positive. Despite the hour, I was awake then.'

Hank ignored the dig. Ailsa was trying to attract his attention. 'I'm putting you on hold again.' He muted Alexander before he had time to argue.

'Can I speak?' Ailsa whispered.

'Got something for me?'

'Maybe.' She thumbed over her shoulder. 'Could Alexander be the shooter?'

'Only if he was standing where you are now. The science indicates that he didn't shoot them from his position across the road. The trajectory of the bullet proves that. Why d'you ask?'

'Am I standing where he alleges the shots came from?'

'Yes, he told Lisa and I that Lee Bradshaw returned fire in your direction.'

'Corroborated?'

'Not yet, though damage to the hedge backs up his claim.'

Ailsa kept her focus on Hank, her voice low. 'Then maybe you need to reinterview the curtain twitcher next door who I assume is Ella Stafford. My one o'clock. I might be hidden from him across the road, but she's looking straight at me. She's been watching us the whole time.'

52

Lisa trailed Kate from their temporary home, along the corridor to Jo's office, then stood aside as Kate tapped on her door. The profiler had her back to them, feet on her desk, head snuggled into the upright. She could've been listening to someone on the phone, except there was no movement, no pen in hand or notes being taken.

Kate smiled at Lisa. 'Are you hearing what I'm hearing?'

Lisa tilted her head to listen at the door. 'Oh please, even my nan didn't listen to Bing Crosby.'

The volume increased as Kate turned the handle and crept inside, Lisa following her in. Jo's eyes were closed. Kate leaned forward and cut the radio. Jo almost jumped out of her skin, her face turning red. 'Hey, how long have you been standing there? I didn't hear you come in. I was concentrating.'

'On the back of your eyeballs?' Kate was teasing her.

'Oh, y'know, this and that. I've got a lot on.'

There wasn't a thing on her desk except a used coffee cup and a plateful of dark crumbs. It was a sad reflection of what Christmas had been reduced to this year. Nelson, her Labrador, was asleep at her feet, sending the zeds up, his upper lip twitching with every soft breath out.

Kate looked at Lisa. 'Do we believe that?'

'You're a terrible liar,' Carmichael told Jo.

'I'm busted. What can I say, the boredom got to me—'

'I told you not to come in,' Kate and Lisa said simultaneously.

'And I told you two the same. Did it make a difference?'

'If you're here to hold my hand in case I fall apart, I won't,' Lisa said.

'She won't,' Kate confirmed. 'Besides, I'm here.'

'I can see that.' Jo yawned. 'Question is, what for?'

'There's no one in the MIR. They're all out making enquiries and we're about to leave too. Fancy a trip to Whitby?' Kate knew what the answer would be. The Yorkshire seaside town was one of Jo's favourite places, around an hour and a half's drive away. She was already on her feet, grabbing her coat, picking up Nelson's lead.

Hank didn't look up, for fear of tipping off the nosy neighbour that they were onto her. Ella I-saw-nowt Stafford could wait a few moments longer. He kept his focus on Ailsa. 'The shooter will have scoped out this place before he shot the Bradshaw boys. Even so, I'm stumped. How the hell did he escape without being seen? Alexander claims Christine arrived outside within seconds of hearing gunshots. There were no reported sightings by anyone we've spoken to. All of those we identified had legitimate reasons for being in the vicinity, as in they live or work round here.'

'How is that even possible? Someone must have spotted our guy.'

'Not necessarily. He'd hardly use the main roads if he could avoid it.'

'Yeah, but that requires knowledge of the area, the ability to evade the cameras around here, an individual who knew the place well enough to navigate the back lanes and stay out of sight.'

'If the glove fits,' Hank said.

'Word is, we looked the other way on purpose. Five hours is quite a head start.'

'Keep that thought to yourself please, Ailsa.'

'The offender can't have vanished into thin air, can he?'

'Alexander claims he ran down the stairs to help. It's feasible that it may have been the very moment the shooter chose to walk away. As you pointed out, someone on this side of the road had a better viewpoint. Come on, I don't think Stafford has told us all she knows.'

Carmichael sat in the front with Kate, Jo and Nelson in the rear. They had been heading south for the best part of an hour discussing the investigation. Hundreds of enquiries had been generated. Few produced anything like a breakthrough. If Kate had learned one thing as an SIO, it was that you had to know which questions to ask if you wanted to elicit the right answers.

She condensed her thoughts for the other two.

'Other than the finder, in-depth interviews Curtis conducted were few and far between. Two women had seen a couple of lads leaving the riverside that morning, one wearing a retro jacket.' Even in the North, where kids went clubbing in a state of undress, that was unusual for a December morning.

'He assumed it was the Bradshaw boys?' Jo asked.

Kate caught her eye in the rear-view mirror. 'One of the female witnesses described them as shifty looking, not local. She couldn't photo ID them. Unless Curtis knows something that I failed to spot, no one else saw them at the riverside. Within hours of the murder, Lee and Jackson had gone through passport control at Newcastle Airport, pre-booked tickets paid for in cash having been left at the check-in desk by a female I reckon was Christine.'

'Was she questioned?' Jo asked.

'No,' Carmichael said.

'Why not?'

'CCTV was inconclusive.'

'She may have paid someone to do it for her,' Kate said. 'Assuming Lee and Jackson were running from a murder charge and not something else.'

'You're not convinced, are you?' Jo said.

'Making assumptions was Curtis's thing. I prefer hard evidence.'

'What are the chances of them flying out within hours of her murder being coincidental? Kate, they may as well have held up a placard with the words WE DID IT written in Georgina's blood.'

'Circumstantial isn't enough, Jo. We need to link them to the scene.'

'Where did they fly to?'

'Paris, Charles de Gaulle. According to Curtis, French police were too slow and lost them. They could have gone anywhere from there, or even doubled back to the UK via boat. Anyway, Curtis never found them. If he had, they'd probably still be alive . . . in prison, but still breathing.'

They all went quiet.

A call alert broke the silence.

Andy Brown's name popped up on Kate's mobile.

Kate took the call on the hands-free. 'Speak to me, Andy.'

'Sorry to disturb you, guv. I can't get hold of Hank.' He sounded rattled. 'He was heading for the crime scene with Ailsa, but his phone is constantly engaged. I thought he might have been calling you.'

'I've not heard from him. Did you try Ailsa?'

'Yeah, I'm getting voicemail. I left a message. She hasn't responded.'

'Is it urgent?'

'You could say so. The bodies are piling up. Hazel Sharp is dead.'

53

The door was an unusual shade of pink, Ailsa thought. Grossly inappropriate for such a lovely period house. She rang the bell and stood to one side. Seconds later, Stafford opened the door slowly, a pair of anxious eyes peeking through the narrow gap afforded by the security chain. Ailsa held up ID. 'Hello there, I'm DC Ailsa Richards. You'll remember my colleague Detective Sergeant Hank Gormley. We're following up on the shooting incident on Christmas Eve. We'd like to ask a few more questions. Can we come in?'

'Um, it's not convenient.'

'It's important,' Hank said.

'I'm not properly dressed.'

'Then go and put some clothes on, please. We'll wait.'

The door closed, the lock clicking into place.

Rolling her eyes at Hank, Ailsa dropped her voice to a whisper. 'Want me to go round the back?'

'Nah, if she's a runner, so am I.'

Ailsa grinned. He'd put on weight since she'd last seen him.

'More likely she's formulating a cock and bull story we might swallow,' he added. 'It won't work a second time. I'd like you to have a go at her. You're more her age, less scary than me.'

'On the outside,' Ailsa said. 'I brought my cattle prod in case.'

'You might need your sunnies.'

'What?'

'You'll understand when we get in there.'

Before Ailsa could probe any further, the bolt slid open and the chain came off. The door swung into a geometrically tiled, narrow hallway. Unlike the property next door, Stafford's home, whether owned or rented, retained many of its original features. She led them into a tidy living room that had wood flooring and a black marbled fireplace with a cast iron surround, inset with a panel of ornamental tiles featuring flowers on a beige background. The room was immaculate, not a thing out of place. Everything in it was a shade of pink – as were the clothes Stafford was wearing.

The young woman had a problem.

Ailsa didn't look at Hank. She wondered if the pink theme continued upstairs. It wasn't mentioned in the statement given by first responders. It didn't surprise her that Stafford had been hiding when they broke in. She was a mouse, in every sense of the word: small, timid, and fragile, like a porcelain doll.

'Please, take a seat,' Stafford said.

They all sat down, the detectives on the sofa, Stafford on the edge of an armchair. She didn't speak, just sat there staring at them, trying to keep her hands still, failing miserably.

'No need to be nervous,' Ailsa said. 'Can I call you Ella?'

She answered with a nod.

'I take it we've repaired your window?'

'Yes, thank you. I didn't think anyone would come until after Christmas.'

'It was important to secure your property.'

Ella drew a hand to her neck. 'Am I in danger?'

'Haven't you been watching the news?'

'No.'

Ailsa spotted the lie and didn't challenge it. Instead, she went the direct route. 'Whoever was shooting at the visitors next door is not Houdini, Ella. He must have come in and got out somehow. I think you saw him.'

She didn't admit or deny being a witness.

'If you're withholding evidence, you realise we won't catch the man. You seem overly anxious, if you don't mind me saying so.'

'Wouldn't you be after a gunfight?'

Ailsa thought 'gunfight' was an odd word to use. 'Yes, I suppose I would. I can now tell you that the gentleman who lives next door passed away and his wife is in custody. Neither of them can hurt you. Besides, by calling us, you were acting in their best interests, as any right-minded member of the public would. We appreciate any help we get, but we need the whole story, not the part you want to tell us.'

'Yes, well I didn't ask for this.' She looked at Hank. 'I told you last time, I don't want anything else to do with it.'

'No, Ella. You specifically said you saw nothing. That's not true, is it?' A hostile witness was not what he wanted. 'You're acting like you know more. Tell us and we won't bother you again.'

'You will, though, won't you, further down the line?' She tipped her chin dramatically. 'I have an important job I can't afford to lose. If I tell you, it'll mean taking countless days off. I'd have to get myself into town. It costs a fortune to park. For what? To get slagged off by a defence barrister or show my face to the scum in the public gallery? I'm young, not stupid.'

'No one is suggesting you are.' Ella had a point though, Ailsa thought. Civic duty was overrated. It inconvenienced the public and sometimes put them in the firing line. Alexander across the road was the perfect example. Nevertheless, the tenant was turning. Ailsa could sense it. Time to give her a nudge. 'Ella, what work do you do?'

'None. It's the holidays.'

'That's not what I asked.'

'Why does it matter?'

'You got fired from the bank for telling lies, didn't you?'

Mortified, Ella dropped her gaze, then raised her head, an angry retort. 'Why are you investigating me?'

'It's what we do. Let's not make that same mistake again, eh? When I was outside a moment ago, you were looking down from the window directly at me. I got the impression you were reliving a nightmare. You saw the shooter, didn't you?'

54

Kate's phone rang as the Q5 crossed the windswept moors heading for the seaside town of Whitby. Hank's excitement filled the car as he came on the line. Ella Stafford had given him a description of the shooter: medium build, taller than Ailsa, shorter than the laurel hedge, which had not recently been trimmed and stood at six five, describing his jacket as shiny, possibly leather. 'Alexander must have missed him when he ran down the stairs.'

'Stafford could see that in the dark?'

'There was light coming from the hallway, which also means Lee and Jackson were backlit, giving our man the perfect aim. His face was hidden under a peaked cap. Ella said he was wearing light trainers and was dead cool. He made no attempt to run as he left the scene. He walked east. Unless Stafford is misleading us – and I don't think she is – it rules out Charlotte.'

'Don't be too quick to rule her out.'

'Stafford was adamant the shooter was male.'

'I could look like a bloke if I wore a cap on a dark night. Stafford's description could fit any number of people: Nico, Oscar, Alexander, half the bloody force.'

'I don't think she made it up. She was precise on clothing.'

'Then we're in business. How was Ailsa?'

'I can't fault her. She was the one who spotted Stafford watching us from upstairs. She also got her to open up. She's too good to be on loan, Kate. You should secure her in the January transfer window.'

'I'll see what I can do,' Kate said. 'Are you heading back to base?'

'No, Ailsa and I are seeing Johnson. If his camera on the

gable end has a live feed, we're throwing a party tonight and you're invited.'

'Hang on. Have you spoken to the incident room in the past hour?'

'No, why?'

'Andy's been trying to get hold of you. Hazel Sharp is dead. They're calling it an overdose, but smacks of Christine rubbing out a witness. I can almost hear her giving the order: "If I get lifted, do what you have to."' Kate met Jo's worried gaze through the rear-view mirror. That morning, while Carmichael was sleeping, she'd warned Kate that Christine might choreograph an escalation of violence while on remand.

The search team found nothing incriminating at Christine's gaff they could hang on Harvey, so they let him go. When the cops left, he returned to the house to find cupboards and drawers hanging open, floorboards up, no sign of any technology. Tossers! He flew into a rage, kicking furniture, smashing everything in sight. Don, Lee, and Jackson were bad enough. With Christine gone, who'd step up?

Helping himself to a large measure of Macallan, he sat down, lifting dirty trainers onto the white sofa, savouring the thought of living there in his boss's absence. If Christine was going down, she'd be drawing her pension by the time she came up for air. Harvey thought he was in with a shout for the top job, until Tony arrived, ordered him to turn the screws on Hank Gormley, as per their boss's instructions.

Harvey glared at him. 'She said nowt to me.'

'You want it word for word?' Tony looked up at the ceiling, as if searching for the answer. 'You know, I can't remember. Mind you, she was in the bath at the time.' As he said it, he noticed Christine's car coast through the front gates, crunching on gravel as it parked out front. Montagu got out, buttoning his jacket, Jacob handing him his briefcase – all very official.

They heard the front door open and close.

Voices getting closer . . .

'Decision time,' Tony said smugly.

'You're suddenly Soprano?' Harvey scoffed. 'Do me a favour.'

Although Harvey was Christine's muscle, Tony washed her dirty money and was therefore fundamental to the cause. Harvey made up his mind there and then that he couldn't work for a money man. Still, there were other candidates within the organisation. The odds of him taking the top job were quickly dissolving.

The million-dollar question was, who had she chosen?

Montagu walked into the room, shocked to see the state of it, taking photographs for reference, explaining that it would demonstrate police insensitivity to the bereaved and therefore help Christine's case. Harvey failed to mention that he was responsible for most of the damage.

Montagu sat down at an antique writing desk.

Clicking open his briefcase, he stood up, handing them each a sheet of paper, with a note from Christine naming her temporary successor, someone who she said she could trust with her life. Harvey and Tony looked up from the note, eyeballing each other: *Is this a joke?* The signature was Christine's. The name on the contract was Jacob Burrows, The Tank. The man was dangerous.

'Where was Hazel found?' Hank asked.

Kate changed down and took a bend in the road. 'Her usual squat.'

'She wasn't there yesterday, I checked. Any evidence that the body had been moved?'

Kate smiled. 'You psychic now?'

'It doesn't take a genius to put it together, Kate. She hasn't been seen at the squat for a week. It occurred to me that Christine's crew might be keeping her company. What better way to make her evidence disappear than feed her addiction, then dump her body, making it look like an OD.'

'Yeah, talk later.'

'Wait a minute.' Hank paused. 'What about Sam?'

'Sam?'

'Her kid. Two years old, blue eyes, blonde curly hair.'

'Removed by social services six months ago,' Carmichael confirmed. 'Sorry, I should have passed that on. Ash . . .' She almost choked on his name. 'Ash said that was the sob story Hazel gave her new landlord when she took on the tenancy. Suffice to say, he didn't like the look of her, so she played the sympathy card. She begged him to put a roof over her head so she could get her toddler out of care. He told her to sling her hook. When she offered him cash in advance, the mercenary git took it.'

Hank thanked Lisa. 'The kid's safe, that's all that matters. Kate, do we know who's doing the PM?'

'Not yet. Andy will confirm.'

'Make sure it's someone who knows what a murder looks like.'

55

On his first visit to the crime scene, Hank had noticed the CCTV camera he now knew belonged to Paul Johnson. It pointed directly into the back lane, which suited Hank down to the ground. It was where he suspected, hoped, that the killer went to escape the attention of any passers-by.

'Not that there were too many of them at the time of the shooting,' he told Ailsa. 'Most right-minded folks tucked up in bed, trying to get some kip before the festivities began, their offspring hyped up and impatient, with only one more sleep until a reindeer arrived pulling a heavy sleigh.'

As they walked up the road, Hank stopped to listen, then swore beneath his breath. There was an ear-splitting racket coming from the house they were heading for. When no one answered their knock, Ailsa banged on the window, pointing towards the front door, yelling at someone to let her in.

Music blasted into the street when it was eventually pulled open by a weird-looking bloke with a mop top the Beatles would have been proud of in the sixties, a rollie hanging from his mouth that smelled suspiciously like weed, and a bit of white powder visible around his right nostril that wasn't icing sugar from a mince pie.

Curtis lived in a brick-built bungalow with a red pantile roof and panoramic views over Whitby Sands. Unlike his neighbours, he hadn't built up, only out. He didn't need to, not for a better perspective anyway. The house was high above the beach, practically on the cliff edge. Ignoring the glorious vista on her side of the car, Kate drove past it, parking on the bend further down the street to let Jo and Nelson out of the car.

Without waiting to be asked, the Labrador jumped out and

sat obediently on the pavement, wagging his tail, keen to be off chasing waves. Jo crouched down beside him, attaching a new lead to his collar. Then pulled on a grey beanie that matched her warm jacket, tucking a loose hair in at the side. Her eyes briefly caught Kate's as she stood upright, a non-verbal message passing between them: *wish we were all going.*

'I'll text you when we're done,' Kate said.

'Where shall we meet?'

'Here's fine.' Kate locked the car, handing her the keys. 'Lisa and I could do with some fresh air. We'll walk from here. I'd like to tell you we won't be long, but I'm not sure that's the case. Depends on what reception we get.'

Jo looked down at the dog. 'We'll be fine, won't we, Nelson?'

Carmichael smiled. 'Enjoy yourselves.'

'I'd say you too, but Kate's in battledress.'

Kate grinned. 'I have no idea what she means.'

'Watch your BP is all I'm saying.'

'I'll be the epitome of calm, as always.'

Jo tugged on the lead and set off without a backward glance.

Kate stood a moment, watching as they made their way down a tarmac path that dropped down onto the sand. Making friends with other dogs was Nelson's speciality, a joy to watch. She turned to face Carmichael, an idea occurring. 'Seeing Curtis isn't a two-person job if you'd like to join them.'

Carmichael shook her head. 'I'm fine.'

'I have a spare hat you can borrow.' Kate pulled it from her pocket and held it out. 'Not quite your style but who'll see it?' She scanned the empty sands. 'Go on, catch them up. It'll do you good.'

'It'll do me more good watching you take Curtis apart. If he'd done his job, Ash would still be here.'

'Lisa, I'm so sorry. Till now, that hadn't occurred to me.' Kate's judgement was usually sound. She was having doubts about bringing Carmichael along. 'I don't know what I was thinking? Why didn't you say?'

190

'I'm fine, boss.'

Was she though?

'Lisa, as I told you before, this could go one of two ways. Plan A is to go in easy, not to rile him. I want him to think that we're here for a general chat, to lull him into a false sense of security, not castigate him for a murder he never solved. We'll get nothing from him by going in hard.'

'And if he doesn't play ball?'

'Follow my lead. In fact, don't follow mine, follow his. There's no version of an interview that doesn't involve changing direction at a moment's notice. Go with the flow. Just make sure he shows his arrogance before we show ours.'

There was movement in the window of the house they were heading for. It was a female, probably Curtis's wife, acting as lookout, ordered to stay put until he told her otherwise. Kate rang the bell and took a step backwards – no copper's knock this time.

Curtis showed surprise as he opened the door. Kate had specifically asked North Yorkshire police not to tell him who to expect, only to advise him that he would be getting a visit from detectives by close of play in relation to an old case.

Even he could work out which one.

'Kate, I wasn't expecting two of you.' He looked Carmichael up and down, like she was shit on his shoe. 'And you are?'

Lisa's eyes were cold and unfriendly. 'DS Carmichael, MIT. Who were you expecting, Professional Standards?'

He'd made a fatal mistake in setting the mood of the conversation before introductions were complete. Already, he was regretting it. He chuckled nervously and stuck out a hand towards the woman he'd wronged.

Carmichael didn't take it. With Kate's warning ringing in her ears, she covered her indifference seamlessly and deliberately, so that her sleight would appear unintentional. It was beautifully executed, accompanied by an apologetic smile.

'I don't think anyone does that any more, do they, sir?'

Curtis dropped his arm.

56

It had taken the best part of an hour to get any sense out of Johnson. After a cocktail of drugs and alcohol, the detectives were amazed that the waste of space even remembered his name, let alone possessed the skill to install a surveillance system that would be of any use to them. He'd customised the camera, angling it with a wide view of the narrow lane to the rear, hoping to catch an image of the persons responsible for several thefts in the area, to alert the cops, he said.

Ailsa checked out his story with her colleagues in the MIR. The evidence was on the incident log for the postcode, confirming that there had been several incidents reported lately – bikes, tools, kids' toys, anything with a resale value that an opportunist could carry or ride away with – justifying the cash Johnson had shelled out on the private security to capture any suspicious activity he might pass on.

It surprised Hank that he had the wherewithal or means to finance such a device. Maybe he was more than a user; stolen bikes a cover for dealing from his premises, justification for the camera should a nosy cop query it.

Smart move.

A note to the drug squad could wait.

Hank was after bigger fish.

'A motion sensor triggers the camera?' He was hoping Johnson had the sensitivity and threshold levels set correctly, otherwise there would be no evidence and he was sunk. The guy was struggling to stay awake. 'Yes, or no?' Hank pushed. 'It goes on when someone moves, right?'

'Yeah, it pings my phone.'

'What you've got could help us with a major crime,' Ailsa said, stroking his ego. 'The sooner we're done, the sooner you can get back to your mates. My colleagues at the nick will be well-impressed with your technical know-how, as will a judge if you give us credible evidence we can put before a court.'

'You think?'

'I know—'

'Will I have to get in the witness box?' He was thrilled by the prospect.

Ailsa had stumbled on the trigger that would make him talk.

Reverting to plan B, Kate asked Curtis if they could talk inside. What she had to say wasn't a doorstep conversation. Reluctantly, he stepped aside, allowing the detectives in. The living room reflected his personality. It was drab, old fashioned and untidy, uninspiring in every way. He turned to face them, addressing Kate directly. He'd never acknowledge her as his equal – not if his life depended on it.

'Your timing is off,' he said. 'The wife and I are heading out. A family gathering.'

His wife presumably had a name. Whatever it was, she was watching from the kitchen, a worried expression on her face. She saw Kate looking, and stepped forward, offering the visitors a seat at the dining table and refreshments after their long journey, irritating her husband in the process.

He wanted rid of them.

Declining the offer, Kate and Lisa thanked his wife for her kind hospitality and sat down. Grudgingly, Curtis followed suit, taking the carver chair. He'd see that as a demonstration of his dominance. It was a confrontational stance, the table acting as a barrier between them. 'What's this about? If it's going to take all afternoon, I need to call my son.'

For a moment, Kate thought he was going to say: lawyer.

He might need one yet.

'It'll take as long as it takes,' she said. 'Murder doesn't recognise holidays. I assume you've seen news of the shooting?' She didn't wait for an answer. 'It's hard not to these days with TV, radio and social media on a continuous loop.'

He gave a resigned nod. 'I'm surprised anyone's putting themselves out over it. Even a workaholic like you. There won't be many who live in and around Newcastle mourning the death of anyone with the surname Bradshaw.'

'That's the difference between us, Gordon. You see dead scum. I see two young men whose lives have been cut short, who may or may not have caused the death of a police officer.'

His laugh was hollow. 'That's hilarious.'

'We never did communicate well,' she said. 'This is no longer about professional jealousy or point scoring. You're retired and I'm far from it. I'm not here about the Bradshaw boys, or to warn you of the shitstorm heading your way. I'm here to discuss Georgina Ioannou's murder investigation.'

'Why? Do you have new evidence?'

'I'm working on it.'

'Make it quick. As I said, I'm expected elsewhere.'

'You want it brief? That we can manage.' Kate nodded to Carmichael.

She bent down, lifting her bag from the floor. Throwing open the flap, she took a message spike from it and placed it deliberately and dramatically in the centre of the table between them, with handwritten notes attached, a pile as thick as an old telephone directory, with almost as many entries.

'What's that?' Curtis glared at her.

'If it looks like a message spike . . .' Carmichael left it there. Kate had asked her to bring the item along as a prop. 'More specifically, it's a number of queries relating to the high-profile case you failed to solve.'

'You ladies don't know how to make a list?'

'Oh, we do.' Kate let him sweat a moment.

The spike contained a comprehensive list of queries. She didn't intend going through the lot, only those he couldn't dispute, errors and omissions that would produce the very reaction she was after . . . him on the back foot, exactly where she wanted him.

'Read them,' she said.

He didn't.

Counting on that, Kate sat forward, elbows on the table, hands clasped together. 'You know, on every murder investigation I've been involved in, there's always been one or two things I wish I'd done differently, but your handling of Georgina's case trumps them all—'

'If you're suggesting I fucked up—'

'Stating, not suggesting.' She gestured towards the spike. 'Your enquiry into Georgina's death was a dog's breakfast from start to finish.' Removing the first message, she pushed it slowly across the table for him to read: **Bradshaw boys pinned as guilty from the outset.** 'As the current SIO, I must consider alternative scenarios. Georgina's arrest rate was high. She worked at a busy nick—'

'So?'

Removing another message, Kate slid it towards him: **Little evidence that Curtis looked at anyone else.**

'I didn't have to.' He screwed up the message and tossed it on the floor. 'It was clear who'd killed her. Everything you need to know is in the files. It's ridiculous to suggest that anyone other than the Bradshaws were responsible. They went missing within hours of her death.'

'So people keep telling me.'

Carmichael said, 'I think he's missing the point.'

A third message landed in front of him: **No involvement of Interpol.**

He read it and said nothing.

'My question is, why? You knew the Bradshaws had flown to Paris. I'd have thought a trip to Interpol HQ in Lyon would've been right up your street, a chance to show off with your international colleagues. If you'd kicked it upstairs to your mates on the top floor, I'm sure they'd have coughed up.'

'I didn't need to kick it upstairs. I was SIO.' He'd played right into her hands.

'So why didn't you use that authority?'

He didn't answer.

'Likewise, if you'd consulted with the regional organised crime unit, they would've told you that Christine owned several properties abroad. Did it not occur to you that her boys were living in one of them? Christine's real estate is the first place I'd have looked.'

'You can't lay that at my door. French police carried out the search.'

'Without a steer from you,' Carmichael said. 'It's a big country. Did you think they'd rock up with your suspects without any intelligence to go on? You didn't try very hard to find them, did you?'

57

When he was in service, Curtis hated being spoken down to by any female, let alone by an officer a rank below his own. He was a ticking bomb, which was unfortunate for the family pet, a border terrier, who arrived at his feet at the most inopportune moment.

It yelped as Curtis kicked it away.

He flinched as Carmichael got up suddenly, her chair scraping across the wooden floor, her right hand balled into a fist. Kate tried to catch her arm before she leapt across the room. The young detective was quicker, striking Curtis full in the face, knocking him off his chair before Kate could intervene.

He got up, wiping blood off his lip with the back of his hand.

'You had it coming,' Kate said.

'I'm making a complaint.'

'No, you're not . . . and I'll tell you why. I have so much on you, it would take a fortnight to write it down.'

'And you can't touch me for it.'

'You can't hide behind your retirement forever, Gordon. If I connect you to Christine Bradshaw, or anyone who works with her, you're going down for conspiracy to pervert the course of justice.' Kate turned her head slowly, smiling at Carmichael. 'Nice right hook . . . I never saw shit.'

'Mary, get this fucking dog out of here, now!' Curtis yelled.

The terrier ran to her, shivering in fear, a trail of urine soaking the floor.

Kate wanted to deck him too, and might have done, had his wife not rushed in to save her pet. The front door slammed as she left the house. Kate glanced out of the window. It was only 3.05 p.m. and already the light was fading. Mary was shrugging on her coat, underdressed for the depressing weather.

Or just depressed.

Living with Curtis would do that to any woman.

As Mary walked past the window, she caught Kate's eye, a clear expression that required no interpretation: *Help me by not riling him.*

'Lisa, go and see if Mrs Curtis needs help, please. She looks upset.'

Curtis yelled, 'There's no need for that.'

'There's *every* need.' Kate nodded to Carmichael, handing her a business card. 'Give her this. Tell her that if he uses hands or feet in an aggressive manner again to call me.' She wasn't only talking about the dog. In her experience, those who attacked defenceless animals wouldn't think twice about decking a human.

Curtis got the message.

He didn't argue as Carmichael left the room.

Her absence gave Kate the opportunity to pressurise him further. She was keen to get across something she'd rather not say in front of Lisa. 'So, if the Bradshaws were guilty, where's the evidence? *If* they had been arrested and *if* you've done your job properly it would have prevented their deaths, their father's death, and a vicious attack on a police officer who sadly did not survive.'

'How is any of that my fault?'

Kate's silence spoke for itself.

Carmichael re-entered the room – a nod to Kate. She scowled at Curtis and sat down. Kate didn't allow the interruption to distract her. Eyeballing Curtis, she said: 'Without a shred of hard evidence, you led the Ioannou family to believe that those boys were guilty. No wonder they were up in arms at your handling of the case. For three long years they endured pain and suffering while the Bradshaws were living the high life, God knows where, doing God knows what, laughing their cocks off.'

'You're obscene.'

'No, I'll tell you what's obscene. The first complaint you made. I saw it, Gordon.'

'Then you'll know Oscar threatened me with physical violence.'

'A moment ago, I could have done the same, except you're not worth it.'

He got up and poured himself a drink.

With his back turned, Carmichael spread her hands: *What complaint?*

Asking Curtis to sit down, Kate handed him another note: **No enquiries made at Strangeways?** 'Prigs can't keep their gobs shut, Gordon. Especially when it involves the opposition. You knew how well connected the Bradshaws were. Any one of their crew could have been watching Georgina, taken note of her routines, her shift pattern, where she shopped, when she'd most likely be home alone. Did it not occur to you that Lee Bradshaw might be bragging about that to a cellmate?'

'No.'

'Why not? He was his mother's son. Deluded. Brought up to believe that he was invincible. And yet at no time did you send anyone to speak to the people who were close to him or his brother while they were inside. I'm talking about their personal officers, medics, probation team, all of whom had access to other prisoners who also like to boast and may have given us a clue.'

She slid another note across to him: **Samples not entered in evidence or sent to the lab.** Kate wasn't finished yet. 'I have it on good authority that you ignored a rookie who came to you with samples you dismissed out of hand, as witnessed by your 2ic, Zac Matthews. That's a clear breach of protocol.' Kate paused. 'Christine too scary for you, is she?'

Curtis glared at her. 'That's a slanderous allegation.'

'Not if it's true.' She used her hand like a paddle. 'Thumb drive. Hand it over.'

Curtis hadn't seen that coming. His body language was giving him away, eyes wide, lips parted slightly. 'I have no idea what you're on about.' He knew she meant the footage she'd provided of Georgina's funeral.

Kate turned her gaze on Lisa, a cue that she was up next.

Carmichael couldn't wait to hammer in the nail. 'You don't remember me, do you, sir?' When Curtis didn't answer, she continued. 'I was the one who covered every inch of the crematorium, inside and out on the day Georgina was buried, as well as the reception afterwards – covertly, of course. I was also the one who handed you the thumb drive.'

'Where is it?' Kate said.

'In the exhibits room, where it belongs.'

'Try again.'

He couldn't look at her.

Kate glanced at the message spike. His eyes went that way too. He was nervous, wondering if it contained a mountain of other evidence. The slips of paper at the bottom were all blank. When she invited him to look through them, she knew he'd refuse. She could add predictable to corrupt and incompetent.

'Vital evidence has disappeared,' she said. 'It would be a dereliction of duty not to look for it. I know who took it and why.' She didn't. 'Was there something or someone on it that Christine Bradshaw didn't want us seeing? I hope she paid you well to lose it, because you're about to lose a whole lot more.'

Carmichael turned her head toward Kate. 'Do you think he was *always* on her payroll?'

'Fuck off!'

'Let's not sling wild allegations,' Kate said. 'It could've been a mishap. The thumb drive accidentally slid into his briefcase by mistake on his way out the door.'

Curtis found his voice, a pathetic attempt at holding his bottle. 'You came here asking for proof. Where's yours?'

'Oh, we're way beyond that,' Kate said. 'You may be an ex-cop with friends in high places, but I don't need any. My guv'nor is sunning himself in LA. I'm standing in for him. I have all the resources I need to take you down and I'll wager a year's salary that I can find a search warrant quicker than you can find the Chief on a Bank Holiday. However, if you were to produce that thumb drive right now, this all goes away.'

58

Hank was standing in Kate's office, staring out at the horizon, thinking about Ash and his distraught parents. Had he made more progress during the day, he might have felt less drained. He was up against it with no clue in terms of a suspect for his double-hander, other than confirmation that the shooter was an average male. He was hoping that might change when the team returned to base for the evening briefing.

Feeling the need to call home, he pulled his mobile from his pocket. Before he had a chance to speed-dial Julie, the device began to vibrate in his hand, Kate's name showing on the home screen, his work wife barging her way into pole position. Turning from the window, he sat down, lifting his feet onto her desk before taking the call.

'Hey, stranger. How's it going?'

'Getting there . . .' Kate was upbeat. She was in transit, speaking hands-free as she drove. 'How about you? Unlike almost everyone else on the planet, I hate surprises at Christmas. Anything I should know?'

She listened as he filled her in on his chat with Johnson, including the small matter of the witness being off his head, totally hammered when he and Ailsa arrived.

'Was the camera feed live or not?'

'Only during the night. Which means we won't see our guy scoping out the place during the day. Assuming the sensitivity and threshold levels were set correctly, motion sensors ping on Johnson's phone.'

Brake lights illuminated the car in front for no apparent reason Kate could see. Traffic ground to a halt. Hank had too. 'Hank, focus. Was there anyone on it?'

'One male—'

'So why the flat mood? That's one more than you had yesterday.'

'The footage is grainy and ambiguous. I doubt it'll take us anywhere. I don't think video enhancement is a realistic prospect,' he said. 'Put it this way, Johnson's mobile phone isn't the best on the market. I'll let you know when technical support examines it. Half the department are on leave, the rest busy on other jobs.'

'None more urgent than ours. Tell them to bump us up the queue—'

'I already did, but I wouldn't hold your breath.'

Hank put the phone on speaker, searching Kate's desk for a pair of nail scissors to snip off a thread he'd noticed hanging loose on the sleeve of his jacket.

'How poor is it?' Kate was asking.

'It's a shadow, nothing more. No distinguishing features that I can see.' Not knowing the identity of the mystery figure made his job more difficult and suited him in equal measure. 'I'm praying it's no one we know.'

She didn't answer.

He knew she was as concerned as he was that they might be looking for a cop, worse still if it turned out to be someone they were currently or had been close to. It sounded like she was travelling at speed. He could hear muted conversations going on. For a split second, he thought that Kate had Curtis in the car, then dismissed that theory. She wouldn't have called him if that had been the case.

She was talking to Carmichael.

Hank wanted to ask how she was. He thought better of it in case it upset her. Safer to wait until they saw one another in person. 'Did you retrieve the thumb drive from Curtis?'

'You think I drove all that way to come home empty-handed?'

'This is why I prefer being on your team, not running it. It's more fun.'

Kate laughed and so did Lisa, which pleased him no end.

'I'm serious,' he said. 'Bright can't get his arse back quick enough for my liking.'

'Hey, the fact that we're winning doesn't make you a loser.'

'I wish I believed that.' Hank heard Jo's voice. He didn't catch it all, though he could swear she'd mentioned animal cruelty. 'What is this, a girls' jolly? I thought Jo had gone home hours ago.'

'We can't get rid. She begged us to let her tag along.'

'I did not,' Jo said. 'Hank, don't listen. She's talking rubbish.'

He tuned them out. They were quite the double act, putting on a show to keep Carmichael's spirits up, her mind off Ash. That's what he loved about those two, Kate especially. Whatever shit she was dealing with, her team were her first and only priority.

'Hank, it's starting to snow here so I doubt we'll make the evening briefing. You'll have to manage without us. Fancy a pint at the police club on the way home? I'm buying.'

He spoke. 'I could murder one.'

'Lisa will call you when we're close.'

59

Waiting for his team to show their faces, Hank wandered into the empty incident room with his briefing sheet. Turning on the TV, he changed channels, hoping to catch the early evening news. He was in luck. The familiar face of the BBC's *Look North* presenter Jeff Brown filled the screen.

He was in full flow.

'A Northumbria Police press official confirmed this afternoon that detectives will be working round the clock in the hunt for those responsible for the brutal doorstep shooting of two young men in the East End of Newcastle. Both victims died at the scene. Peter Harris can tell us more . . .'

The footage switched to an outside broadcast.

Harris wore a shirt and tie under a brown hooded jacket, his breath appearing as small clouds as it hit the cold air. 'Sadly, we've seen such horrific crimes before in our region. This was an audacious attack carried out in the early hours of Christmas Eve.' He drew attention to the street behind, including the front door of the Bradshaws' temporary home and flowers attached to the railings outside, Hank noticed. For a moment, he wondered who'd sent them, but with cameras rolling, perfect strangers seized the opportunity to get on TV. This outpouring of grief pissed him off.

Scum like the Bradshaws didn't deserve it.

Harris was still talking. 'Residents of this quiet street are in a state of shock. Acting Detective Inspector Hank Gormley, the Senior Investigating Officer, was unavailable for comment.'

Hank swore.

He'd been 'unavailable' for most of the day. In his head, the reporter had made it sound like he didn't give a shit, except

Hank knew that wasn't the case. The truth of it was *he* was becoming over-sensitive in his old age.

Harris was stating a fact, not having a dig.

They knew each other well.

On screen, Harris held a telescopic microphone towards a woman with her back to the camera. She was wrapped up warm in a pink coat and pink scarf, ready to make the most of her moment of fame. He knew who it was before the reverse shot kicked in.

It was a master stroke to allow everyone in the organisation to view Jacob as Christine's driver, not a valued confidante, her close protection, always carrying a lethal weapon and prepared to use it. Lee had seen him as the hired help, whereas Jackson had treated him with kindness and respect, as a friend of the family.

Christine's voice arrived in Jacob's head: 'No one looks at the chauffeur.'

They had laughed about it.

Jacob wondered if she was laughing now.

With that depressing thought lingering, he turned on the TV, instantly recognising the street the news presenter was standing in. He watched for a moment, then said, 'Hey, you two, get over here and make it quick. You need to see this.' Harvey and Tony did as they were told. All three fixing their eyes on the girl being interviewed.

Nervously, she looked to camera, then focused on the man in front of her, who thanked her for taking the time to talk to him.

'I understand that you're a long-term resident,' Harris said.

She nodded. 'I've been here seven years, longer than most.'

'People are calling it an execution. How has the incident affected you?'

'Naturally, we're all devastated for that poor family, especially at this time of the year. I didn't know them personally.

They had only recently moved in. Things like that don't happen around here. None of us are safe. We won't rest until the person responsible is off the streets.'

'Neither will we,' Jacob whispered.

'Knowing that he's out there . . .' The girl's voice broke. She was welling up. Again, she turned to camera as if realising that she was being watched.

She was.

'What do you reckon?' Jacob said. 'Witness or concerned neighbour? Let's find out. If the BBC can find her, so can we. We need to know what she knows.'

'Send Harvey,' Tony said. 'He's in the market for a new skirt.'

'Fuck off!' Harvey said.

Jacob told them to get out.

Jesus! Hank slammed his fist down on his desk. If Christine's crew had a lookout – and knew that Ella Stafford had already spoken to police – they'd be on it like a shot. It wouldn't take them long to find her. The piece cut to the studio. If Ella had said anything else, it had been edited out, but in talking to the press the girl had inadvertently dug her own grave.

This was Hank's worst nightmare.

The anchor's expression was solemn. 'News is also breaking that the officer in charge of the firearms team who suffered a serious assault in that protracted incident has since died in hospital. He's been named as Sergeant Ashley Norham who was thirty-five. His family have been notified.' The screen flickered as an image of Ash in uniform was uploaded into the top right-hand corner of the TV. 'Speaking at a press conference earlier today, Northumbria's Chief Constable described the officer as outstanding, dedicated to serving his community. The Chief extended her heartfelt thoughts to his family, friends, and colleagues, adding that it was another dark day in the history of the force. We will bring you more as and when we receive an update. In other news—'

Hank killed the set.

He felt for Ash's parents, more so for Carmichael, but his attention was on Ella. He was still thinking about her when Ailsa arrived at his shoulder.

'Did you catch that on the TV?'

Hank was already dialling Ella's number.

Jacob sat back. If the MIT had watched the same broadcast, they'd be spitting bullets now. They'd have dissected every word, every sentence, making the same jump as he had. If Hank Gormley had already interviewed the girl as a witness, he'd have warned her to keep a low profile. The silly bitch should've taken his advice.

Now she'd have to face the consequences.

He looked out of the window in time to see Harvey's car disappear, then sat back, pleased with himself. His cigarette had burned out in the ashtray. Before the spiral of smoke vanished, he lit another, savouring the hit, applauding Christine.

She didn't miss a trick.

Since her temporary arrest on Christmas Eve, she'd been fuelling the fire, sending instructions via Montagu to record the local news feed. Jacob picked up the TV remote and accessed the piece. He watched it again to see if he'd missed any nuance that would take him any further in his quest to find and speak to the witness personally.

The girl had obviously been instructed to keep her focus on the presenter. Inevitably, facing the media for the first time, her eyes darted to the cameraman before she began to speak. Jacob rewound and pressed play.

Seven years.

That was his first clue.

It was a start . . . but only if her home was her own.

Pulling a new laptop towards him, he logged on, googling Zoopla. It took him seconds to find the only mid-terraced property sold in that street in 2014. Elated to find that it was right next door to the crime scene, a house Christine's brief now had the keys for, Jacob picked up his burner and called Harvey, filling him in on the good news. 'Collect the keys. You know what to do.'

'Where d'you want her?'

'Take her to my place.' *My place* was code for a trap house in the West End. 'Bung her in the cellar.'

Job done; Jacob hung up, savouring an image of Harvey letting himself in, moving through the roof void into the neighbouring property, grabbing the girl. He pushed his laptop away, staring at her frozen image on the TV screen, then replayed the whole thing. On the third viewing, he took note of her sympathy. That wouldn't be enough to save her. There was a certainty in the way she said *he's* out there, not *they're* out there. She saw the killer. Soon she'd wish she hadn't.

60

It was three deep at the bar of the police club. Not a lot of social distancing going on. Only the double-jabbed were allowed in. Kate and Hank were squeezed in at one end, trying to attract the attention of bar staff. Lots of the women were dressed up for a night on the town, all heels and glitter, the men smart casual.

All Kate wanted to do was go home and crash. For as long as she could remember, she and Hank had found time to raise a glass at some point between Christmas and New Year, no matter what else they were up to.

This year would be no different.

They had to beg Carmichael to join them. Reluctantly she agreed, in exchange for being treated as an adult and being allowed to return home afterwards. She was fine, she said. Kate wasn't convinced, but what could she do that she hadn't already done? Carmichael squeezed her way in beside her, raising her voice above the hum of conversations. 'Jo and I are round the other side of the bar. We managed to grab seats from a couple who were leaving. Want a hand?'

'I wish . . .' Kate stuck a finger in her left ear and raised her voice above the din. 'What do you have to do to get a drink around here?' She rolled her eyes at Carmichael. 'We haven't placed an order yet.'

Phil, one of the barmen, overheard. 'You're next, Kate.'

Smiling a thank you, she turned to face Carmichael. 'Keep Jo company. I need a quick word with Hank. We'll be there in a mo.'

As she moved away, Lisa avoided Hank's gaze. He watched her edge out of the huddle of bodies. Kate noticed his expression go from positive to negative in a flash.

'What's wrong?' she asked.

'How's she doing?'

'Honestly? She never ceases to amaze me.'

'Any concerns?'

She waggled her hand from side to side. 'No histrionics in the office, if that's what you mean. Out of the office? Well, apart from decking Curtis, she's doing great. Knocked him right on his arse.'

'Seriously?'

'Seriously.'

'What for?'

'There's no one more skilled at putting people under pressure than she is. She did that and he took umbrage. Disrespect she could handle, but when he kicked the dog, she saw red and so did I—'

'What did you do, push her out of the way so you could get there first?'

'Not far short. You should hear the way he talks to his missus.'

'How did you get him to own up to the thumb drive?'

'I lied. Told him I knew who'd taken it. I knew squat and he swallowed it. How he ever made DCI is beyond me.'

The barman arrived to serve her.

Kate ordered the drinks.

'Shall I put it on a slate?' Phil asked.

'Nah, we're at work at seven. We're only having the one.'

'No problem. I'll get you the machine.' He moved away to collect it.

While they waited for their drinks to land, Hank took the opportunity to ask a question he'd been wrestling with since they had arrived. 'Is Lisa talking to you?'

'She is . . .' Kate looked at him oddly. 'We decided to compromise—'

'What?' Hank rubbed his ear as if he was trying to shift water. 'For a minute there I thought you said compromise.'

She punched his arm. 'At her request, I promised no light duties.'

'In exchange for what?'

'Jo's office is hers if she wants to let go.'

'Well, it's not working. She's holding it in, Kate. She can't look me in the eye.'

'Lots of people are brave at the point of crisis, then lose it in the company of those they love. Don't crowd her. She'll come round.'

Kate used her card to pay contactless. Phil put their drinks on a tray, wishing them all the best for '22. She threw him a smile. 'You too, Phil.'

Hank shook his hand across the bar.

Kate turned to leave.

'Hold on, Kate.' Picking up the tray, Hank said: 'I don't want to talk shop when we sit down. The team are flat out. We're on top of things and Ailsa's a diamond, but we could use your help, Lisa's – and Zac too if you've managed to persuade his guv'nor to release him.'

'I did try.'

'He's not having it?'

'No.' Kate hid her irritation. 'Zac's a big part of Operation Strike. He's keeping them abreast of developments and pursuing leads on the Bradshaws—'

'And you're the head of CID—'

'I know, and I could pull rank, but we've already taken Ailsa. Besides, Zac is working for us, only not where we'd like him. I've agreed he can come and go as and when. Relax, you have everything under control. This is not a race. We'd like nothing more than to link the incidents and run them as one, but we're not there yet. Let's slay a few more dragons, then we'll surface and give you a hand.'

Harvey had one eye on his rear-view mirror. A driver since he was twelve years old, he'd grown up able to spot and outrun police. It had taken him a while to perfect his skill, an apprenticeship with his father who, in his day, would give Lewis Hamilton a run for his money. Harvey got there in the end, developing a sixth sense when it came to those who might do him harm – friend or deadly foe.

For some time, he'd suspected that he was under surveillance. It wasn't unusual. On more than one occasion Christine had put someone on him, keeping track of his movements. She trusted no one. Now she was out of the equation, he knew that the vehicle two cars behind was a cop.

Harvey had also developed a photographic memory when it came to number plates. The other day, a vehicle had followed him into Northumbria's Specialist Emergency Care Hospital. He'd gone there intending to put the frighteners on the paramedic who lived across the road from Christine's RV rental in Heaton. As he sat there watching the cops watching him, Harvey invented a story should they choose to stop and question him. The best he could come up with was that he was waiting for a nurse he'd met in a club. He didn't know her name, only that she worked there. There was no law against trying to find her.

The fact that no one had questioned him spoke volumes.

When Christine told him to call it a day, the trailing car lost sight of him temporarily as another in a long line of ambulances arrived, blue lights flashing, only to be replaced by the car behind him now.

Did they think he was fucking stupid?

Harvey slowed, leaving the bypass towards Wolsington Village, approaching from the south. His luck was in. As he made the turn, an amber light at an unmanned, ungated level crossing was replaced by double lights flashing red. He had less than thirty seconds to cross before the Metro wiped him out.

Audacity was everything in his game . . .

With his heart in his mouth, he floored the accelerator, timing his run perfectly. His tail end had cleared the railway

213

line when the train flew across the road behind him, cutting off his pursuers and any that were behind them.

Harvey laughed. 'Dumb fucks!'

He lived for an adrenaline rush.

It's what made him feel alive.

He sped off, taking roads with multiple exits he knew would scatter the observation team in a race to find him, eventually doubling back, dumping his vehicle in Bank Foot car park, hopping on a Metro going in the opposite direction, calling for his own reinforcements to meet him on an industrial estate close to the airport, less than half a mile from where he lost his tail.

Jumping into a freshly stolen vehicle, Harvey took the wheel, heading for Montagu's place to collect the keys to Christine's rental in Heaton. The solicitor was in his PJs, shaking like a leaf when he answered the door shortly after midnight.

If he was under the impression that Christine didn't know where he lived, the man with gravitas in a court of law showed himself to be woefully lacking in common sense. The dozy fuck had moved four times in as many years. Unlike the woman who paid him to keep her out of trouble, he had no anti-surveillance strategy.

Arriving at his Heaton destination, Harvey got out, telling his sidekick to jump in the driver's side and await his signal, then leapt over the rear wall, letting himself in. Using a small Maglite to find his way around the property, he crept upstairs so as not to wake the neighbour he'd come to snatch.

If she wouldn't come quietly, he had a plan B.

Climbing into the roof void was easy. Conveniently, there was a pull-down ladder. The attic floor was partly boarded, the loft empty. Harvey inched his way toward the gap in the party wall. Moving through the crawl space was a mare for a man his size. With no intention of going out that way, he ploughed on. Once he had the girl, he'd text his co-driver to bring the car round and meet him out front.

Harvey would bundle her in and spirit her away.

On the other side of the party wall, he had to be careful. No boarding here but plenty of insulation. Sweat poured off him. To reach the hatch, he had to move stealthily across the ceiling joists. One wrong foot and he'd end up downstairs on his arse quicker than anticipated, tipping off his target that she had company.

No handy roof ladder here.

The hatch creaked as it lifted . . .

Harvey remained motionless, listening for movement on the floor below. Silence. Satisfied that he hadn't disturbed the girl, he put the torch in his mouth, hefting himself over the edge, legs dangling for a few seconds, then a short drop to the carpeted floor beneath, a smooth and soft landing.

The house was a mirror image of next door.

He didn't need a diagram.

Turning himself sideways, Harvey slid along the wall, opened one bedroom door. Nothing but piles of junk in there. Further down the hallway, he turned the handle to the second bedroom. Pushing it ajar, he swore under his breath as he shone the torch around. The bed was made up. No one in it. He checked downstairs, then called Jacob.

'The girl's not here.'

Jacob exploded. 'Find her!'

61

As soon as Kate arrived in the incident room, she was made aware that Harvey had managed to lose the obs team. She called them off. Now that Christine was in custody, and her crew were wise to police, there was no point continuing the surveillance operation. Arriving in Bright's office, she gave Carmichael an important task. She worked away quietly as if it was a day like any other.

Last night, she'd insisted on sleeping in her own bed after what turned out to be a pleasant couple of hours spent in the police club. It was a shame Ailsa couldn't join them. It might have been good for Lisa to chat with a detective her own age, someone who was and would remain unaware of her relationship with Ash, unless Lisa chose to confide in her. She'd made her position clear. The only way she'd move on was if people backed off and let her deal with her emotions in her own way.

Kate could relate.

She stopped watching Carmichael, her focus returning to her computer screen. On the day Georgina's body was found, a witness had come forward. His name was Ronny McCall. He was an angler friend of her father.

Pulling his statement, she gave him a bell.

Identifying herself, Kate asked him to run her through what he remembered of that day.

'There's not much to tell, Detective Chief Inspector. I was walking my old retriever. Georgina and I said good morning, but that was the sum of our exchange. I tipped my hat and she moved on.'

'Was that normal?'

'For her it was.'

Something about the man's tone struck Kate as odd, as if he

was holding back. She gave him a gentle nudge. 'Mr McCall?'

'I, I don't want to speak out of turn.'

'It won't go any further,' Kate said. 'She's dead, sir. Please cast your mind back. Anything you can tell me, no matter how small, might help me catch her killer.'

McCall took a moment to answer.

'I must admit, I was worried about her,' he said finally. 'As a child, she used to fish there with her father. A chatty little thing, she was. Then, quite suddenly, she didn't fish any more. I didn't see her for a very long time after that.'

'For how long?'

'Years. When I did see her, she was polite, but different.'

'In what way?'

'I put it down to teenage angst. Not the most communicative group, are they? She seemed unnaturally withdrawn. I couldn't help thinking that something awful had happened to change her. I didn't ask. How could I?' He paused. 'I guess she grew up, found other things to keep her occupied.'

He didn't believe a word of it . . .

Neither did Kate.

McCall's was not a baseless claim. Georgina's life had been overshadowed by a dark secret. Kate had always known that.

'Wish I had now,' he added. 'Maybe I could have helped her.'

'I doubt that, sir.' Kate paused. 'How did she strike you the last time you saw her?'

'Same.'

'You saw her regularly?'

'As an adult, yes. Though she never stopped to chat.'

Kate thanked him for his time and hung up.

Georgina's coolness towards McCall could be interpreted as distraction, given what she'd found out at roll call the night before she died. Unless she had reason to believe that she was being followed, in which case she wouldn't want to endanger the old man and that's why she'd gone on her way. Except that didn't fit or explain the sudden change in her demeanour.

There was a missing link here.

All Kate had to do was find it.

The deterioration McCall had spoken about had her tearing her hair out. According to the house-to-house team, no one saw her arrive home in Rothbury, let alone enter her house before walking the riverside path. That didn't mean she hadn't. Kate made another call, then hung up, heart pounding in her chest.

Sensing a change in her mood, Carmichael looked round. 'Boss?'

'Tell you later.' Kate got up suddenly. 'I'll be with Jo if anything urgent comes up.'

As she rushed into the corridor, Ailsa was walking towards her, a big smile on her face. Kate was in a hurry and didn't want to blank her. They spoke briefly, Kate asking how she was settling in, Ailsa saying that it felt like she'd never been away.

'I'm looking for Jo,' Kate said. 'Have you seen her?'

'She was in her office a moment ago.'

'That's where I'm heading . . .' It was a bloody big hint that their conversation was over. Kate was about to walk away, then turned, delivering news that she knew would please her temporary recruit. 'If you're looking for a permanent move, you'd be a good candidate for the MIT.'

Ailsa was elated. 'Really, you mean it?'

'On Hank's recommendation. He rates you and so do I.'

'Guv, I don't know what to say.'

'Yes would do.'

In her peripheral vision, Kate caught a glimpse of Jo exiting her office, locking the door behind her. So she didn't run off, Kate called out to her, then glanced at Ailsa. 'Can you give us a minute? If you have any questions about what I said, come and find me later.'

'I don't. May I go and thank Mr Grumpy?' She meant Hank.

'Sure. What's wrong with him?'

'He's buried in a mountain of paperwork. He told me that sometime today he might get some detecting done.'

They both laughed.

'By the way, that's a big fat yes, guv.'

62

As Ailsa moved away, Jo unlocked her office and disappeared inside. Moving swiftly, Kate pushed her way into the room, trying to organise her thoughts as she entered. She slumped down in the armchair Jo had brought from home to make her visitors more comfortable. Nevertheless, Kate felt tense. Jo wasn't going to like what she was about to say.

Nor, it had to be said, did she.

'Am I keeping you from anything? You looked like you were on your way somewhere.'

'Nothing that can't wait.'

'Good, I'd like to run something by you before I dump it on Hank and the team. You're the best sounding board I know.'

'I thought you weren't going to interfere in his enquiry.'

'It's a theory, nothing more at this stage, but it has implications for his investigation and mine. It gives me room for doubt. It gives him a valid reason to interview Nico for the double-hander, I mean over and above the obvious.'

Jo gave Kate a black look – she loved Nico.

Everyone loved Nico.

Jo said: 'Can I get you a drink?'

'Not unless it contains alcohol.'

'There's a pub a short walk from here.'

'No time.'

'C'mon . . .' Jo made a face. 'Doesn't the head of CID get a break?'

Kate made an excuse that she didn't want to leave Lisa too long.

Jo accepted it. 'Any more talk of a resignation?'

'No, and you're not supposed to know about that.'

'Then you shouldn't have told me.'

'I trusted your integrity.'

'Past tense? Blimey, I wasn't expecting that.'

'Don't be daft. I'm sorry, I didn't mean anything by it.'

'Well, judging by your current mood, I'm also in need of alcohol. Sadly, I only have caffeine.' Jo got up and made tea. Handing a cup to Kate, she sat down, rolling her chair away from her desk, ready to listen.

Kate explained that she'd just got off the phone with Nico. 'I was trying to establish if Georgina had parked her car on the driveway and gone straight to the riverside on the morning of her death.'

'Isn't that in the file?'

'In a fashion.'

Jo frowned. 'Either it is, or it isn't.'

'Her car was on the drive when Curtis called on him, just after I delivered the death message. Nico told him that she used to park up and go for a walk to clear her head before going inside, a daily routine. Based on that evidence, and the fact that she was in uniform when she was found, he made a judgement that she hadn't gone into the house.'

'And that bothers you?'

'It does.'

'Sounds perfectly reasonable to me. You often park up at home and nip up the road for a newspaper or croissants before coming in. Why would Georgina be any different?'

'I'm coming to that.' Kate paused. 'I can't prove if she went into the house or not. I probably never will. She was late signing off duty that morning after a tough shift. Her uniform had more than one offender's blood on it, one of whom was in custody, the other fighting for his life in A&E. Under those circumstances, I'd have gone inside, keen to shower and change, even if it meant going out in the cold with wet hair afterwards. I still need to know if she saw or spoke to Nico that morning.'

'Did you ask him?'

Kate gave a nod. 'He swore he hadn't seen her since she'd set off for night shift on the eve of her murder.'

'You don't believe him?' There was irritation in Jo's tone.

'To be honest, I don't know what to believe. It reminded me of a conversation he claims preceded Georgina's departure at around nine o'clock the night before: his secret plans for their retirement in Greece, hers to stay in the UK and spend more time with their grandchildren, something they talked about over dinner.'

'You think they argued?'

'They did.' Kate took a moment. 'When I saw him on Christmas Eve, he made light of it. I think the words he used were "not a row exactly"—'

'You think their difference of opinion was more serious than he was making out?'

'He thought Georgina was having an affair.'

'What?' Jo's eyes widened. 'No way.'

'That was my reaction too.'

'Kate, she'd have told us if that had been the case.'

'Would she? I'm not so sure. We shared a lot, but there are things we all hold back. I just don't understand why he said it. By the way, none of this is in the original file. According to Curtis, they were the perfect couple. The fact is, they were an ordinary couple who rowed and made up afterwards, like you and I do, sometimes over nothing.'

'A third party isn't nothing, Kate. Nico would have been devastated.'

'Not to mention angry.' Kate left the implication hanging a while before proceeding. 'We both know that jealousy can lead to murder. We also know Nico. I can't believe that a lovely, gentle man like him could turn into a killer, but he's given himself a motive and I can't get it out of my head.'

'Kate, relationships are fragile. When trust is broken, there's a spectrum, with suspicion at one end and rage at the other, fear and humiliation somewhere in between. Distrust is a key motivator, a trigger for extreme violence, especially in men. They don't deal with infidelity very well. You witness that every day.'

'Not quite. Ordinarily, I have no personal knowledge of the people I lock up, but I've known Nico for years. In all that time, I've not witnessed so much as a spark from him, let alone the level of anger it would take to shoot the person you love in the back. Have you?'

'No, but real or imagined, that level of threat is enough to push *anyone* over the edge. Think of it as two sides of the same coin: the upside is the strength of a person's love; the flipside the same level of hate. If I can't have you, no one will.'

'I needed to hear you say it,' Kate said.

'Are you sure about this? I'm sensing doubt. In what context did he mention an affair?'

'He said she spent so much time at the riverside, he began to think she was cheating on him.'

'A throwaway remark, surely—'

'I don't think so. It felt like he'd engineered the conversation to go that way.'

'It doesn't mean he killed her.'

'Nor does it mean he didn't. Jo, I don't want this to be the case any more than you do. As I said, it's a theory I simply can't afford to discount. If there was no affair, why invent one? Why tell me one thing and Curtis another?' Kate dropped her head. 'Nico had the perfect opportunity to follow Georgina that morning.'

'How? You said she was late coming off shift.'

'Doesn't mean he wasn't waiting for her. She'd known from roll call that Lee and Jackson Bradshaw were out. If she called and he was still angry from the night before, she may have handed him the perfect opportunity to kill her and blame it on a couple of low lives who'd very publicly made threats against her.'

63

Hank listened carefully as Kate repeated her theory, adding one important detail: that Nico may also have murdered the Bradshaw boys to prevent their capture and, by extension, stop them proving their innocence if caught. Hank could see the sense in what she told him. 'Bloody hell, Kate. That's quite a stretch. I hope you're wrong.'

'There's nothing in the file to suggest that Georgina called home on the morning she died.'

'Did she?'

'Yes, when she finished her shift, a call lasting three minutes. That's time enough to tell Nico that the Bradshaws had been released and yet he told me that she hadn't mentioned it.' Kate didn't blink as Hank stared across the desk at her. Her suspicious mind had made, and was still making connections that had never occurred to her predecessor, all or none of which might be on the money. 'I need to know what was said. Only one party is alive to ask. I appreciate this is part of my investigation, not yours, but I want you to handle it.'

'Why?'

'Because Nico won't be expecting it from you. When you speak to him, chuck it in as a lowballer and see what reaction you get.'

'Will do.'

He watched her go, then sat for a while contemplating what he should do next. Signing off on his briefing notes, he walked into the MIR, collaring Andy Brown. 'Hand these out. Let the team know I want them all here at six. No excuses. We'll be reviewing all the outstanding actions and I expect results.'

The MIT were being told to up their game.

'Leave it with me . . .' There was no resentment in Brown's

tone. In Hank's current mood, the DC wouldn't dare give him any lip. 'Anything else I can do while you're out?'

'Yeah, when you're done, come and find Ailsa. I have a job for the two of you.'

Back in Kate's office, Hank summoned Ailsa by text. He'd sent her to chase technical support on Johnson's video footage. She'd been gone a while. When she entered a few minutes later, she was brimming with excitement. For a split second, he thought she had positive news. She did, only not the kind he was after.

She thanked him for his faith in her, repeating the conversation she'd had with Kate about transferring to the MIT on a permanent basis. Becoming a murder detective was a dream she never expected to come true so soon after leaving her home force.

'The next vacancy is mine,' she said.

'That's great, Ailsa. You deserve it. The boss doesn't give out praise unless she means it.' He changed the subject. 'The techies have nothing to report?'

'Not yet. They're hoping to respond tomorrow at the latest.'

'OK, keep me posted. As a result of information received' – Hank didn't say where from – 'I have an interview to conduct with Nico. If it was with anyone else, I'd take you with me, but it's complicated and highly sensitive, given that his dead wife is ex-job. I think two of us would be overkill.'

She looked disappointed.

'While I'm out, I want you to visit Ella Stafford. I've called her several times and she's not picking up. Andy's going with you. Don't take any shit from her. If she's out, camp on her doorstep until she comes home. If she's there, tell her to stay the hell away from the press or she might get more than she bargained for. Is that clear?'

'Crystal, Sarge.'

225

64

Carmichael was where Kate had left her, in Bright's office with the door shut, eyes pinned to the thumb drive footage from Georgina's funeral. Lisa hadn't spotted anything untoward on the first run-through. She paused the tape. Relaxing into her seat, she stared at the screen, hands clasped behind her head, a quizzical look on her face.

Kate was intrigued.

'What is it, Lisa?'

'There's something here that's trying to grab my attention and it's driving me insane. I've watched the tape several times already. It won't show itself. I tried visualising the route I took at the crematorium that day. It's unlike me not to piece it together.'

'It'll come to you. I have something else I need you to do that won't take long.'

'Fine by me, I'm going crazy anyhow.'

'I'd like you to get hold of two things: Georgina's shift record going back six months before she died and her phone record for the same period. What I'm specifically looking for is how often she called home after her shifts, particularly if she was late finishing. Make it a priority, please. If I'm not here, call Hank with the results, as quick as you can. This involves him too.'

Nico had told Hank that he'd be at his restaurant for a few hours. He was in the middle of a VAT return due in on New Year's Day. Given that he'd done little business this quarter, it wouldn't take him long to finish. He said he'd love to chat over a drink before he opened for the evening crowd.

Hank felt sorry for him.

Trade had been so slow to pick up – if it ever would when the pandemic was over. Nico no longer bothered catering for lunch. It wasn't worth it for the trickle of customers prepared to eat inside in what was traditionally his busiest period of the year. Hospitality was only starting to recover when the Omicron variant arrived like a big fat party pooper. Nico, like every other business owner, was struggling to get by. The city centre was always heaving.

Not this year.

Hank switched off the radio; talk of rising cases, genomic sequencing and a hypocritical government treating the people who'd elected them as idiots was as depressing as it was contemptible.

No one believed a word they said any more.

Pulling up outside the restaurant, Hank yanked on his brake and killed the engine, remaining in the car. His mobile began to vibrate on the dash. It didn't surprise him that the call was from Carmichael. Kate had told him to expect her to make contact. She'd choreographed last night's drink in the police club. She was doing the same now, ensuring that Lisa couldn't give him a wide berth for long.

He lifted the phone to his ear. 'So soon?'

'You snooze, you lose, Hank.'

He was on strict instructions to treat her no differently. They were over the awkwardness people often feel when someone dies. In his experience, friends, family and colleagues fell into one of two categories: those who carried on as normal; those who, rather than say the wrong thing, said nothing.

Thanks to Kate, Hank had found Lisa.

He wouldn't risk losing her again.

'Go on, then. Hit me with it.'

Carmichael said, 'In the six months prior to her death Georgina was kept late on twenty-one separate occasions, nine of which were night shifts. She only called home once.'

'The day she died—'

'Correct.'

Hank took it like a punch to the gut.

He peered through his windscreen, his emotions all over the place. Across the street, the windows of Nico's ground-floor restaurant were in darkness. There was a dim light on in the office on the floor above. 'Lisa, I wouldn't normally ask this, and wouldn't do so now if we weren't talking about people we love. Are you sure?'

'One hundred per cent. I had Andy double-check it.'

'How far back did you go?'

'A year, double what Kate asked for. We got the same result. Not one call. It wasn't just unusual. It was unheard of.' A long, ominous silence stretched out between them. 'Hey . . . you still there?'

'Yeah, I hear you.'

'We have proof of a call, Hank. No content.'

'You're not convinced she told Nico the bad news that morning?'

'Are you?' Carmichael said. 'Far be it from me to contradict the boss, but it doesn't seem likely. Knowing that he was home alone, I doubt Georgina would worry him with news of that magnitude, news that they were no doubt dreading. Surely that was a conversation they would have face to face. We're not talking about your average offender's release. We're talking about two kids into torture and intimidation, who were intent on doing her harm.'

65

Jo tapped her fingers on the desk. She was being paid very well to sit around and do nothing. She got up. Grabbing her coat from the peg behind the door, she put it on, checked her pockets for car keys, scooping her bag off the floor. Turning the light off on the way out of her office, she stormed along the corridor.

She'd had it with Middle Earth for today.

When Jo burst through Bright's office door unannounced, Carmichael was on the phone.

She looked up. 'Gotta go, Hank. Jo's here.' She hung up, eyeing her visitor. 'That was some entrance. Are you coming or going?'

'Definitely going,' Jo said. 'Sorry, I didn't mean to disturb you.'

'You're not.'

'Any idea where Kate is?'

'Haven't you seen her?'

'If only.' Jo regretted the words as soon as they left her mouth. Carmichael would never see Ash again. And here she was, sounding off at nothing that mattered. 'Lisa, forgive me. I'm so sorry. That was insensitive.'

'Forget it.'

Jo didn't know where to put herself. 'How are you doing?'

Carmichael sidestepped the question. 'Kate was looking for you earlier.'

'Yeah, we spoke briefly.'

'Anything I can help you with?'

Jo shook her head. 'Could you tell her I'll see her at home?'

'Why don't you sit for a bit? I could do with a break and may have the thing to sort us both out.' Carmichael tugged at

Bright's top drawer. It was locked. Her expression went from mild disappointment to furtive in a flash. 'Shall we break in? The guv'nor has shot glasses and a secret stash of alcohol for special guests. I could murder a drink.'

'Fill your boots. I can't, I'm driving.'

'So, what's wrong?'

'Kate has a lot on. She left home early and told me she'd probably stay late. I wish I had that problem. I'm fed up . . . we're supposed to be on leave.'

'Have you tried telling her how you feel?'

Jo met Carmichael's gaze. 'Not lately.'

'Maybe you should. You're too accommodating.'

'Out of necessity.' Jo exhaled. 'Falling out with Kate before she goes on duty or works late doesn't help her or me. I never want her driving to a grim crime scene with my shouty voice in her ear or greeting her with a disappointed face when she gets home. It's not like you guys have a choice, is it?'

'She's lucky to have you.'

'I'm the lucky one. I'm also bored rigid.'

'Why's that then?' Kate said from behind.

Jo turned to look at her. 'Want a list?'

'Bored and argumentative. Must be serious.'

As Kate entered the room, Jo moved to one side, putting a distance between them, a glance at Carmichael's desk. From her current position, she saw something that disturbed her, something that required Kate's intervention and possibly her own.

She didn't let on.

Carmichael closed her laptop. 'I'll give you two some space.'

'Stay put,' Kate said. 'I might need a witness.'

Jo seemed to have lost her sense of humour.

Kate apologised for mocking her. 'Why don't we all sit down, and you can tell us what the problem is?'

'You're all so busy . . .' Jo tried not to think about what she'd seen. 'You seem to have forgotten that I'm in the building, let alone ready and able to assist. To put it mildly, I feel surplus to requirements. I'm sick of sitting in an office smaller than a police cell, twiddling my thumbs and staring out of the window at an industrial landscape.'

'I consulted with you earlier, as I recall—'

'Yes, but you didn't ask me to do anything. Hank hasn't requested an offender profile either—'

'Because it would fit half the force,' Kate said. 'I'm not saying you're not needed, Jo. You're essential to this team, as well you know, but the psychology of revenge is understood among my lot. We deal with it every day.'

'Kate's right,' Carmichael said. 'I feel vengeful right now.'

'That's no surprise.' Jo gave her a hard look that Kate didn't see.

'No, it isn't,' Kate mistook Jo's meaning for Lisa's predicament.

Jo was between a rock and a hard place. Sharing what she'd viewed on Carmichael's laptop seemed like a betrayal of a friend with whom she had a close working relationship; not sharing it would compromise her loyalty to Kate. In the end it came down to the simple fact that her duty was to the organisation, not one individual she loved like the daughter she'd never had. She couldn't ignore what Lisa had been looking at.

'It won't help you,' Jo said, looking directly at her.

Carmichael's eyes were pleading with her not to drop her in the shit.

Kate eyed them in turn. 'Will one of you tell me what the fuck is going on?'

Jo stepped forward, flipping open Carmichael's laptop. It was password protected. She stared at Kate, urging her to help.

Kate received her unspoken message loud and clear.

'Unlock it,' she said.

'Boss—'

'Lisa, I won't ask again. Unlock it . . . now, please.'

Dropping her head, Carmichael typed in her password, revealing a video on the screen in pause mode. It was a copy of Ash's headcam footage, taken inside the crime scene. Don Bradshaw, on his knees, right arm outstretched, the gun in his hand pointing directly to camera, his dead offspring on the floor beside him.

No one alive, bar Don, was in shot.

Kate rewound the tape and pressed play.

There were shouts of 'Clear! Clear!' presumably from upstairs. When Don raised the gun, there was a loud bang. He fell backwards, a short pause before Christine yelled. The image shook, moved towards the floor, then stopped with a view along the carpet to the doorway.

For a long moment, Kate didn't speak, her focus shifting from Jo to Lisa, then to the memory stick plugged into the laptop. 'I'm not even going to ask you where you got this.' She extended her arm. 'Hand it over.'

Carmichael did as she was told.

'Promise me you haven't made a copy.'

'I haven't, Kate. I swear.'

'Go home and don't come back.'

'Kate, stop it.' Jo was appalled by her reaction. 'You can't—'

'Stay out of this, Jo. This is not your business—'

'Then I wish I'd never told you.'

'Fine, make it my fault. You could have kept it to yourself.'

'You're her boss.'

'Exactly, and I will deal with my detectives as I see fit.'

'Shut. Up.'

Kate and Jo stopped trading blows.

Carmichael had both hands to her ears, her eyes squeezed shut, tears soaking her shirt as the floodgates opened. She was shaking uncontrollably.

'Lisa, c'mon, you're not in trouble.' Kate stepped forward, pulling her into a hug, her voice little more than a whisper. 'I'm not angry with you. I'm trying to protect you. You can't unsee stuff like that. Those images will haunt you for the rest of your days.'

'Don't you think I know that?' Carmichael choked on her words, begging Kate not to send her home. 'Whatever you think I'm feeling, triple it. I'm trying . . . really I am, but I'll be honest, the need to punish Christine is eating me up. I can't fight it, control it, let alone describe it. A prison sentence will never be enough. Never. Even if she goes down, it won't be for the rest of her life, will it? One day she'll be out – and it's driving me insane. If I could kill her and get away with it, I would.'

'Lisa, it'll pass,' Kate said. 'We're all hardwired to think that way.'

'I know. I don't expect you to believe me, but I viewed the footage for professional reasons, not personal ones. I *needed* to see it. I *had* to see it. If anyone we know was driven to avenge Georgina's death, they'll be as racked by guilt as I am. It'll manifest itself in their behaviour, as it has in mine. They are the signposts we should be looking for.'

Kate lifted a hand to her mouth, stifling a grin. 'Lisa, that is the biggest load of bollocks I ever heard come out of your mouth, but top marks for trying.'

66

Hank knocked gently on the door and waited. The restaurant lights came on simultaneously as Nico made his way slowly down from his office to let him in, moving towards the front door like it was a normal meeting between friends, except it wasn't. As he got closer, he looked nervous. It seemed that neither man was overly keen on this rendezvous.

The door was pulled open.

'Hank, good to see you. Come in.'

'Would you mind if we walk? I've been stuck inside all day.'

'I'll get my coat.'

Hank stood guard while Nico alarmed the restaurant, aware that he'd have to ask his friend a few pointed questions in the next hour or so. Tucking his keys into the inside pocket of his coat, Nico pulled on a hat. They set off across the road. Taking the post-medieval Dog Leap Stairs leading from Castle Garth to Side, they turned right at the bottom and were soon on the Quayside.

Hank, who'd never been good at small talk, tried. 'Did you finish what you were doing?'

'Aargh.' Nico threw up his hands dramatically. 'Your English taxes do my head in.'

Hank smiled. 'Do my head in' sounded strange in his accent.

'How're Julie and Ryan?' Nico asked.

'I wish I knew . . .' The question made Hank uncomfortable. Even though they were heading to the pub, he wanted to keep off the personal stuff. He explained: 'When this kicked off, all leave was cancelled.'

'For that scum?' Nico gave him a dirty look. 'Curtis—'

'Let's not go there, eh?' Hank stopped him venting. 'He was a disgrace. Those of us who do our jobs properly are ashamed of the way he ran the investigation, no one more so than Kate. Georgina deserved more and now she's getting it.'

They walked on.

Hank had taken the liberty of reserving an outside table at the Pitcher and Piano, a bar overlooking the Millennium Bridge. It was table service only. As they waited for their drinks, he wondered what the Ioannou family would think if they knew that Curtis had walked away with vital evidence supplied by Carmichael at the time. It was now in safe hands. If anyone could get something from it, she could.

Their drinks arrived, removing his pathetic excuse not to get to the point.

Nico had noticed his reticence.

'Hank, it's OK,' he said, without preamble. 'Kate warned me that you'd have to talk to me and the kids. I get it. You have a job to do, so let's get it over with and we can enjoy this.' He held up his Guinness.

Hank tipped his glass towards it, appreciating his friend's attempt at making a difficult conversation easier. He took a long draw of his beer, using his hand to wipe froth away from his upper lip. Nico had sidestepped Kate's attempt to find out where he went after he closed the restaurant on the night the Bradshaw boys were blown away.

Hank put his glass on the table. 'I have only four questions.'

'Ask them.' Nico waited.

'You told Kate you were working on Christmas Eve, is that right?'

'Yes, if you want proof, we can go to the restaurant.'

'At the moment, that's not necessary . . .' Best to leave him in no doubt that they might need to talk again if his story, when he told it, didn't hold up to further scrutiny. 'Where did you go afterwards?'

'Home to bed. Living alone, I realise it's a weak alibi. Fortunately, the house alarm doesn't lie.'

Hank had only two questions left to deliver, one Nico

couldn't possibly avoid by saying he didn't remember. The answer would be etched on his memory for the rest of his life. Kate's request echoed in Hank's head: *chuck it in . . . see what reaction you get.* He met the eyes of the man sitting beside him, who was, in his opinion, a dubious suspect for three murders, even though he didn't yet know it.

'Georgina rang you when she finished her night shift, didn't she?'

Nico's body seemed to stiffen. 'Yes, how did you know?'

Hank sidestepped the question. 'What did you talk about?'

That one hit Nico on the blind side.

67

Kate and Jo left Middle Earth via the rear stairs, Kate thanking her as they reached the car park. 'If you hadn't spotted Lisa with that footage, I might never have known about it. Despite the reason she gave for acquiring it, she'd have watched it on a loop until it drove her round the bend.'

'Will she hold a grudge?'

'Against you? No, you did the right thing . . . and she knows it.'

'I hope you're right.'

'I am, don't worry about it.'

'For what it's worth, she made a lot of sense trying to worm her way into your good books – when she talked about revenge, I mean. The desire to right a wrong must be overwhelming. It's bound to affect those driven to kill. Not that I'm suggesting she'll go that far. Will you let her carry on?'

'I'll sleep on it.'

'She didn't have to tell you about her run-in with Zac.'

'No, I must thank him in the morning. As for your role in the enquiry, I need you, even if Hank doesn't. While I have doubts about who killed Georgina, most of the MIT don't.'

'That's never bothered you before.'

Kate used her fob to unlock the doors and spoke to Jo across the roof of the vehicle. 'The team are probably right on this one, but I need to tick *all* the boxes, not only the ones that happen to be convenient.'

They climbed in and buckled up.

Kate turned the engine over and drove towards the exit barrier, waiting to move forward in the queue that had formed in front of it.

'Where did you say we were going?' Jo asked.

'Kingston Park. Zac found our mystery rookie, the one whose samples were ignored by Curtis.'

'She's expecting us?'

'Yeah, we spoke on the phone. I'm hoping she has intel for me.'

'And I'm here because . . . ?'

'It might stop you whining.' Kate grinned at her. 'Joking! I have a job that's right up your street. Any chance you can use your Home Office contacts to gain access to the staff at Strangeways?' Following riots in the nineties, the prison had changed its name to HM Prison Manchester. Kate was betting the regime would be the same.

'I think so,' Jo said. 'What do you need?'

'Sight of Lee and Jackson's prison records. All paperwork: personal officer notes, probation and parole reports, anything written about them you can lay your hands on. If you can swing an interview with their wing SO, that would be great. You'll have to travel. I don't have the time. The names of cell-mates would be the icing on the cake. If any of them are still there, find out if they're willing to talk. If you can do that, I'll love you forever.'

Jo looked at her. 'I thought you were doing that anyway.'

'I'll add in extras.'

Jo's laughter was fleeting. 'Strangeways had extras. I once wrote a paper on it. Did you know it was one of few prisons with its own gallows. There were a hundred hangings there – mostly murderers. Eighty per cent of their victims were female, twenty per cent of whom were killed by their husbands – a sickening statistic.'

'Unfortunately, it's still happening.'

'Do you really think Nico might have killed Georgina?'

'No, but he had motive and opportunity. I can't see him organising the means at such short notice. Unless he owned a gun and had been planning to kill her for a while. If he thought she was having an affair, maybe that's why he wanted to go home to Greece, to get her away from the person she was seeing.'

'I worry that you're overthinking this, Kate. Aren't you a tad curious as to why he'd offer up a motive if he was guilty of a crime? He didn't leave the country, did he? He's still here. Doesn't that speak for itself?'

'Maybe. Or maybe asking her to leave everything behind and move abroad was a last-gasp attempt at keeping her. When she refused to go, he snapped. I'm praying that's not the case, but who knows what goes through the mind of a killer?'

68

Ella Stafford's cheeks were on fire. Like a small child who'd been ticked off by her head teacher in front of the whole school, she helped herself to another chocolate treat to cheer herself up. She'd just closed the door to DCs Brown and Richards and returned to the living room when the doorbell chimed again.

She stopped chewing and looked around.

They'd forgotten something.

Seeing nothing that didn't belong, she trooped into the dim hallway, her new slippers swishing on the hardwood floor, her mother's voice arriving in her head: *Stop dragging your feet, girl.* Defiantly, she dragged them even more, traipsing to the front door. Pulling up sharply, she zeroed in at floor level. On the WELCOME mat, a small square envelope caught her eye. It wasn't there when the detectives left. She was sure of that.

Curious, she bent down to pick it up.

It had no name or address.

She turned it over.

Nothing.

A Christmas card, she decided, hand-delivered by a kind neighbour who'd forgotten her name. She'd done it herself, more times than she cared to admit.

Better late than never.

She was about to open the card when she spotted a smaller one on the newel post, about the size of a credit card. She peered upward, her eyes taking in each stair until they reached the dark landing above, and further still to the hatch into the attic. Fear gripped her, a shiver travelling the length of her spine. When she'd arrived home, she'd had the distinct impression that someone had been inside.

Now every creak in the old house made her nervous.

She glanced again at the small card, then reached for it, relaxing when she saw the crest of Northumbria Police, the name of DC Ailsa Richards – Regional Organised Crime Unit. She'd left it without asking. Still, it had given Ella pause for thought, acting as a reminder of the warning the officer had come to deliver. Her home security left a lot to be desired and she was to stay away from the press.

She swung round, the door chime echoing in her head, a question arriving. Why leave a card and ring the bell?

Retracing her steps, Ella helped herself to another treat on the way to the living room window, before inching the blinds apart to see if the person who'd left the mystery post was standing outside, waiting for her to open the door.

She glanced up and down the street.

Not a soul about.

Her anger grew.

The police had done nothing to reassure her and everything to scare her in the one place she felt safe. Releasing the blinds, she turned from the window, sliding a finger beneath the flap of the envelope, watching blood rush to the site of a papercut. With her back turned, she missed the shadowy figure passing her window.

69

The flat Kate was looking for was north-west of Newcastle, a twenty-minute drive from their Wallsend base. Technically, Jo wasn't required – and could have travelled separately in her own car – but Kate wanted her along. She had an important question to ask. She planned to drop her at home later and drive her to work in the morning. They wouldn't get a lot of time together in the coming days.

Kate pulled over. 'It's this one, first floor.' The building she was looking at was mid-seventies, four flats in a block, red brick on the ground floor with slate cladding on the top half, tired on the outside, as was the garden.

'Shall I wait in the car?' Jo asked.

'No, Hamilton won't mind.'

'You know her?'

'According to Zac, she knows me.'

Jo smiled. 'Who doesn't?'

They got out and walked to the front door, watched by the person who lived downstairs. Kate rang the bell. Seconds later, the door was opened by a woman with brown hair and eyes so dark it was hard to see her pupils. She was wearing figure-hugging Nike tracksuit bottoms and a grey vest. Her arms were fit, her feet bare. A healthy film of sweat glistened on her body.

'Guv, it's great to meet you.' Her face flushed slightly.

Kate hadn't seen a reaction like that since the day she met the woman standing next to her. 'Likewise . . .' She thumbed left. 'This is my colleague, Jo Soulsby, Northumbria's criminal profiler.'

'Hello.' Hamilton stuck out a hand. 'Fay . . . Hamilton. Come in.'

She led her visitors upstairs.

With her back turned, Jo gave Kate a sneaky look: *It's great to meet you?* She did this whenever other women paid Kate compliments, perceiving a threat, even if it wasn't there. She was messing around, pulling Kate's leg.

Kate shook her head: *Behave.*

The flat was small, nicely furnished, perfect for a copper in her twenties, close to a Metro station and the airport, a stone's throw from the city.

It reminded Kate of her first property.

Fay turned to face her. 'Sorry, guv. I didn't think you'd be here so soon. Excuse me while I grab a towel.'

As she left the room, Jo kept her voice low. 'Wonder if she needs a rub-down.'

'How old are you?' Kate whispered. 'I'm working.'

Jo pressed her lips together, suppressing a giggle as Hamilton returned.

'Grab a perch,' she said, kicking her exercise mat into the corner. All three sat down, Kate and Jo on a two-seater sofa, Hamilton cross-legged on a square leather pouffe, keeping her bare feet off the cold wooden floor, her back straight. She practised yoga.

'I hope I'm not wasting your time, guv.'

'I'll tell you if you are. What have you got for me?'

Oozing confidence, Hamilton dived straight in. 'Three years ago, when I was a probationer, I attended the scene of Georgina Ioannou's murder.'

'Yeah, Zac Matthews told me. That's why I'm here. Was it your first?'

A nod from Hamilton. 'I noticed evidence of a scuffle not far from where her body was found. It was beyond the outer cordon. I brought it to the attention of the SIO. DCI Curtis wrote it off, refusing to listen. He said there were fights in parks every day. Without putting too fine a point on it, I was young and bright and, how can I put this, of the wrong persuasion.

If I'd offered up a gun with prints on it, he'd have ignored that too.'

Kate felt the past rear its ugly head.

It was now common knowledge that she was gay. It hadn't always been the case. She remembered that sinking, gut-wrenching feeling she'd experienced as a young officer having been marginalised by guys like Curtis. Now she understood why Hamilton had asked to meet her outside of work.

'I appreciate your honesty,' she said.

'Thank you. I realise I should've done something about it—'

'Like end your career before it started?' Kate scoffed. 'Fay, I understand. Believe me, I've been there. You did nothing wrong. Zac mentioned you knew or knew of the Bradshaw brothers.'

'Yes and no. I told him there was a power struggle between the brothers. They were known to fight, verbally and physically.'

Kate wasn't expecting that. 'You knew this, how?'

'Interesting that you should ask. Curtis never did. Too busy pulling rank.'

'Well, now *I'm* asking.'

'My younger sister attended the same school as them. She was a year above, but their names were rife in our house. Our young 'un was terrified of them. She'd miss the bus if they were waiting to get on. Their differences of opinion were legendary, in and out of school. It was much more than sibling rivalry. Lee bullied Jackson relentlessly and anyone else he was jealous of. He was a thug as a kid, an even bigger one as he grew up. If this doesn't sound stupid, I could almost sense them at the riverside.'

Kate's intuition told her that Hamilton wasn't done yet. 'Go on.'

'I looked around. Close to the road, I found a small area of soil that had been disturbed. It occurred to me that someone had been standing there, perhaps waiting for Georgina. The tree next to it was old and gnarled. In several places, fags had been stubbed out on the trunk. An innocent smoker would dump their fag ends on the ground nearby or flick them into the undergrowth. There was nothing there, I checked. Curtis discounted my theory out of hand. The second time I approached him, he told me to get the hell out of his crime scene.'

'If it's any consolation, he told me the same,' Kate said.

'The brothers were impatient little twats. I can imagine them smoking their heads off while they waited for Georgina to show. Honestly? I thought Curtis was on their payroll. I didn't have the guts to do anything about it.'

'Did you record the exchange?'

'I did.' Hamilton paused. 'You don't remember me, do you?'

Kate kept her expression neutral. Had Hamilton been older, Kate would have been dying inside, terrified of what she'd say next with Jo there to witness it. Before she came into Kate's life, her relationships had been brief, on some occasions nothing more than a one-night stand. She was relieved that Hamilton wasn't one of them.

'Should I?' she said, eventually.

'Not really. You gave a lecture about four years ago at headquarters. I was there.' Hamilton's focus left Kate briefly and landed on Jo. 'She was seriously impressive.' The yoga queen looked at Kate. 'You taught me a lot that day, guv. The thing I remember most was always to cover my back.'

70

Hank had a mountain of outstanding actions to get through and was hoping to make headway. The MIR was heaving, everyone remaining at their desks, in line with current protocol, rather than gathering in the briefing room where they were packed in like sardines. He was about to call the team to order, when Kate, Jo and Carmichael slipped unexpectedly into the rear of the room. Curious as to why they were there, he approached. 'You know I love an audience, and it's lovely to see you, but what are you all doing here? I'm sure you have loads to do.'

'We have a lot less to do now than we did this morning,' Kate said.

'Thanks to her new flexible friend,' Jo said.

Clueless, Hank said, 'Did I miss something?'

'In-joke,' Kate said. 'Take no notice of her. The good news is, we might all be joining your team sooner than you or I anticipated when we decided to run the investigations separately. Don't panic, I won't take away your big boys' toys, like my chair and desk. I'm more than happy to sit this one out.'

'Not on your life. I'm knackered.'

'You'll appreciate me more from now on then?'

Kate stopped teasing and told him of her out-of-office meeting with Hamilton, adding that the rookie had been treated appallingly by Curtis while trying to do her job properly. Kate handed him an A4 sheet.

'Read this. It's hot off the press.'

Hank took it from her and began to read:

WITNESS STATEMENT
CJ Act 1967, s.9 MC Act 1980, ss 5A (3) (a) and 5B; MC

Rules 1981, r70

Statement of: Police Constable Fay HAMILTON

Age if under 18: If over 18 insert 'over 18': Over 18

Occupation: Police Officer

This statement (consisting of 1 page(s) each signed by me) is true to the best of my knowledge and belief and I make it knowing that, if it is tendered in evidence, I shall be liable to prosecution if I have wilfully stated in it anything which I know to be false or do not believe to be true.

Date: 24 December 2018

Time: 13.25

Signature: F. Hamilton

At 11 a.m. on Monday, 24 December 2018, I was on duty at the scene of an incident on the riverside in Rothbury. I was deployed to secure the footpath and area to the north of the crime scene. Whilst carrying out my duties, I noticed an area of land that I have indicated on a map I drew at the time: FH1.

This area had been disturbed and was rutted. There were no clear footprints, but the grass had been trampled and flattened. It looked like a disturbance or fight had taken place. On closer inspection I noticed that a nearby tree, indicated on exhibit FH1, had been used to stub out several of what I believed to be cigarettes.

The residue left on the bark of the tree was grey in colour and some of the bark had several small round burn holes which equate to the size of a cigarette. As the ash hadn't been washed away, I concluded that it had been deposited recently.

I counted ten burn holes on this tree. I took photographs on my private mobile which I have retained in a separate album. These images have not been enhanced or altered in any way.

Exhibits FH2, 3, 4 and 5 show the trampled area

outlined above. Exhibits FH6, 7 and 8 show the grey material and damage to the tree I have described as burn marks. Exhibit FH9 is an image of a red cigarette lighter (in good condition that contained fuel) which I found and photographed in situ on the disturbed ground where I believe a scuffle had taken place.

I recovered the following exhibits:

FH10: a cigarette lighter

FH11: the grey material

FH12, 13 and 14: soil samples and debris

I have indicated on FH1 where each of these exhibits were collected.

I formed the impression that person(s) unknown had been in the area for some time and had smoked several cigarettes. That they had removed the butt ends to prevent leaving their DNA and that the lighter had been left at the scene by accident – possibly as a result of the scuffle mentioned above.

Signature: F. Hamilton

'Not bad for a rookie,' Hank said, looking up.

'Now there's an understatement if ever I heard one. Gold is what it is. And, unlike the thumb drive Curtis half-inched from the exhibits room, I found Hamilton's exhibits sealed in evidence, correctly bagged and labelled. And she sent me her images and a photocopy of the map she sketched while at the scene.'

'Blimey, Superwoman.'

Jo laughed. 'Hank, you don't know the half of it.'

He focused on Kate: 'Did anyone raise an action as a result?'

'The statement reader did,' Carmichael said. 'The receiver put it in for referral.'

'Why would he do that?'

'No choice,' Kate said. 'The samples that were to be examined, and those that were to be put in for referral, were set out in Curtis's policy document. And if anyone argued with his decisions, they were ignored or booted off the investigation. Zac confirmed that the samples Hamilton collected were in the woods, beyond the outer cordon, outside of the parameters laid down by the SIO. Anyway, I've now sent them for examination.' Her eyes sparkled with excitement. 'I have a good feeling about this, Hank.'

71

The briefing finally got underway at 6.15 p.m., late on account of Hank's unexpected visitors. Since Hamilton's evidence might prove that one or both Bradshaw brothers had been lying in wait for Georgina, Kate had decided to throw her lot in with him, so that all personnel were up to speed on who killed the two of them.

Hank told her he was ready to shake up the team if necessary. They weren't dragging their feet, but neither had they made much progress. He was keen to get eyes on the offender whose surname, he was praying, wasn't Ioannou. He was about to start when he noticed that Ailsa was missing. Irritated, his eyes scanned the room, eventually landing on DC Brown's desk. 'Andy, what's the story with Ailsa? Why isn't she here?'

'Dunno. We went out to see Ella Stafford, did the business, got back an hour ago. She took a call, grabbed her coat, and shot off again.'

'You didn't ask where?'

Andy shook his head. 'I thought she was meeting you.'

'She knew I wanted everyone here?'

'Yeah, like everyone else.'

'OK, she must be held up.' Hank switched his attention to Maxwell. 'Neil, where are we with the taxi that parked in the adjacent street to the crime scene?'

'The driver has been found and spoken to. He remembers the fare. Two gay boys – his description, not mine. He said they were pissed, as in drunk not angry. They didn't flag him down. He was pre-booked to take them to the street where he dropped them off. The booking came late so they had to wait a while. Don't get excited. The timing is wrong. It was four in the morning, so nothing to do with our incident.'

'You found them?'

'Not personally. I alerted the house-to-house team. They were on their second run-through, knocking on doors where no one was home on Christmas Eve. I tipped them off that we were looking for two young guys, passing on a general description. They weren't hard to find. They were out at a party that night and at home with their respective parents on Christmas Day.'

'Lucky them,' a detective mumbled. 'My old lady had to eat alone.' He was close to his elderly mother and had lost his father recently.

While Hank sympathised, he ignored the interruption, refocusing on Maxwell. 'What reason did they give for heading into the adjacent street?'

'They saw flashing blue lights and went to investigate. They scarpered when one of the firearms team shouted at them to stand clear. That's confirmed, guv. Sounds like a referral job to me which is already taken care of.'

Ailsa rushed into the MIR, apologising. Spotting Kate and Carmichael, her face changed colour. She took off her coat and scarf, then said to Kate, 'I've got a good excuse, guv. It's about Ella Stafford.'

Kate looked at Andy.

He frowned: clueless.

'What about her?' Kate said.

'She was warned, as per Hank's instructions. After we got back, she called me. She was in tears, claiming that we'd hardly driven away when the doorbell rang. She found a card pushed through the letterbox you all need to see.'

'And you didn't think to tell me?' Andy was miffed.

'Sorry, no.'

'Ailsa, you should have let him know where you were going,' Hank said. 'You might have needed backup. That's the very reason I sent you there double-crewed.'

'I didn't think . . .' She walked forward, handing Hank two

evidence bags, one containing a small envelope; the other containing the card that went with it. 'I don't think Santa sent it, Sarge.'

Hank took it from her, then addressed the team. 'For your benefit, the message is typed in capital letters, quote: "STAY AWAY FROM THE PRESS AND POLICE".' He noticed Ailsa's expression darken. 'There's more?'

'I'm not sure.'

'Of what?'

'On the one hand, Ella seemed genuinely spooked—'

'I sense a "but" coming.'

Ailsa grimaced. 'She owns a typewriter.'

'You think she sent it to herself?' Kate asked.

'She has issues, guv.'

'Issues?'

Ailsa explained about Ella's pink palace.

Hank confirmed it. 'She's . . . odd . . . and lonely, a Walter Mitty character. I wouldn't be surprised if she *didn't* see the killer. Maybe she fantasised about seeing him to get attention, not that it makes her any less vulnerable or deserving of our protection.' He held up the card. 'This isn't a threat from Christine's mob. They don't warn people in advance. They would have stormed in there, dragged her out, and beaten her senseless until they got a description of the shooter.'

'Then we have a problem,' Carmichael said. 'Assuming Ella is telling the truth, it's a threat from the killer. Maybe he saw her TV debut and decided that she'd seen him, just as Ailsa did when she saw her looking down from the window onto the crime scene. That's not a dig, Ailsa. It was a good call . . . one I'd have made.'

Kate's heart swam with pride. Carmichael knew how to handle people and led by example.

'There is another scenario,' Hank suggested. 'The perpetrator we're looking for could be one of Christine's cohorts. She had to rely on *someone* in her sons' absence. Maybe that person didn't fancy a demotion when they arrived in the UK. Someone like that would blow Ella Stafford away and enjoy doing it. Ailsa, do we know who Christine's 2ic is currently?'

'Last I heard, Tony Bullock fell out of favour. His dick isn't big enough, apparently.'

Harry spat out his tea.

Like a Mexican wave, a chuckle of laughter reverberated around the room.

Ailsa pushed on. 'It wasn't him though, Hank. A ROCU surveillance team had him on camera at the time the Bradshaw boys were killed. By the way, he's not running the show. Zac has it on good authority that Burrows is. My lot are doing a job on Christine's properties as we speak. I'll give them a call, let my partner know what's happening this end. If they've come up with anything of interest, I'll update you.'

'Where is Ella now?'

'Downstairs in reception.'

'I knew I liked you.' Hank grinned. 'Until we have more intel, we treat her as a key witness. She may be the only one able to pick out an offender in an ID parade. You did good, Ailsa. Whatever we think of her idiosyncrasies, we can't ignore this. Her security is a priority. Organise a direct alarm on her place and covert cameras, front and back. Do it now. She can't go home until they're fitted. I'll authorise it.' He glanced at Kate for reassurance.

She gave a surreptitious nod of approval, then asked: 'Is there anywhere else she can go in the meantime?'

Ailsa shook her head. 'She has no immediate family, guv. None she'd give the time of day to, or maybe it's the other way round. I got the impression that she didn't have a very nice upbringing. She had a sleepover at her nan's home in Gateshead last night. It was her eightieth birthday, but the woman is terminally ill. She can't go there.'

'Friends?' Hank asked hopefully.

Ailsa shook her head. 'No support network whatsoever. It

took all my time to persuade her to come with me.'

'Sort her out with overnight accommodation then,' he said. 'I'll bring you up to speed later.'

72

Harvey sank down in his seat as a Traffic car sped out through the gates of Northern Area Command HQ, blues and twos engaged, a hostile sound he was as familiar with as the garage bands he listened to. He remained calm, unfazed by it. Half an hour ago, a female detective left the house in Heaton with the shocking pink front door, escorting the girl into her pool car. Furious for missing her a second time, Harvey followed, keeping a safe distance, Jacob ordering him to clean up his mess.

Now parked on a side street, with a view of the exit, Harvey watched and waited, unable to shake the feeling that he could be picked up at any moment. This close to danger he was still able to control his breathing, normalise the rhythm of his heart. Not so earlier when Jacob turned on him, a warning to grab the girl or face the consequences.

There was nothing ambiguous in his words.

Until now, Harvey had never seen him packing a weapon. Gone was the chauffeur facade, the gentle giant act and jokey personality. Swearwords spilled from his mouth like dragon fire. Speaking to the pink girl could be a game changer. He could not have been clearer as to what would happen should Harvey fail him.

The guy was a psychopath . . .

Harvey's eyes fixed on the exit. Every time the door swung open, throwing an arc of light out into the night, he lifted his binoculars to see if it was the pink witness. And then it came to him in a flash, a lightbulb moment. Had she noticed that someone had been inside her home and reported a burglary? Although he'd not touched a thing without gloves last night, he may inadvertently have left a clue, a smudge of dust, a drip of sweat on the carpet as he left her attic. If police were in possession of his DNA, he was fucked.

Had they taken her into protective custody?

Why else was she there?

Why was he?

Whatever sympathy he felt for the girl, the responsibility for what happened next was hers, not his. She should've kept her gob shut. The door opened again. This time Harvey was in luck. Hers was not a face he'd forget in a hurry. She looked scared on the TV. She looked terrified now as she made her way out along the pavement. If he was a betting man, he'd wager that she'd left of her own accord. She was not walking. She was running.

The police wouldn't be far behind.

Harvey knew how they thought, how they worked, better than anyone.

He had one shot before the cops picked her up and threw a cloak of protection around her. He started the car and moved off, closing on his target . . . fifty yards . . . forty . . . thirty . . . looking for the best place to pick her up. When she suddenly stopped running, he braked as another scenario presented itself.

It dawned on him then that the girl's presence might not be a happy accident, but a trick to draw him from the shadows. The thought angered him. If they thought he was stupid enough to walk into an ambush, they were wrong. Checking his rear-view mirror, he spotted a vehicle pulling slowly into the street behind, its headlights blinding him. His eyes shifted to the girl, potentially his and their sole eyewitness. It was impossible to predict her next move.

Even harder to predict his.

73

Hank checked his watch, keen to finish the briefing. Most of the footy-loving MIT detectives had tickets for tonight's home game at St James's Park. Newcastle United were desperate to avoid relegation from the Premiership. Eddie Howe, in post as manager for only six weeks, had said there was no time to waste in the club's bid to boost the squad. Hank would pray if he thought it would do any good. Against Man U, what they needed was a miracle.

What *he* needed was to go.

An image of the Bradshaw boys lying dead at the crime scene entered his head. They would have been there too if they hadn't been shot. Hank cracked on, asking for feedback on the TIE action Kate had raised on Georgina's ex-boyfriend-ex-stalker, Alan Crawford.

Harry Graham raised a hand, advising everyone that after an extensive record search, DC Gerry (aka Supermodel) Hall, had managed to find an address and phone number for him in Berwick-upon-Tweed.

Kate was stoked. 'What's he got to say for himself?'

Harry shook his head. 'Nothing yet.'

'Why not?'

'He wasn't in. Gerry left his details with a message that we need to speak to him urgently and followed it up with a couple of calls to his landline. He didn't respond. I wasn't happy, so I sent the action out again. More messages were left. Gerry got a bad vibe when Crawford eventually returned the call. He point-blank refused to talk about Georgina and rang off.'

'Then it's time we paid him a visit.'

Hank looked at Kate expectantly. 'Maybe we should both go, assuming you haven't ruled him out as an alternative suspect for Georgina's murder, based on Hamilton's evidence.'

'I think you know me better than that. If the Bradshaws were waiting for her, and I'm pretty sure they were, we can't ID them unless forensics come up with something.'

'I'll text you his address,' Harry said.

'Can I clarify whose investigation we're on about here?' Maxwell asked.

'Both,' Kate and Hank said simultaneously.

'How's that for synchronicity?' Kate said. 'Keep up, Neil.'

Hank noticed Jo trying to attract attention and gave her the nod to proceed.

'I don't like the sound of Crawford,' she said. 'And I haven't even met him. Anything you want to share, over and above the information you already passed on, Kate? You said he stalked Georgina. What form did that take?'

'Phone calls, notes through the letterbox, that sort of thing. It was years ago when she confided in me. We were dealing with a case of harassment. It was hardly an offence then.'

'It's hardly an offence now,' Carmichael grumbled. 'As shameful as it sounds, it's part of the aggro women put up with every day.' Kate had allowed her to remain at work, but she'd been super quiet . . . till now.

'The case Georgina and I were dealing with was serious,' Kate continued. 'That's how it came up in conversation, though she went out of her way to stress that in her case it was mild.'

'So, the stalking was remote then?' Jo said.

'Not always. Crawford followed her from work a couple of times, tried to engage her when she was out doing her job. What bothered her the most was that he'd start a row in public. It's easy for us. We can hide in plain clothes. She couldn't. The rest she took in her stride. He wasn't trading insults or threatening her with violence. From memory, pathetic and harmless were the words she used to describe him.'

'Yeah,' Jo scoffed. 'We've all met women who've used the same adjectives when discussing disgruntled romantic partners who can't or won't let go, some who lived to regret it. Sadly, a lot more haven't. I'll wager that Crawford would have been the first person you'd have looked at for her death if you'd been in charge. It's where Curtis should have looked, had he not been so blinkered.'

'That we can all agree on, though I'd have expected there to have been a gradual escalation of intimidation over the years, I mean between Georgina meeting Nico and her death. There was none. If there had been, she'd have told me. Besides, he'll be knocking on now, won't he?'

'A reason to use a gun,' Brown said. 'He'd never have overpowered Georgina.'

A few detectives laughed nervously.

Georgina's party trick had been to arm-wrestle male detectives.

'Are you lot listening?' Jo said. 'I'm making a serious point here. I've worked with guys who have morphed from old flame to murderer in a flash, others who've taken years to get there.' She looked at Kate. 'Berwick is what, thirty-five miles from Georgina's home in Rothbury, no more than sixty from Hank's crime scene. Let's assume he didn't kill her. He's local enough to have heard about her murder. It was broadcast far and wide. His obsession could easily have switched to those who took her out. Let's face it, fingers were pointing one way only. Up to now you've been looking south of Rothbury for your suspects. Maybe you should be looking north.'

'I'll bear that in mind.' Hank waited for the murmurs reverberating around the room to fade. The team were jaded, in need of downtime, a yawn here and there despite the open windows. He couldn't send them home yet. 'Let's move on. What else has anyone got for me? C'mon, there must be something. What's the hold-up with Hazel Sharp's post-mortem report?'

'There is none,' Carmichael said. 'It should be on your desk.'

Hank could tell by the look on her face that she'd handed

the job to someone to pass on and didn't want to drop them in the shit. Not wanting to pressure her, he let it go. What did it matter anyhow, so long as it had come into the MIR?

'And the outcome was?'

'Inconclusive. Tim Stanton said she was like a pin cushion and that her overdose could've been intentional, accidental, or administered unlawfully by a third party, adding that there were no injuries on her body to suggest the latter, though he's firmly convinced that she was moved after death.'

There wasn't a detective among them who didn't believe that she was taken out by Christine's crew as soon as she was no longer of use as a bogus tenant. OCGs didn't like loose ends. They got rid of anyone who might blab to the first person willing to tip them a few quid. Hazel was used and discarded, as simple as that.

'Well, I hate to sound cruel, but that's one less incident on our plate,' Hank said.

'He's right.' Kate rose to her feet. 'If there was any proof to be found, Tim would have found it. So that's that. We move on and let Hazel rest in peace.'

74

Kate crossed the MIR and stood at the front. 'What I'm about to say goes no further than this room. It's highly confidential. If any of you breathe a word of it, you'll be wearing an itchy blue suit.'

The team waited for the revelation.

'After I saw Oscar on Christmas Eve, I took the liberty of requesting his personnel record. There's stuff in there that I wasn't aware of. Did anyone know that his marriage broke up since his mother passed away?'

'I did,' Harry said. 'Jenny wants a divorce. He's not in a good place apparently.'

'That explains a lot.' Kate scanned the room. 'Oscar has been issued with blue forms on several occasions for insubordination. He's lost everything bar his job, and only kept that because his supervision put a good word in for him on compassionate grounds. On a final warning, he was ordered to get help for anger management from the force psychologist. He failed to show. Charlotte didn't escape unscathed either. She received a PTSD diagnosis after her mother's death. She's been undergoing counselling and is said to be recovering well.'

'Nico never mentioned any of that to me when I met with him,' Hank said.

'Nor to me. I don't suppose he wants to talk about it. Would you?'

'No, I suppose not.'

'How was he when you spoke to him?'

Hank shared the bare bones of their chat, stopping short of describing it as an interview with a suspect. 'He claims he went home to bed after closing the restaurant on Christmas

Eve. He was specific on timings. CCTV cameras have him walking towards his car and ANPR have the car heading north on the A1, though the driver cannot be identified. There's a sophisticated alarm at Nico's home he seems to think will prove that he entered the premises when he said he did.'

'Unless someone else drove the car home, entered the house and turned off the alarm for him and they're all in it together.' Neil Maxwell had stuck his head above the parapet, sharing an opinion unpopular within the MIT. 'I mean, I hope that's not the case. It's the theory we're all trying to avoid, right?'

'Except you,' Harry said.

'Someone has to say it,' Maxwell bit back.

Hank intervened. 'It's a definite maybe, Neil. Friends or no friends, we're ruling nothing out, not Nico, Charlotte and certainly not Oscar in view of what Kate told us.'

Maxwell visibly relaxed. It wasn't often that his opinions got the nod. Kate was of a similar mind. Had bereaved relatives formed a vigilante group and taken revenge? There were parts of the city where it was almost mandatory.

'Guv, were you going to speak?' Hank asked.

'Only to reiterate that over and above the obvious revenge motive, which incidentally we all share, we have zero evidence to connect them to the Bradshaw killings. We need hard evidence and there is none. As it stands, there's more to connect Nico to Georgina's murder than to this shooting and even that is circumstantial. Did you ask him about Georgina's last phone call?'

Hank nodded. 'He got a bit upset. Said she wanted to be sure he wasn't still angry.'

'It begs the question, how angry was he?'

There was silence in the room.

'OK, wrap it up . . .' Hank's mobile rang, stopping him from finishing his sentence and the squad from moving off. No one rang an SIO in the middle of a briefing unless there had been a development. He pulled his device, checked the home screen:

Ailsa. He noticed five texts that weren't there a moment ago, all from her.

He took the call.

'Quiet!' he yelled.

Kate knew instantly that something was up.

Hank lifted a forefinger to his lips to silence everyone. Ailsa Richards' breathless voice arrived in his ear. 'Sarge . . . I'm so sorry . . . Ella Stafford is gone.'

The police had warned Ella that she knew stuff others might kill for, not in so many words, but as good as. Ailsa, the female detective, had gone above and beyond to explain and reassure her, taking her into protective custody, telling her to sit tight. If only she'd done as she was told, not bolted the second her back was turned. She should have told the cop that she'd rather not spend the night alone in a hotel.

What woman would?

Now she was outside, she felt even more frightened in an area unfamiliar to her. She looked left and right, wondering which way to the main road where she could catch a bus home. She'd rushed headlong into danger and now wished she'd accepted Ailsa's offer, never leaving the safety of police HQ.

She quickened her step.

A dark car pulled up beside her.

At first, she thought it was Ailsa.

When she realised it wasn't, she screamed, hoping someone would come to her aid.

The driver got out, bundling her into his car, telling her he wasn't going to hurt her if she did as she was told.

Yeah, like she believed that.

As they moved off, another car crashed into them, knocking her sideways. Her high-pitched screams were drowned out by the sound of metal on metal as the same car rammed the one she was in, again and again, sending the vehicle careering onto the pavement, bouncing off it, throwing her around in her seat like a doll. Was this the police? Caught up in a violent confrontation between opposing sides – one wanting to kill her, the other to save her – she banged the windows, begging to be let out.

The cars zigzagged across the road.

Her driver yanked the steering wheel suddenly, shoving the other car into the path of one coming the other way. They clipped each other. One lifted off, landing on its roof. The other spun three-sixty degrees and was heading straight for them. Ella braced herself for impact, then her lights went out.

'What do you mean, gone?' Hank locked eyes with Kate.

'Speaker,' she said.

Tapping his mobile's home screen, he placed the device down on the nearest desk, so he didn't muffle the sound with his hand, then repeated the question into the phone, in verbal shorthand.

'Gone where?'

'I don't know,' Ailsa was panicking. 'When I left you, I told her to sit tight while I organised her security and booked her hotel. When I went to collect her from reception she wasn't there. The desk clerk said she'd gone out for fags and wouldn't be long. I waited half an hour. She didn't show. I'm told she left on foot, though she might have phoned for a taxi or flagged one down.'

'What makes you think that?'

'One was seen driving by a moment later.'

'Wait there. I'll come down.'

'I'm not there, Sarge. I'm at Ella's.'

'What part of "you should have let us know where you were going" did you not understand?'

'You were in the middle of a briefing—'

'That's no excuse.' Hank swore loudly. 'When I tell you to do one thing, I don't expect you to do another. You do not enter that property, you hear me? Under no circumstances.'

'I won't . . .' There was a long pause. 'Hank, the door's wide open.'

Kate pointed at Carmichael, making a C-shape with her hand as she spoke into the phone, her voice calm and measured. 'Ailsa, listen carefully, stand down and wait for backup. If you ever want to work for this team permanently, *do not* enter that house.'

Carmichael was already informing Control. 'Officer requires urgent assistance . . .' Her voice was drowned out as a row erupted in the corridor outside the MIR. It sounded like a punch-up taking place.

All heads turned in the direction of the double doors.

'Christ,' Hank said. 'It's like nightshift in the Wild West.' He meant the west end of the city. 'Andy, whatever that is, tell them to keep it down. I can't hear myself think.'

He got up to sort it, so that Carmichael could hear Control without having to stick her finger in her free ear. As he opened the door, Oscar Ioannou broke free from a couple of uniformed officers trying to block his way, hurling insults as he struggled to shrug them off and push his way into the room. His face was scarlet, his fists clenched, a glance at the murder wall on the way in.

He made a beeline for Hank.

Instinctively, Kate stepped forward. 'Oscar, you can't be in here.'

'The fuck I can't!' He pushed her away, his spittle concerning her more than the shove had. He pointed over her shoulder. 'Did you know Hank's been questioning my old man? Asking him about my mum, treating him like a suspect? I want a word.'

'You got it.' Hank was livid. 'Cells or interview room? Your choice.'

'How about outside?'

Hank's laughter riled Oscar even more. 'Get out of my incident room.'

'Make me.'

Hank grabbed him, shoving his arm up his back, bundling him out into the corridor with little effort. As the door slammed shut behind them, an uneasy silence descended on the room . . . until Ailsa's voice boomed loudly over the phone Hank had left on the desk.

'Guv? What's going on?'

75

Hank was sweating on the fate of Ella, concerned about Ailsa too. She'd taken it badly that a vulnerable young woman had gone missing, though like him she was relieved that officers entering her house found no dead body. Nothing was disturbed inside. No signs of a struggle. Ailsa had tried calling Ella several times. On each occasion, the calls had cut to voicemail. There had been no response to the messages she'd left. The fact remained that in the process of finding her a place of safety, she'd disappeared.

Taking a key from his pocket, Hank homed in on the attached label: Interview Room 1. Desperate to protect Ailsa from her own enthusiasm, he hadn't thought through the potential consequences of his actions when he left Oscar in there to calm down. Now, as Hank hurried along the corridor towards the interview suite, it occurred to him that his decision to lock the door was bordering on stupidity.

Oscar had three choices: sit and wait; break down the door; the third option was unimaginable. The guy had exhibited behaviour that was unbecoming an officer, displaying a complete disregard for rules and regulations. It didn't need a psychiatrist to ascertain that he was under extreme psychological distress, out of control, a rogue policeman with mental health issues brought on by his mother's violent death. What would Jo make of it?

Suicide risk was the answer Hank came up with.

Quickening his pace, he decided to consult with her in the morning. Despite Oscar's appalling behaviour, Hank felt sorry for him. The man was clearly ill, his grief compounded by serious mistakes in the murder investigation that followed, evidence ignored or overlooked by an incompetent SIO – who may or may not also be bent – and who'd failed to exercise professional curiosity.

No wonder Georgina's son was in a state.

Hank was breathing heavily as he approached the locked door with visions of an avoidable suicide by a man who'd reached breaking point. If he'd ended his life, Hank would never be able to live with it on his conscience. Taking a deep breath, he peered in through the small window of the locked room.

Oscar was on his feet, pacing the room.

No harm had come to him.

Hank wished he could say the same about Ella. She'd still not surfaced, nor answered her phone. Suspecting that she may be in grave danger, he tried not to think about what might be happening to her. All he could hope for was that she'd be found before it was too late.

It was a big ask.

Sensing a presence, Oscar glanced at the door, standing his ground as it was unlocked and pulled open. Hank stepped over the threshold, assessing his mood. Oscar was jumpy as well as wary. He was in the vicinity of Middle Earth when Ella went missing. Was his dramatic entrance into the incident room a ruse, an excuse he could use if his car had been spotted in the area? Could he have abducted her, hidden her, and got here in time to cause bloody mayhem, giving himself an out?

Hank parked the thought.

He'd return to it later.

76

'Took you long enough,' Oscar barked. 'You know what time it is?' He threw himself down on one of two chairs placed either side of an oblong table, the only furniture in the room. He was wrung out. The bottle of water Hank had provided before he left was empty, crushed and lying on its side in the centre of the table. The room reeked of nicotine. The floor was littered with cigarette butts. It was a wonder the fire alarms hadn't tripped.

Hank replaced the water with a fresh bottle.

Oscar drank greedily.

He didn't look or act like his father, a much gentler man, but there had always been something about him that bugged Hank, no more so than today. A moment ago, he'd sympathised with his plight, cut him some slack, tried not to think too badly of him.

The guy didn't make it easy for anyone to like him.

He was hurt all right – as anyone would be – but dancing around him wouldn't help. As a mark of respect to his mother, loved by everyone who knew her, too many people had made allowances already.

Hank would treat him as he would any colleague who was out of order.

'You're a bit far from home, aren't you, Oscar?' Hank pulled out the remaining chair and sat down, resting an elbow on the table, lifting his right foot onto his left knee. 'Were you passing, decided to call in and give me a mouthful? Did throwing your weight around make you feel better?'

He didn't answer, though the blush of guilt arrived on his face.

Hank studied his body language. He was rigid in his seat, a

clue that he was hiding more than the row he'd instigated two hours ago. 'Now you've had time to think about it, you want to tell me what you were doing?'

'I already did. You've been hassling my old man.'

'Have I shite. The Nico I know didn't tell you that, not in a million years.'

Oscar glared at him.

'Is this the part where you say, "no comment", I ask another question and get the same response? That game bores me. Can we play another?' Hank waited. There was no response. 'I'll go first, shall I? If you *ever* manhandle my guv'nor again—'

'You'll do what?'

'You do not want to find out.'

'You're out of your mind if you think my father offed that scum.'

'It's my job to interview anyone of interest, Oscar. That includes close relatives and anyone with a grudge. You, your dad, Charlotte, all score highly on both counts. Whether you like it or not, you will be investigated. I did speak to Nico, but since when does that give you the right to burst into my briefing and assault a senior detective? You want to thank your lucky stars it was Kate, otherwise you'd be in a cell, mate.'

'Are we done? Because I have a home to go to.'

'That's a provable lie, right there. Word is your missus threw you out. Couldn't wait to get shot of you because of your mood swings.' It wasn't like Hank to rub salt into an already gaping wound. It would never have happened with the tape running. He hadn't said it to hurt Oscar. He'd said it to demonstrate what he had to lose, what he'd already lost if the rumours were true. 'If you were struggling, why didn't you come to me? I'd have been happy to play peacemaker. We're mates, right? Well, we were. You're testing my patience, behaving like a prick.'

Oscar glared at him.

'It's obvious you're not coping. You're entitled to feel aggrieved. That's normal, but I'm warning you, this is where it stops. You're law enforcement. You can't keep pissing people off. Carry on like this and you'll be out on your ear. It'll destroy you, Jenny, the kids. You want that? Because if you do, you're going the right way about it. I understand—'

'Really? Your colleague was murdered. She was my mum.'

'And Kate is her friend and my boss. If anybody's going to do this job properly, it's her. So, push her around, why don't you, you dozy fuck. Can you not see the irony in mourning one woman and abusing another? Look, I know how you must be f—'

'You know bugger all.' Oscar had a weird look on his face. 'You've gone through this, have you?'

'Seriously? A thousand times, mate. I see and speak to the bereaved every day I turn up for work, every time I close my eyes, so don't tell me that I don't know what I'm on about.'

Oscar pushed his chair away from the table and stood up. He faced a blank wall, fists clenched, shoulders rising and falling steeply. He was breathing heavily, having an episode of some kind. Hank didn't know what to say or do. He should have brought Jo in sooner. She'd have known if Oscar was suffering or faking it. Too late. A woman's life was at stake. Hank decided to ask him outright.

'Oscar, are you ill?'

Complete silence.

'Oscar, talk to me. You need help, if only you had the sense to realise it. Surely even you know that you're making the same mistakes, over and over.'

When Oscar turned around, there were tears in his eyes. No fight left in him. 'I came here because I wanted you to know . . .' His voice caught in his throat. 'I *needed* you to know that my old man wouldn't hurt a fly.'

'I haven't accused him of anything.'

'As good as.'

'I don't see him in here ranting and raving, do you?'

'He didn't kill the Bradshaws—'

'Did you?' Hank had to ask.

'No, why would I? I wanted them to suffer. I was mid-shift when they were blown away. You think I snuck off, committed a double hit, then returned to work acting as if it never happened?'

Hank dropped his head on one side. 'Did you?'

'C'mon, Hank. Look at me. I'm a wreck. I wasn't responsible, except for shoving Kate, and I bitterly regret that. I'm sorry—'

'Tell her that.'

'I will.' He looked right through Hank. 'You'd think I'd be glad the Bradshaws are dead. I'm not, even though we didn't get the satisfaction of seeing them go down for life. Reaping it up again in the newspapers and on TV is what's doing my head in. You're not going to arrest me, are you?'

'Any reason why I shouldn't?'

'Hank, please. If I lose my job, it's over. My lass will never forgive me. She's already threatening to piss off with the kids to her folks in Devon. I'll never see them again. I'm begging you. I'll apologise to Kate. I'll do it now if you call her. I'll do anything you want, but I need to get out of here . . . tonight.'

The way he stressed 'tonight' set Hank's mind racing. Ella still hadn't been found or he'd have heard about it. Dead or alive, he couldn't take the chance that Oscar had spirited her away. He sat for a moment assessing his next move.

'Where's your car?'

'Downstairs. Why?'

'I've got a missing witness. You're going nowhere until I establish that she's not in the boot.'

77

When they got home, Kate and Jo inevitably ended up discussing the investigation they had been working on during the day. With Ella Stafford missing, there was no time like the present. Dinner over, they tidied up the kitchen, took their wine into the living room and sat down, side by side on the floor, toasting their feet in front of the newly fitted log-effect gas stove that, despite its pretensions, would never replicate the look and smell of the real thing Kate had grown up with in the Northumbrian countryside.

Over a bottle of red, they dissected Oscar's loss of control, Jo sharing a theory she'd formulated as they cobbled together a meal that turned out to be well below par, neither of them eating much of it. Jo shuffled her body around until she was sitting cross-legged, facing Kate, the better to judge her reaction.

Kate smiled. 'I swear I can hear you think sometimes.'

'I can't see Oscar killing anyone or even conspiring to do so.' Jo expected to be shot down. Kate said nothing, allowing her to theorise without interruption. 'It's more likely that distrust has been building over the last couple of days – within his family, I mean. Feelings have been running high for years. In the heat of the moment, if one or all of them had so much as hinted at a vigilante killing, it wouldn't surprise me if it hadn't been blown out of all proportion, especially by Oscar.'

'Are you saying he's delusional?'

'He's ill, Kate.'

'He'll be suicidal if it turns out that his dad killed Georgina.'

'Let's hope that never becomes a reality.'

'You mean proper ill, as in unfit for duty?'

'I think it's come to that, yes.'

Kate put her wine glass on the hearth, then sat back, resting her head against the soft cushion of the settee, eyes fixed on Jo as if she was trying hard to keep them open. 'Thanks for the insight, but mentally unstable suspects are not what I need right now.'

'I don't see him as a suspect.'

'Based on what?'

'Paranoid thinking isn't unusual in situations like these. The family are as close as any we know. Georgina's death literally blew them apart. Oscar was always temperamental. That's a whisker away from highly volatile. In my opinion, the person you're looking for is the exact opposite. Someone who, at the time of the shootings, was in absolute charge of their faculties, methodical and calm, most probably a person with ice running through his or her veins.'

'Not Oscar then,' Kate scoffed.

'It seems to me that the subject of his hatred was Curtis, not Lee and Jackson Bradshaw. Isn't that what Nico told you?' Jo raised an eyebrow. 'Maybe Oscar isn't the only one who distrusts a family member.' She paused for a moment. 'Has it not occurred to you that they all suspect one another?'

'You're supposed to be cheering me up, not kicking my legs out from under me.'

'Just offering you what I've got. Didn't you say that Oscar was on duty when those boys were shot?'

'Yeah, and the crime scene is on his patch,' Kate reminded her.

'Assuming for one moment that he's innocent of any wrongdoing, and was working as he said he was, he has no way of knowing what his father and twin were up to that night, does he? In his present state, the uncertainty of not knowing will be unsettling him. He may already have reached the point where he believes that one or both killed the Bradshaw brothers in cold blood. In which case, he'll see what he wants to see, anything that confirms his bias. He'll also project his anger onto anyone who gets in his way, as he did in the incident room. He has no off switch, does he? Hank was the cause of his discontent for daring to speak to Nico. You just got in his way.'

Jo took a sip of wine, eyeing Kate over the rim of her glass. Her eyes sparkled in the darkness, reflecting the lights from the Christmas tree and the church candle on the mantelpiece. Anyone looking in through the window would see two women very much in love, enjoying each other's company, but the romantic atmosphere was an illusion. Tonight, they were work colleagues, no more, no less.

'You once suspected me of murdering my ex,' Jo said. 'Your lack of faith may have been temporary, but you and I both know it was there in that hospital room following my accident. And, if my memory isn't too fuzzy, it altered your behaviour considerably.'

'You know how to kill a moment.'

'Nice sidestep. Since when did talking shop become a moment? Kate, I'm not saying that your suspicions lacked foundation. You're a cop who couldn't ignore the fact that I had obvious motive—'

'Then what are you saying?'

'I think you know . . . Or perhaps I'm not explaining myself very well. What I'm trying and failing to get across is that at the time you knew details of my history with Alan you couldn't get past—'

'You're saying I amplified it and decided you were guilty?'

'No, Bright did that all by himself.'

'Yes, he did.'

'His condemnation changed the dynamic between you and him, between me and him, between us. That's how suspicion works. It eats away at your insides. Once the seed of doubt had been planted, it grew, until it was impossible for you to excise it from your brain. And when you eventually managed to convince yourself that I was telling the truth, out of loyalty to me you went against everything you believed in to prove my innocence. There was us. And there was them . . . the police.'

Kate sat up straight, hugging her knees.

She didn't say anything because Jo was right.

She was still talking. 'In the same way that you protected me, it's possible that Oscar is now protecting a person or persons he truly loves. And, just as you cast aside what Bright thought of you at the time for going AWOL in the middle of a murder investigation, Oscar won't care what you think of him now, so long as you leave his father and sister out of it.'

'Well, acting like a prick won't help.'

'He's irrational, Kate. He could even be dangerous if anyone threatens his family.'

78

Hank didn't blink as Oscar reached into his pocket. Withdrawing his car keys, he clashed them down on the table. He was incensed, his jaw set like stone, his mouth firmly shut. He knew that if he kicked off again, he'd be charged with assault and thrown in a cell, despite Kate's insistence that she wouldn't press charges. Hank gestured to the door, a quick flick of the head, telling Oscar to move it, then followed him down the corridor, texting Brown as he went, hoping he was still in the incident room.

Hate doing this. You still around?

Brown answered immediately . . .

Walking out the door. What's up?
Oscar and I, heading your way. I'm going to search his car. When he leaves, follow. I want obs on him until further notice.
I'll keep you posted.

Pocketing his phone, Hank fell in step with Oscar. As they entered the dark car park, they walked right past Andy's vehicle. He was the perfect detective for the task, skilled in the art of surveillance, young enough to cope with a double shift when called upon to do so. He'd have scoped out the parked cars, locating Oscar's vehicle, and made sure he remained out of sight while the search went on.

Hank blipped open the doors of Oscar's vehicle, including the boot.

Oscar stepped between him and the car, stalling. 'Is this necessary?'

'Would I be doing it if it wasn't? Shift, or I might get the impression that there's a reason you don't want me in there.'

'Look, give us a lift home, keep the keys, do a forensic job on it, do whatever you want, but let's kill it, now.'

Oscar's expression was impenetrable.

If he was bluffing, expecting Hank to back off, he had another thought coming.

Shaking his head, Oscar moved to one side. He didn't look like he was getting ready to run. Then again, Hank had searched for bodies before while the killer had stood calmly by while he did it.

Taking a small torch from his pocket, he felt the rush of adrenaline in his veins in anticipation of what he might find. Inhaling deeply, he opened the tailgate, unhooking the retractable boot cover. There was the usual rubbish in there: a foot pump, a set of jump leads, de-icer sprays, a child's trainer, a muddy glove, and other evidence that Oscar had kids. No Ella. No blood. Nothing that would suggest a hasty body disposal or any weapon either, as far as Hank could tell.

Oscar showed his frustration as Hank took the opportunity to carry out a more thorough search for a weapon, removing the contents, before lifting the cargo liner, then the flooring, exposing the spare wheel housing. With the torch between his teeth, he carried out a fingertip search, including any pockets that could hold a small firearm.

It was clean.

Perhaps too clean.

Hank closed the tailgate, searching the interior of the car with as much care. The fact that he'd found nothing, meant nothing. Whoever had killed the Bradshaw boys was well organised. They had to be. It was that or certain death. Oscar could easily have grabbed Ella, then switched vehicles.

'Satisfied?' His expression was a mixture of I-told-you-so and arrogance.

Handing him the keys, Hank kept his cool. 'You're not alone, mate.'

Oscar opened the driver's door and climbed in, dropping his window.

Hank peered into the vehicle. 'If you need help, say so. We're on your side. Get your act together, then we'll talk.'

Oscar started the engine and drove away.

79

Before she left the house, Kate called Hank to alert him that she was on her way to his place for an early start. It was still dark when she arrived. Even though it was wet, he was waiting outside when she got there, diving into the car before it had properly come to a standstill. Kate turned right, heading for the central motorway, then glanced into the passenger seat. Hank looked knackered and was scoffing his usual bacon butty.

There was no news of Ella. She wasn't with her parents or her nan. An officer had been posted outside her address overnight. She'd failed to show. Hank updated Kate on his interview with Oscar, the futile search of his car, his decision to ask Andy Brown to keep him under observation until further notice.

'Where did he go?'

'To an address in Stobhill, a new build. There was a vehicle on the driveway. It's registered to Charlotte.'

'What?' Kate slowed the car, looking across at him. 'She lives in the Allen Valley.'

'Not any more, unless they're staying with a mate or, with my cynical SIO head on, a co-conspirator.' Hank licked his greasy fingers. 'I called Andy at two a.m. He said the lights were on till around midnight, then it seems everyone inside went to bed.'

'Enough time for them to get their story straight if they have anything to hide.'

'Precisely. I told him to stay focused while I organised a replacement obs team. He insisted on sticking with it. The poor bugger is still there.' He held up what was left of his butty. 'I feel guilty eating this.'

'Yeah, right. Did you ask Julie to make him any nosh?'

'No . . . I forgot—'

She noticed the plastic container on his knee. 'Is that mine?'

A nod. 'It's my job to keep *you* fed, innit? You want it now?'

'No, save it for later.'

Hank placed the container on the dash.

Kate had intended on a quick stop at Middle Earth before heading to Berwick to visit Georgina's stalker. She made a split-second decision. Pulling hard on the wheel, she steered her Q5 onto the A1, heading north, flooring the accelerator. 'Change of plan,' she said. 'If Oscar hasn't emerged from Charlotte's place, let's give them an early knock. Crawford can wait.'

They arrived at the address as dawn broke, Kate stopping short of the property. It was a red-brick detached house off East Lane End Farm, north-west of the historic market town of Morpeth, close to the River Wansbeck. On the very edge of the estate, backing onto fields, the street was quiet, not a breath of wind through the trees. A veil of early mist added an ethereal quality to the surrounding landscape, though it would never match the tranquil, otherworldly setting of Charlotte's stone-built cottage in Sinderhope.

The curtains were closed.

There were lights on inside.

As they got out of the car, Kate scooped the plastic container off the dash and a small bottle of water from the side pocket, ignoring Hank's joke that she should perhaps wait until they got back in the car to eat her breakfast. Her focus switched to Andy Brown's vehicle, parked behind two cars at the very edge of the cul-de-sac with good vision of the exit junction. Hank knew fine well what she was up to. She moved towards the car, the window winding down as she approached.

She handed Andy the refreshments.

'Enjoy,' she said. 'Hank and I are going in. If I'm not entirely satisfied with Oscar and Charlotte, or I get the sense that they might be involved in Ella Stafford's disappearance, I'll call out the CSIs and have the house and their vehicles searched. An obs team will be here to relieve you within the hour. Hank wants them both followed till the girl is found.'

80

It was Oscar who answered Kate's knock. She acted as surprised to see him as he was to see her. He was wearing pyjama bottoms and a T-shirt, both too big for him. Kate suspected that they belonged to Charlotte's current squeeze, a semi-professional footballer who'd moved in after only one date, whose physique, it had to be said, was impressive. Oscar was shamefaced, practically begging for forgiveness when his twin walked down the stairs.

Unlike her brother, she was fully dressed.

Charlotte was happy in her job in the marine unit, a gregarious, liberated woman, the life and soul of any party. Single, no kids and no wish to have any, she'd lived life to the full until the day her world came crashing down. Although she'd undoubtedly suffered like any family of a murder victim would, unlike Oscar she had kept her shit together. She was, and always had been, a credit to the memory of her mother.

The likeness to Georgina was uncanny.

Both women had that dreamy quality movie stars have. Two of Kate's namesakes, Cate Blanchett and Kate Winslet, had it in abundance. Like them, Charlotte was a woman with an enigmatic smile, a faraway cast in her eyes, even when she was looking directly at you. As a youngster, she was smart and fiercely independent. As an adult, she had an air of self-assuredness that said, *Don't mess with me* and required no practice to pull it off. As a police officer, she was instantly suspicious.

'What's going on?' she said.

The atmosphere was awkward.

Oscar didn't look at his twin, which made Kate think that Charlotte genuinely didn't know what had happened in the incident room the night before. If that wasn't the case, she deserved a BAFTA for her performance as an innocent extra, happening upon a scene that she found incomprehensible.

Kate relaxed.

The first thing people do when they conspire together is to share every tiny detail with each other, so that if they are ever questioned, they put up a united front. No matter how small or seemingly insignificant, any contact with the police would be dissected and discussed ad infinitum until they had their story straight.

This didn't appear to be the case here.

'Kate? I asked what's going on?'

Now Oscar turned to face her. 'Stay out of it, Charlie. This is not your problem, nor is it anything to stress about.'

She glared at him. 'Do I look stressed to you?'

'That's not what I—'

'So, tell me.' Charlotte took no shit from anyone, certainly not from him. 'If you're in trouble, you made it my problem by coming here.' She gave him an icy glare. 'You didn't lock yourself out, did you?'

'No,' he said sheepishly.

'What have you done?'

The twins were close in looks and mannerisms but, like any other siblings, they could scrap. As kids, they drove Georgina crazy with their constant bickering. Charlotte had always been the dominant one. She almost always came out on top, as she would this time.

Oscar caved under the weight of her gaze. 'I've been an idiot.'

'So, what's new?' She laughed.

'Not funny.' He hung his head in shame, then looked up at her. 'I had a go at Kate in the incident room.'

Whatever Charlotte had expected, it wasn't that. 'What the hell for?'

'Doesn't matter,' Oscar said.

'It does to me. And why is she still on the doorstep? Have

you lost your manners, as well as your mind?' Charlotte ushered Kate and Hank inside, along a short hallway and into a smart living room. Apologising for her brother's impropriety, she invited them to sit, asking for a proper explanation.

Kate and Hank remained standing, holding onto their authority.

Oscar tried to fill the silence. 'I didn't know Kate would be there. It was Hank I had a beef with.'

'Why?' Charlotte waited.

'He questioned Papa.'

'And that surprises you? For Christ's sake, he's the SIO in the Bradshaw killing. Were you not expecting that? I sure as hell was.' Charlotte didn't wait for a reply. 'Have you been online lately? Our names are plastered everywhere. It's called guilt by association. To be honest, I'm surprised we haven't been asked to take leave while it all cools down. With the press fuelling the fire, we could end up dead if you-know-who is planning a backlash.'

Oscar seemed to shrink under her gaze.

Kate studied the dynamics between them. Had Charlotte thrown in that last remark to gain sympathy from her visitors? It was true, of course. There was no telling what Christine's deputy would do in retaliation. Tony Bullock was a money launderer, but he'd grown more and more dangerous since he got involved with her.

The Missouri Ozarks sprang to mind.

Charlotte had run out of patience. 'What does Hank's questioning have to do with Kate?'

'She got in the way.' Oscar didn't tell her all of what went down.

Kate could see that he was struggling. It was difficult to admit that part. He wasn't acting like the prick he was yesterday. Quite the opposite. His anger had subsided. She was about to speak when he beat her to it.

'I was completely out of order. Kate deserves an apology—'

'And now I have one,' Kate defended him. 'Drop it, Charlotte. It's unimportant.'

'Is it? Mum loved you so much. She'd have been appalled by his actions, as shocked as I am.'

The comment jarred with Kate. Charlotte didn't yet know what his actions were. Or did she? Kate had already decided that if these two had anything to do with doorstep executions, Charlotte was the instigator, the one quite literally calling the shots. Had she told him to say as little as possible and let her deal with the police if they turned up? Was he hiding behind her strength, taking advantage of her protection?

It seemed that way.

Someone was moving along the hallway.

Kate was about to make an excuse, giving herself an opportunity to check him or her out, when Charlotte's footballer player, whose name she couldn't recall, made his way into the kitchen. Their eyes met for a split second – a temperamental stare – then he was gone. How long might he have lingered behind the door? Had he overheard their private conversation? The word 'accomplice' entered Kate's head. In her line of work, professional curiosity turned everyone into a potential villain.

A question from his girlfriend made her pay attention.

'Kate, is that why you're here . . . . to charge Oscar?'

'Let it go, Charlotte. I have. This is a welfare visit, nothing more.'

'At this hour?' Charlotte checked her watch and didn't try to hide her cynicism. 'It's five past seven.'

'Hank and I are on our way north to interview a witness.' Kate was keen to get going, to see what Georgina's stalker had to say for himself. 'We wanted to make sure that you were all right before we left.'

'Why wouldn't I be?'

'I also wanted to reassure you that what happened at the incident room isn't going to be a problem in case you thought it might be. We understand what you're going through as a family. All we ask is that you allow us to do our jobs, unhindered. You know how this works. As you said, it's no surprise that we have questions. Like it or not, they need answers.'

Charlotte didn't speak.

Aware that she was no slouch, Kate could almost see the wheels turning in her head. She got ready to deflect the blow that was surely on its way. It didn't take long to arrive and was accompanied by a scowl.

'How did you know that Oscar would be here?'

'We didn't,' Hank said. 'We came to see you.'

'I have a mobile phone.'

'We thought you might have a word with Oscar on our behalf. Charlotte, he needs help.'

'No, I don't,' Oscar said. 'And stop talking about me like I'm not here.'

Hank gave him the side-eye. 'Yes, you do. And if you don't get it soon, you can kiss goodbye to your police career, your pension, and probably your family.' He turned his attention to Charlotte. 'We didn't want to worry Nico with this. He has enough to cope with. Knowing how close you are to Oscar, we thought you might be able to help. These conversations are best done in person. On each occasion I've visited, you've been out.'

Kate didn't look at Hank.

He was lying through his teeth, giving Charlotte far too much to chew on. From the look of her, she wasn't buying his bullshit reply. Smart enough to know when she was being played, she spoke again, a hard edge to her tone.

'You left no message.' Her eyes switched from Hank to Oscar. 'This is no welfare visit, is it? What are you not telling me?' She waited, angry with all of them.

'They're looking for a missing witness,' Oscar confessed.

'Witness to what?' Charlotte's eyes scanned all three suspiciously, before landing on the weakest link. Her brother flinched as she raised her voice. 'I asked you a question, Oscar. What witness?'

'I don't know. A woman . . . a girl. Hank searched my car last night. He found nothing and let me go. He obviously had me followed. I'm sorry, I should've anticipated that and warned you.'

'Yes, you should. In fact, you shouldn't have come here. Can't you see how it looks?' Charlotte showed her contempt for Hank, though the black look she doled out wasn't only reserved for him. Slowly, she turned her head, hate-filled eyes landing on Kate. 'And here was me thinking we were friends.'

'Charlotte, we are.'

'You reckon?'

'Don't be silly, I've known you since—'

'Why the hell didn't you ask if you thought Oscar and I had something to hide? Did you think we'd stand in your way, knowing a witness was missing? Did it not occur to you that we want this circus over and done with as much as you do?' She was far from done. 'I could tell you to get a warrant, but I have nothing to hide. Do what you must, then take your lapdog and get the fuck out of my house . . . ma'am.'

81

They had found nothing untoward in the search. All their unscheduled visit had achieved was putting Charlotte's back up. She didn't speak again, or follow them to the door as they let themselves out. Kate felt the weight of her gaze as she walked down the garden path towards her vehicle. The two women had seen each other infrequently since Georgina's funeral, though they had spoken on the phone more often. At first Charlotte hadn't been keen to talk about her mother. It upset her too much. Kate could relate. When her own mother died of cancer, she wanted the whole world to do one.

Despite a PTSD diagnosis, and ongoing counselling since, by all accounts Charlotte had made a miraculous recovery. Kate wondered if their relationship stood the same chance of repairing itself.

She didn't think it likely.

That made her sad.

While in the house, Kate had noticed a life-size headshot above the fireplace. Georgina's smiley eyes appeared as if they were looking directly at her. The image was taken at a house party years ago. At around midnight, they had gone out into the garden and got wasted on Ouzo Georgina had brought home from one of her frequent trips to Halkidiki. She'd joked that as it cost half the price, they could drink double.

Happy days.

Kate missed her friend.

Though she felt no obligation to protect her adult children, investigating cops left a bad taste in her mouth. For a moment, she felt like she'd woken up in Professional Standards. She was angry with herself. If she'd handled Charlotte better, she might not have taken it so personally. Charlotte was a police officer.

So was her twin. It seemed unlikely that either of them would involve themselves in a double murder, conspiracy to kidnap, not to mention the numerous associated firearms offences they might be charged with if they were ever linked to the victims, acting alone, together, or God forbid with their father.

None of the three held a licence to hold a firearm.

Hank had already checked.

'What do you reckon?' he said.

'I honestly don't know. The fact that Ella's not there means nothing. I'm pleased we had the opportunity to see them together, to see how they react as a pair. If they are involved in this, I'd have expected them to have been of a similar mind, and they're not. Did you notice how angry she was with him for lying about locking himself out? Oscar was embarrassed by it.'

'Double bluff?'

'Possibly.'

They got in the car.

'She's angry with me, not you, Hank. You'll get more out of her than I will.' Kate yanked her seatbelt so hard it locked in the retractor mechanism. She had to repeat the motion slowly, pulling it across her chest, clipping it into the seat buckle. 'I want you to try and talk sense into her. What time are you interviewing her?'

'Three o'clock.'

'She'll have calmed down by then.'

'I doubt that. She gave me a choice: a neutral bar or Middle Earth, refusing my offer to conduct the interview in the comfort of her own home. She made it quite clear that neither of us are welcome. Now we've pissed her off, she'll be difficult to reach.'

'Then be persuasive,' Kate said. 'You're good at that.'

She drove out of the estate, giving Andy Brown a nod as she passed his car. Kate was listening to her gut. Her instinct was to leave the observation in place, to split the detail and have Oscar and Charlotte both followed, except they were wise to a tail now. Worrying. If, together or separately, they had abducted Ella, leaving her tied up in some disused shitpit, they wouldn't risk returning to check on her.

82

Ella must have fainted when that car careered towards them, waking as he carried her quickly into a house. Woozy, she remembered going down a flight of stairs, a room with a dead light switch. He told her not to make a sound, that he'd return, and then left immediately. It seemed like days ago.

It was probably a matter of hours.

She lay in the darkness, staring at nothing. Unable to see or hear anything, she waited for the key to turn in the lock, wondering why he hadn't returned and what would happen when he did. He didn't seem like a man with murder in mind.

Could she trust herself to make that judgement?

Questions arrived, thick and fast. How long would he keep her in captivity? Was anyone looking for her? More to the point, would they find her before it was too late? She had no means to call for help. He'd taken her mobile, so police couldn't pinpoint her location. It was clear that he feared them.

Ella curled up into a ball and sobbed.

She didn't want to die here.

'Somewhere remote,' Kate said under her breath.

Hank snapped his head around. 'What?'

'There's nowhere more remote than Charlotte's old place at Sinderhope.' Fishing her mobile from her pocket, she handed it over. 'The address is in there. Get on to Control. I want it searched.'

As he made the call, Kate drove on, her fear for Ella's safety growing with every mile travelled. Debris from Storm Arwen was everywhere. Fallen trees, flooded fields and damaged property.

Single-track sections of the A1 thwarted her progress,

slowing traffic to 45 mph. Kate caught a glimpse of majestic Bamburgh Castle and Budle Bay in the distance, a view that never failed to lift her.

It seemed no time at all before they reached the outskirts of Berwick. Kate had always thought that residents weren't quite sure which side of the Anglo-Scottish border to align themselves with. Due to its strategic position on the mouth of the Tweed, the most Northerly market town in England had been fought over and changed hands several times.

Kate loved to visit.

It was a place she could live in for two reasons: its proximity to the sea and because it was equidistant, give or take a few miles, from her two favourite UK cities: Newcastle and Edinburgh.

As they sped across the Royal Tweed Bridge, the sky was Mediterranean blue, the town bathed in brilliant winter sunshine. Crawford's home was a smart, double-fronted Grade II period townhouse, inside the Elizabethan old town walls, with wonderful views over the river and estuary to Tweedmouth.

Kate parked her Audi on the adjacent quay, a stone's throw away, taking a moment to appreciate the vista. After her bust-up with Charlotte, she looked forward to her chat with Georgina's ex. She wasn't looking for a fight, unless one came looking for her, in which case she'd oblige.

The man who answered the door was distinguished looking, with thick, dark, grey-flecked hair and deep-set blue eyes. He looked younger than she expected, smartly dressed in a green V-neck cashmere sweater over a checked shirt, moleskin trousers and brogues. No wedding ring, Kate noticed.

'Alan Crawford?' Hank held up ID, identifying himself and Kate.

Kate said, 'Can we come in, sir?'

'Detective Chief Inspector, I told your colleague, more than once, that I don't wish to discuss my relationship with Georgina Hart.' It was strange to hear him refer to Georgina by her maiden name.

'Mr Crawford, I've always found people this far north to be friendly, knowledgeable, pro-police. Is there a reason you don't want to talk to us?'

'I don't have to, do I?'

'Technically, no.'

'Then, I decline. I have an appointment soon.' He began to push the door to.

Hank stuck his foot in, ready to curb any further resistance. 'Mr Crawford, we're murder detectives with questions. We can ask them here or sixty-five miles away at Northern Area Command, in which case you'll probably have to rearrange your whole day, not just part of it. It's entirely a matter for you. What's it to be?'

Resentfully, Crawford allowed them in.

Hank stepped aside for Kate to enter before him, rolling his eyes as she walked past, expecting the next hour or so to be a complete waste of effort, unworthy of the hour and a half it had taken to get there.

Crawford led them into a large living room that was stylish, exquisitely furnished, the walls covered in contemporary photography Kate liked a lot. He turned, hooking a thumb over his trouser pocket, his other arm hanging loose by his side. He looked more uncomfortable than nervous and offered no refreshments after their long journey, a heavy hint that he wanted them gone.

Kate got straight to it. 'We are investigating a double murder, an incident which you may or may not know resulted in two further deaths. One of the victims caught up in the drama was a police colleague—'

'Yes, I read about it. I'm sorry for your loss.'

'Thank you.'

Crawford added, 'Before we go any further, can I say that

I'm not trying to be awkward or uncooperative. My thing with Georgina was brief. It happened a very long time ago, 1987 in fact. She was nuts. One minute, she was all over me, then next she wouldn't talk to me or tell me what I'd done wrong.'

Kate tried to put him at ease. 'May I call you Alan?'

'Please do.'

Crawford was a lot less prickly from that point on. He seemed nice enough, not what Kate was expecting, not a man she believed would cause them any trouble. But was he the type to stalk a dead female colleague?

She explained, 'I used to work with Georgina. She told me that after you broke up, if that's the right way to describe it, you followed her around for a while, wouldn't take no for an answer. Is that correct? Am I, or was she, mistaken?'

'You see, this is exactly why I didn't want to discuss my association with Georgina. Refusing to "take no for an answer" sounds predatory. It wasn't, I can assure you. I don't want you, or anyone to think that my behaviour was in any way weird.'

'Alan, we're not here to make judgements or accuse you of anything.'

'I'm pleased to hear it. You'd better sit down.'

Kate and Hank did as he asked.

Crawford sat too. 'Let me provide you with context. I was six years younger than Georgina. That might not seem like a lot, but it's a big deal when you're seventeen, in love for the first time. Not to put too fine a point on it, I fell for her from the moment we met. It wasn't hard. Everyone melted if she paid them attention, as you will know if you were close.'

He struggled emotionally.

'I adored her. She ripped my heart out. It sounds melodramatic when you say it out loud, especially at my age. I promise you, that's the truth of it.'

His eyes found the floor.

Kate used the brief pause to check out the room. There were no photographs of family on display, nothing to suggest a partner either. If she was a betting woman, she'd take a punt that he lived alone. Jo's warning about old flames taking years to wreak revenge echoed in her head. This seemingly mild-mannered man had admitted that he was a one-time lovesick puppy. Was he also a ticking bomb, waiting to explode with devastating consequences?

'First cut?' Kate said.

'And last, in my case.' Unable to hold her gaze, he looked away.

Seeing him in profile, a memory clicked into place. 'Did I see you at Georgina's funeral?'

'You may have done. I was there.'

'Did anyone from the Murder Investigation Team speak to you in the weeks and months following – the SIO, perhaps?'

'No, though I thought he might when he looked into her background, assuming she told anyone about me.'

'She told me.'

'Not the good bits. We had a lot of fun together.'

Kate wanted to keep him on track, to build rapport and put him at ease. 'Did you go to the funeral reception too?'

'No, I didn't . . .' Realising what conclusion she might draw from it, he added, 'I didn't know her friends and family. And I'd hardly attend if I'd hurt her, would I?'

'What about the men who killed her?' Hank said. 'Would you hurt them?'

'I'm a doctor, DS Gormley. I save lives, I don't take them. I assume you've spoken to the other guy.'

'Of course,' Kate said. 'Georgina married him. He was the first to know—'

'I'm not talking about the father of her children. I mean the one before me, the one she was so keen to push me in front of.'

Kate hadn't the first idea what he meant by that. One thing she was sure of, though: Crawford was still not over her. He was visibly upset. 'I'm sorry, you lost me. I thought you split when she met her husband-to-be in Greece.'

296

'Is that what she told you?' Crawford shook his head. 'Doesn't surprise me. I got the impression they worked together. I'm guessing their "thing" was against regulations.'

Kate felt uncomfortable. She could see how painful it was for him to talk, but she needed to push him for intelligence. 'Could you describe this man?'

'Six, six one. Fit body, around Georgina's age, sure of himself like you.'

Like the shooter who took out the Bradshaw brothers thirty years on, Kate was thinking. She exchanged a look with Hank: he thought so too.

Crawford continued. 'It took me a long time to accept that Georgina used me to get at the guy. We went out every night for a couple of weeks to some cool places where people knew her. She was popular, always dressed up, looking gorgeous. I remember thinking she could have had anyone, but she chose me.' He cleared his throat. 'One night, we were in Julies night-club when *he* walked in and everything changed . . .' Crawford's eyebrows moved towards each other, creating two deep creases above the bridge of his nose. 'He was the love of her life, no doubt about it. They couldn't take their eyes off each other. It was obvious they had fallen out. It's hard to describe, but it was as if she'd been waiting for that moment. Waiting for him to find her. I soon realised that she was punishing him, that I was no more than a young stud on her arm, a way of twisting the blade.'

83

Kate thanked Crawford for his cooperation, acknowledging how difficult it had been for him to talk about Georgina. He'd filled in gaps. She appreciated that, though she kept that to herself as she got up to leave. As she followed Hank to the door, Crawford called her name. When she turned to look at him, he asked for a moment of her time alone.

She glanced at Hank. 'You go on . . . I won't be long.'

He hesitated.

She flicked her eyes toward the door: *move it*. She heard the front door open and close again, the mortice lock click into place. There wasn't a hope in hell that he'd left her in that house alone.

Retracing her steps, she wondered what was coming.

Crawford took a moment to find the right words.

'Detective Chief Inspector, I realise that my behaviour might sound off to any woman, especially a police officer, but please don't think of me as threatening. I loved Georgina more than I can say. My teenage ego didn't appreciate being dumped. My attempts to contact her afterwards were ignored. All I wanted was an explanation as to why she'd dropped me so suddenly. There was nothing sinister in it. I was a complete idiot then and I apologise.'

'There's no need—'

'There's every need.' He let out a sigh. 'I want you to know that it was a bruising experience, one that shaped my life from that point on. Unlike Georgina, I never married or had children. I can't hold down a relationship. If things don't run smoothly, I bail.'

'Unrequited love is a killer, Alan. None of what you told me sounds like your fault. Georgina and I were very close. That's how I found you, don't forget.' She left out the circumstances in which his name came up. 'If it helps, she went out of her way not to smear your name. Refusing to take no for an answer were my words, not hers. I said it to get a reaction.'

'Thank you for telling me.'

The reason Georgina described Crawford as harmless was crystal clear. He was that in a nutshell. Kate felt compelled to let him down gently. 'If Georgina treated you badly, believe me she'd have had a good reason. The Georgina I knew would never hurt people, not intentionally. You've given us a lead we didn't have before and for that we're grateful.'

As they walked by the Chandlery on the way back to Kate's car, they passed a mobile vendor, a poor sod trying to eke out a living with potential customers melting away by the day. Hank gave him the price of two lattes without asking him to dispense anything.

The seller looked like he was going to cry.

Touched by Hank's gesture, Kate smiled at him. 'That's why I love you. You're such a softie. In return for your kindness, you deserve a treat on the way home.'

'I'd settle for a public loo.'

'That's included.'

A few miles on, Kate turned off the A1, stopping briefly for refreshments and a bathroom break at the Barn at Beal restaurant. They ate at a picnic table outside, eyes drawn across the causeway to the Holy Island of Lindisfarne, shimmering in the distance. They had been there less than fifteen minutes. Already Kate's mood had lifted.

It didn't last.

On the road again, they were held up briefly by red flashing lights over an unmanned level crossing. As they waited, Brown rang with news from the search coordinator, his voice filling the car. 'No joy at Charlotte's old place, guv. She still owns the cottage but is renting it out as an Airbnb. A couple from the South are staying there.'

'As of when?'

'Christmas Eve.'

'They did search it though?'

'Yeah, course.'

'The outbuildings too?' His answer was drowned out by the LNER Edinburgh to London train flashing by, rattling the car as it rushed past. 'Andy, I lost you. Did they search the outbuildings or not?'

'Every inch. No sign of Ella.'

'Bugger. Did you find Alexander's brother yet?'

'Yeah, Andrew was a cop, until a joyrider ran his Traffic car off the road, leaving him with life-threatening injuries. He spent months in hospital, many more convalescing at the police rehabilitation centre. He no longer works or walks, so he's not our shooter. I'm not saying it gives Martin Alexander motive, but I don't suppose we dare ignore it either. Although Ella would have recognised him, wouldn't she?'

'Sounds like the perfect motive to take her out of the equation.' Hank locked eyes with Kate. 'Told you I wasn't happy with him.'

Kate ordered Andy to bring him in.

'He'll have a job,' Hank said. 'He took leave when I warned him that Christine's crew paid him a visit.'

Kate glared at him. 'Where is he?'

'I have no idea.'

'Tell me you're joking.'

'Firearms were moving in on Christine's gaff when he called, Kate.'

'Andy, I want him found. See if his brother knows where he might be.'

'Will do . . . You want the search team to continue?'

'In the Allen Valley? No, if she's there, we'll never find her. Extend our thanks and tell them to stand down.'

The rest of their journey to their Wallsend base was uneventful, the glorious countryside they passed on the way largely ignored. Kate was unhappy with Hank's failure to secure Alexander's travel plans, but the excuse he gave was valid. She let it go, her focus returning to Crawford. He'd met Georgina at a gym they were both members of. He was adamant that she'd choreographed the meeting with the mystery man in Julies.

'Before my time,' Kate said. 'What was the club like?'

'Class, the haunt of professional footballers and celebrities. Where they went, we followed. In its heyday, it was the place to be seen. I stumbled in and out of there often.'

Kate tuned him out as he continued to reminisce.

As a young detective Hank had to fight women off. It wasn't only his looks that drew them to him, though when Kate first met him, he was considered the office catch, until he met and married a woman with the same name as the club.

'Did you meet Julie there?' she asked.

'Not her thing, but it sounds like Georgina was a party girl—'

'Weren't we all? Now I can barely stay awake after nine.'

Hank chuckled.

Kate was too busy dwelling on her meeting with the witness to lark around. 'Sounds like Crawford never got over the break-up. If he's telling the truth, the night they bumped into the man he described as "her ex" was their last together.'

'Is that what he said?'

'Weren't you earwigging at the door?'

'I scarpered when it became obvious he wasn't going to take you hostage.'

'He claimed that he was duped by her, not to make the other man jealous, but to get him out of her hair for good. Georgina said hello to him, then slipped her arm around Crawford's waist, making it clear they were an item. The guy put his drink on the bar and walked out without a backward glance. Soon after, Georgina complained of a headache. Crawford put her in a taxi and that was the end of their relationship.'

'Ouch,' Hank said.

'What I don't get is why an affair with a colleague, if he was a colleague, bothered Georgina so much. It's not like it hasn't happened before.'

'It used to be mandatory in some nicks,' Hank joked.

'My thoughts exactly. Even if the mystery guy was married, it's not something friends fail to share years after the event when the shine has worn off and it's all died down. Georgina told me all sorts of personal stuff. Why not that? And why was it important enough to involve Crawford in such an elaborate charade? If he's on the level, his intel might be hugely significant to the investigation.'

84

Andy Brown had caught a couple of hours shut-eye at home, having been stood down by a new surveillance team. Surprisingly, after working all night, he was wide awake and jumping up and down when Kate and Hank arrived at Middle Earth. So keen was he to impart whatever was on his mind, he trailed them to her office before they had time to take off their coats, visit the locker room or grab a brew. Hank told him to sling his hook. He and Kate had been on the go since 7 a.m.

'It's important, Sarge. It involves Carmichael too.'

Hank looked out through the open door. 'So where is she?'

'In the Super's office with Zac.'

'You'd better get her then.'

'It might be best if we go to her.'

Intrigued, Kate said: 'Give us five. We also have news to share after an interesting conversation with Dr Alan Crawford. Unless he's a very accomplished liar, he's no longer in the mix as a suspect. Ask Ailsa to join us too, please.'

At half past one, all six gathered in Bright's office: Kate and Lisa at his huge desk; Zac on a side table; Hank, Andy and Ailsa taking seats reserved for guests. Though it was a roomy office, it was chilly in there, Kate insisting on having the window open for ventilation. Five of the MIT, including Kate and Jo, had already been infected with Delta, but Omicron was rampant. Some of the younger detectives were not yet boosted. The team was already down 20 per cent and she couldn't afford to lose more.

If one went down, the rest would fall like dominos.

Hank checked his watch. 'I'm meeting Charlotte at three o'clock sharp. I don't want to rile her any further by turning up late, so can we get on with it?' For the others' benefit, he explained that as of that morning, the MIT were no longer welcome at her place. 'Until then, I'm yours.'

'Where is the meeting?' Kate asked.

'The Blackbird, Ponteland.'

'Outside, I hope.'

He gave a nod. 'The reason she chose it, I imagine.'

Satisfied, Kate began by updating the others on Crawford's revelation. 'He appears to be on the level. Hank and I will sit down later and decide what to do about the mystery cop he described as the love of Georgina's life.'

'Then why was she so keen to dump him?' Jo asked.

'I don't know but intend to find out. If he exists, we need to find him quickly – not that I think he's a danger to anyone else. If, as we suspect, his motive was revenge, he's achieved his objective.' She noticed Ailsa wasn't paying attention. 'Ailsa? Did you hear a word I said?'

'Yes, guv . . .' Apologising, she slipped her mobile into her pocket. 'Sorry, I was texting my contact in the search team.' She was fretting, worried stiff.

From the sad expression on her face, Kate could tell there was no news. 'Ailsa, in no way are you responsible for Ella leaving the station,' she said.

'Guv, she's exposed and vulnerable for all the reasons I outlined. What if—'

'Enough, Ailsa. We have no time for what ifs. Of course, you're worried. We all are. I need you to focus and let your contact do her job. That's what search advisers are for. She won't thank you for checking in every five minutes and she won't report on negatives. There's no time for that, for her or you. When Ella is found, you'll be the first to know.'

Kate left it there, turning her attention to Andy Brown, asking him to go next. He'd been champing at the bit since he entered Bright's office. He could hardly contain himself, though he glanced at Ailsa, checking on her before he began his delivery. Satisfied that she was all right, he turned his gaze on the others.

'While you and Hank were out, technical support reported back on the gable end video feed. The footage of the alley was of such poor quality they were unable to enhance the stills sufficiently to make an ID.'

'Damn it,' Hank swore.

'It's not all grim, Sarge. Three shots can be heard in quick succession before the figure comes into view. It's highly likely that it was the shooter. Using police personnel, they reconstructed the scene and determined that the male or female – they weren't convinced either way – was approximately five nine to six three.'

Hank's mood brightened. 'Coincidentally, a height that fits our new prime suspect.'

'Hold on,' Kate interrupted. 'I thought Ella said the shooter walked off in an easterly direction. Isn't the gable end to the west of the crime scene?'

'He must have used the cut and doubled back,' Andy said.

'He'd have had to walk past Christine's yard. Would he risk that?'

'He might if he was disturbed,' Hank said. 'People were out at all hours letting off fireworks round our way. A great night to discharge a gun and have no one take a blind bit of notice. Besides, if he appeared right after shots were fired, the chances of it being anyone else makes even less sense.'

'Send me a copy of the footage.' Kate looked at Carmichael. 'Lisa, I hope to link the two investigations imminently, but I'm failing to see how this concerns our enquiry.'

'I have something that might change your mind,' she said.

85

It was the first time since Ash died that Carmichael seemed properly engaged in her work. She was the MIT's in-house technical expert. It was early days, but this was the breakthrough in recovery that Kate had been hoping for.

'Let's have it then,' she said.

'I was passing Andy's desk when the report came in. I viewed the live feed. I hadn't seen it up to that point. As you know, I've been working on the thumb drive you retrieved from Curtis. I didn't want to confuse the two or have one impinge on the other. I have something you all should see.'

She typed a command into the keyboard on her desktop.

Kate rolled her chair closer, the others moving in so that they could view it too.

Lisa pointed at her monitor, drawing their attention to a still image of one man she'd captured with his back to the camera at the crem, dark full-length coat, collar turned up, scarf and trilby. 'What do you think of this guy?'

'Looks like a seventies Gateshead detective to me.'

Everyone laughed.

Carmichael rewound, then pressed play. 'Watch closely. As you can see, this is the east chapel, not the west chapel where Georgina's service was going on. He's not engaging with mourners around him.' She looked up. 'Don't you think that's odd?'

'Not especially. The bereaved like their space.' Realising what she'd said, Kate was kicking herself. Carmichael didn't react. Kate moved swiftly on. 'For their own reasons, people like to be close to the person being buried or cremated, without antagonising anyone who has a more valid excuse for being there. I've attended many services when I've not spoken to family, because my relationship with the deceased was our business and no one else's.'

'At first, I thought the guy was shy, or perhaps too upset for small talk. Now I'm not so sure.' Pushing her keyboard away, Carmichael placed her laptop directly in front of the desktop. Ignoring everyone around her, again she typed a command. 'You asked me to walk a particular route, taking in all the buildings, gardens and parking area. In this footage, I've done a loop and I'm heading back to where I started. I think this is the same man.' On screen, as mourners entered the east chapel, the figure made off toward the car park. Lisa paused the video. 'It seems he didn't attend either service after all.'

'Now that is odd,' Kate said.

'Maybe he lost his bottle,' Zac said. 'I've known that happen.'

'Or maybe he was using the east chapel crowd as cover,' Hank said. 'Because he was there to say goodbye to Georgina, not the person being cremated across the way.'

'Good point.' Kate was impressed. 'Maybe he's the cop Crawford talked about.'

'You might be right.' Carmichael ran the footage on. Eventually, the man stopped walking. He was partially obscured by a tree, only the brim of his hat showing, and the bottom half of his left leg. 'Look at the angle of his foot. If I'm not mistaken, he's watching me, watching him. Only a pro would do that. We need this footage looked at.'

'Why?' Kate said. 'There's nowt on it that's of use to us. He might just be an oddball.'

'Watch this,' Carmichael said.

She'd timed the footage she wanted them to see before-hand, scribbling her readings down on a notepad, setting up her grand finale. The others looked on as she lined up both computers, her fingers eventually pausing on the mouse pad. Moving the counters to a predetermined position on each device, she pressed play on both desktop and laptop simultaneously. The desktop footage showed the shadowy image of a figure on the gable end video making off from the crime scene. The laptop showed a moving image of the unidentified man walking away from her at the crematorium car park.

'What do we think?' Lisa eyeballed the others, a smile developing. 'Tell me that's not the same guy.'

86

The Blackbird pub used to be a favourite haunt of Northumbria Police officers. Their HQ was once situated half a mile or so along the road. The outside tables were almost empty on account of the damp and drizzly weather lying over rural Northumberland. Charlotte had bagged herself one under cover, close to the front door.

She was facing Hank, though her head was turned, looking the other way, smoke drifting from the cigarette in her right hand, probably searching for a surveillance vehicle. Hank had noticed one in his peripheral vision when he drove in. He didn't acknowledge the officer inside in case she was watching. She'd chosen to sit with a view of the T-junction where she'd see him arrive, no matter which direction he came from.

He approached with caution, hoping she'd calmed down from this morning's row. He had little doubt that she'd eventually forgive him and Kate for not being straight with her. Cops rarely bore grudges.

They didn't have the time or the luxury.

By all accounts, Charlotte had been helpful when spoken to by Curtis following her mother's death: her parents were happy; they argued occasionally. Who didn't? Georgina meant the world to Nico; he was the best father anyone could wish for, Oscar a pain in the butt. Questioning her this time would be different. From all quarters, the finger of suspicion was pointing directly at the family.

They both knew it.

Unlike Oscar, Charlotte accepted it.

'Hey,' Hank said, trying to keep it friendly, trying even harder to ignore the folded newspaper tucked beneath her bag to prevent it blowing away. The headline stood out in bold capital letters: **GREEK TRAGEDY GOES ON**.

'Hey yourself.'

'Is it safe to sit down?'

'Always the joker.' Charlotte took a drag on her cigarette, taking it deep into her lungs, then blew the smoke away from him. 'I ordered a latte. If you want anything stronger, the waiter shouldn't be long.'

Hank slung his leg over the wooden bench. 'Are we good?'

'You tell me.' She slid the fag packet towards him. 'Help yourself.'

It was an olive branch gesture he had no intention of knocking back. They had been known to share a sneaky one in her parents' garden in the past, hiding in the shed like a couple of teenagers so as not to get caught by her mum or his wife.

Picking up the packet, he took one out.

She leaned in, lighting it for him, a hint of their former secret alliance. It had been a while since he'd smoked. The nicotine tasted rank. It burned his throat, the hit going straight to his head. Was Charlotte trying to manipulate him, reminding him of their friendship, the laughs they'd shared, in the hope that he'd go easy on her?

There was zero chance of that happening.

'Did you find your witness?' she said.

He shook his head.

It was the first thing any genuinely concerned cop would ask. All perfectly normal, unless that cop was guilty, trying to gain access to information a suspect shouldn't have. Charlotte was, and always had been, a game-player, living on the edge.

Hank apologised for what had happened earlier. 'I appreciate how difficult it must be for you to accept us sniffing around. The sooner we can get it done—'

'The sooner it goes away?'

'I wasn't going to say that.'

'Weren't you?' She stubbed her cigarette in the ashtray. 'Because it won't go away. Not for me, my father or Oscar. Not now. Or ever.'

'I know. What I was going to say was, the sooner we can eliminate you from our enquiries the better. Believe me, I'd like nothing more. I'm not here to hurt or humour you. Neither will I lie to you.'

'You won't lie to me *again*, you mean?' She was scoring points, seeing how far she could push him.

'I deserved that.'

'Yes, you did.' Charlotte paused, a sad look on her face. 'I'm not trying to rub it in, Hank. You have a plateful, I imagine . . . and I liked Ash Norham. He was a good bloke. How's Carmichael coping?'

The question threw him.

He feigned ignorance. 'What do you mean?'

Charlotte's eyes turned icy. 'You said you wouldn't lie to me.'

His reply was guarded. 'How did you know?'

'I saw them together in town one night. I'm no detective but I'm a cop who keeps her eyes open. I may not have found true love, but I recognise it when I see it.'

He tried to lift her. 'I thought Ronaldo had moved in—'

She laughed. 'That was last week.'

'He was there this morning.'

'And he'll be gone by the weekend. Believe me, I know when I'm beat.' She acted as if she couldn't care less. 'Let's just say his club aren't happy with the adverse publicity. I don't blame him for taking their advice. He could have anyone. Why pick me?'

'I can think of any number of reasons.'

'You're hitting on me now?'

'I would if I thought I was in with a chance.' He'd missed her. 'No? OK, I get the message. Just so you know, Lisa would rather her relationship with Ash wasn't made public.'

'Done, though if I saw her, others may have. If it gets out, it won't be from me. I can't hang around long. Ask your questions.'

'There are things you need to know first.' He tried to second-guess her reaction to the fact that he knew of her and Oscar's medical history. She didn't explode, though clearly it didn't please her.

He moved quickly on. 'You may have recovered. Oscar hasn't. If you're unaware of that, I probably shouldn't be sharing it – and wouldn't if I wasn't so concerned about him.'

'Tell me or don't – I haven't got all day.'

'He's been displaying a pattern of behaviour that would have resulted in dismissal had it not been for your mum and what happened to her.'

'I knew he was struggling—'

'It's gone way beyond that. Even before he had a go at Kate, he was on a final warning, a psych assessment concluding that he's in need of professional help. He's refusing to accept it. Up till now, allowances have been made.'

'And now he's run out of road.'

'Just about.'

'I didn't know any of that, I swear. I'm serious, Hank. We've not seen that much of each other lately. Our perfect family has fallen apart since Mum died. She was the one who arranged our gatherings, the one around whom we all revolved. Oscar and I let things slide. We both see Papa, not always . . . in fact, hardly ever, at the same time.'

Hank had lost count of the families he'd seen disintegrate in the aftermath of murder. It was depressing to hear that hers had suffered the same fate. Nico was either naive or kidding himself. He'd given the impression that everything was as normal as it could be three years on. Ever the optimist, he was keeping up appearances, doing his best to put the past behind him.

'I understand,' Hank said. 'I'm sorry.'

'I don't want your sympathy.'

Hank studied her closely. If she knew of Oscar's downward spiral, on top of losing her mum, it gave her another reason to hate the Bradshaw brothers. Few officers could bear the idea that they had committed murder and walked away scot-free. Secretly, and in some cases very publicly, many officers on the force were delighted that the scumbags had finally got what they deserved.

'What about Jenny?' Hank asked. 'Have you two spoken?'

'My sister-in-law and I were never that close. Perhaps that's why Oscar chose her, as an antidote to me. She's Mother Earth. I can't stand rug rats. Why d'you ask?'

'They're separated.'

'Since when?'

'I can't believe he didn't tell you.'

'He didn't.'

A waiter arrived with their order, a mobile card reader sticking out of his jeans pocket.

Hank reached for his wallet.

'Put it away, I've got this.' Charlotte paid contactless. The machine bleeped, spewing out a receipt. Tearing it off, the waiter put it down on the table.

'Have a nice day,' he said.

'You too.' Charlotte rolled her eyes at Hank as the waiter moved away. 'When did that become a thing in the UK?' She lit another cigarette, before resuming the conversation. 'I'll speak to Oscar.'

Hank gave a nod. 'Make it quick.'

87

Carmichael yanked out her AirPods and threw them down on the desk. Relaxing into her chair, she stared at her laptop, as satisfied as she could be that no more could be gleaned from the video she'd filmed covertly at the crematorium. Without professional enhancement she could go no further. The image was frozen on the man she was convinced was the same shadowy figure seen on the gable end footage.

Kate wasn't so sure.

Across the desk, only the top of her head was visible. She'd asked Carmichael to examine the video for any audible clues.

'Boss? Have you got a minute?'

Kate looked up from a budget sheet that made grim reading. 'All done?'

Lisa nodded. 'I've listened a dozen times. I can hear no doors slamming, engines starting up, or cars driving away after the unidentified male made his way toward the crematorium car park. If I had to make a guess, I'd say he left on foot. Want me to check the reg numbers of the vehicles I recorded at the time? Unless someone slipped in while I was making my way through the garden of remembrance, I'm sure I caught them all on camera.'

'No, leave it with me.'

'Aren't we revisiting vehicle enquiries?'

'No, we'd have to trace two, three hundred cars, possibly four or five times that many people. Vehicles will have been sold or scrapped. Raise the action and put it in for referral.'

'Are you sure? The fact that I didn't see or hear the guy leave doesn't mean he didn't arrive by car. If I was him, I'd have disappeared PDQ and returned under the cover of darkness to collect my vehicle.'

An incoming text interrupted their chat.

Kate glanced at her mobile. *More bad news.*

'Lisa, I've made my decision. In view of Crawford's revelations this afternoon, our priority is Georgina's early service, who she worked with, who she drank with, who she slept with. The week she went to Julies with Crawford is vital. We need a timeline for that week, the week before and the week after.'

Another interruption – a knock at the door this time.

Maggie Morrison's face appeared at the window. She was one of Northumbria's most experienced forensic investigators. They had worked together for almost two decades.

Kate beckoned her in.

She had a wide smile on her face as she entered, making no secret of the fact that she had good news to share. She didn't wait to dole it out. 'Ask me who got DNA matches on the lighter PC Hamilton found at Rothbury riverside—'

'Matches, plural?' Kate asked.

Maggie nodded. 'For both Lee and Jackson Bradshaw. Looks like they were sharing the lighter, passing it back and forth while they waited for Georgina. It ties one, if not both brothers to the scene.'

'You're a star, Maggie. We'll take that, won't we, Lisa?'

Carmichael was trying not to sulk over Kate's knock-back. 'Absolutely—'

Maggie cut her off. 'I have more.' A flash of regret crossed her face.

Kate realised that she'd said too much in front of Carmichael. First: the forensic investigator was doing her best not to look at the DS directly. Unusual. They got on. Second: the text Kate had received was from Hank, telling her that Charlotte was aware of Carmichael's relationship with Ash. Kate was kicking herself that she hadn't yet warned her. If one person knew, everyone knew . . . Maggie included.

'Lisa, can you give us a minute?'

Carmichael's eyes met Kate's, then Maggie's. 'Something

going on that's above my pay grade?' She was staring at Maggie. 'Is this about the gun Hank sent you? Because if it is, I'd like to stay.'

Kate was about to repeat her request, then thought better of it. Carmichael would find out soon enough. It was impossible to keep secrets at Middle Earth. This was why a few days' leave had been mentioned, breathing space for Lisa to get her shit together. Having declined, she'd have to suck up any condolences coming her way, the one thing she was desperate to avoid.

Kate threw the forensic investigator a nod to proceed.

'There was a rush on the gun,' Maggie said.

'There always is when the rubber-heelers are sniffing around.' Carmichael meant Professional Standards. 'Don't tell me the IOPC are arguing over rules of engagement, the rights and wrongs of lethal force? Don Bradshaw aimed a firearm at Ash. What else was he supposed to do?'

Kate was proud of Carmichael. She'd shown that she could handle anything that came her way. She'd also got the message that her relationship with Ash was common knowledge. And yet, she didn't admit or deny it.

'Lisa, I'm so sorry,' Maggie said.

'Don't let sympathy hold you back.'

'After I finished with the gun, it went off to ballistics and was bumped up the queue. The report is in. The gun Don Bradshaw retrieved from his doorstep, the one he aimed at Ash, has identical markings to the weapon used to kill Georgina. You have all the proof you need.'

88

Up to now, Charlotte had been relaxed, though Hank hadn't yet said anything contentious. Without being prompted, she put her cards on the table, offering a flat-out denial that she had anything to do with the Bradshaw shootings. She checked her watch, a heavy hint that he should finish his questioning so she could get home before dark.

'What is it you want from me?' she said.

'You were off duty on Christmas Eve, right?'

'Cut the stuff you already know the answer to, Hank. I'm a cop, remember?'

'OK. Where were you that night?'

'Out to dinner.'

Given that it was the anniversary of her mother's death, that might have surprised him had he not known since yesterday that she wasn't at home. 'Can I ask where?'

'That's my business.'

'You're not helping, Charlotte.'

'Take my word for it. What I was doing is not relevant to your investigation.'

'It is if you were in the East End.'

She didn't flinch, though he detected a hint of concern. It came and left in a flash, so fleeting he might have missed it had he not been paying close attention. It was as clear as day that she was keeping secrets.

His phone rang.

'Sorry, I'll have to take this.' He excused himself and took the call in the men's room where he wouldn't be overheard if she followed him inside. It was Kate, updating him on the ballistics report.

'How's it going with Charlotte?' she asked.

'Painfully slow. She was out to dinner on Christmas Eve and won't say where.'

Kate was suddenly in a restaurant, wearing a black dress, hair tied up. She'd arrived early, telling the maître d that she wanted to cover the bill. When the Ioannou family arrived, Charlotte was wearing the identical outfit.

'Kate?'

'Hold on.' She was gone a few minutes before she came on the line. 'She was at the Cook House. I've sent you a copy of her credit card slip.'

'How the hell—'

'Lucky guess. It's her favourite eatery, where we celebrated her twenty-first. Jo and I go there a lot. We're on first-name terms with the staff.'

'I'd better go before she legs it.'

'Good luck.' She disconnected.

Hank accessed the email, checking the credit card slip. Heading out of the pub, he slipped his phone in his pocket, in a better mood than when he entered. Charlotte was where he'd left her. 'Sorry. You were about to tell me where you were on the night of the shooting.'

She looked through him. 'Nice try.'

He gave her a nudge. 'Charlotte, you were seen on the Ouseburn.' It was a trendy and popular part of town, less than two miles from the crime scene.

'Says who?'

'You know I can't tell you that. I have a credit card slip for the Cook House, timed at 11 p.m. on Christmas Eve, cost of a meal for two. Who was your dinner guest?'

'I told you, that's my business.'

'Who are you protecting?'

'I have no intention of dragging the person I was with into this shitshow.' She gave him hard eyes, lighting up again, buying herself time before she answered. 'It's ridiculous the way my family have been, are being, treated. None of us are

318

crying over the Bradshaw brothers' demise. Why would we? It's not *who* I'm protecting, it's *what*. My privacy. And that's the only answer you're getting. I've been in every newspaper from here to Timbuktu in the last three years and I'm sick of it.'

'Was it Oscar you had dinner with?'

'He was on duty.'

'That's not what I asked.'

She laughed in his face. 'You think we were synchronising watches, firming up our plans to kill over a medium rare and bottle of fizz?'

'Were you?'

She leaned in, staring at him. 'How long have we known each other, Hank? You think we're capable?' Her voice caught in her throat. 'Well, fuck you. Fuck the lot of you, the press, the police, and anyone else with an opinion on what went down.' She stood up, grabbing her newspaper, slapping it across his chest. 'Have you seen this garbage?'

'Charlotte.'

'Don't you dare touch me.'

He raised both hands, backing off.

She turned and fled, not even a glance over her shoulder.

He called after her, but she was halfway to her car already. The engine roared into life. The vehicle sped away. Hank looked down at the newspaper in his hand. The subheading of the article mentioned the family by first name only, though in Nico's case some idiot thought it a good idea not to use his real name, but the one his children affectionately referred to him by. The reporter had picked out the first letter of each name in bold font:

The misery goes on for **C**harlotte, **O**scar, **P**apa

89

Finally, Kate could join forces with Hank and apply for the investigation into Georgina's murder to be closed. On its own, the first piece of forensic evidence might not have been enough. It could still have been construed as circumstantial. The ballistics report sealed it. Kate would make up the file for Bright and request that it be recorded as detected: the guilt of the offender(s) was clear. She felt like leaving it in his inbox tied in a big red bow. His bugbear had always been undetected murders. She had no doubt that he'd rubber-stamp it on his return from LA, transferring it to her in-tray before the ink was dry.

Kate had calls to make to Jo, Hank, PC Fay Hamilton.

Carmichael left the office with Maggie. Kate suspected that they would chat out of her hearing, Lisa trying to establish how many people were talking about her. As soon as they closed the door, Kate speed-dialled Jo's number. The dialling tone stopped. Jo didn't come on the line, though Kate could hear road noise.

She had her foot to the floor. 'Jo? Can you hear me?'

'I can now . . . the signal dropped out.'

Kate heard the click-click of a vehicle indicator. 'Sounds like you're flying. Where are you?'

'About to join the M6—'

'Don't. We have our smoking gun, and I mean that literally. The weapon CSIs recovered from Christine's place was used to kill Georgina. Enquiries at Strangeways are no longer necessary.'

'Great, I'll cancel my hotel then. I'm an hour and a half away. You want me in the office, or shall I head home?'

'Head home . . . and go easy on the accelerator.'

'Yes, Mum.' Jo was laughing as she hung up.

Kate wasn't.

She was worried . . .

Jo's good humour was an act. Last night, the woman she loved with a passion admitted that she was struggling. A doctorate in forensic psychology didn't make her any better equipped to deal with her job than anyone else. For the first time in her life, she wanted to run away. She'd begged Kate to pack a bag and go somewhere quiet, somewhere they could be together for a while, away from incident room noise.

Anywhere would do.

Kate turned her down. With Bright away, and so much on, it was out of the question. She sat for a moment, staring into space, wondering if Jo had turned around or kept driving. She'd gone missing before, needing time to heal, away from everything, a memory Kate had no wish to revisit. She shut her eyes, daydreaming of lying on the sofa watching a movie until she fell asleep, Jo in a more playful mood, giving her a reason to stay awake. There was only one problem with that fantasy . . .

Her day wasn't over yet.

Scooping her mobile off the desk, she tapped on Hank's number. The call cut to voicemail. She left a message for him to call her ASAP, then accessed Hamilton's number, thanking her for the evidence she'd preserved, the statement she'd made three years ago, informing her that her efforts alone had solved the undetected murder of a fellow cop, a stain on the reputation of the Murder Investigation Team.

'I can't thank you enough,' she said.

'It's my job, guv.'

'There's a difference between doing it and doing it well in the face of resistance from a senior officer who won't give you the time of day.' Kate didn't use the word homophobia. She didn't need to. Hamilton knew exactly what she meant. 'It's a strength all officers require, and few possess without a few years in.'

'You spoke, I listened, guv. The fact that I covered my back is down to you.'

'Take the credit, Fay. To have such wherewithal as a probationer says a lot about you. Take it from one who knows. You're wasted in uniform. You've shown an aptitude for detective work. Any application to the CID will be considered favourably.' Hamilton was ecstatic. 'In the meantime, report to my office in plain clothes. I need bodies.'

90

Hank arrived as Kate ended the call, updating him on developments, good and bad. He reciprocated, then tossed the newspaper Charlotte had given him on Bright's desk. She picked it up and read the headline. It didn't impress. Nor did the byline: *Gillian Garvey, Chief Crime Correspondent.*

'I should've known,' she whispered under her breath.

Hank guessed she'd seen the name of the writer. 'Looks like she's gone up in the world.'

Kate's expression was ice cold. 'I was thinking the opposite. This is a new low, even for her. You know what the worst thing is? Gillian is a clever journalist, a workaholic, able to dig up information that others can't. How she goes about that is anyone's guess, and frankly I don't care. She's so much better than this.'

'That's not the impression you gave last time you two saw each other.' Hank was referring to Kate's fury after Garvey abused the privileged position of a shoo-in at every Northumbria Police press conference. With TV cameras rolling, she'd given Kate a hard time, posing awkward questions, forcing her to suck up her bullshit until the conference ended. 'From memory, she was in shreds after you'd finished with her.'

'Yeah, well she deserved it.'

'Didn't she hold up the white flag afterwards?'

'I don't recall.'

'I think you'll find she did.' Hauling himself out of a chair that was far too comfortable to be in an office, he got ready to leave. 'What do you want me to do about Charlotte? She's not going to tell us who she had dinner with.'

'Doesn't the restaurant have CCTV?'

'Not working on Christmas Eve.'

'Bugger. I wonder if she knew. It's odd that she didn't use her father's restaurant that night. It was open and God knows he needed the trade. I can't help thinking she didn't want him to see her in town. Why won't she say who she was with?'

'She said it has no relevance to our investigation.'

'That's for us to determine.'

'Try telling her that.'

'I will. In view of what I told you, we need to get the family together. Rumours will spread like wildfire now the ballistics report is in. I don't want them to hear the news from anyone but us.'

'I'll see if they're free.' Hank made his way to the door, then turned to face her. 'Now the incidents are linked, can I steal Carmichael?'

'No, she's busy with Georgina's antecedents. What's Maxwell doing?'

'Up to his eyes in airport CCTV.'

'He's swinging the lead.' Kate showed her irritation. 'There can't be more than half a dozen humans flying now. Tell him to get a move on. And ask Ailsa to check the restaurant receipts in case the person Charlotte was meeting arrived before her. Whoever it was may have bought a drink and paid contactless. Who uses cash these days? I can't remember when I last saw real money.'

'It's worth a shot.'

'That's why I suggested it.'

Hank smiled. 'It's good to have you back, Kate.'

91

Alone with her thoughts, Kate considered Hank's take on Gillian Garvey. He was right, of course. If she sounded off at the journalist, she'd be playing into her hands, giving her the satisfaction of knowing that she'd rattled cages. Similarly, if Kate threatened to go to the Press Complaints Commission to lodge an official grievance, it would take forever for them to act – they both knew it.

Kate called Gillian, hoping to talk some sense into her. She suspected it wouldn't go well but felt compelled to try. She would play it by ear. If the crime correspondent was willing to hear her out, Kate would bite the bullet for the sake of Georgina's family. It had been a while since Kate had expelled the journalist from the inner circle. This gave her a bargaining chip. If Gillian played nice, as a gesture of goodwill, she might even allow her back in. And if not . . .

She'd make it up as she went along.

Garvey picked up and took her time to speak. 'Well, well, if it isn't Northumbria's finest.' She sounded triumphant. 'I'm honoured. I miss the old days, don't you, Kate? I'm guessing you're not calling to invite me to dinner.'

In your dreams.

'Sounds like fun,' Kate said. 'Some other time perhaps. I'm in the middle of a double-hander.'

'Oh yes, I forgot. Can I help you with that?'

Kate was on the brink of losing it. 'What is wrong with you, Gillian?'

'Nothing I'm perfectly well. Thanks for asking. You?'

Gillian was smart.

Kate was smarter.

'Your game is fundamentally flawed,' she said. 'Your beef is with me, not a murdered police officer's family. I'm asking on their behalf, and on behalf of any other officers you want to drag into that hole you've put them in, to back the fuck off. Do you think you could do that small thing for me?'

'I thought you'd cancelled our special arrangement. I'm not one to hold a grudge if you're asking nicely—'

'I'm not asking, I'm telling.' Holding her tongue had never come easy. Kate would not, could not, let this cockroach get the better of her. 'And spare me the I'm-just-doing-my-job routine. As for me, I'm tied up tonight. How about I shout you breakfast in the morning?'

They arranged a time and place.

Kate disconnected.

Without knocking, Hank walked in. 'We're on with the family. I have a few things to do. How does an hour from now suit you?'

Kate looked at her watch. 'Fine. Where?'

'Nico's restaurant.'

Kate raised an eyebrow. 'Hardly. We need privacy.'

'They're closed today. Can't afford to keep the lights on.'

The family were waiting when Kate and Hank arrived, a close-knit unit sitting around an oblong table with a dimmed overhanging light at the centre. Candles flickered as always, creating a warm and welcoming atmosphere. There was food and wine on the table and two extra places set for a supper. Nico never missed an opportunity to feed his family or his guests. It was bred into him, part of his Greek heritage, one of the many things that made him special. The smell of the food and the sound of traditional music playing gently in the background sent Kate hurtling back to 2005.

The taxi rattled along the bumpy road that edged the coast, the sun low in the sky, light fading fast, a pink fluffy cloud reflected in the water. The Porto Marina taverna clung to the rocky edge of the shoreline. Picture-perfect in its natural surroundings, it looked exactly as Kate remembered, an open-ended, under-cover restaurant, with pretty lights strung in the pine trees.

Her cab came to a stop.

She paid the driver and got out, the smell of Greek cuisine attacking her senses before she'd closed the car door. In the water, a small boat rocked gently in crystal clear water, anchored to a jetty at the end of which was a flagpole with a ragged Greek flag flapping gently in the breeze coming off the sea. In the taverna, tables lined the water's edge, every one of them taken.

'You made it!'

Georgina was walking towards her, a beaming smile, eyes on fire. She was wearing a turquoise and navy dress, split up the side, sun-bleached hair falling softly around bare shoulders, arms and legs deeply tanned, a pair of strappy flat sandals on her feet.

'Wow! Three weeks of R&R suits you.' Kate took her hands, looking her up and down. 'You look stunning.'

'I feel it . . .' Georgina glanced at the ground. 'No luggage?'

Kate held up a small backpack. 'Two bikinis, a pair of shorts, a T-shirt and flip-flops. All I had time for.' The trip was last-minute to celebrate Oscar and Charlotte turning seventeen, a delayed flight forcing a hasty change of plan. It was Georgina's suggestion that they meet at the restaurant.

She put her arms around Kate. 'Thanks for coming.'

Kate looked past her. 'Do the kids know?'

'They soon will. C'mon, they'll be stoked.'

'Kate?' Charlotte's voice bled into her thoughts. 'Kate, food's ready.'

Kate turned, half-expecting to see Georgina.

Charlotte was returning to her seat.

Nico was pulling out a chair for her.

Kate wanted to bawl.

She sat down, Hank choosing the seat on her right flank. Given his recent dealings with the family, none of which had gone particularly well, they had decided that she should be the one to lead the discussion.

Kate wasn't ready.

There was nothing she wouldn't give to be sitting with Georgina, their legs dangling from the jetty, the warmth and movement of the Aegean Sea slapping gently against their bare feet.

Focus!

As Nico poured wine, inviting everyone to help themselves, Kate glanced around the table. Had she not known otherwise, she could have thought that Hank had given them the news, that all had been forgiven, that the family were ready to celebrate the closure of the investigation into Georgina's death. When Nico took a seat between his twins, Kate was back in that taverna taking part in a different celebration. The image unsettled her. Misreading her expression, he apologised for any bad feeling that had existed between the five of them lately.

'Please don't,' Kate said. 'There's no need. Everyone here understands that Hank and I have a job to do. Believe it or not, we are trying to do it sensitively. We know how difficult it is for you right now. Reports in the press aren't helping, though that's not why we asked to meet with you. As of an hour or so ago, we have hard evidence that the Bradshaw brothers were responsible for Georgina's death.'

For a moment no one spoke.

Oscar broke the silence. 'There was never anyone else in the frame, Kate.'

Charlotte's eyes were shut, a moment of silent contemplation, of heartbreak and sorrow, but also relief. A sob left her throat. She glanced at her father. He had no words. She reached out, placing a hand on his, a gentle squeeze. 'It's over now, Papa. Mum can rest in peace.' Lastly, she looked at Kate and Hank.

'Thank you,' she said.

'I wanted to tell you before you heard it on the grapevine. None of you are going to like what I have to say next.' Kate paused, taking in each face. 'Some of the evidence I've uncovered has been in the system for almost three years. It had not been forensically examined until I took over the case. I'd like you to keep that to yourselves.'

'Sounds like a cover-up to me,' Oscar said.

Nico shot him a dirty look. 'Let Kate finish, please.'

'No, he has a right to say his piece.' Kate looked at him. 'You can call it how you see it, Oscar. I'm being transparent. What I'm talking about will damage us and our organisation if it's made public, prolonging speculation in the press. I can't order you not to talk about it, and won't try to stop you, but it'll aid our investigation if we keep it in-house.' She'd purposely used the words *us, our* and *we* to remind Oscar and Charlotte of their professional obligations not to bring the service into disrepute.

Charlotte asked: 'So, what evidence are we talking about?'

92

Kate was about to pull the pin and throw a live grenade on the table. 'At the original crime scene, a probationer drew attention to disturbed ground near where your mum was found. She told me that Curtis declined to look at it. It concerned her so much, she collected several exhibits, handing them in without his knowledge. She also took photographs and made a formal statement to that effect. One of those items was a cigarette lighter, on which forensics found Lee and Jackson Bradshaw's DNA.'

Oscar was instantly agitated. 'What happens to Curtis?'

'The question is, was he incompetent or was there criminal intent? Unless we can prove that he deliberately conspired with an OCG to throw the case, there's little we can do about it.'

'So, we're meant to suck it up?' Charlotte said.

'That's not what I'm saying. Professional Standards will investigate the matter thoroughly. Just don't expect Christine Bradshaw to assist in that regard.'

Charlotte's tone was harsh. 'She'd sell her granny to get off lightly.'

'Not this time,' Kate said. 'Dropping Curtis in the shit would be bad for business. The cops she has in her pocket will scatter like rats on a sinking ship. It'll also implicate her in an offence of perverting the course of justice in the murder of your mum. That will add to her sentence, not reduce it.'

Kate allowed the family a moment to process what she'd said. It also gave her thinking time. Jo's advice was usually sound. She was probably correct in her assumption that the only thing the family were guilty of was suspecting one another of the Bradshaw shootings, making them act out of character. Even so, Kate had to consider the possibility that Jo was wrong.

In which case, *she* was dining with a killer.

Kate had spent her whole career on shifting sands. With Ella missing, it was make-or-break time. Setting up this meeting was part of a wider strategy to give and to receive transactional analysis. Sharing intelligence with three people who were undeniably still suspects in a double shooting was risky.

She had a call to make.

'I also came to tell you that we now have irrefutable evidence that the gun Lee Bradshaw fired on the night he died is the same weapon that killed Georgina.'

Shifting in his seat, Hank took a sip of wine.

He looked decidedly uncomfortable.

Kate knew why.

Despite the convivial surroundings, an atmosphere of suspicion hung in the air; the detectives wondering if the family's hospitality might be a ploy to ply them with wine in the hope that they would let slip details of the investigation; the family wondering if they were the ones being duped. Kate's reputation for pulling strokes with suspects was legendary.

She made no apology for it.

It got results.

She'd been straight with the family. Now she wanted something in return. Early in the shooting investigation, Hank had decided that if Nico, Oscar, and Charlotte ever became credible suspects he'd ask for DNA samples, believing that they wouldn't refuse if they were innocent. Kate wasn't so sure. Charlotte would probably take such a request as an accusation. Kate went with her gut, aware that she was skating on thin ice.

'While we're on the subject of DNA,' she said. 'We'd like yours—'

Nico's mouth almost dropped open. 'Why?'

'Purely for elimination purposes. Evidence is coming to light every day. We found samples at the scene that are unidentified. Just as I had to prove that the Bradshaw brothers killed Georgina, Hank and I now must prove that one or all of you didn't kill them. It's that simple. Volunteering a sample is the quickest and easiest way to put you in or out of the investigation.'

The anticipated explosion never came.

'So be it,' Nico said.

Charlotte said, 'You're not getting mine.'

Oscar said, 'Get the swabs out.'

As soon as the words were out of his mouth, his twin visibly relaxed. When Charlotte changed her mind, it was clear that she had suspected her brother and had been trying to protect him. She looked earnestly at Kate and said, 'I for one hope you never catch who killed them. If you do, we'll be queuing up to shake their hand.'

93

The evening briefing began at nine. Hank updated the team on the state of play, taking questions from the floor afterwards. Jaded detectives were buoyed by the fact that Kate and Carmichael would be around to assist the investigation going forward, with Zac Matthews and Fay Hamilton helping to ease their heavy workload – as and when they could be spared from normal duties. It was a source of irritation that neither was 100 per cent at the disposal of the MIT. In a depleted organisation, every unit was struggling to keep up.

It was what it was.

When the team found out that it was Hamilton who'd linked the Bradshaws to the original crime scene, they broke into a spontaneous round of applause, Fay receiving a verbal slap on the back from those nearest to her.

She took it like a pro.

When the noise died down, Carmichael kicked off the meeting, informing everyone that she was trawling through Georgina's early service record to ID her mystery boyfriend, pre-Crawford.

'If he exists,' she added.

'I'm inclined to think that he does,' Kate said. 'Fay, you can help with that. Lisa will show you the ropes in the morning. Are you on social media?'

Hamilton's expression matched her words. 'Isn't everyone?'

'Personally, I'd rather eat worms,' Kate said.

A chuckle reverberated around the room.

'Dig up what you can on Julies.' For Hamilton's benefit, Kate explained that the club no longer existed but had been very popular in its day. 'Lisa has the dates we're interested in. Do what you can. People love to share memories. Try all platforms, but especially Facebook and Instagram. It's images we're after. You might find something useful.'

'Good luck with that,' Harry said. 'Everyone who went there ended up shit-faced.'

'Told you,' Hank grinned at Kate. 'If you can remember it, you weren't there.'

Hamilton laughed, too young to appreciate that the joke was old.

Hank asked Zac to give his input.

He didn't look happy as he stood to face the team. 'It's not good. Harvey's gone to ground. He's not been seen since he gave the obs team the slip Monday night. Our snouts haven't seen him either. Given that he likes an audience, the fact that Ella went missing the day after, we need to find her PDQ.'

'Fuck!' Hank exhaled. 'Anything else?'

'Yeah, I found his car at Bank Foot Metro station. Keys still in the ignition—'

'Just the car keys?' Kate asked.

'Yeah. Looks like he jumped out and legged it. The car's still there. Nowt of any interest inside. We'll keep an eye out, unless you want it uplifted?'

'No. Just keep us posted.'

'He won't be back for it, guv.'

'Zac's right,' Hank said. 'Harvey's not that stupid. He'll have left it there so he can say it was nicked when we pick him up.' He scanned the room, asking if there was any more intel to add.

Carmichael held up a finger to attract his attention. 'I consulted a guy who works at Newcastle University. He studies biometrics and has given evidence in criminal trials—'

Hank cut her off. 'We don't have the budget, Lisa.'

'And we all want to go home,' Harry said.

'I was only after an indication.' Carmichael's face flushed slightly. 'I know it wasn't green lit, but he agreed to compare the surveillance video from the crem with the gable end video and answer the simple question: could it be the same man? The scientist said the gable end video isn't long enough or of good quality. He's a great contact and super quick. I thought we could add his name to our database for future reference. If we find any more footage, he might be useful.'

Hank couldn't knock her effort.

'Do you have any more magicians up your sleeve?' he said.

'No.'

'I do,' Ailsa said from the back row.

'Blimey, we're drowning in officers using their nous,' Harry said.

'Yeah, and they're all female,' Jo said.

Everyone laughed.

Ailsa stood up so she could be seen. 'While you were out, I went to the Cook House restaurant like you asked. The description I got from the staff fits Nico Ioannou. Dark curly hair, lovely personality, foreign, just as Hank described him to me. When I checked the takings, there was a credit card payment for a pint of Augustinerbrau in his name, drawn on the National Bank of Greece.'

94

As she drove home, Kate couldn't quite believe what had come out of Ailsa's mouth. Having taken a punt on Nico's innocence, it looked like he'd lied about being at his restaurant till closing time on Christmas Eve. What other explanation could there be for Charlotte not using the family restaurant that night, or refusing to say who her dinner guest was?

What had he done?

Kate turned into her road. Relieved to see Jo's Land Rover parked outside their home, she pulled up behind it, jumped out and made her way into the house before next door's cat could get there. Hanging her coat in the hallway, she called out.

'Jo, I'm home.'

'In here.'

Following the voice, Kate arrived in the living room.

Jo was putting an LP onto an ancient turntable Kate had purchased during the pandemic. Like a lot of people, the nostalgia for vinyl had emerged when most people were re-evaluating, working out what was important, what to discard, what to hold on to, how to spend their free time and, it had to be said, their spare money. There was a wonderful crackle before the first track started playing, an oldie Jo had inherited when her father died: *Back in Central Park* from Earl Klugh's *Low Ride* album.

Kate smiled.

Jo loved New York, even though it now had associations that sent a shiver down Kate's spine. Last night, they had made a pact to visit together when travel restrictions were lifted. She slid her arms around Jo from behind, gently kissing her neck.

'Hey,' she whispered. 'I've been dying to do that all day.'

'Glad you picked me then.'

'Who else would I pick?'

'Hmm . . .' Jo turned, lifting a finger to her lips, a quizzical expression. 'Your new bestie, maybe. Ms look-how-fit-I-am Hamilton.'

'There's only one woman in my life. I'm looking at her. How was your journey?'

'Peaceful. Just me, a long strip of grey tarmac, a big sky and lots of sheep—'

'Heaven. Wish I'd been there.'

'So do I . . . you look wrecked. Tough briefing?'

Kate recounted Ailsa's revelation. 'I feel betrayed. It hurts.'

'You want wine?'

'Whisky.' Slumping down on the sofa, Kate kicked off her shoes, lifting her feet onto the coffee table, watching Jo pour two fingers of Lagavulin into glasses. 'The trouble with this job is I'm not looking for a villain I can hate.'

Jo handed Kate a glass and sat down, twisting her body so they were facing one another. 'If it *was* Nico, there's not a police officer alive who won't understand where he's coming from. Or how difficult it'll be for you to lock him up.'

'I won't let our friendship colour my judgement—'

'Nor should you. Take your emotions out of the equation and this case is no different from any other. If Charlotte and Nico were plotting to kill at the Cook House, they've been making a fool of you. In fact, it's worse than that. If they're guilty, they're taking advantage of your relationship with Georgina. Be angry, be furious, but don't feel sorry for them, or yourself. They don't deserve it and it doesn't suit you. They've been muddying the waters so you can't see clearly.' Jo paused. 'On the other hand, would they offer their DNA voluntarily if they were guilty? Why would they risk the possibility that you'd link them to the crime scene? That makes no sense.'

'It makes perfect sense. Shooting someone from a distance is

337

the best way of avoiding any transference at the scene. They're cops. They know we won't find anything.'

'You have Oscar and Charlotte's prints on record, don't you?'

'Yeah, we all provide them for elimination purposes. We don't have Nico's. In any case, none were found at the scene that we haven't already identified. I just wish they'd stop playing games.'

'If it is them, they can't think there's a hope in hell of getting away with murder. They know how good a detective you are.' Jo threw Kate a smile. 'Why don't we go up and I'll run you a bath?'

'I'm too wired to sleep. There's so much about this investigation that I still don't understand. If only I knew what Georgina was hiding. What could be so bad that she couldn't share it? She was good and kind, prepared to help anyone, close to her family and with a large circle of friends. I can hardly ask Nico about an old boyfriend, can I?'

'You can ask Charlotte.'

Kate shook her head. 'She won't talk to me.'

'How about Molly?' Jo meant Molly Hart, Georgina's mother.

'Did *you* discuss your love life with your parents? I didn't, not until you came along, and what an unmitigated disaster that turned out to be. Telling my dad, I mean, not meeting you.' Kate fell silent for a moment. 'I wish you'd met my mum. She'd have loved you as much as I do.'

'Your old man loves me now.'

'Yeah, after several years of twisting his arm.' Kate rested her head on the back of the sofa, closing her eyes. 'I failed to live up to his expectation of what a good daughter should be. You, on the other hand are goody two shoes, bringing a couple of kids into the equation, something I didn't give him. Tom and James are as close as he'll ever get to being a granddad. You humour him. I don't.'

'Maybe you should try.' Jo gave Kate some space to think on it. She'd never admit it, but she idolised her old man. Ed

Daniels was too stubborn to realise it. Jo would bring father and daughter closer if it was the last thing she did.

Within seconds Kate was fast asleep.

95

Kate woke at 5 a.m. in the living room, a blanket over her, the fire still on. As was often the case, her mind was already in gear as she opened her eyes, on this occasion thinking about Jo's suggestion that she contact Georgina's mother for help. She decided that she would pay Molly a visit. There was no reason why she should run her plan past Nico, though she thought she would. He might find out and jump to the conclusion that she was using a frail old lady to dig up dirt on the rest of the family.

He loved Molly.

They both did.

Kate felt both sad and guilty. Sad for a mother who'd outlived her child. Guilty, because she'd allowed her visits to tail off recently. Every time she walked through the door of Molly's care home her mood changed. She became tense and weepy, Kate's presence a reminder of the circumstances surrounding her daughter's death. Nico had been in such a state at the time, Kate had been the one to tell her. And, as her condition deteriorated, had Molly come to blame the death messenger?

If Nico was responsible for the Bradshaw murders, he might have been tempted to share that with his mother-in-law, reassuring her that they got their comeuppance before her mental capacity declined further. Easing his own conscience for not telling her that Georgina was never coming home, safe in the knowledge that if Molly repeated anything he said, it would be written off as delusional. Even if she was taken seriously, she'd never make a credible prosecution witness.

That was a whole other kind of hearsay.

*

Kate threw off her blanket, got up and walked to the shower, desperate to share her intention to visit Molly with Jo, including the reason why it might prove difficult. All of this she mulled over while she got ready for work. Since the global pandemic, protocols within care homes had been tightened, and rightly so. They were underfunded. Staffing levels worse than they had ever been, carers leaving in their droves, every additional visitor adding to an impossible workload.

At the breakfast table, Jo registered Kate's dilemma: to go or not. 'You're wondering if it's ethical to visit a sick woman for your own ends, aren't you?'

'Am I?' If looks could kill.

'Then don't go.'

'I'm *thinking*.'

Jo was aware of every nuance in Kate's voice, the subtle difference between what she was saying and what she meant, the subtext. 'Stop prevaricating. You have a double-hander to solve . . . and Ella is still missing. If Harvey didn't take her, someone else did. If you suspect that it's Georgina's ex, you need to find him. There may only be a slim chance of Molly helping with that but you must explore it, surely. Are you worried for her or yourself?'

'Don't analyse me please.' Kate looked away.

'Is that what you think I'm doing?'

'No . . .' Kate grabbed Jo's hand. 'I'm not angry with you. And you're right, it's not something I look forward to. Finding Molly floating between two states of consciousness, sometimes lucid, very often not, isn't unusual, though it is distressing, for both of us.'

Kate sighed, caught in the past.

One time when she arrived, Molly didn't recognise her. And yet, when Kate's mother died, Molly had stepped in as surrogate. They were so very close. Then there were the times she'd begged Kate to fetch Georgina, unaware that she was gone. The worst time of all was when Molly thought Kate was Georgina.

Jo squeezed Kate's hand. 'Hey, I was stating a fact. I didn't mean to upset you.'

'You didn't.'

Jo was unconvinced. 'You have an emotional connection to Molly. Your hesitation is understandable, but it's got to be done, Kate. A life is at stake. What alternative is there? If you're worried about Molly, don't be. A lot of people living with dementia remember events that happened decades ago and yet they don't recall what they were doing five minutes earlier. It's the nature of the disease. On this occasion, that might help rather than hinder you. You're examining a past you know nothing about. Look at it this way, do you think Molly would want you to rule her family out as suspects or not? Because, as I see it, Georgina's old boyfriend has as much of a motive to kill the people who killed her as anyone else.'

'Yeah, you're right.'

'Would you like me along?'

'I'd like nothing more. You're good with people, crazy partners included.' Kate managed a weak smile. 'But the home will be in semi-lockdown, one visitor at a time I imagine. Asking for them to make an exception isn't justified because I've lost my bottle. And for Molly's sake, the fewer people she's in contact with the better. Her safety is more important than having a wing man.'

'I agree. With any luck, you'll catch her on a good day.'

'I hope so.'

'Does Molly like music?'

'She used to, why?'

'Dementia patients often exhibit cognitive improvement when listening. The same goes for familiar voices. Keep talking to her, even if she doesn't respond. You never know, something might click.' Jo paused, adding a final reminder of why it was so important for Kate to make that visit. 'Kate, never lose sight of the person Molly once was, the person she still is, despite her confusion. If you remember that, you'll be fine, so long as you take it gently. It might seem cruel to humour her, but if it clears her son-in-law and grandchildren of any wrongdoing, it's what she'd want you to do.'

96

A breakfast meeting with Gillian Garvey was never going to be the most pleasant way to start a working day. For the most part, Kate sat in silence with little appetite for food, unlike the woman sitting opposite. When she'd finished eating, Kate reached down, removing the previous day's newspaper from her briefcase and slid it across the table.

'The headline is bad enough,' she said. 'The subhead is worse, Gillian. Did you think it was clever bolding the first letter of Charlotte, Oscar and Papa to spell out cop? You're inciting anti-police sentiment, pinning a target to the backs of the Ioannou family. It's unethical, irresponsible, bordering on libellous. More to the point, it's killing them. The shooting victims were part of an OCG, as well you know. Sadly, some of them are still breathing. Some of them can even read.'

Garvey laughed.

'I'm serious, Gillian. You'll end up with blood on your hands if you continue in this vein. I have a one-time offer for you to redeem yourself.'

There was flooding on the roads to Middle Earth. While Kate was held up in rush-hour traffic, with no let-up in the angry weather, she took the opportunity to call Nico, explaining that she had a mind to visit Molly, expecting a degree of resistance. She couched her idea in general terms, those that might draw a favourable reaction, without mentioning the mystery man she was now hunting.

'I'm sorry,' he said. 'I don't understand.'

'Well, without rubbing it in, journalists are on a fishing expedition. Their condemnation of police officers—'

'Don't you mean Oscar and Charlotte?' Nico interrupted.

'I mean all of us, me included. Fingers are pointing directly at the MIT. I resent the implication that we're dragging our feet on purpose, because that's what this witch hunt amounts to. We're under enormous pressure to put this case to bed and every police officer is under suspicion.'

'That's not what it feels like.'

'Please, hear me out . . .' The Audi moved forward in the line, a few metres only, adding to Kate's frustration. Time to up the ante. 'When I heard that there had been a five-hour stand-off at the Bradshaws' house, I was ready to tear a strip off a firearms officer because I knew the press were bound to see it as a conspiracy to protect whoever had taken revenge. That officer is now in a freezer at the morgue. Nothing will deter me from finding the person whose actions triggered the incident that resulted in his death.'

'And how can Molly help with that?'

Kate had to think quickly. 'I'm going back to basics, looking at Georgina's early service record to find out who she worked with, to see if I can ID anyone who might have snapped and done something off-the-scale stupid. By the same token, I must trace the friends she hung out with while she was living at home. I'm talking about before you and I knew her, anyone she was particularly fond of who might have avenged her death.'

'That's a long shot, given Molly's mental state.'

'Who else can I ask?' Kate crossed her fingers. 'How is she?'

'No deterioration since your last visit.'

Ignoring the dig, Kate pressed on. 'Then I'd like to try.'

'You could be wasting your time.'

'I'm aware.' She nudged him over the line. 'Anything I can do to take the heat off Oscar and Charlotte is worth doing. Please run it past them and let me and the care home know your decision.'

Nico saw no reason to deny Kate's request, though he warned her that care home staff might feel differently. They had other residents to consider. Visitors had to book in advance so they could keep the numbers down. His text came in at nine thirty, giving her permission to visit. There had been no objections from his son or daughter. Kate hoped that they were finally beginning to accept that she was covering all the angles, not merely considering the family as suspects.

Finishing her paperwork, she called the care home, keen to get there as early as possible. Experience had taught her that Molly was less agitated in the mornings, declining as the day went on.

'Good morning,' said the woman who picked up.

The voice and the accent were familiar to Kate. They belonged to Magda Hahn, the care home manager, a Polish national who'd come to Britain as a child and who had been so kind to Molly when she entered residential care following her diagnosis.

'Magda, it's Kate . . . Daniels.'

'Hello. I was expecting your call. I understand you wish to see Molly.'

'Please. I realise that the safety and well-being of residents is a priority, but I'm fully vaccinated. If you wish, I'll bring proof of my status and, of course, take a test beforehand . . . my visit is work-related, otherwise I wouldn't ask. I'd like to call this morning. Is that possible?'

'Hmm, Molly is an early riser. I'm not happy to interrupt her routine. She usually has a nap around ten.'

Kate checked her watch. 'How long will she be out?'

'Not long. We wake her with a cup of tea around ten thirty. It helps to settle her at night if she's active during the day.'

'I understand. That'll give me time to get there. Would eleven o'clock suit you?'

'Perfect. Her lunch is at noon.'

'I'll be gone by then.' Kate was about to thank her and hang up when Jo's voice arrived in her head, an echo of their earlier conversation. 'Magda, could you put on some soft music after Molly's nap?'

'You've been doing your homework.'

Kate smiled to herself. 'My adviser is a class act.'

97

Kate signed the visitor log, turning back a few pages, establishing that Nico had visited on Boxing Day afternoon, spending half an hour with his mother-in-law. Magda came out of her office to greet Kate, then led her along a wide corridor with grab rails on either side, the interior beautifully decorated in pastel shades that were pleasant on the eye. A huge Christmas tree adorned the residents' dining room, a dozen or so tables being set for lunch. Members of staff were wearing Christmas T-shirts and tinsel in their hair, keeping up appearances after a difficult couple of years.

Kate's job was often traumatic.

She couldn't have done theirs.

Molly's room was up one flight of stairs, at the end of a long corridor. It was larger and more expensive than most, Georgina insisting on giving her mother the best she could afford. It was a mini-bedsit, light and airy, her bed nearest to the door with an en suite bathroom; a lounge area at the far end, two armchairs for guests and a smart TV. Molly was sitting quietly, staring out of the rain-soaked window at the Simonside Hills in the distance, the radio on low, tuned to a channel playing classical music.

'Molly, you have a very special visitor,' Magda said as they approached. Georgina's mum looked at Kate, then at the care home manager, a blank look on her face. Magda threw her a lifeline. 'It's Kate, Georgina's friend. You remember Kate, don't you?'

Molly didn't answer, though her mouth turned up at the edges.

Her pale blue eyes twinkled as she met Kate's gaze for the second time. Her once auburn hair was pure white, tied in a messy bun at the nape of her neck. In contrast to other residents, Molly wore casual slacks, a baggy grey T-shirt, and modern loafers, like the ones she used to wear in her artist's studio. A pair of designer specs hung round her neck. She'd always taken care of herself.

'Hello, Molly . . .' Kate pulled up a chair and sat down. 'I brought treats.' Taking a box of chocolates from her bag, she placed it on the small round table beside Molly's reclining chair. Kate hadn't bought them. They were a gift from Jo's eldest son that she wouldn't miss. She'd grabbed them from home before setting off.

'I'm sorry I've not been in lately,' Kate said. 'I've been working long shifts at the police station.' Jo had told her to be precise.

There was no response from Molly, no outward sign that her interest had been piqued by either the chocolates or talk of police. Not the best of starts, but now she was here, Kate would spend time with the old lady, even if she had no recollection of ever having met her.

There was an open book turned upside down on Molly's knee.

Kate said, 'What have you got there?'

Molly didn't answer.

'It's a picture book, a present from Nico,' Magda said. 'Can I get you a cup of tea, Kate?'

Noticing Molly's empty cup, Kate asked, 'Molly, would you like a top-up?'

She shook her head.

'We're fine,' Kate said.

'I have to go,' Magda said. 'Ring the bell if you need anything.'

'Is it lunchtime?' Molly asked.

'Soon, I'll come and get you when it's ready.'

'I don't like potatoes.'

'Fibber . . .' The care home manager bent down to pick up Molly's empty cup and saucer, then stood upright, a wide smile on her face. 'You always manage to eat them.'

Molly giggled.

It was good to see her smiling.

Once they were alone, Kate found it hard to strike up a conversation. Molly's thought processes were painfully slow. She hadn't lost the capacity to communicate, but her responses were unpredictable and difficult to follow, her attention drifting off. She was staring at Kate now, more confused than ever. Had she forgotten Magda's introduction, or failed to retain the information, Kate's name along with it?

There was a holiday snap in a gilt frame on the windowsill. Georgina dancing in the foreground; Kate and Nico photobombing in the background. Kate got up and lifted it down, hoping it might help. Keeping her voice calm, she reminded Molly ever so gently of the day that it was taken, being careful not to say anything that might upset her.

'Georgina looks lovely in this photograph, doesn't she?'

Molly took it from her and seemed to settle. She hugged the frame. There was a long pause before she said, 'She loved to dance.'

'Yes!' Kate had an in. 'Didn't she used to go to Julies night club?' Not a flicker of recognition. The name meant nothing to Molly. Kate changed tack. 'I hear Nico came to visit recently. Did you have a good time?'

Molly acted as if she hadn't heard the question.

Was that the case or would she rather not talk about it?

Kate dropped the subject. The last thing she wanted was to upset Georgina's mum. It had always been a long shot. Kate would struggle without Jo to point her in the right direction. She was so much better at this stuff than Kate. As those thoughts passed through her head, she felt a slight tug on her hand.

Molly's cool fingers closed around hers, squeezing gently.

'Don't be unhappy, Kate.'

She couldn't speak.

Not only had Molly identified her for who she was, the

octogenarian was showing genuine concern for her welfare, as she'd always done. The thought made her want to weep. Holding hands felt fragile, like a frayed rope bridge across a vast ocean. However tenuous, it was a connection Kate was desperate to hang on to. Keen to keep the memory alive, and the conversation going, she finally found her voice.

'Hey, you know me. I'm always happy.'

'Not when your mother passed, dear.'

'No, I was very sad then, but I had you to help me over it.'

Molly's expression changed, in a positive way, as if in the depths of her subconscious she remembered that they were once close confidantes, that Kate was someone she loved, someone she could trust. Then her expression darkened. She became extremely agitated, wringing her hands, unsure of where to go next.

'Sometimes Georgina was sad too.'

'I know,' Kate said gently. 'Do you know why?'

Molly hesitated.

Kate gave her a moment. 'Molly, why was she sad?'

'It's a secret. She wouldn't come out of the bathroom. The door was locked.'

Kate had no clue where Molly had plucked that from, what day or even what decade she was in. A scenario entered Kate's head that made her blood boil.

This might lead somewhere.

Kate took Jo's advice to keep talking. 'Do you remember when that was, Molly?'

'In the summer. You know that.'

Kate knew squat. 'Did you tell me about it?'

'Yes.'

She hadn't. 'I'm sorry, I forgot.'

Molly said, conspiratorially. 'You weren't always her best friend you know.'

'I'm sure that's true . . .' Kate picked a random name from the air. 'That was Sarah, wasn't it?'

'No, silly . . . It was *Cally,* Cally Fitzsimmons. Until . . .'

Until?

The word was loaded. It floated in the air like a dark cloud. The expression in Molly's eyes could only be described as anguish. Kate didn't want to add to her distress. She'd have to tread carefully. 'Till when, Molly? Did Cally and Georgina fall out?'

A nod, a frown. 'I told her not to say anything. She said she had to, to keep Cally safe.'

Where Molly went, Kate followed. 'She wasn't safe?'

Molly's gaze returned to the window. Without looking at Kate, she said, 'They came home early, without eating their picnic.'

Kate was clueless.

She stroked the old lady's hand to soothe her. It seemed to be working. Molly's mind wasn't the only one in turmoil. Kate's thoughts were all over the place. She walked her way through the conversation in an attempt to make sense of it. Her guts were telling her that this event, whatever it was, had happened when the girls were relatively young. Could it have been the root of Georgina's sadness, the deep secret Kate had always known she was hiding?

A leap it may be, but it was plausible.

Going by her own experience as a youngster, falling out with mates was a regular occurrence. The source of discontent was usually petty jealousy of one kind or another. The girls had been out for a picnic and argued. What about was anyone's guess. Had a new kid edged Georgina out of Cally's affections or the other way around? Was their spat over a boy, perhaps? Was Cally mixed up with someone Georgina felt compelled to warn her about?

To keep Cally safe.

Before she moved into care, Molly had lived in the same home all her married life. When Kate's mother died, Molly took her in. She'd given Kate the key to Georgina's old room.

So why had she locked herself in the bathroom? Kate's nausea turned to revulsion as instinct took over. The answer was staring her in the face.

'Molly, did someone hurt Georgina?'

The old woman nodded.

A tear arrived on her eyelid. Like a small balloon on a piece of elastic, the weight took it over the edge, splashing onto her blouse. Silent tears turned to sobs as she relived the trauma. 'She was a child,' Molly said. 'I should never have let her go with him.'

'Who? Molly, help me understand. Who did she go with?'

'Cally's father.'

It all fell into place.

'Molly, listen to me—'

'I'm tired now.'

'I wouldn't ask if it wasn't important. Do you remember Mr Fitzsimmons' first name?'

'I want Magda.'

With great effort, Molly turned her back on her visitor, slamming the portal shut. Whatever the truth of it, Kate didn't have the heart to delve further. She pressed the call bell, convinced that Molly's memory was real. Cally's father was the secret Georgina had been keeping all those years. Whatever he'd done to her, it was so traumatic she'd taken it into adulthood, unable to share it with anyone, not even Kate.

Magda entered the room, shocked to see Molly so distressed.

Kate mouthed the word: *sorry*. 'Should I stay or go?'

'Go . . .' The manager dropped her voice to a whisper. 'Don't worry, she's unlikely to remember.'

98

Kate raced away from the nursing home, keen to reach base and liaise with Jo. Molly's cognition may be impaired, but her confusion was real, so too was her agitation. Kate was convinced that what Molly had told her, albeit disjointedly, was based in fact. Reaching the A1, Hank called, asking her to rendezvous in the centre of Newcastle. She agreed, too preoccupied to ask why, then hung up and speed-dialled the MIR.

The phone was answered immediately. 'Carmichael.'

'Lisa, I'll be longer than anticipated. I'm on my way to meet Hank in town. Drop what you're doing. I need you to trace someone as quick as you can. Her name is Cally Fitzsimmons. She'll be the same or similar age to Georgina, so a good place to start would be the schools we already have in the system. If you draw a blank, widen the field.'

'Who is she?'

'She may not even exist. If she does, it's her father we need to find.'

'First name?'

'No idea – assuming he's still alive. I'll explain later. Tell Harry to raise an action and put it down to me.'

'And if I can't find her?'

'Link it to the action I raised on Georgina's early police colleagues. It's a long shot, but someone she used to hang out with may know who Cally is and where we might find her. I'm not hopeful. I don't recall Georgina ever mentioning her, which may sound odd, but her mum seems to think they were best friends as kids. When they were kids there was a parting of the ways. It needs investigating.'

*

Harvey was shadowing Kate Daniels. Word had come through from his contact that she was now in charge. He kept his distance in the traffic, the peak of his cap pulled low. On second thoughts, he took it off and threw it into the footwell.

Caps at the wheel were a red flag to a cop.

Dropping the visor as the sun sank beneath the horizon worked equally well. Daniels was no slouch. If he got too close, she'd spot him. Depending on her mood, she had options: pull off and see if he followed, double back to ID him or call for backup, assuming she hadn't done that already. There was no sign that he too was under surveillance.

Yet.

Hank was waiting with his own updates when Kate arrived at Finnegan's, a traditional long bar not far from Nico's restaurant. He got a brief glimpse of her as she poked her head in. When she saw that the boozer was heaving, with standing room only, she stepped out, allowing the door to slam shut, leaving him in no doubt that he was drinking alone.

His phone rang.

He glanced at the screen.

Kate was listed as: Guess Who?

He tapped to answer. 'Boss.'

She was already in full flow. 'Drink up. I'm outside.'

'I saw you. You're not coming in?'

'Not on your life.'

She disconnected.

Finishing his half, he ordered another, placing a tenner on the counter. Telling the barman to keep the change, he made for the exit. Despite the fading light, he took in Kate's disapproval. She didn't need to say anything – her eyes were doing the talking – homing in on the full glass in his hand.

'You do know we're understaffed, right?' She didn't wait for an answer. 'I can't afford to lose you, temporarily or

355

permanently. What were you thinking? Couldn't you have chosen somewhere less risky?'

Harvey pressed his body hard against the wall, with only a slim view of what was going on across the road. Though he was too far away to hear what was being said, it was obvious that Daniels was tearing a strip off her DS.

Wondering why, Harvey moved in.

Crossing the road, he squeezed himself into a tight space where he wouldn't be seen. Daniels yanked Gormley off the main street and into a scruffy alleyway that ran down the side of the building, spilling his beer over the sleeve of his jacket in the process.

'Well?' Harvey heard her say. 'This had better be worth the detour.'

'Keep your voice down,' Hank said. 'It's where my informant hangs out.'

'Along with a deadly virus,' Kate reminded him. Hank had more strengths than weaknesses. Like a lot of the guys, he thought he was bulletproof. History had shown that he was not, so why put his health in danger? He had a wife, a son. Kate thought he had more sense than to hang out in crowded bars and told him so. 'Besides, you cannot be seen drinking in public. You'd better hope you weren't followed. I just got Garvey onside, though she'd love an opportunity to plaster your face across the front page with a pint in your hand. All she needs is a zoom lens and you'll be centre stage in Partygate 2—'

'It's a half.'

'Same difference.' Kate wasn't laughing. 'You're the SIO of a double-murder case.'

'Am I? The team would rather it was you—'

'Either way, the shooter is still out there. There will be a bloodbath if Christine's mob get hold of him. And in case you forgot, Ella's still missing.'

'And I'm working on it,' he said.

'Garvey will make it look like you're not.'

'Why do you think I'm here?'

'How many have you had?'

'One, I swear.' He held up his glass. 'And this one.'

'Where's your car?'

'I didn't bring it. That's why I rang you.'

'I'm not your personal taxi—'

'You've never minded before.'

'I don't mind now—'

'Your face does.'

Kate sighed.

How could she stay angry with a grown man who looked like a schoolboy caught behind the bike sheds? She dropped the subject. There were more important things to discuss. While he finished his beer, she smoked half a cigarette. This time she enjoyed it. A delivery lorry sped by on the main road, drowning out their conversation.

A wide arc of light flooded the street as three guys exited the pub, laughing and messing around, giving Harvey the once-over as they passed by, clocking the fact that he was earwigging someone else's conversation.

He pulled down his zip, urinating against the wall.

The men moved away.

Harvey swore under his breath. He'd missed some of the chat between Daniels and Gormley, information obtained from someone called Molly that Daniels said might lead somewhere. Was Molly Gormley's informant, Harvey wondered. His crew worked all over, in various jobs, but none in Finnegan's Bar as far as he was aware. From memory, none were called Molly either. He'd have to check with Tony.

He was the paymaster.

If anyone knew, it would be him.

Daniels had already changed direction, asking Gormley if

there was any other news that she should be aware of.

None she was going to like, he told her.

He leaned against a scaffold pole, shading his eyes from a security light that was pointing right at him, his back against the wall. 'Christine's gaff was clean, Kate. I mean the real one, not the temporary one . . .' He went on to tell her that ROCU had stormed the place with a warrant, backed up by armed support. 'It had been stripped of anything incriminating. Christine's mob shifted their operational HQ.'

'Do we know where?' Daniels asked.

'Bishop Auckland.'

'It didn't work for Cummings.' Daniels peered along the darkened alleyway. 'They may have a new address, but they won't be a million miles from here, Hank. They won't stop looking until the shooter is no longer breathing.'

She was right about that.

Gormley drained his glass. Daniels stubbed her fag out on the wall, flicking it into a nearby skip like a navvy. Harvey half-expecting her to light another. He'd learned something to his advantage tonight, something that would earn him Brownie points with Jacob. Someone in their organisation had grassed.

99

Martin Alexander was found by Police Scotland a couple of days later. He was with his wife and daughter, walking on the stunning coastal headland of St Abb's Head on one of the mildest New Year's Days Kate could ever recall. For generations his family had owned a small second home in Eyemouth. His brother had pointed the MIT in the right direction.

Outraged by the fact that police had picked him up in relation to an abduction, there and then Alexander had given detectives permission to search his car and holiday home. When they were done, the paramedic rang the MIR to speak with Hank. And when told that he was unavailable, he left a message that his brother Andrew had a spare key to his Heaton home, insisting that Hank have it forensically examined, so desperate was he to rule himself out of the investigation into Ella Stafford's disappearance.

It was not the police that bothered him.

Alexander was smart.

He'd seen Ella talking to a reporter on a local newsfeed. If she was linked to the shooting and he was linked to her, then it stood to reason that he was also being looked at for executing two OCG members. Alexander was in no doubt that their cohorts would act first and ask questions later.

Until Hank made an arrest, he was a marked man.

Alexander wasn't the only one Kate felt sorry for. The MIT were jaded, losing hope of ever finding Ella alive. If Alexander hadn't taken her, who had? Ailsa Richards was panic-stricken. The team rallied around, trying to lift her. She was in a bad way. Kate had known good people leave policing over less.

Kate sent Jo a text: **Need your help**.

The reply was instantaneous: **With?**

Ailsa's struggling. Don't want to lose her.
Leave it with me.
Let me clear it with her first.
Good plan. x

Kate invited Ailsa into her office for a chat.

She listened carefully, then said: 'Guv, I don't want special attention.'

'You're not getting it.' Kate studied her. 'We all need a sounding board occasionally. At the risk of sounding ancient, there was a time early in my career when I needed support. It came from a uniform sergeant who is no longer with us, a woman I've not forgotten. I'm not sending you to the force psychologist. Speak to Jo, off the record. Only the three of us and Hank will ever know. I guarantee it will help.'

Ailsa gave a resigned nod, got up and left the room.

As Kate watched her go, Neil Maxwell caught her eye through the doorway. Unlike Ailsa, he had a smile on his face. Unsure if he was trying to attract her attention, Kate pointed at her breastbone: *Me?* He nodded, beckoning her over. She got up, marched into the incident room to his desk. She sat down on the edge of it with hope mounting.

'What is it?'

'Is Ailsa all right?'

'Perfectly. Why?'

'She's not herself.'

Kate played dumb. 'She seems fine to me. You, on the other hand, look like shit.' She glanced at his computer screen. It was on pause mode showing Lee and Jackson Bradshaw walking beneath a green Customs Nothing to Declare sign in an unidentified airport, along with other passengers.

'You found them.'

'Yeah. No place to hide with so few travelling.'

'Is that *our* terminal?'

'Edinburgh.'

'About time. I was beginning to think you'd been asleep on the job.'

'Unfair, boss. I've had problems getting the footage. Half the staff have been laid off. I've had my eyes on the prize ever since.' He ran the footage on. 'Get a load of that swagger. They're off a flight from Alicante. Thought they were home and dry, until someone intervened. I wonder who knew they were coming.'

'Someone did,' Kate said.

'What d'you need, boss?'

'A sequence of events from the moment they touched down until the moment they were shot.'

'Is that all?'

'Cut the sarcasm. Get someone to confer with Alicante. What we're after is who dropped them off at the airport, who they spoke to, if they made any calls.'

'You have someone in mind?'

'Yes.' Kate glanced into the corridor. 'I've asked Ailsa to do something for me. Allocate it to her when she returns. I want you to focus on what happened this end. Either they were seen on arrival in the East End of Newcastle, someone tipped the killer off beforehand, or they were followed from Spain.'

'Understood.'

'Keep your eyes peeled, Neil. What I'm after is a timeline of their arrival, a minute-by-minute update of their movements through the airport terminal, including whether they got a bus, taxi or were picked up. If we can get a reg number that would be a bonus. And remember, we're not the only ones anxious to find this out. Bullock has financial resources we don't have. Money talks. He'll be on a spending spree trying to identify who dropped Christine's kids in the shit.'

Kate hung around while Maxwell switched between cameras, trying to keep up with the Bradshaw boys as they made their way through the terminal, two pairs of eyes trumping one. She stood, about to leave him to it, when something she saw on his computer almost knocked her sideways.

'Wait,' she said. 'Rewind a frame or two.'

He did, then pressed play.

'Stop. There.'

Kate narrowed her eyes, held her breath. As other passengers moved through the busy arrivals hall, a man was leaning against a pillar, checking his phone, or pretending to. Though his head was bowed, from a distance it looked like Nico. Eventually, he looked up, pocketing his phone.

'Jesus. Of all the scenarios, I didn't figure on this.'

'You're going to have to give us a clue,' Maxwell said. 'What or who am I looking at?'

She picked one guy out. 'You don't recognise him from Georgina's funeral?'

'I was nominated to mind the shop, remember? Who is it?'

'Nico's brother, Nils. The man I suspect Charlotte had dinner with on Christmas Eve, the reason she couldn't or wouldn't say who she was with. Till now, it never occurred to me that the Ioannou family might have hired a hit man from abroad. If this is what I think it might be, I suspect no money changed hands.'

'At least it's not a cop—'

'Not a British cop,' she corrected him. 'He's what the Greeks call special services division. I can think of no innocent scenario that involves him arriving in the UK off a Spanish flight . . . if that's what he did. I want a copy of the passenger manifest on my desk PDQ. And find Hank urgently. He needs to know we have another suspect.'

100

Kate had much to be grateful for. A lot had happened in the last few days. A briefing had been hastily arranged to discuss the way forward. She picked up her notes, glancing at the electronic murder wall as she entered the MIR. While the open-unsolved investigation had been concluded, the MIT were convinced that the shooting incident was a revenge attack. The diagram on screen looked like a big wheel with an image of Georgina at the centre, and spokes fanning out in all directions, listing her family, work colleagues, close friends, and other associates.

The HOLMES system listed many more categories.

The diagram contained the names of persons of interest for the shooting, more than she could count on one hand. Taking them chronologically and in order of importance, under the family heading were Nico, Charlotte and Oscar, Nils Ioannou having been added to the mix. When picked up by Greek police, he claimed he'd arrived in the UK to spend Christmas with Charlotte.

She later confirmed it.

Initially, Hank didn't believe a word of it. He changed his mind for two reasons. One: Nils had agreed to fly to the UK to be questioned on the next available flight and was in the air at this very moment. Two: he was not on the passenger manifest from Alicante to Edinburgh. He was on another flight altogether and had tickets to prove it.

Whether he'd flown into Edinburgh by chance or been fed intelligence and choreographed his arrival to coincide with the Bradshaw brothers landing in the UK was a question no one had an answer for. Was Nils playing games? Was Charlotte? The family had always been, and still were, the most likely suspects, acting together or separately.

The weak link was Oscar.

For days Kate had pored over the investigation, viewing Hank's notes with the sharp eyes of a surgeon. She shifted her gaze to the category containing Georgina's work colleagues where Hank had scribbled **How long is a piece of string?** This was a statement of fact, not an attempt at sarcasm. In a time period approaching three decades they were simply too numerous to mention by name. Despite extensive questioning of those closest to Georgina, not a shred of evidence had been found against any police officer.

Not one of them was acting odd.

No one was discounting Christine's crew. Unless he'd been superseded by Harvey, Tony Bullock stood to benefit the most from Lee and Jackson's rapid exit from their mother's criminal enterprise. Had one of them taken objection to their home-coming, fearing that they might have to step down, pushing them out of the action? Had someone else? Was it an unknown gang trying to rid the area of the competition? These were all possibilities. Either way, no hard evidence had come to light to sway the enquiry one way or the other. Proof, it seemed, was hard to come by, even from Hank's trusted informant.

The smart money was on the cops.

Kate felt physically sick.

Setting her papers down on a nearby desk, she rubbed at her temples. She had a raging headache, physically and metaphorically. Martin Alexander arrived in her thoughts unbidden, a man whose only involvement was that he had the misfortune to live near the crime scene. Other than that – and the fact that his brother was an ex-cop – there was nothing to link him to the shooting. He'd done his civic duty by coming forward as a witness, only to be picked up by police, forced to explain himself.

He wouldn't step up again.

Another random individual took his place in Kate's aching head: Dr Alan Crawford – the man whose heart Georgina had so cruelly broken, if he was to be believed. He'd also been eliminated, having provided a watertight alibi for the time of the shooting, which left the mystery ex-boyfriend he claimed was someone Georgina was keen to distance herself from all those years ago.

His ID was still unknown.

Did he even exist?

The more Kate thought about this, the more convinced she became that the answers were born of historical events. How that linked to the shootings was less clear. As investigations go, this one had been a mare from start to finish for Hank and their team of detectives.

Kate glanced at him.

He was at his own desk, happy among his colleagues.

Due to the complexity of the case, he'd stepped aside as SIO. His decision, not hers. It was viewed by the team as a good move, in no way a reflection of his expertise. In drawn-out enquiries such as this, detectives needed their leader. Kate had taken over officially. Unofficially, she would ensure that Hank took the credit when the case was resolved.

It would be . . . it was only a matter of time.

It had to be said that even before she left her office, her brain had been scrambled, except for a glimmer of light that had arrived in the darkness, delivered by Carmichael when her boss most needed it. Lisa had finally traced Cally Fitzsimmons. For reasons Kate didn't entirely understand, she was convinced that this woman – whose birth certificate named her father as Richard – held the key to unlocking the case. That's where she'd go next.

101

Carmichael briefed the team on her discovery, circulating her written notes as an aide-memoire. Cally lived in the coastal village of Low Hauxley, a fisherman's cottage she owned jointly with her husband, Maurice Bainbridge, whose name she'd taken. The couple had lived there for twenty-five years since getting married. Kate decided to pay them a visit without announcing her intention beforehand, giving Georgina's childhood friend no time to prepare for the questions coming her way.

To some, that might sound unethical, but if Molly had been right about the breakdown of Georgina's relationship with her childhood friend – more importantly the reason for it – Cally would most likely work out why a high-ranking detective wanted to speak with her urgently, even after all this time. Kate was keen to avoid stressing her out before she got there. If indeed she knew what her father had been up to.

No matter which way their conversation went, she was mindful of the fact that the woman would need support, assuming the picnic Molly had alluded to was more than a figment of her imagination.

Had she got her wires crossed?

Could Kate rely on anything she said?

The most direct way to Cally's house was the A189 coastal route north that took Kate past Northumbria Hospital's A & E, where Lee and Jackson Bradshaw would've been taken had they still been alive when the firearms team stormed the temporary residence their mother had rented as a hideaway – a place of safety for her fugitive sons. Kate still couldn't understand Don's decision to drag his boys inside the house, or Christine's lack of action immediately afterward. If she'd dialled 999, it would not have helped Jackson. It might have saved Lee. As it was, neither had survived. Lee had stopped breathing, as had his father, on the same floor where Ash lay unconscious hours later.

What a waste.

As the miles rolled by, wind turbines revolving over lush green fields on either side of the road, Kate's thoughts drifted to the crime scene, then to the footage from Ash's headcam as he made that fatal shot to save himself, a video Carmichael would have watched a million times since. There wasn't a hope in hell of her not having retained a copy. Kate would give anything for her not to have seen it.

Focus.

Kate had allowed her attention to wander from her current assignment. That was testament to the seriousness of what she faced when she ran out of road in Low Hauxley. The small village was literally on the beach, facing the North Sea, one of many coastal villages where Jo and Kate dreamt of owning a home when they retired.

Reluctantly, Kate contemplated her upcoming interview with Cally Bainbridge, certain that she held the key to what happened to Georgina when they were the best of friends. Post-briefing, Jo had warned Kate not to begin there. Before she could explain what she meant by that, she received an urgent call and rushed off, leaving Kate none the wiser.

She slowed down, calling Jo's mobile to check on her.

She picked up immediately. 'Hey.'

'Hey, you. Everything OK?'

'Yeah, sorry I had to dash . . . false alarm. Where are you?'

Kate checked the road sign. 'Woodhorn, on my way to see Bainbridge. Have you got a moment; I need your advice—'

'It's New Year's Day.'

'If I'm working, you're working.'

'I meant Cally. She could have a houseful—'

'Then we'll go somewhere quiet. Unless you'd rather I wait until she's at work, to have some line manager poking his nose into her business, wanting to know why police want to speak to her?'

'No, of course not.'

'Today it is then. I've been weighing up the odds, trying to organise my thoughts. If Georgina had been the victim of a sexual assault, perhaps Cally had too, though that is by no means a given—'

'Either way you need to build a rapport before tackling the subject head-on. Historical abuse allegations require careful handling—'

'I'm not a complete idiot.'

'Did I say you were?'

'That's what I heard . . .' Kate grimaced. 'Sorry, I know you mean well, but I've done this more times than I care to remember. Don't worry, I'll proceed gently.'

'I know you will.'

'Upsetting Bainbridge on the first day of a new year is not something I look forward to, Jo. What if Georgina got cold feet about telling her? If she doesn't know what her father was up to, I'm about to break her heart.' Kate fell silent for a moment before adding, 'I wish Molly had been clearer about why and how the girls fell out. I can't breeze in there assuming that an allegation was made and rejected, can I?'

'It might be the case—'

'Yeah, and it might not be.'

'If Georgina did warn her, the fallout would be messy. Most girls idolise their fathers. Even you did, once upon a time. Imagine your reaction if a friend had called Ed an abuser. What kid wouldn't flip under those circumstances? It would explain their sudden split, wouldn't it?' Jo abruptly stopped talking.

Kate knew she had more to say. 'Jo? Talk to me.'

'There is an alternative scenario—'

'Which is?'

'Cally already knew what her father was capable of.'

'And didn't alert Georgina to watch herself around him? Some friend.'

'Did Georgina share it with you? No, and you were best mates. Sexual abuse is shrouded in secrecy, always has been, always will be. You know that.'

'How does that help?'

'It doesn't. You're going to have to play it by ear. I once interviewed a kid who admitted that when her father moved on to a younger child within the family, the only thing she felt was relief – and still she didn't say anything. She was so tortured by guilt and shame, she attempted suicide.'

'Noted . . .' Kate took a sharp bend in the road. Prompting disclosure was never easy. She'd give anything not to do it. 'I'm hanging up now. I have ten minutes to get my head straight. If I don't manage that before I arrive, the minute Cally opens her front door, she'll know I'm not first-footing.'

102

A force ten was blowing inland when Kate parked up twenty minutes later, the blustery wind shaking her Audi like a toy. The car door almost flew off its hinges as she got out and slammed it shut. She glanced at the sea, deep blue today and shimmering in the sunshine. It was another world up there, far removed from her working environment a mere thirty-seven miles away.

She felt calmer now, and not only due to her surroundings. Chatting with Jo had been incredibly helpful, allowing her to see the big picture, the grey areas, the possible consequences for all concerned. She'd given Kate the right steer on multiple occasions. It was good to have her perspective. They supported one another, but for the next few hours Kate's duty of care was to the woman she'd come to see.

Pulling her coat around her, Kate approached the house, as ready as she would ever be to find what she'd come for.

The truth would do.

The house was pretty, yards from the beach, a square of decorative film applied to the centre of the living room window depicting a Christmas wreath to welcome guests. On a day like this, Kate could see why. If a traditional one had been hanging on the front door it would now be twenty miles away. She noticed that residents had placed large stones on top of dustbins and exterior letter boxes to stop them blowing away.

A smartly dressed woman opened the door, holding down her skirt so it wouldn't fly up. She looked younger than Georgina, a friendly face, intelligent eyes behind designer specs. Above the roar of the wind, Kate could make out piano music. For a split second she had visions of a family party going on.

'Mrs Cally Bainbridge?'

'Yes.'

'I'm so sorry to disturb on New Year's Day.' Kate held up ID. 'I'm Detective Chief Inspector Kate Daniels, Northumbria Police. I'm hoping you might be able to help me with something that I'm afraid can't wait.'

Her face said: *Today, really?*

Her mouth said: 'You'd better come in.'

Kate detected no nervousness as Cally stepped aside, hanging on to the door as she entered. The house was warm and cosy, the distinctive smell of cinnamon and cloves permeating the air. Kate would give anything to be at home with a large glass of mulled wine. In the hallway, she turned to face the woman she'd come to see.

'Apologies if you're entertaining,' she said.

'I'm not any longer. My company just left.' Cally retrieved half a glass of red wine from the hall table and held it up. 'Happy New Year!'

'And to you.'

A noise from the kitchen drew their attention. The man filling the dishwasher didn't look round. With his back to Kate, she was unable to establish his age. Husband . . . or father? Christ, that's all she needed. If this was Richard Fitzsimmons, things could turn ugly. Kate showed no emotion as she refocused on Cally who seemed to have read her mind.

'My husband,' Cally said. 'Maurice.'

Kate felt the tension drain away.

'You saved me a job.' Cally dropped her voice low. 'It's time he got his finger out.'

'Is there somewhere we can talk privately?'

'Can I get you anything before we sit?'

'A day off,' Kate said.

Cally laughed.

Opening the door to the living room, she ushered Kate inside. Apologising for the mess, she disappeared for a moment, presumably to tell her husband that she had a visitor and not to disturb them. She reappeared seconds later, pointing to the sofa.

Kate sat and so did she.

Crunch time.

103

Cally was open, friendly, the type of person Georgina would choose to associate with. The big question was, would she come across or stall? Kate could ask herself the same question. Reminding someone of a trauma they had spent their whole life trying to forget, felt cruel. It would leave a bad taste in the mouth of any detective. Unable to postpone or shy away from tackling these serious issues, Kate bent down, taking a notepad from her bag, buying herself time, remembering the warning Jo had left her with.

Tread carefully.

'How can I help you, Kate? Can I call you that?'

'Of course . . .' Since her host was using first names, Kate would too. 'I'm investigating the murder of two young men who were shot on their doorstep a week ago. You may have heard about it on the news?'

'Yes, dreadfully sad, but I'm struggling to see what that has to do with me.'

That was her first mistake.

There would be more . . .

If Cally had been reading up on the case, or watching TV, she'd have seen the associated images, Georgina's face plastered everywhere.

Impossible to miss.

'The civilian victims were suspected of killing a police officer three years ago. You may remember it triggered a man-hunt and was a protracted and complex case that has only just been resolved. I can't go into detail, other than to tell you that the officer's name was Georgina Ioannou.' Kate never took her eyes off Cally. 'You may have known her as Georgina Hart.' Kate could tell from Cally's reaction that she knew something.

373

'I'm speaking to everyone who was familiar with her. Friends, family, colleagues, particularly those who knew her prior to or shortly after she joined the police, those she worked with early in her service. I'm background-checking, that's all. Anything you can tell me about her would be helpful. You do remember her?'

'I do. Georg . . .' Her voice caught in her throat, the first sign of stress. 'We went to the same school.'

Even though Cally had taken her there, Kate was wary of touching on her childhood just yet. Keen not to panic her, she reached for a way to steer the conversation in another direction. Before she grasped it, her interviewee filled the silence.

'Naturally, I was very sad to learn of her death.'

'What was she like?'

'Lovely . . . she was lovely . . . as a kid, I mean.'

Kate nodded, without giving away the fact that she already knew that the two had been close friends as children. Cally wasn't at the funeral. Kate had already checked. 'And as an adult?'

'No clue, sorry. Sadly, we lost touch.'

Kate wanted to ask when, but she'd be walking into a dead end. Instead, she chose a related question. 'When was the last time you saw her?'

'We didn't see each other through our teens.'

'And later?'

Cally shrugged. 'I saw her in Newcastle once or twice when we were in our twenties. Georgina was hard to miss. We never spoke. It was in a crowded club. I was with a bunch of mates. She had company. I didn't want to interrupt.'

Or couldn't face her, Kate was thinking.

She took a moment to digest what Cally had said, wondering if Georgina's company was male or female, if this might be Dr Alan Crawford or the mystery man he'd spoken of, who the MIT had yet to ID, let alone trace.

'A club? Would this by any chance be Julies?'

Cally's eyes widened in surprise. 'Why d'you ask?'

'Was it?' The witness didn't reply. Kate gave her a nudge that might divert her from the wrong answer, an untruthful answer. 'My team are analysing photographs as we speak, identifying people who were there.'

Cally fell for it. 'Is that how you found me?'

Kate could have put her mind at rest. She chose not to. She wouldn't dream of telling her the truth. Bringing Molly into the conversation wasn't a road she wanted to go down. Kate could've blamed the school register, which would also be the truth, but then she'd be heading into another blind alley involving Cally's childhood.

'Was it Julies?' Kate repeated.

'I think it was, yes.' Cally picked up her wine, took a discreet sip and replaced the glass, avoiding Kate's gaze. After a while, she looked up and said, 'I'm not sure I can help you, Kate. As I said, we'd gone our separate ways. Georgina and I were never that close, even at school.'

Molly's voice arrived in Kate's head . . .

You weren't always her best friend, you know.

Cally was a terrible liar.

Kate let it ride . . . for now. She needed to keep her onside. There were valid reasons why a victim of abuse, or the child of an abuser, would wish to distance themselves from their past, even from a police officer, some might say especially from a police officer. Victims had not always been taken seriously or treated well. Kate had no intention of making that mistake.

'On the contrary,' she said. 'You are helping . . . a lot.'

Cally visibly relaxed.

Kate probed further. 'As I said, I'm interested in the company Georgina was keeping. On the nights you saw her, was her "company" male or female?'

'Georgina wasn't gay, if that's what you mean.'

'How do you know if you'd lost touch?'

'I, I don't . . . I know what I saw though . . .' Cally became

375

flustered. 'They were on the dance floor, unable to keep their hands off one another.' Her expression changed from intrigue to alarm. 'You're looking for the man who avenged her death, aren't you? The person who killed those boys. I thought . . . I mean . . . no offence, but the press suggested it was a police officer.'

The witness was smart, like Georgina.

'Is that what you think happened?'

Cally shrugged. 'Why else are you here?'

'My team are following a number of lines of enquiry.' Kate gave her a moment. 'Cally, I'd like you to think very carefully. Can you describe the man you saw her with?'

'Now you're asking. It was a long time ago.'

'You seemed to have a very clear image of them dancing. Please do your best. It could be important.'

Cally got up and stood at the window looking out, as if the sea crashing onto the beach beyond would give her the answer, then she turned and shook her head. 'I'm sorry, Kate. He was taller than her . . . handsome.'

'Age wise?'

'Same as her, I guess.'

'Not younger?'

'Not that I recall. It's something you notice, right? I'm not being rude, but I'd like you to go now. I don't want to talk about this any more.'

'I can understand you not wanting to get involved. I do—'

'It's not that,' she snapped.

'What then?' Kate was struggling to decipher her expression. 'A few minutes ago, you said that you didn't know Georgina that well, which is interesting. I have already spoken to a witness who seemed to think that you were inseparable.'

The woman shrugged, colour rising.

She hadn't expected that and didn't know how to respond.

'We fell out. Girls do.'

'Is that what's upsetting you?'

'Why are you making such a big deal of it?' Cally's tone was brittle. 'We both had other friends.' She was struggling not to cry. Returning to her seat, she bent down. Reaching for her glass, she took a drink.

Kate gave her a moment to compose herself.

Georgina's advice arrived unbidden . . .

When you're talking to victims, it's all about them not you, Kate.

'Cally, I didn't come here to upset you.'

'Didn't you?'

'No, I would never do that. Is there something you'd like to tell me?'

'No, but there's something you'd like to ask me, isn't there?' She began to cry, silent tears. 'It's my father you should be asking, assuming you can find him. Isn't that who you're looking for?'

'I am now,' Kate said.

'Good luck with that. The selfish bastard left my mum and me penniless when I was twenty-three. I thought he'd fled because he was about to be outed as a child abuser.' Cally paused for a long moment. 'That night in the club, I'd seen how happy Georgina was. I thought she'd met a man she could trust, someone she'd confided in, someone who'd given her the courage to go to the police for what my father had done to her.'

'She told you what he'd done?'

Cally nodded, a tortured expression. 'I didn't believe her at first. Why would I? He'd never laid a finger on me. I've been over that day a million times. We were eleven, sitting side by side in the back of my father's car on our way to the riverside to fish. Georgina was wearing shorts and a vest, a purple ribbon in her hair, a big smile on her face. Her mum had packed us a picnic: sandwiches, cake, and home-made lemonade. We'd eaten the cake before we got there.'

She was sobbing now.

'Take your time,' Kate said gently.

'We sat on the bankside, bare legs dangling in the water.

377

My father set Georgina up with a rod and line, then took me further along the riverbank, a hundred yards, maybe more. I begged him to let me sit with Georgina. I couldn't even see her. He refused, saying we'd disturb the fish we were there to catch. When she told me what he'd done to her, deep down I knew that he'd choreographed the whole thing and that she was telling the truth. I'm so sorry.'

'You have nothing to be sorry for.'

'Oh, I do. In the months and years that followed, I stood by and watched her suffer, unable to keep up with schoolwork, failing her grades in subjects she excelled at. She was so bright. It was agonising watching her decline. And still, I couldn't accept that my father was a monster. I did nothing to help.'

Kate's eyes felt like deep pools of hot water. Blinking away tears, she kept her gaze on Cally. Georgina's best friend deserved her support. More than that, she needed to see that her story mattered.

'You can't blame yourself, Cally. You were a child.'

'I should've *done* something.'

Kate leaned forward, taking her hand. 'It wasn't your fault.'

Another sob. 'For years, I buried it. When he left, I told my mother, begging her to go to the police. She denied it too, until she checked her bank account a few days later. He'd pissed off with twenty grand, their life savings. To save face, she let the neighbours believe that they had decided to separate and didn't report him, as an abuser or a missing person. She was so ashamed and went to her grave believing that he'd left the country.'

104

Kate summoned Jo to Bright's office. They sat down, Kate resting her head against the wall, staring at the ceiling. As she left Low Hauxley, she wondered why Richard Fitzsimmons had hung around for so long after abusing Georgina.

'You want to talk about it?' Jo said gently.

Kate blew out a breath, rolling her head sideways, tired eyes meeting Jo's. 'This job sucks sometimes, but I did something good today.'

'You managed to get Cally over the line?'

Kate gave a nod. 'The woman has never talked about Georgina or what her father did to her when they were kids. Now she has.' Jo listened attentively, acting as a sounding board as Kate explained how the discussion went. 'She begged me to hunt him down and punish him, in case he's still abusing kids.'

'He must be some age now.'

'Late seventies. You think that'll stop him? He took twenty grand in cash from the marital bank account. Nothing since. He's not used or updated his passport or driving licence. He made no application to change his name legally, though he may have done so informally. I imagine he had everything in place in case anyone blew the whistle on his disgusting behaviour. He had no intention of changing his ways. Cally hasn't heard from him since the day he walked out. Not a word. No Christmas or birthday cards. He just took off, end of. If he is alive, even if he's abroad, I intend to keep my promise and bring him to justice. He blighted the lives of his wife, his kid, Georgina . . . and probably countless others. If I have anything to do with it, he will pay.'

'Oh, Kate. You look utterly spent.'

'It was worth it,' she said. 'For no other reason than to give Cally the opportunity to offload. You helped me face the dragon too. To be honest, I was more emotional than I ought to have been going in.'

'Too close to be objective?'

'Something like that. I could have sent someone else, but it was something I had to do myself.' Kate's bottom lip trembled. 'I had the strangest sensation that Georgina was with me as I walked through the door, urging me on.' Tears pricked her eyes. 'There was a moment when I was barely hanging on. I nearly lost it when Cally crumbled. It was painful for both of us. I laid it on thick, told her what an amazing police officer Georgina had become, how she'd married a lovely bloke and had a family she adored, that she was a survivor who hadn't allowed an abuser to ruin her life.'

'That was the right thing to do. I'm proud of you.'

'Cally will never be guilt free. I only hope that one day she's able to forgive herself or at least come to terms with her silence. If she'd spoken up, her old man would probably have gone to jail, but it would also have broken her mother's heart. She was a kid in an impossible situation.'

'The guy she saw Georgina with. Do you think it's the one Crawford talked about?'

'A definite maybe. She described them as besotted with one another.'

There was a knock at the door.

Kate looked up to find Zac standing there.

Pulling herself together, she waved him in.

He entered, followed by Hank, Carmichael and Ailsa.

'What's with the delegation?' Kate said.

Zac looked at Hank. 'After you.'

'DNA results are in,' he said. 'Assuming any of the DNA we collected belongs to the shooter, the good news is that Nico, Oscar and Charlotte don't appear to be implicated. Given the familial connection, I'm guessing it rules out Nils too. None of the samples match. We can't link them to the scene.'

380

Carmichael added: 'You should also know that Nils provided the relevant documentation to support his claim. His arrival in Edinburgh at Christmas *was* coincidental. He booked at short notice. There were no direct flights to Newcastle. He was offered Thessaloniki – Munich – Heathrow – Newcastle at a huge cost, not far short of two grand. As opposed to Thessaloniki – Munich – Edinburgh for three two five. No brainer. Besides, he doesn't have the gait of the man seen in the lane behind the crime scene. He picked up an injury. Surgery was required. His leg is in a brace, guv.'

Something was off.

Kate took in each one in turn before asking, 'So, if the family are out of the equation, why am I not seeing relief on your faces?'

'Oscar's sample matches one taken from Ella's house,' Zac said.

'Fuck!' Kate wiped her face with her hands, staring at him, an expression of disbelief.

For a moment no one spoke, including Jo who – by the look of her – was also in denial, unable or unwilling to accept irrefutable forensic evidence that Oscar might have done something bad, something that could put him away for a very long time. It was Ailsa who eventually broke the silence with questions for Hank.

'Didn't you say Oscar was a twin? How do we know the DNA isn't Charlotte's?'

'They're not genetically identical,' he said.

Kate asked, 'Where was it found?'

'On a mug CSIs lifted from the draining board in the kitchen and his dabs are all over it.'

'You're asking me to believe that he sat down, had tea with Ella, then abducted her without taking the bloody mug with him? For Christ's sake, he may not be the brightest, but he's no halfwit. Find him, NOW!'

'Already happening,' Carmichael said.

'Good work.' Kate's mood lifted momentarily.

Hank hated dragging her down again. 'It gets worse.'

105

'How could it possibly get worse?' Kate was almost yelling.

'Nico is not their father,' Hank said.

She exploded. His revelation was the worst possible news. She got up and paced the room, her mind racing through the implications – and not only for the investigation. She swung round to face them.

'Who else knows about the DNA results?'

'Only the six of us,' he said. 'And the lab.'

'Get on to them. Tell them if this gets out, heads will roll. If any of our lot ask, the results are not yet available. Lie if you must. Say they've been mislaid. I don't care. You cannot share this. It'll have devastating consequences for Georgina's family. They have enough to cope with, which will only get worse when we bring Oscar in.'

'They'll need to be told at some point,' Carmichael said.

'We'll handle that when we get there, Lisa.' Kate was on a roll, thinking on her feet, moment to moment. 'We have work to do first. Ella is out there somewhere. I refuse to accept that we're too late.' Kate noticed Richards filling up. 'Ailsa, there's still hope. Hang on to that thought.'

She panicked. 'If Oscar has her, and we arrest him, he won't cough to her abduction. Why would he?'

'Which means we're on the clock. You're good for this. Don't let me down.'

'I won't.' Ailsa stood tall, showing what she was made of. 'Give the results to me. I'll sit on them. When they need to be resurrected, I'll mysteriously find them paperclipped to something else. If the wheel comes off, I'll take one for the team.'

Kate had suddenly come alive.

'Pull up a pew.'

They all sat down.

'I know what this looks like regarding Ella's disappearance, and I accept that possibility. I'm not buying the rest. This shooting is not about a son avenging his mother's death. There's more to it than that. One, Oscar hasn't got the balls. Two, there's a historical element that's not been fully explored.'

The others weren't following.

'What did we miss?' Hank said.

Kate abridged what she'd just told Jo about her meeting with Cally Bainbridge. 'The upshot is, we haven't yet found Georgina's abuser and we're not likely to. Richard Fitzsimmons appears to have disappeared off every official radar without trace. He probably has a completely new identity. We'll keep looking, but I now have two independent witnesses who claim that around the time the twins were conceived, Georgina was infatuated with a man they both saw with her in Julies. That guy obviously wasn't Nico. I checked the timeline. She went on holiday to Greece soon afterwards and met him there.'

'Two witnesses?' Carmichael said.

'Crawford and Bainbridge,' Kate said. 'Until Oscar is in custody, we have one priority. That's to find the man Georgina was seen with at Julies, the person who, deep down, I believe may have avenged her death, the guy I now suspect shares the same DNA profile with Georgina's children. Lisa, I want you to create a timeline from nine to twelve months before Charlotte and Oscar were born. I want to know about everyone who was in Georgina's life, anyone who might have known this guy. Pay particular attention to the women you find. Men are less likely to notice these things.'

Hank said, 'If Crawford and Bainbridge saw her, the whole world probably did.'

'Then it won't take long to find him. She was young, could have dated any number of guys. I'm less interested in who she may have been seen with. More interested in finding a confidante, someone who can confirm our guy's identity.'

'I agree with Kate,' Jo said. 'It's one thing being turned on by someone on a dancefloor when you're half-cut at two in the morning in a sweaty nightclub. It's another, sharing your most intimate details of that relationship with someone else. Females quickly learn to hold back, especially at work, right?'

Kate didn't let up. Her brain was fully in gear, sifting intelligence gathered during the investigation, none more pertinent than actions completed in the past few days, beginning in Berwick with Dr Alan Crawford. 'If Georgina was seen once with the guy Crawford gave us, we could write it off as a good night out. She was seen twice, by different witnesses, on separate occasions: once when they were into each other, once when they weren't. Deep down, I know that we are closing in. And until I can question Oscar, we have two lines of enquiry: this and finding Ella Stafford. Get to it.'

106

There were no arguments. Ailsa asked if she could help in any way. Kate shook her head, telling her that she'd have to complete the action on Lee and Jackson's arrival in Alicante, a question of dotting i's and crossing t's, due diligence no SIO could afford to ignore.

Hank agreed.

'I've done it,' Ailsa said. 'It's now with Harry.'

Kate smiled at Hank. 'Didn't I tell you she was good?'

Ailsa continued: 'It was a last-minute booking made directly with the airport. A taxi dropped them off. They made it through security in the nick of time, ran through the concourse, arriving at the check-in gate with minutes to spare. Maxwell said they used the loo when the plane touched down in Edinburgh, then jumped in what looked like a cab. Only it wasn't.'

'Makes you so sure?'

'There were two men in the front and the so-called cab had a dodgy plate.'

'Have we got them en route from Edinburgh to Newcastle?'

'No, guv. They swapped vehicles. The cab was found abandoned on Ingliston Road, not far from the airport. Nearest CCTV is the Holiday Inn Express, but there's nowt on that. I had it checked.'

'Well, we know they didn't go straight to Christine's gaff.'

'That I can help you with. Between leaving the airport and arriving at the crime scene, I suspected they might have been out celebrating. Zac suggested I check out their usual haunts with ROCU. They gave me a few pointers.'

'You found them?'

'Out on the hoy in Livello cocktail bar. I pulled the CCTV. Christine's driver was waiting outside. He drove them to

Heaton. She'd obviously warned him not to drop them off at the door, which is how they arrived on foot with no luggage.'

'Great work!' Hank said.

Also acknowledging a job well done, Kate welcomed Ailsa to the madhouse. She was chuffed that she could now take part in the priority actions.

'Did you have something specific to say in relation to that?' Kate asked.

'Not really, I was just wondering if Georgina and her bloke had met at school.'

'I don't think he was a classmate. I asked Cally if the man she saw Georgina with was anyone she recognised. She said not. Don't rule it out. Crawford told me that the guy was of similar age to Georgina. Cally seemed to think he was older.'

Hank said, 'Some guys my age look ten years older—'

'Don't you mean younger?' Jo quipped.

He pulled an imaginary dagger from his heart, making them laugh.

Kate steered them to where she wanted them to go. 'Lists have been generated by HOLMES: one for Julies; the one Lisa put together of her early service record that includes colleagues deployed to the same shifts; another for her classmates. I'd like two more: one of the kids in the years above her at school. And finally, the candidates who shared the same recruitment intake in case they joined the service together. Crawford seemed to think they might have been colleagues. Scrutinise the lists. I want them cross-checked immediately.'

Carmichael raised a hand.

Kate gave her the floor.

'Regarding police personnel, I assume civilians are to be included?'

'Yes, everyone. I'm loath to admit it, but fingers are pointing at it being a cop. Cally described him as a bit cocky. Sure of himself was the way Crawford put it. A bit like me, he said.'

Hank chuckled. 'He got that right.'

Ailsa asked, 'Won't Curtis already have checked her personnel history?'

Kate evaded the question. 'Check it again.'

'Yes, guv.'

'Most females have a confidante,' Kate continued. 'If we can find Georgina's, we nail her boyfriend. She may not have told me about him when I joined the force years later but, at the time they were together, she'd have no reason to hide him, unless he was a married man, and that's unlikely. She was dead against extras.'

Jo's expression was deadpan. 'Probably because she'd been burnt. I was once married to a serial philanderer, so I know how it works. His affairs rarely lasted. I know for a fact that on several occasions he hid his marital status, then used our marriage as an excuse to end them. Maybe Georgina's bloke did the same. Maybe he'd learned that she was pregnant, also a good excuse to cut and run.'

'No,' Kate said. 'Crawford was adamant that she was the one ending it.'

Jo gave a disparaging look. 'Unless *he* was the one ending it. My ex could look me straight in the face and lie for England.'

'Jo has a point,' Zac said. 'He's had years to practise his pitch.'

107

They took five, then resumed the briefing, Kate leading from the front. 'I take on board all you've thrown at me so far, including Zac's suggestion that Crawford may have fed me disinformation to throw us off the scent. He's still in the mix but, for what it's worth, I've never been more certain that a witness was telling the truth. Instinct is driving me to follow his lead, so bear with me. It's the only line of enquiry we have. And if I end up with egg on my face, it won't be the first time. Assuming Crawford is on the level, we know that Georgina used him to get rid of another man. We don't know why. We will find out. Merge those lists. Let's see how many hits we get.'

'Yes, guv,' Ailsa and Carmichael said in unison.

'Go.'

They got up to leave.

'Hank, meet me in my office in five. Zac, take care of the lab technicians.'

When they left, Kate turned to Jo and blew out a breath. 'We're close, I can feel it.'

'Can I say something?' Jo didn't wait for a reply. 'I think it's unwise to withhold the DNA results from the family. If it gets out, you can kiss goodbye to a relationship with any of them in the future. You and Georgina . . .' She stalled. 'You were tight. I know that you wouldn't want to lose them all.'

'It's a risk I'm prepared to take. I care less about Oscar, he's his own worst enemy, but as soon as I tell Charlotte, she'll jump to the same conclusion I, or should I say we, have. By that I mean that her real father is also a potential killer who will spend the rest of his life in prison. Imagine what finding out about him, then losing him days later will do to her. I can't do it. I won't. Not yet. I'd rather have him identified, if not detained before I go down that road.'

'Fair enough.'

'Whatever happened between Georgina and the father of her unborn babies – doctor or cop – must've been heavy, because the woman we knew was not the kind of person to keep a secret like that from the family she adored. There is a very good reason she didn't come clean. I intend to find out what it was.'

The MIT worked through till 9 p.m. It had not been the New Year's Day anyone had planned. No one complained. Kate had spoken to Crawford. He didn't object to providing a DNA swab for comparison with other samples, the actions of an innocent man, in Kate's opinion, though she didn't mention that she was intending to do a paternity test.

Sending a local officer to collect it, she stood her exhausted crew down for the night, discreetly inviting Hank, Lisa, Ailsa, and Zac to her place, having first checked that Jo had no objections.

She was happy . . .

And so was Hank. His wife, Julie, was out with friends, an annual tradition. He wouldn't be missed and there was no way Kate was letting Carmichael face a cold, empty house. Ailsa had already mentioned that she was at a loose end. In any case, she was now part of the inner circle. Despite this, her face was tripping her.

Kate knew why.

Her temporary recruit was appalled that she was being asked to engage in a get-together when they could all be searching for Oscar, and by extension, finding Ella. Kate told her to let it go. It was a task for others. A hunt was underway across the force. Having established that Oscar was not at work, officers were checking all his known haunts, others were stationed outside his home. Technical support had pinged his phone, locating it on the move in a remote part of north Northumberland.

'It's impossible to tell exactly where,' Carmichael added. 'But he will be found.'

Reassured, Ailsa accepted Kate's offer.

'I'm out,' Zac said.

'Me too,' Hank said, 'I'm wrecked.'

'What?' This wasn't what Kate expected.

'I'm pulling your leg, man. When have I ever turned you down?'

'When have you ever turned down a free bar, you mean?' Kate looked at Zac. 'You sure you won't join us?'

'Heavy date. She's lush, but thanks for asking.'

'Lucky man,' Hank said. Eyeing Kate with suspicion, he shifted his attention to the others. 'The rest of you, consider yourselves warned. I know a game plan when I see one. This drinks invitation will mutate into an extension of the evening briefing. I'd bet my car on it.'

'Your car's worth squat,' Kate said.

'Are you denying it?'

'Yes.' She was lying. After an irritating call with journalist Gillian Garvey, an idea had been percolating, a way the MIT might bring their mystery man out of the shadows, without having to wait until the MIT came up with a name they could pursue – and if Garvey wanted war, she'd get war.

108

Carmichael and Ailsa waited patiently on the corner of the Groat Market, where the offices of *The Journal* newspaper were located. The detectives were poised to get into a role play that Kate had devised over a couple of drinks late last night. Every time someone left the building, they held their collective breath, only to be disappointed. This had happened several times. Finally, their target emerged from the building, turning right in the direction of the Black Gate and Castle Keep.

'That's her,' Carmichael said. 'Get going.'

Ailsa crossed to the shady side of the street. She was a clean skin, a detective who wouldn't be recognised by the woman walking slowly towards her. Not that Garvey was paying attention. Her eyes were on her iPhone. She seemed oblivious of everyone around her.

That was about to change.

As the gap between the two women shrank, Carmichael called Ailsa's name. Simultaneously, Ailsa turned to the voice and Gillian Garvey looked up from her mobile, stopping dead as she spotted Carmichael over Ailsa's shoulder.

Carmichael pretended not to see her.

The crime correspondent couldn't help herself. She darted into a doorway. Sideways on, she leaned against the wall, playing a game of her own. Slipping on her shades, she checked her watch, glancing up and down the street, as if waiting for someone. Tapping her phone, she turned away briefly. Raising the device, angling it, she tilted her head as if taking a selfie with some of Newcastle's most historic buildings as a backdrop, snapping the detectives in the process.

She was a piece of work.

'You still in the Comms team?' Carmichael said.

'Professional Standards.' Ailsa regretted her words the moment they were out of her mouth. Of all the departments she might have chosen, that was the wrong one to throw at Carmichael. These were the very officers investigating Ash Norham's use of lethal force.

Carmichael was struggling.

Ailsa was kicking herself. She'd heard rumours that Ash and Carmichael were more than just friends. Parking that thought, she focused on their task. Kate had instructed them to make it look genuine, an everyday exchange between detectives who'd accidentally bumped into one another on a city street.

As the seconds ticked by, that request seemed unattainable.

Carmichael seemed weirdly disoriented, as if she'd lost the signal and forgotten where and why they were there. With Garvey earwigging their conversation, Ailsa had no choice but to continue with the act. She didn't have to simulate embarrassment or regret. She genuinely felt it. Carmichael seemed to be teetering on the edge of rational thought, leaving Ailsa wondering which way she'd jump. The only thing she could think of was to ad lib, hoping that her colleague would come to her senses.

'I heard your guv'nor has Oscar Ioannou in custody for the shooting,' Ailsa said.

Carmichael didn't respond. This was bad. This was very bad. Ailsa had one aim now: to extricate her from the situation as swiftly as possible. Shifting her position so that Garvey couldn't lipread what she was about to say.

Ailsa whispered. 'Lisa, what's the matter?'

'You are . . .' Carmichael was acting as if Ailsa was Professional Standards, not pretending to be. What she said next was designed to injure . . . and it did. 'Ash dying made your job a damned sight easier, didn't it? That's one case off your desk. He was a hero. Anyone saying different is a fucking liar!'

'Lisa, they're not saying anything. Let's not do this. Not here.'

Garvey edged along the side of the building. She was only feet away. Of all the people Carmichael wouldn't want party to this conversation, it was her. Taking her arm, Ailsa guided her toward the Cathedral café on the other side of the street. As they reached it, she caught Garvey's joyful reflection in the window. She'd taken the bait . . . but what else had she overheard?

109

When she arrived at Middle Earth, Kate was depressed to learn that Oscar had not yet been apprehended. It was ten a.m. already. Calling the control room, she asked for an update. Oscar's car had disappeared off the radar, leaving a hell of an area to be searched. Kate wondered if, suspecting a DNA match, he'd gone to ground. Was he holed up somewhere with Ella or was there an innocent explanation? Unable to go home to his wife and kids, perhaps he was dossing down with a pal, sinking a few. She summoned Hank, telling him to meet her in the car park.

Carmichael sat quietly in the car, worried about what Alisa might tell Kate when they returned to Middle Earth. The boss didn't need the aggravation of another detective going sick. When she conveyed that thought to Ailsa, the ROCU officer kept her eyes on the road and didn't reply.

Carmichael was in a trance when they left the city. Ailsa made her hand over her car keys, insisted on driving while she got her shit together. Lisa did feel odd, though she tried glossing over her 'episode' in the street as a symptom of fatigue. She said, 'As far as I'm concerned, we lured Garvey into a trap, which is what we were asked to do.'

'We?' Ailsa wasn't fooled. 'Dress it up any way you like, just don't ask me to forget what happened or cover for you. You're not well. That's a risky place for any copper to be.'

'What does it matter?'

'It does if Garvey heard what you said.'

'Who cares? The boss won't believe a word she says. I admit, I've not been sleeping. I'm ready to drop, aren't you? With so many detectives down, we've all put in extra hours. On top of everything, it's knocked me sideways. I swear that's all there is to it. Please, I'm asking nicely. If you tell Kate, she'll say I'm unfit for duty—'

Ailsa's eyes flashed. 'You are.'

Carmichael's phone rang on the dash, not quite her 'get out of jail' card, but a truce she intended to hang on to for as long as humanly possible. She listened, then hung up. 'Put your foot down. Oscar's car was spotted on the A1 near Alnwick. A Traffic cop stopped his vehicle ten minutes ago. He's on his way in for questioning. The boss and Hank are incommunicado. The office manager wants us to deal.'

Kate and Hank had been for a walk in the open air, a chance to discuss the plan they had put together last night and how it might impact the enquiry going forward. It was impossible to do that, even in her office with the door closed and blinds drawn. Assuming Ailsa and Carmichael had completed their mission, they needed time to consider next steps.

As they arrived back at base, Kate spotted Ailsa entering the secure car park. Pulling hard on the wheel, she shot into a space, braking sharply. She jumped out, slamming the door shut. Intrigued, Kate remained in her vehicle. Carmichael got out too, though she seemed to be in less of a hurry to enter Middle Earth than Ailsa.

Kate looked at Hank. 'What do you reckon is going on there?'

He shrugged. 'They don't look happy.'

'I mean the car, divvy.'

'What?'

'When have you ever known Lisa let anyone drive her motor?'

Kate scanned the MIR. Carmichael and Ailsa were nowhere to be seen. The buzz of conversations was deafening. She sensed a mixture of sadness and relief: sadness that they hadn't yet nailed the shooter who'd set off a chain reaction leading to more deaths; relief that they could smell a result.

Everyone was talking about Oscar.

He was now a credible suspect for abducting Ella Stafford.

Whoever had taken her had to be connected to the murder of Lee and Jackson Bradshaw. No question. Kate urged her team not to let their guard down, to keep going with the action to trace Georgina's ex, until Oscar's guilt was unequivocal, every other possibility exhausted.

She turned to find Hank racing out into the corridor, ignoring Carmichael and Ailsa as they emerged from it, a frosty atmosphere between them.

Kate approached them: 'How did it go?'

Carmichael stalled.

Ailsa didn't. 'Garvey is on the hook. Tomorrow's headlines should be interesting. If there's one thing I know about journalists, they love the limelight. Depending on how far the smug bitch stretches the truth, it could end in a lawsuit. She'll get no sympathy from me.'

'You get what you give.' Carmichael's comment was loaded.

Ailsa looked away.

Kate eyeballed Carmichael. She hadn't been talking about Garvey. She was having a dig at Ailsa. The dynamic between the two was as low as it had ever been.

Kate let it go . . .

For now.

Knowing she'd been rumbled Carmichael quickly changed the subject. 'We were summoned to interview Oscar. Now you're here, I assume you want us to stand down?'

'Yeah, but Hank shot off somewhere.' Kate checked the room. No sign of him. 'I can't afford to wait. Besides, Oscar may kick off if he sees him. Ailsa, make yourself useful. Lisa, come with me.'

A flash of resentment crossed Ailsa's face.

Carmichael noticed it too. 'I've got the beginnings of a

migraine, guv. Would you take Ailsa instead?'

Kate shifted her gaze. 'Ailsa, you up for that?'

'Always, guv.'

'Great.' Kate glanced at Carmichael. Ordinarily, she'd be raring to go. This was her making amends. 'Make sure you see the MO for that headache. Is that why Ailsa was driving your car? I saw you when you drove in.' Both detectives had blank faces. 'Know what I love about you two? You've always been team players. Whatever happened between you today, you left it outside. Make sure it stays there.'

110

Kate didn't have the first idea what had happened between Carmichael and Richards, but it was the end of the matter. They had sorted it. She moved on. 'We'll debrief on Garvey later,' she said. 'In the meantime, I want that timeline completed ASAP, Lisa. Oh, and tell whoever is merging the historical lists that I'm expecting an update on my return.'

'Yes, guv.'

Collecting a fresh notepad from her desk, Kate gave Ailsa the heads-up on how she intended to handle Oscar's interview. 'If you think of anything, write it down and show me. If he asks you anything, make your own judgement on whether you answer. Rule one: we are there to ask questions, not answer them.' They were still talking as they reached the corridor. Someone was thundering up the stairs towards them. DC Brown entered from the stairwell in a flap, his red hair matching the shade of his face.

'Guv—'

'Not now, Andy.'

He stopped walking, breathing heavily. 'You should know that Charlotte is at the front desk asking for you.'

'Damn it. Does she know that Oscar is here and why?'

'She's in uniform. Looks done in. I'm guessing she's end of shift.'

'Then she'll know what everyone knows.' Kate tied her hair up loosely. She didn't need this now. 'Any idea where Hank is?'

'No, guv.'

Kate turned to face Ailsa. 'Looks like we're the only ones doing any work round here. Prep the custody sergeant that I'm on my way. Make sure Oscar's been fed and watered. Wait for me there.'

She walked away, the weight of two pairs of eyes on her, all the while thinking of what she might say when she got to reception on the ground floor. If she'd been able to find Hank, she could've sent him to deal with Charlotte, except she felt a responsibility to do it herself, for Georgina's sake.

In a moment of unmitigated sorrow, Kate stopped short of reception.

Through the door's reinforced glass panel, Charlotte struck a pathetic figure that made Kate's heart ache. She was sitting, elbows on her knees, head in her hands, the weight of her uniform dragging her down, high-vis jacket and black boots scruffy, as if she'd pulled a heavy shift. This was her best friend's child. Kate had watched her grow into the woman Georgina was so proud of.

Kate pushed the door open.

Sensing a presence, the duty officer manning the desk lifted her head, a pained expression, like she didn't envy Kate the task in front of her. If Oscar was found to be guilty of the shootings – and Kate was a long way from proving that – some officers would no doubt applaud his actions. An eye for an eye was human nature whether employed to uphold the law or not. That didn't make it right. Kate would rise above it.

There was no justification for murder.

111

Kate took Charlotte to a room set up for victims, rather than an empty office or interview room. Her body language was stiff. Otherwise, she was in complete control of her emotions. She slipped off her jacket, unbuckling her utility belt, dumping it on the table. Pounds lighter, she took the seat Kate was offering.

In SIO mode, she didn't hang around. 'You heard,' was a statement, not a question.

'That every polis was instructed to stop and detain Oscar last night? Yeah, I heard it from Control, like everyone else. I was on duty, single-crewed, my entire shift trying to avoid me. A heads-up would have been appreciated.'

'You know I couldn't do that.'

Charlotte crossed her long legs, hanging one arm over the back of her chair. 'Can I ask you something?' She took in Kate's nod. 'If Oscar and I are in the frame, why aren't we suspended? Oh, I forgot, this week you're the big cheese, head of CID, what you've always dreamed of. It would be an embarrassment if you accused one of us and it turned out that you were wrong. We understand. You have your own arse to cover.'

'I have a job to do, if that's what you mean. I don't suspend officers unless I have hard evidence of wrongdoing.'

'Don't pretend you're trying to support us, Kate.'

'Charlotte, there are no sides.'

'No? Mum would have expected more from you.'

Kate looked away. If Charlotte had slapped her it couldn't have stung more.

'I take it the DNA results are in?'

Kate turned to face her. 'Makes you say that?'

'Because I know stuff you don't. Oscar's an idiot. He sought out your witness, *before* she went missing. Why do you think he came to my place after Hank searched his car? He was shitting himself. If it's any consolation, I told him what a knacker he was. Kate, he's made himself look guilty. He'd never hurt a fly.'

'Charlotte—'

'I know, I know. I also wish I had a quid for every time I've heard those words from an offender's mum, dad, or sibling, but I swear it's true. I could've told you sooner. I should have, just as you could have told me stuff. We both chose not to for all the right reasons. I appreciate that it's no defence for withholding information in a murder-abduction case, and I'll take what's coming for that. I'm telling you now, before it gets any worse for Oscar.'

Kate had enough experience to spot the difference between the truth and a lie. Charlotte was displaying no tell-tale signs of anxiety. She'd spoken from the heart. Her delivery was natural, not mumbled or confused. Kate was as sure as she could be that her story had not been fabricated or rehearsed. Besides, she'd have to have known about the DNA match, and that wasn't possible, unless it came from Oscar.

'Is he here?' Charlotte asked.

Kate nodded.

'Can I see him?'

'You know that's not possible.'

'Kate, I'm begging you to believe me. Check his phone.'

'For what?'

'An audible message from me.'

'Warning him that he was the target of a manhunt?'

'Begging him to hand himself in.' Charlotte paused. 'Do you think Oscar has the guts to take out half an OCG? C'mon, how likely is it? I could have shot them dead and enjoyed doing it. I could even have taken your missing witness and dug a hole to bury her in to save my skin. He couldn't. He doesn't have it in him.'

Kate could only hope that was the case.

Ella Stafford might still be breathing.

112

Hank's phone pinged an incoming text from an unrecognised number. He was about to ignore it as spam, until curiosity got the better of him. Leaving the MIR, he wandered into Kate's empty office. Nicking a bottle of water from her mini fridge, he sat down. Unscrewing the top, he lifted his feet onto her desk, reclined her seat and took a drink while tapping on the message icon on his home screen.

Lay off Oscar. You're wide of the mark.

Intrigued, Hank keyed a reply.

Says who?
Nice try, Hank.
Mate, you're boring me. It'll take more than that to convince me.
No can do.
Is this you, Nico?
Trust me, it's not.
I don't even trust myself.

Hank stared at the screen for a long while.
When the messages stopped, he hit the keys again.

Fancy a beer? We should talk.
Not possible.
Washing your hair, Charlotte?
Keep up, big man. She's downstairs talking to your boss.

That hit Hank like a body blow. He got up suddenly, sending

the bottle flying, spraying water across the room as it hit the desk, soaking everything on it. Loud swearing brought Carmichael to the threshold to see what his problem was.

'Whoa.' She grinned. 'You do know there's a shower in the men's locker room?'

'Very funny.' Hank grabbed some tissues. 'Where's the boss?'

'Interviewing Oscar.'

'You sure?' He began to relax.

'That's where she was heading when we last spoke.'

The tissues were disintegrating. 'Then why aren't you with her?'

'She took Ailsa.'

He didn't have time to debate why Kate would favour a DC who'd been commandeered to the squad over his and her favourite DS. Ailsa was good. Carmichael was outstanding. 'Call her and confirm, would you?'

'Call her yourself. Kate will fire me if I interrupt.'

'Text Ailsa then.'

'Why?'

'Do it.'

Frustrated by his secrecy, Carmichael tapped out a message and pressed send.

You and the boss still with Oscar?

A reply arrived instantly.

No, she's with Charlotte. Oscar is next.

Carmichael immediately relayed the info to Hank. 'Does that satisfy you?'

'No.' Without another word, he handed her his mobile.

Carmichael read the text stream, eyes widening in surprise. 'Jesus!' She looked up. 'Well, if neither Charlotte nor Oscar could've sent that text, they have an accomplice. Or we're looking for a cop, only his name isn't Ioannou.'

113

Charlotte's unscheduled arrival at Middle Earth had given Kate the opportunity to explain that there were other things going on that she needed to be aware of, namely that stuff might appear in the local newspaper soon that might be upsetting. She couldn't see a way of stopping it.

'You think we give a shit what the press are saying?' Charlotte scoffed, a contemptuous glare. 'They've hounded us for years. In their eyes, we're guilty. We had hoped that you might champion our cause. It looks like we were mistaken.'

'That's unfair. I wanted to warn you—'

'Makes a change.' Charlotte looked right through her. 'Don't go doing us any favours, Kate. Anyhow, now that Oscar is in custody, he won't be reading newspapers, will he?'

'Nico will.'

'And you think a warning would be best coming from me. Why not? Who needs sleep? And while I'm at it, I can tell him that his son isn't getting out anytime soon. I'm sure they'll both appreciate your thoughtfulness.'

Kate ignored the sarcasm. 'Do you think Oscar is a suicide risk?'

'No. He's stronger than he looks. And if you have his DNA results, you must have mine.'

Kate's stomach rolled over. Since they had sat down together, she'd been dreading this. 'I do have them. All clear. No link to any samples at the murder scene.'

'I could have told you that.'

Kate didn't bite. 'I had to check.'

'Did you?' Charlotte palmed her brow. 'I need to crash. Hand them over and I'll be on my way. All of them. Our prints too. If Papa and I are eliminated, they shouldn't be in the system.'

'They'll be destroyed. You have my word.'

'You think I trust you? No thanks.'

'Watch your mouth. There's a limit and you reached it. You can have yours if you insist, though I choose not to share them at this moment in time. I'm not finished with them entirely.'

'That makes no sense.' Charlotte was no fool. 'You gave me the all-clear.'

Kate stood her ground. 'That's correct.'

'So why could you possibly need them?'

They stared at each other for a long time.

Picking up on Kate's reticence, Charlotte was no longer the sister of a suspect. She was her mother's daughter, a smart cop sifting credible reasons for withholding DNA. She got up, pacing the floor. It took her a while to get there. Finally, she made the jump. Every cop on the force had a tale about surprising, sometimes earth-shattering DNA results. 'Oh. My. God . . .' Charlotte swung round, hard eyes on Kate. 'Nico's not our old man, is he?'

114

Hank couldn't imagine what was taking so long. He'd expected Kate to touch base with Charlotte, then kick her out. In the meantime, he and Carmichael had been over that text conversation several times and come up with a few bullet points to fire at Kate before she disappeared to deal with Oscar.

The detectives had been watching the door to the quiet room for over ten minutes. Suddenly, it burst open. Charlotte rushed out. She sprinted down the corridor, looking like she might puke, disappearing into the women's restroom, the door banging shut behind her, causing Kate to wince as she arrived in the open doorway, meeting the gaze of her 2ic with tired eyes.

'She knows?' Hank said.

A nod. 'She demanded the DNA results. Didn't trust us to destroy them. I don't blame her. We'd have done the same in her shoes. I tried talking her out of it. It raised suspicions. She guessed the rest. She asked me a direct question. I had no choice but to confirm it.'

'Poor bugger.'

'Want me to go after her?' Carmichael said.

'No, give her some space. What did you want, Hank?'

He handed her a photocopy of the text he'd received.

'What does it prove?'

'Only that Charlotte and Oscar weren't on the other end of it,' Carmichael said. 'He's in the custody suite, she was with you. You can schedule a text. You can't hold a conversation without being present. I'd say it proves that we are looking for a cop. Who else knew you were with Charlotte?'

'Andy Brown,' Hank said.

Carmichael almost laughed. They were good mates.

'And Ailsa,' Kate added. 'And if she mentioned it to Harry, everyone in the world will know.'

Hank dropped a bombshell. 'It's a retired cop or someone who's been around a while.'

Kate looked at him. 'What makes you so sure?'

'That text came from a burner, and I've not been called Big Man since I was one, a decade or more ago. If he has my number, pound to a penny I'll have his.'

'Change of plan, Hank. Give me your phone . . .' Kate took it from him, explaining what had gone down with Charlotte, specifically that Oscar had coughed about visiting, not abducting Ella Stafford. 'I want you to interview him and confirm it. Ask him where his DNA might have been found in Ella's home. We can't let him go, though I believe Charlotte was telling the truth.'

'What are you going to do?'

Along the corridor, a door creaked open.

Charlotte emerged, calm and composed. She headed towards the three detectives, her focus mainly on Kate. 'What you told me changes nothing. Let's face it, I've had worse news. As far as I'm concerned, Nico is still my dad, but it'll crucify Oscar if he finds out that he's not. I'm not going to tell him, unless one of us needs a transplant and Nico decides to put himself forward.'

Hank and Carmichael laughed.

Kate put her arms around Charlotte, catching Hank's eye over her shoulder, sending him a non-verbal message: Police humour in her darkest hour meant Charlotte was going to be fine.

115

In the quiet room, Charlotte stuffed her utility belt and high-vis jacket into her backpack, then retook her seat. A moment later, Kate arrived with a tray of refreshments, setting it down on the table. She'd already indicated that she had other urgent questions to put to her if she felt up to it. They could do it later if she preferred.

Charlotte sighed.

How could she sleep now?

Kate shared that she was close to a resolution that didn't involve Oscar, explaining that intelligence had arrived while Charlotte was pulling herself together in the restroom after receiving such shocking news. Kate had a theory that the current case had a history that she didn't yet understand.

That made two of them.

'Crack on.'

'Are you sure? You're exhausted and I don't want to upset you.'

'I think we're way past that, don't you?'

The sun came out from behind a cloud. It streamed in through the open window at an angle, blinding Kate, accentuating the lowlights in Charlotte's hair, turning it auburn like her mother's. Georgina was in Kate's head, urging her on as she used to . . .

It's OK . . . she won't break.

Human resilience never ceased to amaze Kate.

'Did your mum ever mention life before Nico?'

Charlotte frowned. 'In what context?'

'Generally. When she was a kid, when she was single, what she got up to, clubs she went to and stuff.'

'I suppose she must have. I wasn't usually listening.'

For the first time for a long time, Kate laughed out loud. 'You were a bugger at times.'

'I've got news for you, I still am.' Charlotte softened. 'I was training to be you.'

'Not your mum?'

'Nah, you were cool . . . she was . . . Mum.'

The tug on Kate's heart almost moved her to tears. 'I never wanted kids—'

'As I said, too cool for school. So, now we're on the same page, I might behave. Why do you need to know about Mum? You two were joined at the hip. I thought growing up that she told you everything.'

'No one shares everything . . .' Kate levelled with her. 'I have two witnesses, one a close childhood friend, the other a man who dated your mum for a while. Both have mentioned another man we'd like to trace, a man I believe loved your mother very much.'

'Who you think may be my real father.'

Kate nodded.

'A bloke who never showed his face.'

'They broke up. I don't know why. Would you want to meet him?'

'No chance.' Charlotte changed her mind. 'On second thoughts, I would, so long as he agrees to a paternity test. If it turns out that he's my biological father, all well and good. Just don't try facilitating a meeting. I have a dad. I don't need another. What I do need is an opportunity to thank the real one for offing the Bradshaw scum. That's what they deserved. If I could, I'd pin a medal to his chest.'

116

As soon as Charlotte left the building, Kate turned on her mobile, checking for messages. Andy Brown had left a voicemail. 'Guv, I'm in the observation room watching Hank's interview. It's going well. Oscar is undoubtedly sweating. Who wouldn't be in his situation? He's saying nowt to indicate he's lying. He's admitted his conversation with Ella and no more. Hank's quizzing him on his movements in the house and where he may have left his DNA. I'll keep you posted. End of message.'

Kate took the stairs two at a time, arriving in the MIR with high hopes and pumped full of adrenaline. Grabbing Carmichael, she gave the team strict instructions that they were not to be interrupted, for any reason. Maxwell immediately waved to get her attention.

'What did I say, Neil?'

'Your urgent DNA request on Crawford is here, guv. No match.'

'In that case, you're forgiven.'

It was good to have the confirmation.

Adjourning to her office, Kate asked Carmichael to log on to HOLMES where they could access the lists they had talked about, with a plan to cross-reference them with Hank's contact list.

Lisa reminded her that they hadn't been able to speak to anyone at Georgina's school over the weekend to ask for names of the pupils in the years above hers. She'd arranged for someone to contact the keyholder and was awaiting an update. 'Otherwise, we're good to go,' she said.

'We can't help that. Let's work with what we have.'

Carmichael's fingers flew across the keys to get where she

needed to be. All set, she looked up at Kate. 'Where do you want to start?'

'Let's look at her classmates. See if any of them joined the police.'

'That's a negative, boss. They had more sense.'

'What about her recruitment intake? Give me those who've since retired.'

Carmichael brought up the alphabetic list. 'Five names: DS Robert Cooper, Detective Superintendent Graham Edwards, PC Marianne Johns, Sergeant Dave Osgood, Sergeant Asif Qureshi.'

'Bob Cooper is dead, so we can discount him,' Kate said.

'Really?' Carmichael was horrified. 'How did that get past me?'

'No one could go to the poor bastard's funeral. He died in 2020.'

Kate was in the zone, scrolling through Hank's contacts. 'His name is in here, as it happens.'

'Then I'd raise another action in case someone got hold of his address book, boss.'

'Good call.' Picking up a pen, Kate wrote a reminder: +RA: Cooper's address book. She continued searching. 'No Edwards in Hank's contacts. Oh, here we go: PC Marianne Johns is here.' She tapped the O in the contacts list and found Dave Osgood (Sgt). 'No Qureshi,' she said, 'though I'm pretty sure Hank knows him. Maybe they weren't close.'

'They were.' Carmichael looked up. 'Try "Scottish". That's his nickname.'

'Nope, no Scottish either.'

Lisa closed the list, accessing another, this one headed 'Julies nightclub'.

Repeating the process, Kate came up with two names linked to Hank's address book, which she added to the others: Mick Goodwin (DS), and Nigel Wolstenholme (DC) a guy everyone referred to as Woolly, which was how he was listed in Hank's contacts. A third: David Osgood had appeared on two lists.

'Hank knows a lot of people,' Kate said. 'Try Georgina's shift colleagues.'

Again, Carmichael was lightning fast. The list that uploaded on screen was different to the others, split into the Area Commands and broken down into the stations where Georgina had been posted. Collectively the names ran into the hundreds. Many were highlighted, some more than once. Only this time, as expected, they were mostly uniform staff. On one of the lists, she homed in on a name that was not highlighted.

Kate's heart skipped a beat when Lisa pointed it out: PC Kate Daniels.

If emotions were colours, hers was black.

Kate had felt the loss of Georgina from the moment she took over the enquiry into her death. Now it was threatening to overwhelm her. She took a deep breath. However bad she felt, Carmichael must feel ten times worse. Having given her the same advice Georgina had extended to *her* as a young officer, Kate simply couldn't allow herself to go there.

Be strong.

'You shout the names out,' she said. 'I'll check the phone. Let's see what we've got.'

With meticulous attention to detail, Kate and Lisa worked on, finding five more retired officers: Sgt Jane Holliday; PC Terence Kelly; Insp Michaela Portman, DS Richard Thomas, DC Alan Humphries. Of the five, only the last two were also in Hank's contacts. More importantly, they had both worked with Georgina very early in their careers. Kate could only remember two people she'd gone to training school with and subsequently worked with. Northumbria was one of the largest forces in the country.

She looked down at her scribbles.

'How many have we got?' Carmichael said.

'Seven – six if we minus Cooper.'

Working her way through them, Kate marked Cooper as

deceased, placing a tick next to the ex-detectives who'd appeared more than once. She stared at the yellow Post-it Note. Two hits were better than one. She wanted more.

Robert Cooper (DS) – deceased
Marianne Johns (PC)
Dave Osgood (Sgt) √√
Mick Goodwin (DS)
Nigel Wolstenholme (DC)
Richard Thomas (DS)
Alan Humphries (DC)

She looked up at Carmichael. 'Who did you ask to contact the keyholder at the school?'

'Neil's doing it.'

'Right, I'm going to leave you on your own for a mo. Lock the door if you must. I want all the intel you can lay your hands on for Osgood, as quick as you can. He joined with Georgina, has since retired, *and* was known to frequent Julies. I'd like you to check him against Georgina's personnel record too. She had commendations, one or two for acts of bravery. From memory, she wasn't alone on either occasion. One last push, Lisa. Let's see if we can nail this.'

117

Unable to find Maxwell anywhere in the MIR, Kate practically ran from the room. Crashing through the double doors into the corridor, she turned left into the men's locker room, kicking open toilet doors. Nothing. She was about to walk out again when an old sergeant entered, pulling his flies down even before he crossed the threshold, turning every shade of puce when their eyes met.

'Vinnie.'

'Ma'am?' He was trying to sort himself out, snagging his zip in the process, getting more and more flustered.

'Have you seen Maxwell?'

'Uhm, I think I saw him—'

'Either you did, or you didn't.' How could a copper look so guilty? Kate could smell tobacco on Vinnie's clothing. 'Doesn't matter. I know where he is.'

Kate rushed out, using both hands on the push bar of the emergency exit to open the reinforced steel door. Maxwell was leaning over the fire escape, taking in the view, such as it was at this time of night, like he had all the time in the world to waste while Ella Stafford's life hung in the balance.

She was incensed.

He glanced over his shoulder, straightening up when he realised who'd caught him in the act. 'Guv?' He binned his smoke, crushing it under his foot, sending sparks flying everywhere. 'I'm sorry—'

'Save the excuses. I'm not in the mood. Did you manage to get hold of the school keyholder?'

'Better than that,' he gloated. 'I spoke to the deputy head. She sent me what you asked for.'

Kate spread her hands in frustration. 'So where is it?'

'On my desk. You said no interruptions.'

He had a point. 'Show me.'

She spun on her heel, heading for the incident room. He arrived soon after. The newly printed list was on top of a bundle of current actions in his in-tray. Kate took it from him, returning to her office. Without speaking to Carmichael, she sat down, running her finger down a long list of school pupils in the year above Georgina, one of whom was also in Hank's phone book.

Oh God.

Of all the people on that list, she didn't want this man to be the one she'd send to jail for the rest of his life. When he was in the job, he was one of Bright's closest friends. They drank together, played golf together, attended matches together at St James' Park. This could not be true . . .

Kate was staring at the image of a teenage child, a boy who'd grown into one of the most revered detectives on the force, a man of integrity, a man everyone loved to be around. He'd retired not long after Georgina's death.

Kate stood.

Lisa was staring at her. 'What?'

'Get a pool car. I have a call to make. If it comes off, I know who we're looking for.'

118

Kate drove at high speed on a blue light, killing it as she closed on the target property. The last thing she needed was an audience or to alert the suspect that he'd been rumbled. Carmichael hadn't said a word all the way there. Like Osgood, the man they were on their way to arrest had ended up with three ticks against his name. Not only was he retired, and in the year above Georgina at school, he also appeared as a contact in Hank's address book. He was responsible for Ash Norham's death, even if that was not and had never been his intention. Sadly, Lisa's boyfriend had ended up as collateral damage in someone else's fight.

Braking hard, Kate turned the corner and slowed to a crawl. The house was in complete darkness. She coasted by, checking it out. At the end of the street, she did a U-turn, then pulled to a stop with a good view of the front door.

No movement.

'I need a lookout. Stay in the car and warn me if I get company.'

'Boss, you need to wait for backup.'

'I don't have that luxury.'

Carmichael was about to beg. 'Kate—'

'Don't argue, Lisa. Ella's been gone six days. Every second is vital. If she's in there, I must get her out.'

Switching her mobile to silent, Kate grabbed her only weapon, a police-issue expandable baton. Getting out of the car, she crossed the street. There hadn't been time to expedite a search warrant. Slipping stealthily down the path at the side of the building, she arrived at the rear, waiting a second with her ear to the door.

Silence.

Using her elbow to break the glass, she listened for any activity, doors opening and closing from neighbouring properties. When no one came to investigate, she reached through the gap, turned the key, and let herself in.

Pushing the door open, she stepped inside, switching on her Maglite, casting an arc of light across a remarkably tidy kitchen. Glass crunched beneath her feet as she moved further into the room.

She stiffened as something shifted above her head.

Extending her baton, she made her way toward the hallway, then the worst thing happened. Her torch flickered . . . and died. Swearing under her breath, she shook the thing violently. It burst into life, then died a second time. Kate glanced over her shoulder to the rear door, considering her options: return to the car for another flashlight or put the kitchen light on, risking giving herself away if her target arrived home.

She chose to do neither.

Picking her way into the hallway, she crept blindly up the stairs, glad of the moonlight on the top landing. Carefully, she turned the handle of the first door she came to. It was locked, like Molly's bathroom when Georgina was a kid. Kate leaned against it, unsure if she heard whimpering from the other side, or if her imagination was playing tricks.

She listened again.

Silence.

Kate tried the door opposite.

It creaked as she pulled it open.

She stood a moment, allowing her eyes to adjust to the darkness, her guts flagging a warning that she was not alone. Through a chink in the curtains, she could see the outline of a head, backlit by a streetlight. She swallowed hard, panicked by what she was about to see: a dear ex-colleague who had gone off-piste and couldn't live with what he'd done.

Focus!

She shivered violently, didn't want to think, didn't want to imagine. She steadied her breathing, intuition telling her that whoever was sitting there was also drawing breath. She wished she'd taken Lisa's advice and waited for backup. She wished she knew how far away they were. She wished she could get out of there. A cop turned cold-blooded killer was a dangerous combination. And still the ominous figure hadn't moved an inch. Sucking in oxygen, Kate raised her arm slowly, flicking on the light switch.

Nothing happened.

A sound she didn't recognise arrived from over her shoulder, like furniture being moved, or maybe a body being dragged across a wooden floor. She dared not turn her back on the man in the chair. She took a sideways step, leaning down slowly to turn on the bedside light, no sudden movements.

Ex-DI, Zac Matthews showed no remorse.

If anything, he looked relieved.

Tired and sad, not crazy.

And calm . . .

Too calm.

119

It was then that she saw the gun in his hand, resting loosely on his knee. Until now, it hadn't occurred to her that he'd have kept his firearm after the shooting, never mind that he might use it.

She held her bottle. 'What happened to you, Zac? You crossed a line. There's no coming back from this, you know that, right?'

He didn't answer.

'What have you done with Ella?'

'The girl is fine. She's here of her own free will.'

'Yeah? She's locked in.'

'Failsafe. If Christine's crew came looking, I needed time to get to them before they got her.'

They stared at each other for a long moment, Kate wondering if he'd argue over the weight of evidence against him. Kate's phone vibrated in her pocket. She pulled it out and tapped to answer, lifting the device to her ear as Carmichael yelled down the line. 'Kate, get the hell out. Two heavies at the front door. Backup on its way, including armed response.'

'ETA?'

'Three minutes.'

'Make it two.'

Kate didn't have to warn Zac. He got the message as his front door was kicked in, those entering at ground level announcing their arrival and their intention.

'You're a dead man!' a disembodied voice yelled.

Kate recognised it as Christine's de facto boss. 'Shit!'

'Was that Burrows?' Carmichael was alarmed. 'Kate, I think he has Harvey with him. They'll kill Zac or die trying.'

'Blues and twos, Lisa. Now. Get out the car. Keep everyone

away. Leave the line open and update me.'

'On it.'

In the street outside, all hell broke loose as a siren screamed and blue lights lit up the night sky, which flashed in every room in the house, causing untold panic from downstairs. Kate expected a stampede toward the rear exit. She was out of luck. It all went quiet, except for the girl in the next room.

She became hysterical.

What Zac did next blindsided Kate.

He reached for his phone, which had a two-way radio app installed.

Pressing to transmit, he spoke quickly to his house guest. 'Ella, stay calm and stay put. The police are here, but so are the people we've been expecting. Remember what I told you. They want *me*, not you. You're safe.'

Ella was scared, her voice croaky. 'Promise?'

'I promise . . .'

'Roger that.'

Zac smiled at Kate.

She was too relieved to laugh.

Zac focused on Ella. 'Good girl. No more talking. Over and out.'

He'd always been one of the good guys. He'd spoken to Ella with the tone of a concerned father she never had, no trace of agitation in his voice, just the wisdom of a professional who'd spent his whole career preserving life, not taking it. That was the detective Kate had been proud to know, the Zac she would remember. 'Give me the gun . . .' She gestured for him to hand it over. 'Burrows isn't getting up those stairs and you're in enough trouble.'

120

Ash's crew arrived on scene first, closely followed by uniform patrol vehicles and MIT personnel. With Kate armed and poised to protect Zac and Ella at the top of the stairs, and firearms officers bursting through the front door at ground level, Burrows had nowhere to go. He was captured in the garden, too heavy and too slow to climb the fence, Harvey taken down by Hank on the other side of it.

Ella was finally safe, on her way to Middle Earth. Zac was cautioned and arrested at the scene, then transported to the same place by a Traffic car, Kate keeping him company in the rear. He didn't want a brief. He intended to make a full and frank confession, as keen to get it over with as she was.

At his request, they did that.

'Zac, you know how this works,' Kate said when they sat down together in the interview room, formalities over with. 'I need to know it all. Why don't we start at the beginning?'

'I've known Georgina since I was a kid, though at middle school she went out of her way to avoid me. She was different, aloof. A big turn-on when you're that age. It took me a long time to pluck up the courage to speak to her. I first asked her out in high school. She told me to do one. I backed off. She'd never dated. I began to think she was into girls. By chance, we met on a course, which is how I assume you found me. I never doubted that you would.'

'We're not all Curtis.'

His expression darkened. 'He was a dick.'

'Did you think you'd pull it off?'

'Not for a second.'

'Then why?'

'She was the love of my life, Kate. As simple as that.'

'For how long?'

'Not long enough.' Zac paused, stuck in a memory. 'If I could bring her back for just five minutes and tell her that, I would. It wasn't all plain sailing. She had trust issues I didn't understand.'

'Did she tell you why?'

'Not initially. We'd been together a year before she finally moved in. Night after night, she'd wake, sweating and screaming, "Run! Run!"' Zac wiped his face with his hands, then shut his eyes, on the verge of breaking down, the painful memory hard to share – even harder to shake. 'I tried talking her down. As time went on the nightmares got worse. It didn't take a genius to work out that she'd suffered an unspeakable horror.'

Georgina kicked out, gasping for breath, then threw a punch that struck his right eye with such force, his neck almost snapped. Zac struggled to restrain her. Then, in a moment of clarity, he realised that in her nightmarish state, she was unable to differentiate between a dream and reality. His hands had become those of an attacker. The thought nearly killed him. The noise that came from her mouth reminded him of an animal snared in a trap.

'Dear God!' Kate's heart broke a little as Nico's voice bled into her thoughts: *She used to dream about the threats they made. She'd wake in a cold sweat, lashing out, like they were in the room with us.* Kate made the connection. It wasn't the Bradshaws Georgina was trying to get away from, it was Fitzsimmons.

Maybe it was both.

'Zac, do you need a break?' Kate did. 'Shall I stop the recording?'

'No, I'm fine. I realise this must seem strange to you—'

'It doesn't,' Kate interrupted. 'It's making perfect sense.'

'I used to hold her until she stopped panting. Her heart was beating so fast I worried that she might have a coronary.

I thought, wrongly as it turned out, that when she spoke my name she was properly wide awake. Often, she wasn't. I've never seen that before, someone who looks awake but is stuck in nightmare, unable to break free.'

'Sounds terrifying.'

'For both of us . . .' Zac's bottom lip quivered. 'When she woke in the night, Georgina would cling to me, frightened that he was there, hiding in the shadows. I'd get up, put on the light, pull back the covers. She'd be drenched in sweat. I know fear and so do you. This was something else. I could smell it. She told me it began when she was eleven years old.'

121

Kate shuddered. Zac hadn't chosen the age randomly. *Like Cally, he knew.* Hank had cautioned Kate that interviewing Zac might be unwise, too close to home for a friend of Georgina, that she might struggle to hear confirmed what she'd discovered from Molly during the investigation. Jo agreed with him, warning her that graphic details were going to hurt. Kate ignored their advice. This was one dance she'd have to do alone.

'His name was Richard Fitzsimmons,' Zac said.

'I know. Her mother told me.' What came next stunned her. The background he was about to share was more shocking than anything she could have imagined.

'You won't find him unless I tell you where he's buried.'

'He was her best friend's father,' Zac said. 'Thirty-five at the time. He raped Georgina. I didn't find out till years later. I couldn't let him get away with it. She was in terrible pain, Kate. She joined the police to protect girls like her from guys like him.'

Kate sat quiet for a moment, giving him space.

Giving her space.

'Once she told me, I couldn't live with it,' Zac said. 'I wanted to rush out of the house and find the disgusting pig who'd done that to her.' For a moment he couldn't speak. He was dying inside. 'I suppose you want to know where he is now and how I did it.' It was a question that required no answer. Zac was still talking, but he was someplace else.

'Twenty grand by tomorrow or I go to the law.'

Fitzsimmons didn't admit or deny abusing Georgina. Why would he? He had a good job, a position of trust. He had a wife, a kid, a nice life. Georgina had night terrors and would until he was six feet under. This was blackmail, serious shit that carried a maximum prison term of fourteen years. As a copper, Zac knew he'd get the full whack. He'd risk everything to give Georgina peace. He was well prepared. She'd thank him for it.

'It was never about the money,' Zac said. 'That was to lure Fitzsimmons to the riverside where he'd pay for what he did to Georgina. He fell for it. Job done, I walked away. I figured the missing cash would give the impression that he'd done a runner. I kept my eye on the PNC for months. He was never reported as a misper.'

'You were home and dry—'

'Not quite.'

Now Kate understood. 'It backfired, didn't it?'

'Spectacularly. When I came off shift the night after I told her, she'd moved out. George couldn't live with it. Said it was all her fault. Blamed herself for telling me. She was terrified that I'd get caught. I guess that's why she kept her distance.'

'It must've taken a lot to walk away from you. She loved you, Zac.'

'Not enough.'

'By then she was pregnant, right?'

'I guess so.'

'You didn't know?'

He shook his head. 'Not until I saw Oscar's photo in the paper after her death. I had a full head of hair once too.'

Kate had the exact same epiphany the moment Zac's name had popped up on the schools list in the year above her and also in Hank's contacts. It all came together, Zac's fifty-seven-year-old face morphing into Oscar's. As a final confirmation, Kate had asked personnel to email the original image Zac submitted when he joined the police. He looked nothing like it now, but there were similarities.

No wonder Georgina loved her son.

'I put the past behind me and got on with the job,' Zac said. 'There was always a chance that we'd bump into each other. If I saw George from a distance, I'd walk the other way in case it made her feel uncomfortable. I watched her from afar, regretting everything, thinking of what might have been. When she was murdered there was no longer a reason for me to stay. I retired.'

'To plan your revenge.'

'They deserved it.'

Kate didn't tell him he was wrong.

He read it on her face. 'I'd do it again,' he said. 'Nothing to lose, Kate.' He dropped his head in his hands and wept as the emotions he'd suppressed for three decades came flooding out, relieved that Georgina could rest in peace at last. After the longest goodbye in living memory, Zac's grieving was over.

122

Kate's heart broke as she charged him with murder. She'd never been more choked in her life. For most of hers, Georgina had carried more than one heavy burden. But, she'd made a fist of it, despite the dark shadow hanging over her.

Zac Matthews was that shadow.

Kate thought of her guv'nor.

Bright was due back from the US soon. How would she tell him that one of his closest pals would shortly lose his liberty for three murders? Kate knew one thing: he wouldn't condone Zac's behaviour, any more than she would. Then again, neither would he condemn a man who'd lost his way.

Despite everything, their close friendship would survive . . . as had Kate's with Georgina, the bond between them unbreakable. The saddest thing of all struck her. In taking Fitzsimmons' life, Zac had lost his own and taken away her right to justice. Out of loyalty to him, a man she once loved as deeply as he loved her, Georgina couldn't tell anyone her secret – especially Kate, in case she went looking for a ghost and found Zac.

Before she went home, Kate sat down with Oscar, explaining that Ella had been found safe and well. He was visibly relieved. There was another reason she wanted to talk to him personally, one he might kick off about. Already he was on his feet, grabbing his coat, getting ready to leave.

'Before you go, I need to tell you something. I'd like you to hear me out before you comment.'

He sat down, meeting her gaze.

She chose her words carefully. 'You might be linked to the shootings in tomorrow's press. I leaked the fact that we had someone helping with enquiries and a positive DNA match.'

She took full responsibility, not mentioning the detectives she'd used to leak the information. 'Your name was not mentioned, but a certain journalist didn't let that stop her. I think we both know who I'm talking about.' She could tell that the name Garvey was in his head. 'I did it to draw out the real culprit before Ella came to harm. Then everything changed. Zac sent Hank an anonymous message, telling him to lay off you, and we worked out who it was. He's now in custody.'

Appreciating her motive, Oscar showed no resentment.

Kate hoped he would also take on board the fact that she was inviting him to return to the fold, making him feel that he was part of the wider organisation. 'Garvey will be spitting bullets when she finds out she got it so wrong.'

Oscar shrugged. 'It's not the first time she's been accused of wild speculation, is it?'

'I should imagine it's a weekly thing.'

He laughed.

'She'll try and wriggle out of it. It won't work. I'll tell her you want a grovelling public apology. How does that sound?'

'That'll do me.'

'Oscar, I know this last three years has been unbearable for your family. It's been hard enough for me.' *He didn't know the half of it.* 'I want you to know that everything we did was to get at the truth. All I ever cared about was letting your mum rest in peace.'

Thanking her, he left the station.

Kate immediately called his twin to let her know.

'I've been thinking about the DNA results,' Charlotte said. 'I decided not to mention the grenade you threw my way to my dad or Oscar. I don't think it'll occur to either of them to ask for a physical copy. If they do, we'll deal with it as a family.'

Whatever the rights and wrongs of it, Kate supported her decision.

What good would come of it? Charlotte didn't want to know her biological father's name, though she would find out soon enough, and if Kate knew anything about her, she would eventually meet the man who had avenged her mother's death, even if it was across a crowded courtroom.

123

Kate was dazed and exhausted as she drove home. The investigation had touched many lives. The likelihood of ever proving that Hazel Sharp's death was murder, not an overdose, deliberate or accidental, was minimal. With Christine Bradshaw, Burrows and Harvey in custody awaiting trial, Kate hoped that new evidence would be found. Informants needed cash. With the big players out of the way, they might seize the opportunity. She wouldn't hold her breath.

One way or another, Hazel's drug addiction had ended her life.

Kate was grateful to the witnesses who'd aided the investigation, especially Martin Alexander, Dr Alan Crawford, Molly Hart, Cally Bainbridge. If Kate had anything to do with it, PC Fay Hamilton would receive a commendation for her assistance in a complex investigation that had gone on too long.

If Curtis had listened to her – he might've got one too.

There was no doubt that the reputation of Northumbria Police had been severely damaged by his incompetence. And even though Zac was retired and now a civilian, it would sink further still, reaching a new low. Zac would face two kinds of justice. He would undoubtedly receive a life sentence on all counts, but his days were numbered.

If Christine couldn't get to him, others would.

Kate wiped her eye.

Having seen how Zac was with Ella when she emerged from her hiding place, Kate had no doubt that he would have made a brilliant father. She thought about that for a moment. Nico was a brilliant dad too, a decent bloke. He'd have continued to love Georgina, even if she'd come clean about the children.

Maybe she had.

The fact that Charlotte and Oscar hadn't been told, meant nothing.

If things had been different, they would have gone looking for their biological father, curious about his absence from their lives. It might have forced Georgina to face the man she was passionately in love with. She probably didn't trust herself not to show her contempt for what Zac had done in her name.

Besides, she loved Nico.

Georgina's voice had come to Kate often during the enquiry, guiding her, keeping her on track. This time it lifted her, answering the last part of the puzzle: *I never dream, or if I do, I don't remember.* Kate would make it her business to let Zac know that he'd rid her of the nightmares.

He'd find solace in that.

As one investigation closed, another opened, beginning with a search for Richard Fitzsimmons, the child abuser who'd faced summary justice at the hands of Zac. A vigilante killing he probably deserved. Kate had no sympathy. He'd blighted Georgina's life and that of his own daughter in the process. The late call from the search team leader was expected.

Kate snatched up her mobile. 'Did you find him?'

'It wasn't hard, guv. Zac's map took us right there.'

'Thanks for letting me know.'

'What do you want me to do with the twenty grand?'

'It's there?'

'Yup, wrapped in plastic, gaffer-taped.'

'Bag it as an exhibit. It needs to go to his daughter after the trial.'

If there was one thing this case had taught Kate, it was that love was everything. The rest was superfluous. Carmichael had lost someone very dear to her and would never get him back. Kate's job now was to ensure she received the support she needed, even though she'd probably decline it.

Lisa had already called Ash's parents, telling them that she'd

431

shared a great deal more with their son than frontline policing. His mother wept and so did Lisa. Losing Ash had broken her heart. If there was such a thing as 'the one', then Ash was as close as she'd ever come to finding a partner to share her life with. Being with him made her whole. He felt the same. When they were together, everyone around them seemed to fade from view.

It was like no one else in the world existed.

As Kate turned into Holly Avenue and stopped the car, Zac's last words echoed in her head: *Look after Jo. Without her, you're nothing. Without you, she is.* Kate looked up at the house. Jo waved from the window. Kate got out of the car. She was about to push her key in the lock when the door was pulled open.

'Hey!'

'You were right,' Kate said, stepping inside. 'From start to finish, this investigation has been too close to home. I'm shagged out.'

Jo gave her a big hug, hanging on for a moment longer than usual, then stepped away.

'Drink?'

'Make it a double.'

Kate dumped her coat on a chair in the hallway as Jo went to fetch the drinks. Seconds later, she arrived with two tumblers containing a generous measure of neat Macallan, a treat Kate's father had bought them for Christmas. They took their drinks into the living room and sat down on the sofa, swivelling round on opposite ends to face one another.

'I tried calling you,' Jo said. 'When you didn't pick up, I called the office. Andy told me that Zac had been charged and Ella found. I'm in shock that he took her.'

'He hasn't been charged with abduction.'

'No?'

'No. It was clear that the note he posted through Ella's door was a warning, not a threat. Once he saw her on TV, he knew others might pick her up, similarly if she was talking to us.'

'He was saving her?'

'From herself . . . at great personal risk.' Kate sipped her whisky. 'Zac followed Ailsa and Ella to Middle Earth the day she disappeared. He wasn't the only one. He couldn't say for sure that it was Harvey who tailed them from HQ. He wasn't waiting around to find out. Let's face it, who else would want to abduct a human candyfloss?'

Jo laughed.

'Zac managed to lose the other car in the traffic after it rammed his several times. Ella confirmed it all. She's taken a shine to him. She said he stopped and offered her a lift, which she accepted. She also said she'd never seen him before. It's bollocks, of course, but who cares now?'

Kate emptied her glass.

'You want another?'

'No, I'm done.'

They climbed the stairs and fell into bed.

Sleep didn't come, despite Kate's exhaustion. She turned this way and that, unable to settle, Jo stroking her back gently to make her relax. It didn't work. Rolling over, Kate kissed her goodnight, telling her to go to sleep.

Jo returned the kiss in the way only she could.

Kate asked, 'You know the other day when you rushed off and told me it was a false alarm? Where did you go?'

'Where did that random thought come from?'

'Dunno, a loose thread that popped into my head.'

Turning on the light, Jo produced the unopened sparkly box from the drawer of her bedside table. 'I brought this upstairs in the hope that you'd deserve it at some point between now and next Christmas,' she teased, handing it over. 'Go on, then. Open it.'

Kate sat up, pulling at the silver bow.

She'd thought about the box once or twice since Christmas

Day, wondering if there was a proposal to go with it and what she'd say if there was. When the box vanished, she thought that the woman who kept her world turning had got cold feet and changed her mind.

Kate lifted off the lid.

Inside was a key, a motorcycle key.

'Oh my God!' She'd lost her beloved Fazer in the explosion that took out their front door, wrecking the hall and staircase during their last investigation. 'Is there a bike to go with it?'

'That's why I rushed off, to postpone delivery. You can pick it up whenever.'

Kate threw her arms around her. 'Did you open yours?'

'Nope.'

'Wait there.' Kate jumped out of bed, thundered down the stairs and into the living room. Twelfth Night had been and gone, but the tree was still up, awaiting a celebration at the conclusion of their case. From underneath, Kate grabbed a box of a similar size to the one Jo had given her. Retracing her steps, she leapt onto the bed, handing it over. This one had a small note attached: *Marry me?* x

Acknowledgements

THE LONGEST GOODBYE is my fifteenth book. It concerns the death of PC Georgina Ioannou, the fictional friend and ex-colleague of my series detective, DCI Kate Daniels. It's written with love and respect for the police family whose tragic deaths touch us all, some of whom have sadly fallen on duty, far too close to home. I give enormous shout out to officers who've shared their stories with me over the years, including and especially my partner Mo, a former murder detective.

There are more people who collaborate in a finished book than you can possibly imagine. Thanks must go to my friend and agent, Oli Munson, always there for me. And to my editor, Sam Eades, whose insightful notes on early drafts pushed me to lift this one to the best of my ability. Enormous gratitude must go to my copy-editor Anne O'Brien – with me since day one – sharing her expertise, making me look better than I am. To Becca, Lucy, Sahil and Tomas, I couldn't do without you.

Thanks to my fellow authors whose books I've enjoyed. Like any reader, I need to escape into the fictional worlds you create. To booksellers, librarians, bloggers, reviewers and readers who share my work, your emails and social media posts blow me away sometimes. Word of mouth makes an enormous difference to any author. It helps to know that you are out there, waiting for the next title and the next . . .

Much love to those who keep me going when we're together, and with hilarious group chats when we're not, my family, at home and away . . . you are the best.

Credits

Mari Hannah and Orion Fiction would like to thank everyone at Orion who worked on the publication of *The Longest Goodbye* in the UK.

Editorial
Sam Eades
Snigdha Koirala

Copyeditor
Anne O'Brien

Proofreader
Linda Joyce

Audio
Paul Stark
Jake Alderson

Contracts
Dan Herron
Ellie Bowker
Alyx Hurst

Design
Tomás Almeida
Joanna Ridley

Editorial Management
Charlie Panayiotou
Jane Hughes
Bartley Shaw

Finance
Jasdip Nandra
Nick Gibson
Sue Baker

Marketing
Lucy Cameron

Production
Ruth Sharvell

Publicity
Becca Bryant

Sales
Jen Wilson
Esther Waters
Victoria Laws
Toluwalope Ayo-Ajala
Rachael Hum
Ellie Kyrke-Smith
Sinead White
Georgina Cutler

Operations
Jo Jacobs
Dan Stevens

STONE & OLIVER SERIES

THE LOST
Alex arrives home from holiday to find that her ten-year-old son Daniel has disappeared. It's the first case together for Northumbria CID officers David Stone and Frankie Oliver. But as the investigation unfolds, they realise the family's betrayal goes deeper than anyone suspected. This isn't just a missing persons case. Stone and Oliver are hunting a killer.

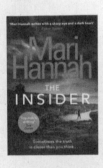

THE INSIDER
When the body of a young woman is found by a Northumberland railway line, it's a baptism of fire for detective duo DCI David Stone and DS Frankie Oliver. The case is tough by anyone's standards, but Stone is convinced that there's a leak in his team – someone is giving the killer a head start on the investigation. These women are being targeted for a reason. And the next target is close to home...

THE SCANDAL
When *Herald* court reporter, Chris Adams, is found stabbed to death in Newcastle with no eyewitnesses, the MIT are stumped. Adams was working on a scoop that would make his name. But what was the story he was investigating? And who was trying to cover it up? When a link to a missing woman is uncovered, the investigation turns on its head. The exposé has put more than Adams' life in danger. And it's not over yet.

When Detectives David Stone and Frankie Oliver are called to Kielder Observatory to investigate skeletal remains found inside a barrel dumped in the water, they learn they're dealing with a death that happened decades ago. But days later when another body turns up floating in Kielder Water, they realise this case is perhaps not as cold as they think...

OUT NOW

MARI HANNAH

DCI Kate Daniels Series

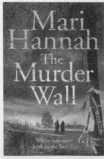  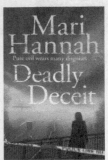

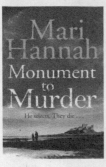  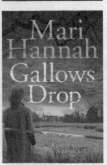

Matthew Ryan Series

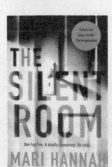 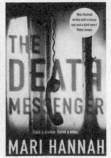

More from the DCI Kate Daniels Series

WITHOUT A
TRACE

A fatal crash.
A private tragedy.
A search for the truth …

'A stunning novel'
M.W. CRAVEN

'Compelling and incredibly moving'
ELLY GRIFFITHS

'A deft blend of emotional drama and crime procedural that
kept me hooked to the very end.'
ADAM HAMDY

HER LAST
REQUEST

**A hidden clue.
A desperate plea.
The Countdown is on...**

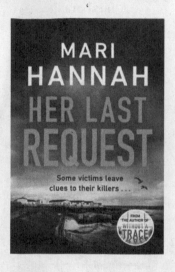

'Involving, sophisticated, intelligent and suspenseful – everything a great crime thriller should be'
LEE CHILD

'A gripping, twisty police procedural – fans of the Kate Daniels series will love this one'
SHARI LAPENA

'Compelling, page-turning suspense. Kate Daniels is a character to cherish, and Mari is a writer at the very top of her game'
STEVE CAVANAGH